Also by the author

The Pie Man

Booklocker.com, 2009

Republished as

Redemption Mountain

Henry Holt and Company, 2013

Much Love,
Glenda
Dec. 2021

The Last Mountain

For Mick and Benjamin

No grandparent deserves to be this lucky.

Marilyn,
I will always cherish the night
when we met Gerry Fitzgerald.
I still have the pictures of
the Heron Mines that you
got for our event. I often play
the soundtrack of the music
we put together. It took
Gerry a lot of years to finish
his second "mountain book"; I
told him to do it, if not for
him, for his future grandbaby.
And he did! Happy Hanukah!

Preface

Only fourteen mountains in the world rise to a height of over 8,000 meters. All are in the Himalaya and Karakorum ranges of Central Asia. Beginning in the mid-1800's, intrepid explorers, soldiers, surveyors and adventurers (they wouldn't yet be called *climbers*), started writing the long history of attempts to reach the summits of the giant mountains. The 1920's and 30's saw numerous failed expeditions and the start of the long list of fatalities on the mountains, which, today stands at over 1,020.

World War II brought on a hiatus of expeditions to the mountains, then, in June, 1950, two French Alpinists, Maurice Herzog and Louis Lachenal, fought their way to the top of Annapurna, and the *Golden Age* of mountaineering was on. In 1953, Kanchenjunga, Everest, and Nanga Parbat were summited, and over the next seven years, nine more of the 8,000ers were conquered. The last to fall was Shishapangma in 1964, located entirely in China and long closed off to western climbers.

The 8,000-meter mountains: (In order of first summiting)

Annapurna	8,078 meters	June 3, 1950	Maurice Herzog and Louis Lachenal
Mount Everest	8,850	May 29, 1953	Edmund Hillary and Tensing Norgay
Nanga Parbat	8,126	July 3, 1953	Hermann Buhl
K2	8,611	July 31, 1954	Achille Compangnoni and Lino Lacedelli
Cho Oyu	8,201	Oct 19, 1954	Herbert Tichy, Sepp Jochler and Pasang Dawa Lama
Makalu	8,481	May15, 1955	Jean Couzy and Lionel Terray
Kanchenjunga	8,598	May25, 1955	George Band and Joe Brown
Manaslu	8,163	May 9, 1956	Toshio Imanishi and Gyalzen Norbu
Lhotse	8,501	May18, 1956	Fritz Luchsinger and Ernst Reiss

Gasherbrum II	8,035	July 7, 1956	FritzMoravec, Sepp Larch and Hans Willenpart
Broad Peak	8,078	June 9, 1957	Marcus Schmuck, Fritz Wintersteller, Kurt Diemberger, Hermann Buhl
Gasherbrum I	8,068	July 4, 1958	Pete Schoening and Andrew Kauffman
Dhaulagiri	8,167	May 13, 1960	Kurt Diemberger, Peter Diener, Albin Schelbert, Ernst Forrer, Nima Dorje, Nawang Dorje
Shishapangma	8,012	May 2, 1964	Chinese team led by Hsu Ching

In 1986, Italian climber Reinhold Messner, universally regarded as the greatest mountain climber in history, summited Lhotse, the fourth highest mountain in the world, to become the first climber to conquer all fourteen of the "8,000ers" (all without the aid of supplemental oxygen). In the next twenty-four years, only nineteen more climbers achieved the fourteen summits, including Ed Viesturs, the only American to have accomplished the feat.

By the end of 2009, no woman had summited all fourteen.

The Last Mountain

A NOVEL

Gerry FitzGerald

BookLocker

Trenton, Georgia

Print ISBN: 978-1-64719-835-0
Ebook ISBN: 978-1-64719-836-7

Published by BookLocker.com, Inc., Trenton, Georgia.

Printed on acid-free paper.

The characters and events in this book are fictitious. Any similarity to real persons, living or dead, is coincidental and not intended by the author.

BookLocker.com, Inc.
2021

First Edition

January - 2010

Chapter 1

The snow was starting to fall out of the gray afternoon sky. Slowly now, the big flakes that blew in off Lake Champlain and piled up quickly. In a few minutes the cars in the lot would be covered. In an hour there would be five inches of snow on Route 7 and getting back to Fayston tonight would take Jack Finley over an hour.

He looked back down at the paperwork on his desk and then up at the older couple sitting patiently at the front of him. "Okay, we're almost done here, uhm ..." he glanced back down at the papers, "Henry, uh Jean. Just need you to initial a few spots here." He slid a form across the desk and handed a pen to the man. "Saying you're declining the extended warranty, right there," he pointed out the spot, "and the rust proofing ... the clearcoat, although you should probably reconsider on that one, with these Vermont winters ..."

"Don't want it," the man said gruffly, looking at the paper and initialing where Jack had made the red check marks.

No, of course you don't want it. You weren't born yesterday. Nobody ever wants it. Jack gazed out of the dealership's front windows at the progress of the snow. He could make more commission on the sale of a rust proofing and clearcoat application than he would on the sale of the Buick, but he just wasn't as good at it as the other salesmen. He never would be.

Jack noticed a man sitting in one of the chairs lined up along the inside of the huge plate-glass window. He hadn't noticed him come in or if he'd yet spoken to one of the other sales associates. It didn't concern Jack because the man didn't look like much of a prospect to buy a vehicle late in the day on a snowy afternoon. He had a scruffy look to him with long hair flowing out from under a Montreal Canadiens baseball cap, a well-worn brown winter jacket, heavy-weight work pants and leather boots stained with the white residue of cement work. He sat perfectly still with his back straight to the chair, his hands thrust into slit pockets in the jacket. When

9

Jack looked at him, the man seemed to nod back almost imperceptibly, as if to say he would wait until Jack was through with his business with the older couple.

"Need to get goin' here. Drivin' back to S' Johnsbury goin' to be slow goin' this afternoon."

Jack's customer brought his attention back to the paperwork. He smiled at the taciturn couple across the desk. "You bet. We're all set here. I'll just turn all this in to the business manager and we'll have your Buick brought around. Should have the plates on it now." He gathered up the folder and disappeared around a corner.

The Sales Manager squinted as he went over the paperwork while Jack stood at the front of his desk. "No rust proofing? No clearcoat?" He looked up at Jack with a disapproving look.

"No, they wouldn't go for it," said Jack glancing at his watch.

"Show 'em the DVD?"

"No, they uh, weren't interested.

"Jesus Jack," the Sales Manager closed the file shaking his head, "I had big hopes for you."

"Yeah, well … next time, right boss?" Jack was looking out the one-way window toward the showroom and saw a young couple come in with an older man. The woman was carrying a baby. Jack started for the door. This was a good "up" and he wanted to get back on the floor. The young couple, he knew, couldn't afford a new bicycle, but the old man could write a check. He had seen this setup before.

As he came into the showroom, Manny, one of the older salesmen was just reaching the couple with his hand out. They were inspecting a new green GMC Acadia, the older man putting on his reading glasses to read the sticker. "Jesus Ker-iste!" he exclaimed to what had to be his daughter, "you see what they want for this thing!"

Jack had seen the act before and was kicking himself for not being vigilant and seeing the young couple come in. Manny had himself a layup, and a nice commission, once they'd all done their ritual negotiation dance. *Probably sell a rust proofing and clearcoat too... nothing's too good for that old boy's daughter.*

Through the big windows, Jack saw the four-year-old Buick he'd sold to the older couple come around the corner of the building and stop in the special "just sold" spot in front. His customers were standing outside in the snow waiting. He needed to go out and shake their hands one more time, hand out more of his business cards, and smile as if he really cared whether they would enjoy their used LeSabre.

Jack took his leather sport jacket off the back of his chair and headed for the door. The man with the Canadiens hat was rising out of his chair. Jack smiled at him. "Is somebody helping you sir?" he asked.

The man was tall, as tall as Jack, six foot three, with broad, strong shoulders like Jack's, but heavier by thirty or forty pounds it appeared from the way he filled out his jacket. "Hello Jack," the man spoke softly with a deep voice and a trace of a French Canadian accent.

Jack stopped in front of the man and smiled, examining him. Then he shrugged. "I'm sorry, do I …"

"Charest," the man interrupted, "It's me Rene."

The smile left Jack's face and his eyes went wide with disbelief, his mouth hung open. "Oh my God, it really is, it's you Rene," Jack whispered. He moved forward and the two men embraced. Jack wrapped his arms around his old friend and pulled him close and held him tight, oblivious to how it may look to the other people in the showroom. Rene Charest did the same but with only his left arm. His right hand stayed in the pocket of his jacket. They embraced without talking for several seconds, reaffirming a bond forged from experiences no one else in the showroom, indeed no two people in Burlington that day had ever shared or even conceived of.

A loud rapping on the window made Jack open his eyes. The angry Sales Manager was outside with his customers, motioning for Jack to get outside and go over the Buick with them and go through the final departure routine. Jack nodded and held up one finger. He and Rene Charest separated.

"Geeze Rene, I didn't recognize you. I never saw you without a full beard." Jack smiled at his old friend.

"And with so many pounds, aye?" Rene patted his stomach with his left hand.

11

That was true too. Jack had always known Rene to be thin, with muscles of iron and not an ounce of fat.

"Heard you were here Jack, doing this. Headed back up to Montreal, so, had to come over to say hello." Rene's eyes danced around the interior of the showroom. "And see for myself that this is what you do now."

Jack shrugged. "Not so bad. Got to make a living, you know. Two kids now Rene. Gotta do something." Jack looked down at Charest's right arm, his fist still deep in the jacket pocket. "How about you Rene? How bad was it?" he said softly.

His friend shrugged and pulled his arm away from the pocket. "Well, not so good for me, eh?" All his fingers were gone along with half of his thumb. The rounded flesh of the stump was brownish and pulled tight like leather.

Jack winced and took Rene's hand in his, examining it like a doctor, or like a climbing partner would on the mountain. "Dhaulagiri. That was a hard one, huh. Sorry about your brother."

Rene sighed and put his hand back into the jacket pocket. "Yeah, Dhaulagiri, on the way down." He shook his head slowly with the memory. "Same old story, retold too many times, eh my friend?" Rene smiled briefly. "Too late in the day; our last summit try. Eight weeks on the mountain. Horrible weather." He sighed. "Tired, and no more patience. Almost out of food and fuel." Rene flashed a quick smile at Jack. "You have been there Jack. We've all been there. But this time …" He shook his head ruefully with the memory. "The luck, it wasn't with us. Storm comes … up the mountain, and it takes far too long to summit. Trying to get back to high camp in the dark. We went up light. Not even a bivy sack. No packs, just a short rope, the axes and a water bottle. The wind is so hard, and the snow goes sideways, and it is dark and we're freezing … you know how cold Jack. So," he sighed heavily, "we *had* to get down."

More rapping on the plate glass window. Jack totally ignored it, peering into his friend's eyes.

Rene shrugged. "And so … we fall. In the dark, batteries too weak, three on the rope, we fall. I lose my mitten, torn off trying to arrest. But we stop finally. Desmarais is okay, but Julien," he took in a deep breath to stem the emotional tide, "my brother Julien – you knew him, eh Jack?"

"Climbed with him. He was with us, you and me and the Italians, on Annapurna the first time."

"Oh yes, I forget. I forget." Rene's eyes seemed to cloud over as some distant memory occupied him. Then he was back. "Julien, he lands on rocks and his leg is broken in the fall." Jack winced with the knowledge of what a broken leg meant high on an 8,000 meter mountain.

"We tried to make a splint with Julien's ax. We tie it tight to his leg and wrap a rope many times around it. But … you know Jack … it is only pretend. No one can be carried down from up there. He tries, but he can't climb. He can't walk. Soon he can't move at all."

Jack looked away from Rene's tear-filled eyes. Outside, the older couple was driving away, ignoring the waves of the sales manager and two other sales associates recruited for the ceremony.

"So we carry him to a spot between some rocks and carve out a place to sit in the snow, out of the wind. I stay there, kneeling with him, for…too long, and Desmarais and I, we are freezing. Then … I kiss my brother and we say goodbye. Julien gives me a note he always carries in the mountains, to his wife and to his children. And he gives me his mittens but it is too late for me. It is thirty below zero with the wind. My hand is dead, black, frozen like meat by then." Rene Charest shrugged with resignation. "Then, we leave him there, on Dhaulagiri – forever – and Desmarais and me, we somehow find the fixed ropes and make it down to the high camp, a miracle for sure, and we save ourselves."

The driving snow outside and the darkening sky, along with Rene's story produced a vivid sense of déjà vu in Jack. Anyone else listening to the story would have thought it a horrible, unique tragedy of a lifetime, but to Jack and Rene, it was just part of their history, an all too often experience shared by the small coterie of high-altitude climbers who live for the challenge of the 8,000 meter peaks. The death of friends and loved ones came with the territory, and it came often.

Rene shrugged and flashed a brief smile. "So Jack, what do you do here?"

Jack nodded Rene over to his half-walled cubicle. "I sell cars, Rene. That's what I do..."

"No, no, Jack. I mean *what are you doing here,* selling cars?"

Jack sat in his desk chair while Rene dropped into the metal folding chair next to the desk. Jack glanced out the windows at the snow. "It's not forever. But for now, I need the income until Peggy can go back to teaching. Next September she'll go back and..."

"C'mon Jack," said Rene shaking his head. He leaned onto the desk toward Jack. "This is not right. It's *not right*," he pleaded. "You are the finest high-altitude climber in America. One of the top ten in the whole world. You have climbed all fourteen. In Europe you would be... like a film star, like a rock star. In Korea, they would *give* you a car dealership." He leaned back in his chair and looked about the showroom. "Not selling Buicks and pickup trucks." He turned back to Jack.

Jack sat still, facing his friend, tapping his fingertips on the desk while he pondered his answer. He owed Rene, his friend, an answer. Rene, with whom he had shared a tent in many high camps, indeed, had shared a sleeping bag with for three days in the horrible storm at 7,500 meters on Annapurna. Yes, Rene – his *brother of the rope* as Charles Houston would call him – deserved an answer. But Jack was tired of the question he'd been answering for the last two years, since he'd come home from the Himalaya after summiting Kanchenjunga, the third highest mountain in the world ... the last of the fourteen 8,000 meter mountains Jack had climbed – the grand slam of high-altitude mountaineering, the automatic ticket into the climbing hall of fame.

"Times are different Rene. And America's not Europe. Mountaineering's not of much interest here. The media doesn't care unless there's a tragedy with lots of bodies and beautiful people laying in the snow, with video for the news shows and people to blame." Jack shrugged. "Economy sucks. Bad as it ever was. Sponsors disappeared." Jack smiled at his old friend. "You know me. I'm not a writer. Not a talker. I'm not Viesturs."

Charest chuckled, "Aye, *no one* is Viesturs eh?"

"I can't write books and give slide shows and motivational talks for the big companies." He chuckled. "Shit, I went to the two biggest party schools in the country – UVM and Colorado State, and flunked out of both of them." Jack sighed and turned to watch the snow through the big windows. "All I did for the last twenty-three years is climb. That's all I ever wanted to do." Jack looked back at Rene who leaned forward in his chair, squinting at Jack with rapt attention. "And then … all of a sudden, you're forty years old … and all you know how to do is climb mountains."

"And that is a wonderful thing Jack." Rene implored. "Only a handful of people in the whole world can do what we did, climbing the big mountains. How do you stop? How? When you are still able?" He shook his head in question. "The new routes, the traverses we talked about... so many beautiful smaller mountains…"

"No Rene," Jack interrupted. "It takes money to climb now. It's too expensive to get on permits and to travel, and I need to work." Jack reached across his desk and turned a picture toward Rene. "This is what I do now Rene." The picture was a summer shot of Jack and his wife Peggy holding a baby, sitting on a green lawn with a little boy sprawled in front of them. "Peggy is holding Beth – she's one now, and Ralph is four."

Rene stared at the photograph and smiled. "Ralph," he said softly. "So who calls a child *Ralph* today?"

Jack laughed. "Peggy's father's name. I was getting ready to leave for Makalu. Couldn't argue too much with her." He looked at his watch. "C'mon, let's go have a beer." It was late in the afternoon and with the snow he knew the dealership would be closing up soon.

They drove up Route 7 a short distance to *Jake's* and found a secluded booth. Rene picked the side of the booth where his right arm would be against the wall and then wrestled his jacket off with his left hand. A very attractive waitress, in her early thirties, appeared at the edge of the table. "Hey Jack," she said softly. "Haven't seen you around much lately."

Jack flashed a smile up at the girl. "Yeah, been working a lot." He shrugged. "You know." The waitress stared at him for a few seconds, then nodded and took out her pen.

Jack ordered a pitcher of *Long Trail Ale.* Rene added two shots of *Jack Daniel's* to the order.

Rene picked up where he'd left off. "You know you could be climbing if you would take guiding jobs Jack. You would climb all you want and make some money too. More than selling cars."

The beer and the shots came and Jack took a long pull on his mug of ale. He put it down softly. "No," he shook his head, "I don't guide anymore," he said firmly. "Not going to climb that way." He glanced vaguely around the restaurant. "I get four, five offers a year to guide on the 8,000ers." Jack shrugged. "All expenses, travel, permits, food, all paid, but no, I won't do that anymore."

"Ah, my friend," said Rene, hoisting his mug. "It's how we all climb now," he said, forgetting his tense. "Well, most climbers anyway. It's the way climbing is going. Without the commercial expeditions you have almost no way to get on a permit any more. Who can afford it, eh?"

"Yeah," said Jack, "and it's what's wrong with climbing now... the commercial expeditions, dragging clients up mountains they don't belong on for a big price. It's not what mountaineering should be. And guiding on the big mountains is just a ruse. It's window dressing for the brochures to impress the clients." Jack paused to calm himself.

"Guiding is fine in the Alps, the Tetons, in the Cascades, on Denali, where you can teach, and you can actually help someone." Jack stared into his beer, his mind wandering. "Help someone get down if they're in trouble," he said softly. He looked up at Rene. "But not on an 8,000er. It doesn't work. It's just a bad trick on the clients who think they're okay, think they're safe because a professional climber is standing next to them." He took a drink and then spoke more softly. "And then, at 27,000 feet, when they can't climb up and they can't walk down and they can't breathe or feel their feet anymore, and the snow and the darkness are all around them and cold like they've never in their lives felt before ... and they look into your eyes expecting *you* to get them off the mountain safely and send them home to their families..." Jack shrugged and sipped his beer. "And all you can do is hope to save yourself ... and maybe try to leave your client near the ropes, so someone later will find him and be able to push his body into a crevasse."

Rene leaned across the table and spoke softly. "That was not your fault Jack. There was no way you..."

A figure suddenly cast a shadow onto the table. "Hey, Jack Finley, king of the mountains. What's happening?"

Jack looked up and recognized a sports writer for the Burlington Free Press with whom he had had a few run-ins with and disliked for years.

"John Teller," the man said, introducing himself to Rene Charest, who extended his left hand to him.

"Say Jack," said Teller, pulling a chair from a nearby table up to the end of the booth and settling in. "How about a quote or two about Logan Healy. This is going to be her summer in the spotlight, huh? Vermont girl makes history, huh Jack?"

The mention of Logan Healy made both Jack and Rene Charest smile. They'd both trekked, climbed and shared a tent with her and knew that nowhere on the planet was there a more fun loving, free-spirited, shoot-from-the-hip girl than Logan Healy. Just her name had a positive effect on them. Yes, this would be Logan's year, when the former ski racer and model- turned- mountain- climber summited her 14th 8,000 meter mountain – the *first* woman to accomplish that amazing feat, *if* she could beat her Korean rival, the indomitable Asian climbing machine, Chun Suek Yen, to the top of K2. Right after which, she would come home to wed Rudi Joost, founder and president of Zermatt Sports, and one of the richest men in America. The pop culture magazines, television shows and social media sites were already buzzing about *the year of Logan Healy.*

Jack grinned with an old memory of Logan. "Make sure you write that I was still the only one in the Green Mountain School to ever beat Logan in the downhill at Stratton." Jack smiled at Charest. "That'll frost her ass good," he said with a chuckle. "I was in eighth grade, she was in fourth, and I beat her by a ski pole."

"So what do you think Jack? Logan going to get up there first?" Teller pulled a notepad and pen from his inside pocket and began writing.

Jack took a long sip of beer and his eyes met Rene's in a knowing moment, the humor gone, sharing - they knew - the same thought. The writer wanted to know who would get up K2 first. Jack and Rene were wondering if *either* of them could summit the world's second highest mountain – the hardest mountain in the world to climb and its most lethal – and live to tell about it. They both knew the statistics – that summiting K2, *doubled* your chances of dying on the mountain. It probably wasn't a coincidence that both Logan Healy and Chun Suek Yen still had K2 left on their scorecards. Both women had attempted K2 twice previously and been defeated by the mountain, as so many others also had; as Jack himself had been turned back twice before making its summit.

Jack looked over at Teller. "Write that I wish great success to both Logan and to Sukey, two tremendously talented climbers who deserve a place in mountaineering history."

"Yeah, okay Jack, thanks," said Teller jotting in his notebook. He looked up. "Come on Jack, who do you think will win?"

Jack just shook his head and sipped his beer. He didn't want to talk to the reporter any more. He'd said enough. *Who did he think would win? He knew who would win. No matter what happened, K2 would win. Even if both women summited and made it down alive, there would be a price to pay, personally or by their expeditions. K2 always got its pound of flesh.*

"So how about the mountain Jack. You climbed K2. You've spent more time up there than just about anyone. Something about the mountain," Teller persisted.

Jack held his beer mug up to Rene and smiled. "To K2, the worst weather on earth." He and Rene chuckled and toasted K2 with their beer mugs.

John Teller folded up his pad and left just as Jack's cell phone buzzed. Jack looked at his watch. "Oh shit, I forgot about dinner." He pushed a button. "Hi honey, yeah I'm at Jake's having a beer with…yeah, okay." It was a short conversation. Jack folded the phone up. "Damn. Gotta get going," he said softly.

Rene Charest smiled briefly and nodded his understanding. He picked up his shot of Jack Daniels. "A toast." Jack held up his glass to Rene's. "To our friends Logan and Sukey and their safe return from K2."

Jack nodded in agreement. "To their safe return," he replied somberly. The men downed the Jack Daniels and then cooled down their throats with the last of the beer.

The snow had abated when they got back to the dealership. Jack pulled in next to an old pickup truck with Quebec plates. Standing in snow, in the approaching darkness both men disregarded the icy wind chill. They hugged briefly and promised to stay in touch. As Jack turned to get back into his car, anxious to get home as late as he was now for dinner, Rene's voice turned him around.

"You know Jack, there will be one more on K2 this summer, going for the record also, don't you? Another woman."

Jack shrugged quizzically. He knew there was no woman climber with thirteen of the 8,000 meter mountains, other than Logan and Sukey. "Okay, I give up," said Jack with a shrug. "Who else will be there?"

Rene took a step closer to Jack. "Yes, there is one more." He smiled at Jack, savoring the moment. "Sophie will be there."

Jack laughed and then peered more closely at Rene to see if he was making a joke. "C'mon, Sophie has several mountains to go and she hasn't been active for two, three years. I think she retired."

"Sophie is on Cho Oyu right now. A winter climb. Then to Gash One in the spring, and K2 in July."

Jack Finley raised his eyebrows and drew in a long breath of cold air. This was a surprise to him. It was true, he had been away from mountaineering news for a while, but he hadn't expected or been prepared to hear the name of *Sophie Janot,* the first true love of his life and the source of so many fond memories of their early years of climbing together. Also the source of so much remorse that had been a part of Jack's life for the last ten years. Her name made his heart skip a beat. He swallowed hard. "Wow, Sophie going for fourteen," he said softly. "Cho in the winter, huh." Rene just remained silent. He knew, as did most of the veteran climbing community, of the storybook affair of Jack Finley and Sophie Janot many years ago.

Jack smiled at his friend. "Well, it's going to be quite a circus on K2 this summer." They embraced one final time before Rene climbed into his truck and drove off in the snow, up Route 7 towards Route 89, north to Montreal.

Jack sat in the dark car, the wipers scraping back and forth over the ice-covered windshield, the defroster on high, blowing cold air. He knew there was no sense hurrying. He'd missed dinner and was already in Peggy's dog house – as he usually was. And now that he'd have to go down Route 100, as the old Pontiac would never make it up and over Route 17 in the snow, it would take him at least an hour and a half to get home tonight.

So he sat in the dark and thought about Sophie, the wind buffeting the car as it had so many tents they'd shared – on Everest, and Nanga Parbat, and the magical Nanda Devi; on Aconcagua their first big adventure together after meeting on Everest – two attractive, young, ambitious, adventurous climbers sharing a tent and then a sleeping bag on the South Col. And then so many tents afterwards. Glorious climbs in the Alps, in Sophie's backyard in France, and in Italy and Austria with her father and brothers, sleeping together in the warming huts. The summer in Alaska. Every climb was better with Sophie, as was every memory.

Jack pictured her on the vertical rock walls of Colorado and California where he'd taken her to show her his past, watching her hang effortlessly by one arm while she patiently probed blindly above her for a crack, a knob, the slightest weakness in the wall, her shoulders and arms rippling with sinew, the ink-black hair falling around her face, the quick flash of her smile, unconcerned. A gymnast, like a spider on the walls. Skills learned on the *Petite Dru* and *Grandes Jorasses* her father trained her on before she was a teenager. Jack had always thought he was a talented rock climber until he met Sophie.

He thought about Sophie climbing Cho Oyu – the gentlest of the big mountains and the most popular 8,000er after Everest for the commercial tours charging big fees to deliver wealthy amateurs to the summit. But not now. Not in winter. Sophie's group would be alone on Cho, and it would be cold and the snow deep.

Jack's cell phone buzzed. He looked at it and saw that it was Peggy. He put it back in his pocket and let it ring. He wondered who would be with Sophie on Cho. He hoped Sophie had some strong companions with great endurance and large boots to break trail in deep snow. And a partner she could trust with her life when they went for the summit.

Chapter 2

The wind pounded the tent and found minute openings through which to send the powder-like particles of spindrift, coating the small camp stove hanging from the center support. The frosted inside of the tent sagged inward as the snow outside piled up once more.

"Your turn to shovel," said a deep, tired Slavic voice, muffled by the folds of a brown sleeping bag. "You need to shovel," the man repeated a little louder along with a nudge of his knee against the sleeping bag next to him.

"Bon, okay, je vais," the woman replied weakly. She opened her eyes reluctantly and looked down into her sleeping bag at the luminous hands of her watch. Three-thirty, time anyway for them to start getting dressed and melt snow for breakfast if they were climbing today. But, she feared from the sound of the wind and the snow scratching against the thin tent fabric, that no one would be going anywhere today. *Another wasted day, using up more food and fuel that they would soon be out of. And snow threatening to bury their tent.*

The woman turned on the battery lamp and sat up in her sleeping bag, her wool hat hitting the roof of the tent sending a storm of frost powder into the air to mix with the thick fog of her breath. The tent sagged under the weight of the snow. The woman sighed with the thought of pulling her boots on, and having to pee, as she knew she would have to as soon as she got outside in the cold air. It wasn't always like this. Before two children, her bladder was strong and she could go a day if she had to or at least hold it until a sheltered spot came along. But now ... when she stood up. *This was the real reason why women gave up climbing – not the fear of leaving motherless children that was so often given!* She pulled off her hat and gathered her matted black hair behind her ears. *Another day without a brushing.* She was glad there were no mirrors on the mountain. She pulled her wool cap back on tightly and reached down into the sleeping bag for her boots.

In the dimly lighted tent, she wrestled on her down jacket and gloves and searched for her goggles in the mess of rucksacks, food bags and trash that littered the small tent. "L'enfer avec eux!" she said under her breath, crawling over the large mound between her and the door of the tent.

"What do you mean?" said the voice from the sleeping bag. "What did you say Sophie?"

The woman giggled. "No Victor, it is nothing. Go back to sleep" she said sliding over the large Russian. "Wrap up Victor, I'm opening the flap."

The cold hit her like a slap in the face, and then a gust of wind for good measure – like the mountain was telling them it had had enough of the intruders. *Mon Dieu, minus twenty degrees at least, and so much snow!* The new snow was two feet deep and drifting higher over one end of the tent. She waded through the snow toward the handles of the ski poles that were still just barely protruding from a drift, searching with her gloved hands deep into the snow for the rope that was anchored there. She knew it was probably a needless precaution, clipping onto the rope just to squat in the snow to pee, but the wind was blustery and where they'd been able to dig out a level spot for the tent, the edge of the ridge was only ten feet away. *A fitting end that would be! She could see the headline in Le Monde – Noted French mountaineer, Sophie Janot, lost on Cho Oyu, blown off ridge while...* – Sophie giggled, wondering how they would phrase it.

Sophie found the rope and relieved herself quickly and went to work with the plastic shovel, taking care not to rip a hole in the tent. The work made her breathe deeply in the thin air. They weren't yet high enough for the lack of oxygen to be debilitating, but she *was* worried about how she would perform beyond Camp 3. Though now well acclimatized – from two previous climbs up to Camp 3, two weeks in bad weather at the high camp, and then down again to basecamp to recuperate – it had been over three years since she was above 8,000 meters. *Maybe it was a mistake,* she thought, *climbing Cho Oyu without oxygen, but then it was probably a bigger mistake to climb Cho in winter. And here they were, stuck at 6,500 meters where the thin air was beginning the slow destruction of their bodies and their brains and the storm doing its best to bring an end to the expedition, an end to this foolish idea of climbing her last three 8,000 meter mountains in just six months.*

A low, guttural cough from the tent a few yards away drew Sophie's attention. Ang Phu and Temba would both be up soon to get on with the preparation of liquids and breakfast in anticipation of the climb to Camp 3. They knew, probably better than she did, that it would have to be today, or there would be no summit attempt tomorrow and that would be it for the expedition, and the end of Sophie's quest to be the first woman to scale all fourteen of the world's tallest mountains. The Sherpas would do their part, she was certain. They would be ready to leave at 6:00AM, to go up – or go down one last time.

She shoveled out the small path between the tents, and then the drift of snow leaning against the windward side of the Sherpa's tent. Again she heard the low, suppressed coughing from within the tent. It was Temba. He had been coughing for two days and now sounding worse.

Before crawling back into the tent, Sophie waded uphill through the snow a few meters and held her face up to the mountain before her. Even on an overcast night with no moon and no stars visible, mountain snow always seemed to emit a faint light through the darkness. She could just make out the form of the ridgeline above the camp, the ridgeline they would follow all the way up to Camp 3 on the shoulder – six hours of climbing in the summer over rock and neve snow, but probably nine hours at least in the knee-deep new powder. *Nine hours of high-risk avalanche climbing. Was it fair to ask Victor and Ang Phu and Temba to take such a risk just to help her "bag another peak" in her race? They didn't need Cho – all three had climbed the mountain before, Victor accomplishing it in one thirty-hour solo sprint to the top and down again, several years ago in summer. She would see what Clement said during the radio call. She would leave it to him.* Just before ducking down into the tent, Sophie thought she could feel the snow and wind start to weaken.

Victor had the stove going and a pan full of snow almost melted when Sophie crawled into the tent. She had to push tightly against his broad back to get past him. Settling back onto her sleeping bag, she pulled off her boots. When she had gone outside she hadn't bothered to fully buckle her boots and snow got in over the tops. Now she needed to change her socks and dry the inside of the boots. The winter temperature on any mountain in the Himalaya made frost-bitten toes a very serious concern. She'd already lost the tips of both of her long toes – on Nanga Parbat twelve years ago – and knew then that she had been very lucky there was a doctor at base camp with the proper drugs. She also knew that frostbite was a cumulative malady – exposure to it led to heighted susceptibility. Even in the Alps, Sophie was vigilant over the condition of her toes.

"Good morning Sophie," said Victor, handing her a plastic mug of steaming tea.

"Bonjour Victor. Merci." She held the mug close to her face, breathing in the warm vapor. The stove had warmed up the inside of the tent a little but it was still very cold. Victor unwrapped an energy bar and handed it to her before unwrapping his own. They sat in silence for a while eating slowly and sipping their tea. The small flame from the stove flickered, working hard to melt another pan of snow, casting a dim glow around the inside of the orange tent.

Victor's eyes went up toward the top of the tent, as if he was looking through it into the sky outside. He turned his head to listen. The sound of the snow scratching against the tent fabric seemed to have stopped, and the wind also. "So," he said before taking another bite of his breakfast bar, "will we climb today you think?"

Sophie chewed slowly and took another sip of tea, thinking about the question for a few moments. Everything moved slowly in the mountains, even conversation. She shrugged. "I don't know. We'll see. We'll wait to see what it looks like when the first light comes. I'll call Clement to get the weather and see what he says."

They sat in silence for a few minutes savoring their breakfast before Victor spoke again. "You know," he said with a slight nod toward the entrance to the tent, "they don't climb today."

"Who?" asked Sophie. "Ang and Temba?"

"The Sherpa, they don't climb today."

Sophie smiled with curiosity. "Why Victor? Why do you say that?"

The Russian raised his shoulders and sighed. "They don't climb because it is late in the expedition – only two days more, probably. And the avalanche danger now is very high, and the Sherpa get their money if we go up one more day, or we go down one more day." He nodded affirmatively. "So they go down. I know these Sherpa."

"But we've got two more days to the summit. That's what they came to do."

Victor shook his head. "These Sherpa don't need the summit. They have both been on the top, several times. They are here only to get paid. So today they go down."

Sophie looked over the edge of her cup at her climbing partner to watch for his reaction. "They have been to the top, just like you Victor. You don't need to summit either." She suddenly had a chilling thought that the expedition may be over before she put her boots back on.

Victor looked up at Sophie and smiled. "We will look at the mountain and will see what Clement says, okay? And maybe Ang Phu surprises me, eh."

Sophie hoped that Victor was wrong and that his comments stemmed more from his long-standing dislike and distrust of the Sherpa than from his insight into how men behaved on mountains. It would be a long, hard climb to camp 3 without the Sherpas to help break trail. She thought about Ang Phu and Temba. Unlike the general public, experienced Himalayan mountaineers had long ago stopped deifying the Sherpa as ultra-virtuous, heroic, climbing machines. Some were great climbing partners and wonderful people; some were not. And some didn't belong on the big mountains. In character, the Sherpa were like everyone else. It was a mistake to generalize about them. They were all different. *These two Sherpa were okay though, and she had climbed with Ang Phu many times before.* She hoped Victor had misread them.

Sophie finished her tea and breakfast bar, and began the laborious process of layering up against the cold that she knew, even if the sun was visible most of the day, wouldn't rise above -15° C. She moved slowly, discouraged by her conversation with Victor. He had verbalized the nagging doubts that had been festering in the back of her mind since the beginning of the expedition, indeed since the beginning of the trip, since leaving Argentiere. The doubts that grew on the trek in, setting up base camp, and the pushing of camps up the mountain through the weeks of relentlessly horrible weather. The doubts that she knew were well founded and real, along with the realization that this was unlike any other expedition she had ever been on. It was the realization that she was entirely alone on this expedition – the only person on the mountain not getting paid to be there. Everyone else was a hired hand, an employee, getting paid to contribute to the singular goal of getting Sophie Janot to the top of Cho Oyu and back down again so she could be one step closer to being the first woman climber in history to have climbed all fourteen of the 8,000 meter mountains. *One step closer to the fame, celebrity and wealth that accomplishment would bring – that she now, for the first time in her life, so desperately needed.*

Sophie hated the feeling in the pit of her stomach. The expedition reminded her of everything she despised about the new age of mountaineering – *"peak bagging" for fame and notoriety, and commercial expeditions dragging amateurs up mountains, and their grotesque, self-promoting websites and blogs, Twittering and Facebooking their exploits around the globe ... and yet, here she was, right in the middle of all of it! This wasn't the way she climbed. Sophie Janot, daughter of the great Marcel Janot, an icon of the Alpine school of mountaineering – lightweight climbing with small parties, taking everything you needed up the mountain with you, quickly up and quickly down, leaving the mountain as you found it. The way they climbed in the Alps, and as much as possible in the Himalaya. But she also knew she wasn't the same person she had been when she'd stopped climbing three years ago – before the divorce. Everything was different now.*

The water was ready and Victor was making a pan of noodles. Sophie watched him through the flickering light, emptying an envelope of noodles into the steaming water. He was so capable at every aspect of climbing, from highly technical vertical rock and ice, to mixing a bowl of noodles for breakfast. One of the world's strongest climbers, there was nothing Victor Petrov couldn't do on a mountain. *So why was he here? Just for the money?*

Like a Sherpa. To haul loads up the mountain and break trail and fix a rope up on the ice cliffs above? And of course, to make sure she got to the top and down again, as he'd had to promise Clement and her father when they'd recruited him and Carlos and Toby. High altitude baby sitters! The thought angered her ... that *she* needed professional guides to get to the top of Cho Oyu, the easiest, least technical mountain of all the 8,000 meter peaks.

"Here, eat some noodles Sophie," said Victor, handing her a cup and a plastic spoon.

She grabbed the cup without reply. *The idea that she, one of the most celebrated woman climbers in the world – who had climbed more big mountains than anyone else on the expedition, who had climbed the Petite Dru, Grandes Jorasses and Mt. Blanc when she was still a teenager, and the Eiger north face when she was twenty-two – needed professional guides, enraged her. She didn't need guides. She needed friends and amiable companions to climb with and share the adventure. Or else what was the point of it all?* She ate her noodles in silence.

Ang Phu was walking back down toward the tents through tracks from fifty yards up the ridge when Sophie and Victor went outside. In the dim morning light, they could see that Temba was taking down the other tent and that the Sherpas' full rucksacks were standing in the snow. They were going down.

"No more climb," said Ang Phu firmly when he reached them. "Too much avalanche today. Sun come out. Heavy snow. Too dangerous." He pulled his pack up from the snow. "Temba sick," he said gesturing toward the collapsing tent. "He must go down now."

Sophie smiled at the Sherpa and patted him on the arm. "Okay Ang, take care of Temba. Go down safely." She knew there was no sense in trying to dissuade him and this was not the place to argue.

The Sherpa looked surprised. "You go up?"

Sophie looked up the mountain toward the swirling lenticular clouds at the summit and shrugged. "We'll see what the weather holds," she said. "We'll see what doctor Clement says."

28

Ang Phu looked up the mountain also. He shook his head. "This snow will make very big avalanches. Snow will all come down, and then leave good climbing." He flashed a quick smile but the lines in his forehead told Sophie how worried he was.

The Sherpas started off down the hill with their heavy packs while Sophie pulled the Motorola radio out of her down suit. Dr. Alain Clement, the expedition leader, would be waiting for her call at basecamp, sipping his morning tea, looking into the screen of his laptop.

"Good morning Sophie," he said, cheerfully as always. "How are you and all the boys doing up there?"

"Bon jour doctor. We are fine, Victor and I. Temba is sick and on his way down now with Ang Phu. They are on their way to Camp 1."

"Coming down! They can't leave you …"

Sophie interrupted him. "It is okay doctor. Temba is sick. He needs to go down. They are through.

"Doctor," she said a little louder to change the subject, "what does the weather say for today and tomorrow?

"Well," Clement hesitated, unsure if he should be encouraging her now, "the weather is supposed to be clearing for thirty-six hours and warmer slightly, but without the Sherpas, you cannot continue alone, with just Victor. That's madness in snow this deep."

Sophie looked up the mountain. Victor was trudging up the slope, testing the snow with his ski poles and huge boots. There was a hint of blue in the morning sky and the wind had completely disappeared. Sophie wondered if it wasn't a trick the mountain was playing on them just to lure them up higher. She took a deep breath of the thin air. *This was it then…decision time. If they went down now, the climb was over and all the money she had scraped together to finance the trip was gone, wasted. She would go home broke, a single parent with two children and no prospects. There would be no second chance at Cho. Sponsors had no interest in a mountain called Cho Oyu – all they knew about mountains was Everest and K2 – because that's where people die. Her old sponsors, Evian, and BNP Paribas, and Rolex, they would support an historic climb of K2 in July… if she ever got there. But it wouldn't matter if she couldn't get to the top of Cho tomorrow.*

"Sophie, are you there?"

"We will go up today doctor, and see how it is. Up to Camp 3 for the night and then to the summit tomorrow if conditions will allow. I will call you from Camp 3"

"Sophie, let's talk about … the avalanche danger will be …"

"Thank you doctor, I'll call you tonight." Sophie quickly switched off the Motorola to save the weakening battery.

Victor was walking toward her. "So, Clement, he says to do what?"

Sophie smiled. "He says perfect weather for thirty-six hours. Hot and sunny, seventy degrees. Says we should be wearing our short pants today." She chuckled.

"Okay Sophie, okay," said the big Russian, smiling. "We go up." He turned and looked up the mountain. "The snow is deep, but so light still that it may be possible. We'll see."

They stayed close to the ridge line on their left, trudging slowly, mechanically through the knee-deep powder up the long, gradually steepening snow field. The wind had died completely and the morning sky was a rare shade of light purple as the low winter sun rose through the haze. While they wouldn't have to shed any clothing, the day was already the warmest and best day for climbing they'd had on the mountain in six weeks.

Victor broke trail for the first hour. With his size twelve boots and powerful strides, even in the lead, he was able to stay well ahead of Sophie who needed to push hard on her ski poles taking two strides to his one to keep up. This was the kind of climbing Sophie hated – pushing up laboriously through deep snow – and was least suited for. On vertical rock, frozen waterfalls, or steep ice cliffs, she was a match for any climber in the world, male or female. But in the deep snow, she had to make up for her shortcomings with mental and physical endurance. Staring down at the track in front of her she almost bumped into Victor who had stopped for a drink.

Taking water from her own bottle, Sophie looked back down toward the tent and was discouraged at how little ground they had actually covered in an hour of what would be the easiest climbing of the day. If she had her skis on, she calculated, it would take her under twenty seconds to get back down to the tent.

"Okay Victor," I will lead for a while. Victor smiled down at her without comment, still breathing hard while leaning over his ski poles for a rest.

Sophie started out, up through the unbroken powder kicking through the top six inches, displacing as much snow as possible with her small boots. Victor hung back, resting, knowing that he would catch up to her very quickly at the pace she was limited to. Through his dark goggles, he gazed up the slope to the shoulder and then towards the ice cliff, and beyond it what he could see of the summit snow field. He looked at his watch, and then back up toward the sun rising higher in its low arc to the south, and grimaced. *They needed to be careful.*

Victor let Sophie lead for thirty minutes and then took over again. Sophie reluctantly conceded that they moved far too slowly with her in the lead and took over only for short spells to let Victor rest for a few minutes on his ski poles. Then he would quickly catch up to her and resume the lead.

Soon the slope steepened to the angle it would maintain up to the saddle and breaking trail in the deep snow and thinning air became more arduous. The sunlight hitting the slope more directly also thickened the snow noticeably. They continued climbing at a slow, steady pace with Victor leading, spelled for short intervals by Sophie, until noon time. They had been climbing for four hours and now needed to rest and eat.

They dropped their packs into the deep snow and flopped into seats facing south, down the slope. Sophie treated herself to one of her delicacies, a Fig Newton bar, and drank about half her water. Hydration was a constant concern at high altitude especially with Sophie's propensity to frostbite. After all the work of the morning, her feet felt fine. Keeping on the move was the key; they couldn't sit around too long.

Sophie stood and took out her small digital camera from an inside zippered pocket to take some pictures of the spectacular panorama to the west, with the rugged Gaurishanker next to them followed by a line of majestic seven thousand meter mountains, Langtang Ri, Langtang Lirung, Ganesh Himal, and many others that, transported to the Alps, would tower over Mt. Blanc by nearly three thousand meters, but in the Himalaya remained virtually unknown.

To the south, she could make out the massive Nuptse – just a hundred or so meters short of the big club – and, hidden beyond it she knew was Ama Dablam, just 6,800 meters, but the hardest climb she'd ever been on. *And one of the most satisfying* – she smiled with the recollection – *with Jack, in the old days, when climbing was all they lived for, when they did anything they wanted, went anywhere their wanderlust took them, and climbed the beautiful mountains – Aconcagua, Nanda Devi, Denali, Changabang, Chogolisa and so many others and didn't care about accomplishment, celebrity or notoriety. Just the adventures and living on the edge.*

"Sophie," Victor's deep voice brought her back from her reverie. "From here we rope up." The Russian was on his feet uncoiling the sixty-meter rope he'd been carrying across his chest. He tossed Sophie one end of the stretchable climbing rope.

"Okay Victor, you are right," she said tying the rope onto a carabiner and clipping in to her harness.

Victor tossed the coil of rope into the snow to play out between them, and took up his ski poles once more. He looked up the slope, inspecting the snow with eyes trained by watching the deep snow slopes of the Caucasus, and then turned back to Sophie next to him.

"Now Sophie, listen to me very carefully now. If I turn back to you and yell *go,*" he pointed to the cornice hanging out over the edge of the ridge twenty yards to their left, "you run quickly to the edge and jump over. Don't hesitate and don't wait for me, because if you hear me yell, it may already be too late."

Sophie glanced at the ridge line up the mountain ahead of them and then to her left, at the sheer drop off of at least two thousand feet down the southwest face. She nodded. "I understand Victor," she said, pushing her ski poles into the snow, anxious to get started.

Victor led for the next hour and they made good time. The air was very cold but the lack of wind and the very slight warmth of the low sun made it a very pleasant day to climb. Sophie was encouraged. She still felt strong in the thinning air and her fingers and toes were warm. They'd reach Camp 3 around 5:00pm and if the tents hadn't been destroyed or covered in deep snow, they'd have plenty of time to eat and rehydrate and then sleep for a few hours. At 3:00am, they would leave for the summit – a later hour than usual in order to avoid climbing the ice cliff in the dark – and if the wind and the snow stayed off the mountain, they would be to the top and back down to the high camp by early evening. Sophie was feeling more optimistic about the climb than at any other time since she had been on the mountain. *It was amazing the difference a window of good weather made! At Camp 3, she would call Wanda and Chantal on the Thuraya.* She smiled at the thought of hearing the voices of her little girls and started calculating the time difference in Argentiere.

Again, lost in her thoughts, she almost bumped into Victor. He was bent over his ski poles taking in deep breaths trying to bring enough oxygen into his lungs. He had been working hard all day, breaking trail in the deep snow, doing by himself the job that the two Sherpas should have been doing much of. Now he was exhausted.

"I will lead now Victor," Sophie said moving past the gasping Russian. "You rest for a few minutes and then catch up." She reached into the side of his pack and brought out the water bottle for him. Like hers, it was nearly empty.

Sophie looked up the slope to pick out her line, near the edge of the ridge but not so close where she might stray out onto the cornice and break through the fragile overhang. She pushed her ski poles into the deep snow and started up. It took her twenty minutes to gain thirty yards of separation from Victor.

Stopping for a moment to catch her breath, Sophie looked up the slope to where she could just make out the saddle where Camp 3 was situated. She strained to see through her dark goggles to pick out the small dot that would be the tent in the sea of shimmering white. Then she noticed the cloud on the summit slope high above. *A strange sight on such a clear day,* she thought. And then, a second later, she heard the noise – a deep *ker-ump,* and the mountain seemed to move. *There were no clouds on the summit slopes,* she suddenly realized, *it was the layer of new powder snow being thrown into the air by the avalanche!* Then the snow moved beneath her feet.

"Sophie!" Victor's voice barely carried up to her in the sudden wind. She turned down the slope toward him. *"Sophie!"* He was running up the slope toward her, pointing madly with his left arm toward the edge. *"Go now Sophie. Run!"*

Sophie gripped her ski poles hard, turned and began running and sliding down the trail in the snow she had just come up. She knew why Victor was struggling to get closer to her – to gain more slack in the rope, enough length for him to also make it over the cornice after he planted his ice ax deep in the snow and wound the rope around it. It was their only hope.

The snow was running past her, filling in the trail, as high as her thighs now, pushing her along, faster and deeper. Then the air was filled with snow, and she couldn't see Victor any more. She couldn't see anything.

Sophie turned to her right toward the edge and tried to push her way through the deep, moving snow, using the ski poles to stay erect. She moved slower, and slower as the snow became deeper – up to her chest now – and then the avalanche swept over her, leaving her in darkness. She bent her knees and pushed as hard as she could, and tried to swim through the snow but every step came slower and harder, until she was no longer moving at all. Above her, the avalanche continued to thunder down the mountain, the sound growing more muffled as it built up over her head, applying more and more pressure against her body.

She lay still, trying to breathe, and strained to maneuver her hands up to her chest to see if she could get to the satellite phone inside her parka, to say goodbye to her little girls.

Chapter 3

Tuesdays belonged to Jack. His day off from the dealership, and by unspoken agreement, his day off from Peggy. It wasn't something they ever negotiated. It just came to be, that Tuesday was Jack's day to train and Peggy learned early in their marriage that it wasn't something to meddle with. It was Jack's day to torture his body, to replicate a day in the mountains, if not in height and thin air, at least in exertion, to maintain his stamina. Jack looked forward to the physical pleasures of Tuesdays, but he also had to admit that over the past two years, he had started looking forward just as much to a day without Peggy.

He sat at the kitchen table hurriedly eating a bowl of shredded wheat, a banana and a glass of orange juice. It would be the last real food he'd have until that evening, but he was in a hurry to get started. On the window next to the table he could hear the pinging of the sleeting snow that had started an hour earlier. *A couple of inches of snow was good. At five-thirty in the morning there would be no cars yet and he could ski down the middle of German Flats Road and with enough speed, he could almost make it all the way to the Mt. Ellen access road.*

"Gonna be gone all day again?" Peggy's voice startled Jack out of his thoughts. He looked up to see his wife leaning against the door frame, wrapped in her white bathrobe. She had her arms crossed at her chest for warmth in the cold kitchen.

"I'll be back about six, maybe seven."

"Want me to make dinner?" she asked.

"No, don't wait for me. Eat with the kids."

She frowned and moved to the cupboard and took out a can of cat food. "Wish I had time to go off and exercise all day."

Jack watched her washing out one of the cat bowls at the sink. The puffy bath robe made her look even heavier from behind. She'd put on a lot of weight with their first child, lost some of it, then put on less weight with

Beth and lost none of it afterward. He knew better than to respond to a 'wish I had time to ...' comment. Jack wanted to get going.

Peggy put the cat bowl on the floor next to the radiator, near where Jack had dropped his lightweight pack, and on top of it, a climbing harness with some hardware and two slings clipped on, and a coil of thin, 8mm rope.

"What do you need all that junk for anyway?" Peggy asked derisively, suddenly in one of her moods. "This is just Vermont for cripes sake. You're not a mountain climber anymore." She put her hands in the air. "You're a goddamn car salesman."

Jack continued eating without reply.

"And not selling too many cars either," she said, dropping into the chair opposite Jack. She had something on her mind.

"Jack," her voice softened, "tonight, can we talk when you get back, please?"

"About what?" Jack looked at his watch.

"About dad. About the agency. He keeps asking me why you won't go to work for him. He says you could make four times what..."

"I don't want to sell insurance. Don't want to be an insurance man." *Like your asshole father,* he wanted to add. *Your pompous, obnoxious, look-at-how-successful-I-am, born-with-a-silver- spoon-up-his-ass father.*

"Come on Jack," she pleaded. "Daddy just wants us, and the kids to have a nice life, that's all. We could move to Charlotte. Dad said he'd help us get a nice house, near them..."

"Not moving to Charlotte. You know that Peg. We've been over that."

Peggy arose abruptly and trudged angrily out of the kitchen. Jack knew she'd be waiting for him that evening to take up the assault once again, or at least make it clear to him what a dismal day she'd had.

He looked down at his rucksack on the floor and the "junk" Peggy had referred to, and picked up the old leather climbing harness, thick and heavy, with brass rivets, nothing like the modern, nylon versions he had hanging in the shed. Jack turned the inside of the belt up to the light and examined the inscription, nearly worn away from years of use long before Jack took possession of it. *Marcel Janot,* it said, *Argentiere 1979.* Jack smiled. *The blacksmith of Argentiere.* He recalled the story Sophie's father had told him when he'd given him the old harness. He'd told Jack that he'd made it, a special order, for his friend Reinhold Messner, the legendary Italian climber, who had dropped it off for repair some years later, and never bothered to pick it up. Jack had seen the photograph of Janot and Messner together, on the dining room wall in the farmhouse in Argentiere, and he knew that Sophie's father wasn't the kind of man to tell tall tales. Jack would never trust the old harness in the Himalaya, but once in a while, in Vermont, it felt good to wear a belt once worn by the greatest mountain climber who had ever lived... the first man to summit all 14 of the 8,000 meter mountains, and the first to climb Everest without supplemental oxygen.

Holding the harness in his lap, Jack thought about Sophie's father – "Poppi" to his daughter; simply *Janot* to everyone else, including his wife – a living encyclopedia of the Alps, life-long climbing instructor and guide, mountain rescue legend, and craftsman of climbing hardware once prized by mountaineers the world over.

The memories flooded back, of the glorious summer he and Sophie spent at the farm in Argentiere, where she had grown up, climbing throughout the Mont Blanc Massif, with "Poppi" Janot and Sophie's brothers, cousins and family friends. All expert climbers, exuberant partiers and lovers of life. Jack and Sophie climbed, biked or rode horses during the day, explored the cafes of Chamonix late into the night and slept together in the apartment over the barn – Jack quickly came to appreciate the permissiveness of French parents.

They summited Mont Blanc and Grand Casse and several smaller peaks, and then through the tunnel to Courmayeur and an excursion into the Dolomites. They climbed by common routes, Janot always in the lead, always teaching, always preaching the *Alpine* way of climbing – quickly, efficiently up and down, lightweight climbing with minimal aids, leaving behind as little iron as possible. The old master never missed an opportunity to instruct Jack in proper rope technique, sophisticated belaying systems, or the art of tying life-saving knots with one hand. On the north face of the *Aiguilles d'Arves* Janot gave Jack and Sophie a master class in locating safe rappelling anchors.

Sophie enjoyed watching her father and her lover become friends and trusted climbing companions. And Jack basked in the incredible glow of the knowledge Janot was imparting to him, and in the fast friendship they were developing. It was the summer Jack began deluding himself that one day, Janot would welcome him into the family. Several years later Jack came face to face with the reality that Marcel Janot would never allow his precious, beautiful daughter, a graduate of the Sorbonne, Olympic gymnast at sixteen, and world-class mountaineer, to marry an uneducated, itinerant American rock climbing, ski bum like Jack Finley.

Jack tossed the harness into his pack and tried to ward off the dull pang of heartache he always felt when he reminded himself of Sophie, their breakup, and her subsequent marriage to the Austrian ski racer Tony Linser. The dashing, film-star handsome Olympic champion, from a wealthy family, owned five-star restaurants in Innsbruck, Val-d'Isère, and Cortina, a vineyard in Tuscany, and a villa in Saint-Tropez. It was a marriage made for Hollywood. The paparazzi had a field day.

Passing the wood pile on his way out, Jack tossed two fat logs into his pack bringing the weight up to about fifty pounds he estimated. In the shed off the garage, Jack picked out an old pair of short, telemark skis, and poles. He skied down the driveway to German Flats Road and headed north towards Mt. Ellen, the two inches of icy snow on the road making it possible to get up enough speed in the downhill sections to nearly make it all the way up the next hill. This early in the morning, he skied down the center of the road, enjoying the speed and the cold air of what would be the easiest part of the day.

Starting on the beginner slope to lengthen out his route, Jack skied up Mt. Ellen, pushing easily up the short lower trails, working hard on the steeper intermediates, and then punishing his heart, legs and arms to the breaking point on a couple of black diamonds. The few early ski patrollers and snowmakers he encountered just waved and *knew that it was Tuesday – Jack Finley was skiing up the mountain.* There were no recreational skiers on the mountain until late in the morning when he had reached the base of

Upper FIS. The sleet had turned to real snow that high up, and the wind was whipping across the egg-crate surface of the steepest slope on the mountain. Jack had to claw and scratch and side-step his way up through the icy moguls and was drenched with sweat when he finally reached the top. He checked his time, and pushed off up the goat path trail toward the summit.

At a sharp turn in the narrow trail, just below the platform where the chair lift emptied its passengers, Jack stopped and took off his skis. Wading into deep snow beside the trail, he pushed his way into a large fir tree and planted his skis and poles out of sight until he would need them later in the day. At a six-foot, wooden plank fence marking the boundary of the ski resort, face-to-face with an ominously printed sign warning "Skiers Forbidden Beyond This Point", Jack reached up and pulled himself over the fence, landing in deep snow, his head even with the tips of the evergreens growing below on the steep western slope of the ski area.

Through the thick trees along the top of the slope, Jack hiked for two hundred yards along a trail he was sure, no one else in the world was aware of. When the forest ended at a sheer cliff dropping several hundred feet to boulders and snow covered ridges below, Jack continued up the trail to his left, climbing higher, carefully over ice-covered rocks and fallen tree trunks. Ahead and below to his right, he caught glimpses of the sheer granite face he would soon be rappelling down.

At a landmark boulder, Jack stopped and searched the low rocks for his anchor, an old, rusted piton he'd put in a few years earlier. He tested it with a firm kick, as always, but then also wrapped the rope around a nearby submerged rock for insurance. Whenever he tied onto a piton for a rappel, Jack was always reminded of the incredible story of the legendary French climber, J.C. Lafaille, alone on Annapurna with no hardware, rappelling down a treacherous wall using a scavenged piece of rope and a plastic bottle, frozen in the snow as an anchor!

Jack clamped his descender onto the rope, and yanked hard on the piton one last time, before putting all his weight on the rope. This was a moment of anxiety that didn't change whether it was on an insignificant wall in Vermont, or a legendary face in the Himalaya. A two hundred foot free-fall to the boulders below would kill you just as thoroughly as a three thousand foot tumble down the Rupal Face of Nanga Parbat.

He knew the wall so well, it took Jack less than a minute to reach the bottom. He unbuckled the harness and stowed it in his pack along with the slings and hardware. Leaving the rope in place, Jack made his way carefully down the rocky slope at the base of the wall, found a rock bridge to cross a small stream, and then welcomed the firm feeling underfoot of the old dirt road that would take him out to Route 16.

After a half-mile hike through thick woods, and then past a sleepy, snow covered farm, Jack's legs felt sufficiently recovered from the ski hike up the mountain to begin his run. At the intersection of Route 16, just north of Bristol, he stopped and ate an energy bar, drank half of his bottle of water, pulled the straps tight on his pack so the logs wouldn't bounce around, looked at his watch, and started out on his ten-mile run.

The sleet had turned to light snow, and the breeze had picked up in the afternoon bringing a wind-chill that Jack figured to be around zero. He pulled up his scarf, covering his mouth to warm the air a bit before he pulled it into his lungs. It was turning into a very difficult day for his workout. The snow was starting to accumulate on the road, the wind was pelting him with stinging fingers of icy snow, and the temperature was dropping.

But inside his lightweight North Face jacket, under the hood pulled down tight around his wool hat, Jack smiled to himself. His fingers and toes were warm and comfortable, and the heat he was generating with the pace of his running made the temperature feel unimportant. This was the kind of weather he reveled in. The kind of weather that built toughness and endurance, and separated the serious climbers from the pretenders. He grimaced when he thought about how cold it would be on Cho Oyu that day.

Jack had been to the Himalaya twice in winter. Once to Chang A Bang, to the dreaded north face, in winter to eliminate the hazardous rock falls of spring and summer. And several years later to the Karakorums to attempt Gasherbrum I and Broad Peak. Both expeditions ended abruptly, the unrelenting conditions sucking the enthusiasm, quickly and completely from all hands. Jack remembered the cold that didn't stop, that chilled your bones and never went away, from base camp without sun, to the frozen ridges and snow fields always in shadow, always blasted by the wind. Cold that would freeze your body from the inside out. He vowed never to return in winter.

After a ten-mile loop, the last leg ran down Main Street through Bristol, one of Jack's favorite places in the world, waving back to the few people who recognized him. He left Route 16 and continued his run right up to the base of the granite wall. In spite of the cold and the sleet now pelting him sideways, his inside layer of thermal underwear was now drenched with sweat, and his thigh and back muscles screamed for relief from the heavy pack. But it was late in the day and darkness was closing in and Jack would prefer to have at least a glimmer of light to ski down the mountain in. He quickly donned the old climbing harness, clipped two slings to carabiners on his ascenders, and started up the icy rope. This was a feeling he knew well, as all Himalayan climbers did, making his way up a fixed rope, late in the day in diminishing weather, with another heavy load of supplies needed at a high camp. It was the essence of high-altitude mountaineering. As always, Jack was grateful for the heavy, oxygen-rich Vermont air.

It took Jack twenty-five minutes to get up the wall and hike back to his skis hidden in the pine tree. He quickly stepped into the bindings and set off down the summit path. He stopped at the top of *Upper FIS* and peered down over the edge to see if there was enough light to tackle the difficult slope. Far down the mountain he could see the lights of the snowcats starting up the lower slopes. *Too dark for FIS tonight. No need to break a leg just to cut twenty seconds off the trip down.* As he started to push off to head down the easier path, Jack felt his phone vibrating against his rib cage. He hesitated – it would be Peggy, he knew, to remind him that it was past six-thirty – and she'd been holding dinner for him. He glanced at his phone, saw that it was an unknown number and pressed it hard against his ear to hear over the wind. It wasn't necessary. The reception was perfect, and even from halfway around the globe he immediately recognized the exuberant voice of Logan Healy.

"Hey Finn! Guess where the fuck I am!"

Jack almost dropped his phone, laughing at the first words he'd heard from his old pal in over a year. "Hey Logan," was all he could manage.

He could hear Logan Healy talking to someone near her. "Hey, where are we anyway?" she asked. A mumbled voice Jack couldn't make out answered her. Then she was back.

"We're on the Aegean Sea, right next to Greece. It's about seventy degrees. Where are you?"

"I'm at the top of *FIS.* It's pitch dark and about five below."

Logan Healy laughed. "Hey, what's not to love about Vermont, right? Geeze Finn, you ought to see this boat I'm on. It's Rudi's new yacht, about two hundred feet long and it's incredible."

"So, that'll be *your* yacht pretty soon," said Jack. Over the phone He could hear music, like a band starting up.

"Yeah, I guess that's right," Logan had raised her voice to be heard. "Sorry Finn, we're having a party, for my birthday. Thirty-six today."

"Happy birthday Logan. Sounds like some Dropkick Murphy music playing."

"Yeah, the Dropkick Murphys are here, on deck."

"What?" Jack didn't think he heard her right.

"Rudi flew them over, the whole band, to play at my party."

Jack had to laugh. "Wow, must be nice."

"Yeah, it is. They're great. But this crowd sucks. Too many Europeans and business friends of Rudi's. Not enough of our gang. They don't appreciate DKM. They've all got girlfriends that weigh about ninety pounds and look like Victoria's Secret models. For dinner, they all eat a grape. One girl, I keep telling her she looks chubby, and she goes down and throws up her grape."

Jack laughed. "Same old Logan."

"Yeah, I'll never grow up." The noise from the band diminished and it was apparent that Logan had gone inside. "Hey Jack, listen. You're going to get a call from a guy named Masters, Phil Masters, he works for Rudi. He's going to invite you to a meeting in New York in a few weeks, at Zermatt headquarters."

"Why should I go to New York?" asked Jack.

"Because I want you to. I made them invite you."

"Yeah?"

"It's about the expedition, Finn. This summer... K2."

"Not interested Logan. I've been there."

"Finn, don't be a pig. Just go to New York and listen to Masters, please. Will you do that for me? A favor to me." Logan used her sweetest voice.

Jack shook his head and laughed. Logan Healey would never change. He was too cold to argue. "Logan, I have to go. I'm freezing my ass off. I'll think about the meeting in New York, but I'm not going to K2 this summer."

There was a pause and then Logan spoke again in a serious voice. "I know you're not Jack. But I want you to go to the meeting in New York, for me. Listen to their pitch and meet the people involved, and let me know what you think. Okay Jack?"

"What's the matter Logan? You worried about the climb?"

"Not the climb. It's the expedition I'm worried about. They're turning it into a circus, Rudi and his guys. It's going to be one big merchandising event for Zermatt and it's starting to feel creepy. Christ Jack, The Outdoor Sports Network is going to cover the whole thing and they're flying a trailer right into base camp. They're going to have twenty people there! And the Korean media is even worse. The whole thing's getting out of hand."

"Sounds like it. Well you always wanted to be in showbiz. Maybe they could get Charlize Theron to play your part if you don't want to go."

"Yeah, that's funny Finn. Just go to New York for me, and let me know what you think. Okay?"

"Okay, I'll think about it. Happy birthday Logan."

"Thanks Jack. I'll call after the..." Logan Healy stopped in mid-sentence, shocked by the vision on her laptop on a desk a few feet away from her. It was logged on to ExplorersWeb, the international web site of mountaineering and other adventure pursuits.

"Logan, you still there?"

She lowered herself into the chair in front of the desk and leaned in closer to the screen. "Oh Jesus Jack! I can't believe it."

"What Logan? What's the matter?"

"It's on Exweb Jack. *Oh God.*" Logan clicked the image to full-screen and gazed at the unmistakable image of Sophie Janot in her trademark blue down suit accented in red and white, the colors of her beloved French national soccer team, *Les Bleus.* The team emblem with the *Coq Gaulois* symbol, showed proudly on the breast of her suit. It was a file picture from several years earlier, taken at a high camp, the wind pulling Sophie's hair across her forehead, cheeks and nose red, pale circles around her eyes from the goggles.

Logan scrolled up to again see the simple headline... *Sophie Janot Feared Lost on Cho Oyu.* "Oh Jack, I'm so sorry." The tears ran down her cheeks onto the phone.

"What is it Logan?"

"Jack, it's Sophie." Logan took in a deep breath to cut off a sob. "She's gone. On Cho. A huge avalanche. She and Victor Petrov, the Russian."

Jack Finley couldn't speak. His heart was beating madly and his knees started to buckle. He tried to support himself on his poles, then dropped the phone over the edge of Upper FIS. He watched it bounce its way down the icy moguls, occasionally taking a big leap into the air, until it disappeared into the darkness.

Chapter 4

The morning sunlight streamed through the open window, warming her arm first, then the side of her face, flickering against her eyelids. Sophie woke to the aroma of breakfast cooking in the kitchen directly beneath her. There would be ham and fresh croissants, a platter of chilled fruit, and the thick, strong coffee Poppi demanded.

From outside she could hear Poppi in his workshop, at the end of the barn, rhythmically hammering on his anvil... a horseshoe maybe, a piton, or a part for the old tractor. He would have been at work for an hour at least before breakfast. Sophie loved to help Poppi in his workshop, where he would allow her to throw pieces of coal into the furnace with her small shovel.

She opened one eye and peered through the window at the beautiful blue, June morning sky and traced the distant outline of the summit of *L'Aiguille du Midi*, where Poppi had promised they would climb, next year when she was old enough, when she was ten. Her brothers, only two and four years older than she, had already been on the mountain several times and to the top. She closed her eyes to enjoy a few minutes more of the warm sun before her mother would call to her from the base of the stairs, *'Sophie, Sophie, peu d'oiseaux, venez pour le petit déjeuner.'*

Then the bed moved. Dropping quickly away beneath her, faster and faster it fell, silently through the floor and down through the kitchen, and she couldn't smell the ham anymore or feel the warmth of the sunlight. All she could see was *white*, and then the intense cold engulfed her, and the bed stopped falling and she was jerked violently upward, bent painfully backward at the waist. She snapped open her eyes but was blinded by the whiteout surrounding her. Waving her hands through the air to try to clear a path of vision through the icy powder, she hit the taut rope tied to her harness at the waist, and suddenly knew where she was

Continuing to bounce slowly up then down again on the stretchable rope, Sophie righted herself and did a quick examination of her physical state. She couldn't feel her legs – they had been packed in snow for, *how long?* It couldn't have been more than a few minutes or she would have been asphyxiated in the small air pocket she'd managed to push out in front of her face. She wiggled her feet and bent her knees again and again until she could do a bicycle motion to get as much blood flowing as possible. Surprisingly, her fingers felt good. She must have had her hands up against her chest under the snow.

Her ski poles were gone, but the equipment on her belt, and her rucksack all seemed to be intact and even though she still couldn't see more than a few inches through the continuing whiteout, she quickly felt for her jumars and two slings. She needed to put some weight on her legs and be ready to ascend as soon as the avalanche snow cloud finally settled... after she'd seen if Victor had made it over the cornice, or more likely, dropped through it as she had done. She was very careful handling the carabiners, and the ascenders. To drop a piece of equipment here would be fatal.

She secured her boots into the slings and moved the jumars up the rope a few feet. "Victor!" she called out several times through the snow cloud without answer. Standing in the slings allowed her to bend her knees and start to wiggle her toes, and the feeling began to return to her legs, but it was getting colder. She needed to get up the rope.

After a few more minutes, the fine snow mist finally began to dissipate. She looked down and could see below her a vertical drop of a thousand feet or more until the face sheered out slightly and then fell away again. If the rope broke now, Sophie calculated, in two, maybe three more summers, her body could make it all the way out to the glacier where, with good fortune, it might be found.

"Sophie! Sophie, are you there?"

Sophie's heart soared upon hearing Victor's voice. "Victor, are you okay?" she shouted back through the thinning mist. Then she could see him, swaying at the end of the rope about twenty meters away from her. He was covered with snow but his broad white smile told her that he was unhurt. They had both survived, miraculously, an avalanche of enormous proportions. But, she knew that she had survived only because of Victor's vigilance and experience and his strength. Sophie smiled at him and pointed upward with her thumb. "I'll see you on top Victor."

Sophie made it over the cornice first, and ran down to Victor's ice axe to provide an additional belay for him, coming up the rope. He was a heavy man, and his axe, now sticking out several inches above the snow, had taken a tremendous beating from the tons of snow that had just run down the slope. Sophie wrapped the rope around her waist, then her left arm, and took a hard grip on it with both hands, then dropped down onto the slope, digging in with her heels.

Victor came up over the edge, moving very slowly, and walked over to where she sat in the snow. He dropped to his knees in front of her and smiled, breathing heavily. Sophie could see the sheer exhaustion on his face and realized how hard he must have fought for his life to get over the cornice in the avalanche. Coupled with the torturous day he'd had breaking trail through the deep snow, Victor was now in desperate need of rest and fluids. She rose to her knees and put her arms around him. Victor hesitated, then embraced her, gently, like he was afraid of hurting her with his strength

"I was afraid," he said, "afraid that you wouldn't make it."

Sophie just nodded and smiled. She put her cheek next to his. "Merci Victor," she whispered, now understanding maybe, why the Russian had climbed with her today when the others had gone down. Why he had come to Cho Oyu with her.

Sophie stood and went to her backpack and took out the nearly empty water bottle. She took a small sip and handed it to Victor. "Here, finish this," she said, looking at her watch. "It's three o'clock Victor. We must start down right away, and get you to camp two, to rest and take some liquids." She hoisted her pack to her back.

Victor rose to his feet slowly. He kicked at his ice axe to free it from the snow, and began coiling up the rope. He looked up the mountain. "Sophie, I think we go up, not down."

"Victor, that's out of the question. The climb is over. You can't go higher. You need to rest."

Victor smiled at her. "I can make it up easily to camp three Sophie. Just look at the snow the mountain has given us." He made a sweeping gesture up the slope with his arm. "It is like walking up stairs now, with no trail to break."

"No Victor. It would still take us four hours. It will be dark, and camp-three may not be there anymore. It's over."

Victor reached into his pack and took out an energy bar. He put his gloves under his arm, opened it and handed half to Sophie. He looked up the slope, chewing on the energy bar. "Sophie, it is just as far down to camp two, and that also may not be there. So either way, we may have to bivouac outside tonight."

"But not at seventy-eight hundred meters Victor, if we have a choice."

He knew it was a hard point to argue against. She was right. A bivouac that high on the mountain, in winter, would certainly be fatal if the weather deteriorated at all. He shrugged and popped the last piece of the bar into his mouth, still looking up the mountain. "Okay, so we make sure we find the tent. It will be there. Under the snow, but I will find it."

"Victor! No. This is irresponsible, a foolish risk." She took a step closer to him and searched his face. "You're not a foolish climber Victor, *never*. Why are you saying all this?"

He finally looked down from the mountain and into Sophie's eyes. "Sophie, if we go down, the climb is over. Everything is over. You will not go to Gasherbrum in the spring." He sighed resignedly. "And there will be no K2 in the summer. Your quest will be over." He leaned down a little closer to Sophie. "And no one ever cares about who came in *second*, at anything."

Victor's words hit Sophie like a punch in the gut, forcing her to face the realization that all the money she had raised, along with all of her own savings – everything she had put into the expedition was now gone, wasted by failure on Cho Oyu. She took in an icy breath of air and turned away from Victor to look up the mountain.

"And if we don't go to K2 in July," he continued, "What will I do this summer? How will I ever get to climb K2?"

48

Sophie laughed and turned back to Victor. She smiled briefly, but then a serious look came into her eyes. "Okay Victor, we will go up to camp three, if you are able. If we can find the tents, we will rest and eat and hydrate. But if we can't find the tents, we will bivouac until first light and then we come straight down. Agreed?"

"Yes, Sophie. That will be our only choice. Now, we need to get started and move very quickly." Victor took a step, but Sophie put a hand on his chest stopping him.

"Also Victor, if we find the tents, then early in the morning tomorrow, I will go for the summit... *only me*. I will go alone and you will rest." She could see the disagreement in his face. "Agree Victor, or I will start down right now."

Victor looked down into Sophie's eyes and saw the determination in her face, the face he longed to reach out and touch, but no, he would not do that. *He knew the rules.* "Okay Sophie. Only you. I will sleep and eat and get fat all day while you have all the fun."

She nodded and patted him on the chest. "Okay. Now I will tell Dr. Clement our good news." Sophie switched on the Motorola and heard nothing. The battery was dead. They had been too long on the mountain for the phone. She thought about using the satellite phone, but knew it would take far too long to reach base camp. They didn't have the time. She would call when they were settled in at camp three. She pulled her pack up over her shoulders, brought her goggles down over her eyes, pulled the hood up over her wool hat, and stretched her balaclava up across her mouth. The wind was picking up.

It was dark and cold, and almost eight o'clock by the time Jack made it down the mountain and back out to German Flats Road. It was his own fault, he knew, moving in slow motion, almost a stupor, since hearing the news from Logan Healy. He'd stood at the top of *FIS* for nearly twenty minutes thinking about Sophie, realizing suddenly that he'd never gotten over her. Thinking about how much he still loved her. Thinking about how she was now dead, buried under the snow on Cho Oyu. And in the spring someone would find her body – unmistakable in her trademark blue down suit with the red and white trim. *How she loved Les Bleus!* Jack thought about going to Cho Oyu in the spring, to look for Sophie.

When he'd finally started to ski down, he fell twice, on easy spots, because of his wandering mind. He couldn't remember the last time he had fallen on skis, even in the pitch darkness of night coming down Mt. Ellen – a small, easy mountain he knew every bump on like the back of his hand. Now it was late and Peg would be in a snit, and the plows had scraped down German Flats Road and he had to walk the last mile with his skis over his shoulder, and no energy left.

Peg was waiting for him in the kitchen. "Where have you been all night? You've never been this late. I called you twice!"

He held up a hand to her and shook his head. "Hard day," he almost whispered. He opened the refrigerator, took out two bottles of Long Trail Ale. "Lost my phone on the mountain." He walked past his wife, down the hall to his small office and closed the door. Jack was desperate for a hot shower, but he needed to read the reports himself.

Jack drained half a beer and logged onto ExplorersWeb, where Sophie's picture was front and center. The tragic death of a beautiful, iconic female mountain climber would be big news throughout the climbing community as well as the celebrity-hounding media of Europe.

Jack enlarged the frame and studied her picture, standing between a Finnish climber and a Sherpa at a high camp on Makalu, the caption said. Her last climb before retiring three years ago. A year before her ugly divorce from Tony Linser, the flamboyant ski racer, restaurateur, and as it turned out, international playboy and chronic high-stakes gambler who had for years been investing the family's wealth in Ferraris, large boats, and gambling junkets to Monte Carlo, London, and Las Vegas. When the divorce was finalized, there was nothing left, and Sophie was forced to leave the sprawling chateau in Kitzbuhel and move the girls back to the farm in Argentiere. Back where she started.

The Exweb story chronicled Sophie's storied career, climbing throughout the Alps from the age of ten with her legendary father, Marcel Janot; winning a place on the French national gymnastics team at sixteen; graduating from the Sorbonne at twenty-one; then conquering a long list of the world's greatest mountains, treacherous faces, and difficult routes, over the next fifteen years. Jack was relieved that his name didn't appear in the story. He knew he wouldn't be so lucky in the Burlington Free Press.

Jack scrolled down to a picture from a year ago of Sophie walking the *Champs-Elysees* – an obvious paparazzi shot – hand- in-hand with her daughters, Wanda, 7, and Chantal, 4, named after Sophie's climbing idols. Wanda Rutkiewicz, from Poland, the greatest woman mountaineer ever, who had perished near the summit of Kanchenjunga in 1992. Sophie had cried for a week, and mourned her death for months. And the vivacious and flamboyant Chantal Mauduit, the embodiment of French women climbers in the eighties and nineties. Sophie's idol, and for a short time, her close friend. Killed by an avalanche on Dhaulagiri in 1998.

One small paragraph included Sophie's climbing companion, who, it said, also perished in the avalanche. Victor Petrov, from Stavropol. Twenty-nine years old, married to a teacher, childless. Petrov was a professional climber and experienced Caucasus guide, with several speed records in the Caucasus, Dolomites and in the Himalaya to his credit. He had five 8,000ers on his resume, including a speed accent of Cho Oyu in summer. He had not climbed Gasherbrum I, or K2, the last mountains on Sophie's schedule.

A picture of Petrov from several years earlier, showed him between two other Russian climbers at a base camp on Mt. Elbrus. Jack noted that they all wore brown, or dark gray, rough-hewn clothing, and boots from an earlier generation of equipment – like Russian and Polish climbers everywhere, too poor to afford the flashier, new, light-weight, high-tech equipment, but impervious to weather and difficult conditions, nonetheless. The toughest climbers in the world, Jack was certain. Victor towered several inches over his companions, and draped his long arms over their shoulders. He wore dark glasses in the sun, and had a brilliant white grin, enjoying himself. Jack had never met Petrov, but he felt like he knew him, like he had climbed with him for years. He could see Petrov's strength and determination in the photo, and his love for climbing. Jack had seen it and experienced it so many times, with so many great climbers during his career. A wave of nostalgia swept over him, looking at the picture. He missed the camaraderie and adventure the Russians were sharing. And he felt sadness for Petrov. *So young. Too young to end a wonderful life.* Jack clicked off the computer and sat in the dark drinking his second Long Trail, tears running down his face.

They searched in the dark for an hour, with no sign of the tents at Camp 3. Sophie stopped digging with her hands and fell to her knees in the snow to rest. The work was twice as tiring in the thin air. Her headlamp was growing dim from weakening batteries, as was Victor's. He was ten yards up the slope from her, slashing vigorously into the deep snow with their only axe now, desperate to find the tent that would save their lives. Sophie was shivering and her teeth chattered. She was desperately thirsty, and her toes were going numb.

It had been a fairly easy trek up to the shoulder after the avalanches had scoured the slope, but it had still taken them over four hours in the unrelenting wind that drove the sub-zero cold right through their down suits and into their bones. They found the camp site quickly, beneath a prominent rock outcropping – protection from avalanches – but the snow here was deep and drifted and they had no shovel for digging. Sophie knew that they were both dangerously dehydrated and they had only a short time left, maybe minutes, before hypothermia would overtake them, and then it would be too late to take shelter. They needed to dig out a snow cave and squeeze into the bivy sack together, and fight to survive the night.

Sophie trudged laboriously up to where Victor had disappeared down into the snow. She could see the glow of his head lamp reflecting off the snow. "Victor," she called out feebly into the wind. She came up to the hole he'd been excavating. "Victor, we need to stop and..."

"Sophie! Sophie! I have the tents!" He was backing up out of the hole pulling the bright orange tent after him. The tent, which they had taken down to lay flat in the snow when they'd last left Camp 3, two weeks earlier, was bulging with bags of supplies and their rolled up sleeping bags. Sophie dug away more of the snow and helped Victor pull the tent from the snow. Then they pulled the second, red tent out also. In twenty minutes, they had erected the orange tent down in the hole in the snow, sheltered from the wind, and had two stoves working at maximum flame to melt snow.

The camp had been well stocked, for four climbers, and there was no need now to save fuel or food. They would only be at the camp for two nights, no matter what happened, and then all the way down and off the mountain. They brewed tea, and chicken soup and noodles, savoring the warm liquids and forcing themselves to eat, knowing that it was the altitude that took away their appetite. They took off their boots and Victor massaged the circulation back into Sophie's toes. Then they squirmed down into the sleeping bags, covering themselves with the extra bags from the second tent.

Finally, warm in her bag, hydrated and fed, and feeling optimistic once more, Sophie pulled out the Thuraya satellite phone and called Dr. Clement at base camp. He was shocked to hear Sophie's voice. "My God Sophie! It's really you? You are alive! We had given up. Toby and Carlos and Ang Phu, went up to camp two and beyond, with no trace. The tents at camp two were gone. How did you survive?"

Sophie giggled with a mischievous thought of pretending she was calling from heaven, but no, Clement was too sensitive and, she was sure, extremely distraught. "Yes doctor, we are both fine, Victor and I. We jumped over the cornice on the rope and survived the avalanche, and now we are at camp three."

"Camp three!" Clement was astounded again. "But you must come down. First thing tomorrow morning, straight to base camp. Toby and Carlos will go up to meet you on the way down, around noontime."

"Doctor, at noon tomorrow, I will be standing on the top of this mountain." Sophie smiled at Victor. "I will wave to you."

They argued a bit more but Clement, knowing he was not going to prevail and assuming that Victor would be with her, gave Sophie his blessing. Then she called home and shocked her joyful mother, and talked to the girls for only a minute. Her parents hadn't told them anything, so it was a very normal conversation about when she would be coming home. With tears still in her eyes, she handed the phone to Victor to call home.

Sophie rolled over to give Victor some privacy as he spoke softly to his wife in Russian.

Chapter 5

The black Mercedes came to nearly a complete stop on the icy road before negotiating the turn into the estate. Two massive pillars supported black iron gates blocking entrance to the property. Each pillar was topped with an intricately detailed, white marble sculpture of a snow leopard. After a few moments of idling under the view of two security cameras, the gates swung open and the Mercedes passed through.

Chun Suek Yen's husband, Bhak Mong-hun drove slowly up the long road at a speed respectful of the beauty and serenity of the grounds. The inch of new snow on the pavement added to the quietude. Mong looked over at his wife next to him and scowled as he pulled over to the side of the driveway. He nodded at her without speaking, but she knew why he'd stopped.

She unzipped the dark blue jacket she wore over her black business suit and white blouse, wrestled it off and tossed it into the back seat after folding it so that the white Nike logo on the breast was securely hidden. Her husband wasn't satisfied. He reached over and tapped the pocket of her suit jacket. Suek Yen rolled her eyes, perturbed, and took out her white I-Phone, briefly checked her messages, then put it in the glove compartment in front of her. She was annoyed, but knew her husband was right. This was a meeting you didn't bring Nike or Apple products to. The car moved on.

Suek Yen had never before been to the house of Kim Young-woo, Chairman of *Snow Leopard Industries*, the largest sports equipment manufacturer in Asia. *Snow Leopard* had been the primary sponsor of her climbing expeditions for the last six years, since she had summited Everest, Lhotse and Makalu in one spectacular season and suddenly became a media darling and instant celebrity in climbing-obsessed Korea. In fact, she had only met Young Kim – the westernized name the Chairman preferred – one time, at a photo session at the *Snow Leopard* offices in Busan.

Her husband though, had been invited to the estate several times, and to the Busan headquarters, to negotiate her personal services contracts with

Snow Leopard. Like most Korean businessmen, Young would find it demeaning to negotiate with a woman on business matters and preferred to deal with her husband, an accountant by trade. *That was fine*, Suek Yen told herself. *When they returned from K2, her contract would be up and that would be the end of Mong acting as her agent. And the end of Mong acting as her husband as well.* The car came to a stop under the portico at the massive front entryway to the mansion. Snow leopards were carved into the huge teak doors.

It would probably be the end of her relationship with *Snow Leopard Industries* too, according to the man who would be her new agent after K2. The American sports agent had shaken his head and rolled his eyes in disbelief when she revealed to him the conditions and the penurious financial scope of her contract with *Snow Leopard* and several other lesser sponsors.

She'd met the agent in Los Angeles while visiting her best friend, a golfer on the LPGA tour. The agent represented a dozen golfers, several tennis players and a number of international soccer players. Suek Yen appreciated the agent's experience with European and Asian companies. And though she hated to admit it to herself, she immediately trusted him more than her husband whose interest in her, she had come to know in five years of marriage, was primarily financial. She had long suspected that Mong had been enriching himself with side-arrangements and fees with her sponsors. But now, all of that would come to an end and she could live as she wanted and be free to find love and companionship, and perhaps finally have children before it was too late. The American agent would make her a very rich woman, he told her, if she was the *first* woman to the top of K2 this summer, the first to summit all fourteen 8,000ers.

A valet took the car and they were led through the mansion to a huge conference room with floor-to-ceiling windows looking out over what would undoubtedly be a spectacular garden in the springtime. A group of men stood talking at one end of a massive mahogany conference table. When Suek Yen and Mong entered, the men greeted them cordially with smiles and handshakes – Mong first, Suek Yen noted, as always. Then Young Kim made his entrance to the room followed closely by his secretary. The group parted to allow Young through to shake hands with Mong. He smiled and nodded perfunctorily at Suek Yen. She smiled back politely.

Everyone took their assigned seats at the table, Young at one end as he wouldn't have a lot to say during the meeting, the others toward the middle. The expedition director, Dong Shin-soo, a retired Army officer and now a vice president at *Snow Leopard,* stood at the center of the table across from Mong and Suek Yen and took over the meeting. He introduced the Climb Leader, the representative from the Korean Television Network- KTV, which would be covering the entire climb, and finally, the representatives from *Samsung* and *Hyundai,* substantial but lesser sponsors of the expedition. He warmly acknowledged the generous and patriotic support of two of Korea's finest companies for what would be a "shining moment" for Korea in the eyes of the world.

The *Samsung* rep, an earnest, handsome young man in his late twenties, handed out wrapped gifts to everyone at the table – the latest Samsung smart phone, and a Galaxy tablet. He made a short presentation explaining how Samsung would handle all electronics and communications on the mountain and in base camp and would be responsible for all social media feeds from their communications tent on the Savoia Glacier and from the electronics center in Rawalpindi. He smiled at Suek Yen and added that he hoped to visit the expedition at base camp. The *Hyundai* man smiled benignly and handed out gift envelopes to everyone at the table, presumably for a very substantial discount on a new Hyundai, or perhaps a free car. No one would open their envelope until later. And while Hyundai was a welcome supporter of the expedition, none of the men at the table would ever consider driving a Hyundai. *Maybe a child or relative could use the certificate.*

Suek Yen ignored the gifts and trained her eyes on the expedition director, a man she knew fairly well, having climbed on two expeditions he had taken to the Himalaya since she had become a *Snow Leopard* climber. She studied his face to see if he reacted at all to the revelation by the Samsung man. Tentatively she raised her hand. The eyes of all the men gradually, reluctantly, acknowledged her. Suek Yen had a very soft voice.

"Excuse me Director Shin, but," she turned to the Samsung man, "but why do you say *Savoia*? Why would basecamp be on Savoia Glacier?" Suek Yen had been to K2 twice before. She knew that nearly every expedition located basecamp somewhere on the Godwin-Austin Glacier, the closest access to the Abruzzi Spur, the long-accepted, proven route up the mountain. The Savoia Glacier meant something else.

Shin clapped his hands together and smiled at Suek Yen, taking the Samsung man off the spot. "Yes! We have a great surprise for you Suek Yen, and wonderful news to share." Shin sat down in his chair and opened a folder in front of him. "Yes, we have just recently heard from the Pakistani Ministry of Mountaineering, informing us that our permit for July and August will be for the West Ridge of K2, and we will have it all to ourselves. I'm sure we all welcome this challenge and opportunity to show the high level of Korean mountaineering skill."

Suek Yen just stared at Shin without speaking, waiting for the rest of the story. She knew that at the table, only she, Mr. Shin, and the Climbing Leader seated next to him, had any idea of the impact their assignment of the West Ridge had on the expedition. Shin continued. "Yes, and we also learned that the Americans have been assigned the Abruzzi Spur."

Suek Yen shook her head in bewilderment. "This then, is no longer a fair contest. We have nearly the most difficult route on the mountain, where no one else will have climbed this summer, while the Americans get..." An angry scowl from her husband told her she was out of line.

Shin waved a hand as if to dismiss the issue. "Yes, the American, Logan Healy, will have the easier route, where there will be established campsites from several June expeditions. We *know* all this *Madame Suek*." He was clearly perturbed. "But we will *still* reach the summit *first!*" He closed his file and shrugged. "This is obviously the result of the rich American, Rudi Joost, Miss Healy's fiancé and benefactor, and his political connections put to work, once more bullying their subservient ally, Pakistan, to achieve an advantage. But..." Shin glanced at the Climbing Leader next to him, "we have a plan. And as the greatest climbing nation in the world," he looked around the table at the other men, "Korea will get its female climber to the summit first."

Suek Yen sat unmoving and silent. *Great, can't wait to hear the plan.* She had been put in her place. *The West Ridge, one of the longest, most difficult routes in mountain climbing history. The route that for years had defeated the Poles, and the Russians, and Bonington too, and only been successfully climbed a handful of times in the long history of assaults on K2 since the Italian team's first summit of the mountain on the Abruzzi Spur in 1954. This was the route she was supposed to race up, to beat Logan Healy, a much stronger climber than herself, on the most lethal mountain in the world?* Suek Yen's stomach started to churn. She hoped she wouldn't have to use the bathroom.

The Climbing Leader, Yoon Jin Suk, stood to take over the discussion. Jin Suk was an experienced climber that Suek Yen had been on several expeditions with and had some respect for, even though, like all Korean male climbers, he had always been completely indifferent to her presence on a mountain. He had at least, never shown her outright disdain. Jin Suk revealed the grand plan in his opening sentence. "Utilizing the finest in mountaineering equipment and clothing from *Snow Leopard Industries*," he nodded to Young Kim at the head of the table, "twenty-five of Korea's strongest and most experienced mountaineers and soldier-climbers, will within the first two weeks, force their way up the West Ridge, while putting in place fixed ropes the entire length of the route to the summit snow field, where, we feel Madame Suek will be able to," he hesitated, looking for the words, "more easily finish the climb." He looked down at his notes. "To assist our team in the transport of supplies, rope, and the 400 bottles of oxygen we will be bringing up the mountain, we have also contracted for 30 Hunza high-altitude porters for the expedition."

Suek Yen's head was spinning. *Twenty-five Korean climbers. Fixed rope all the way to the summit snow field. 400 bottles of oxygen. Thirty HAPs. All to get Korea's "female climber... more easily" to the summit.* Suek Yen didn't know whether to be more surprised or insulted. It was evident that the expedition leaders and sponsors had no confidence in her ability to climb the mountain, especially by the West Ridge. *Twenty-five experienced climbers and soldiers. They would, in effect, be short-roping her all the way to the summit of K2.* Suek Yen wondered if they also had a plan to get her down. Or would getting her to the top first and establishing the record, be their only concern?

Jin Suk continued laying out the details of the climb. They would establish four high camps and an advance base camp to be set up on the southern slope at the beginning of the ridge, 500 meters above the base camp on the Savoia Glacier. Each high camp would be fully established and stocked when *Madam Suek Yen* reached it. She would be asked to carry no weight, no pack or equipment on her way up the ridge, to keep her in the "best climbing spirit." She would carry only her oxygen bottle, beginning at around 6,000 meters, or lower if she required.

The Climbing Leader droned on about the amount and quality of the food they would be bringing and the huge amount of equipment, clothing, tents and sleeping bags – the latest models of everything from *Snow Leopard Industries*. Suek Yen had no doubt that she would be thoroughly sick of seeing the *Snow Leopard* logo by the end of the expedition, which, it was now apparent, would be the largest expedition by far, that she had ever been part of. *Twenty-five climbers* and *thirty HAPs!* This would be an expedition rivaling in size the early English *siege style* campaigns of the last century. A veritable army of climbers and support personnel in a massive assault on the mountain.

She knew she was an annoyance to the men, but she raised her hand once again to interrupt Jin Suk. He went silent and everyone looked at her. Everyone but her husband who stared straight ahead, his jaw set in anger. "Climbing Leader Jin," she tried to smile to ease the situation. "With *twenty-five* Korean climbers, and *thirty* Hunzas, and so many tons of equipment to transport from Skardu, I am imagining that this will require maybe 700, or even 1,000 porters to be hired?" Without saying it, she wondered if there were enough porters available in the Baltoro region to outfit such an expedition, especially with the Americans going in at the same time. "This is a very big number for the very long and demanding trek to the mountain."

Suek Yen flashed back to her own experiences of getting to the base of K2, one of the most remote and difficult of the 8,000 meter mountains to reach... the only one not visible from any inhabited settlement. An adventurous flight from Rawalpindi to Skardu, followed by a torturous eight day (if the weather wasn't horrendous) trek through Askole, Jhula, Paiju, Urdukas, and Goro, along some of the most rugged topography on the globe. Up and down cliff sides and chasms on narrow trails of broken rock, and across the raging Braldu River and the Yermanandu Glacier. Difficult enough, without the usual 300 porters and 50 yaks and mules, and the inevitable porter strikes that were almost programmed into their contract. The scope and logistical nightmare of the expedition Jin Suk was describing was like some giant step back in the history of Himalayan mountaineering to the last century.

Before Jin Suk could reply, the Expedition Director, Shin-soo, came to his feet and opened the file on the table in front of him. With a wide smile, he took out two full-page photographs and slid them across the table, between Suek Yen and her husband. "These are the porters of Himalayan expeditions of the future," he said proudly. "No longer can expensive expeditions afford the inefficiency of eight or nine days of trekking to the mountain, and the completely untenable position of negotiating with goat herders and indigent laborers in the middle of a snowstorm a thousand miles from civilization." He closed his file and sat down.

Across the table, Suek Yen and Mong sat staring at the picture of a massive, twin-bladed, CH47 Chinook helicopter. The helicopter was dark green, adorned on the side with the Korean air force insignia. Behind it, dusty brown hills rose in the distance. Mong looked up and smiled respectfully at Shin-soo. Suek Yen just looked bewildered.

"Bagram air force base, Afghanistan," said Shin, pointing at the picture. "Surplus from our years of helping the Americans. One of the largest, most powerful transport helicopters in the world, now being refitted with more powerful engines and rotor blades redesigned for high altitude flying." He glanced over at Young Kim and grinned. "And by summer, it will have been fully repainted with the *Snow Leopard* logo prominently displayed." Young Kim smiled and bowed his head slightly to Shin.

Suek Yen raised her hand timidly, risking another hard look from her husband. "Director Shin, excuse me, but I don't understand how this enormous expense can be justified by this..."

Shin shook his head and looked at Mong for assistance in controlling his wife. Finally, he leaned over the table and glared at Suek Yen. "*Madam Suek Yen,* this is not something that needs to concern you. The helicopter has already been sold to a private company," he started to turn towards Young Kim, and then thought better of it, "that, after our expedition, will be operating a permanent transport service from Skardu in the Karakorums." He reached over and pulled back the photographs. "*This* is the future of Himalayan climbing. Expeditions no longer have time to waste, hiking in to the mountains, nor money to waste on human pack animals. The American expedition will be using a similar helicopter. As will all future expeditions."

"But director Shin," Suek Yen wasn't ready to be quiet, "you need to walk in, to acclimatize. Everyone will be sick if you fly to the base of the mountain."

Shin waved off her concern. "We will deal with the altitude change."

"And what about the porters of the Baltoro region, whose livelihood depends on the expeditions? It's been their way of life for many..."

Shin had had enough. He waved her off. "Now, we need to move on to a more pleasant topic." He nodded to Young Kim's secretary standing by the door. She smiled and went out the door. A few seconds later, she reentered, followed by three very attractive young women, obviously professional models. They were wearing climbing outfits of varying degrees of weight, all in bright red, which had long been Suek Yen's trademark color, accentuated by black and silver trim, the colors of *Snow Leopard Industries*. Each suit was adorned with the *Snow Leopard* logo on the left breast, and smaller logos of Samsung, and Hyundai on the sleeves. All of the suits, even the heaviest down-filled, high-altitude parka, clung tightly to the shape of the beautiful models, and looked like they were created by a Paris fashion designer. The men at the table all smiled their approval as the models circled the table. And Suek Yen also had to grin broadly as she appreciated the beauty of the suits created just for her.

After their trip around the table, the models left by the same door they entered, and Young Kim stood up, capturing the room's attention. He smiled at Suek Yen. "I hope our wonderful star climber is pleased with the fashions that *Snow Leopard* has created for her so that she will look her best for the television and magazine cameras, and for her picture at the summit of K2." Suek Yen nodded and smiled at the Chairman. "And I hope our star climber noticed how attractive the suits looked on women of... more modest proportions than herself, and perhaps can endeavor to, by the summer, approach a more attractive fit for herself in which to display the *Snow Leopard* image." Young Kim shifted his penetrating eyes from Suek, to Mong next to her, looking for some affirmation of his directive. Mong bowed his head slightly, acknowledging that it was his job to see that Suek Yen lost a substantial amount of weight by the time the expedition departed.

Suek Yen stared blankly at the Chairman, and then around the table, and at her husband. There was no one here who would come to her aid in the wake of these insults she had been forced to endure for the entire meeting. And now the Chairman had concluded the meeting by telling her she was too fat! Suek Yen recalled the approving looks the men had bestowed on the slender models as they circled the table, women who had accomplished nothing in life, knew nothing of danger and hardship and sacrifice, who would never be famous for anything. They received respect because they were pretty, and she was not. Suek Yen thought about her image in the mirror that she had always detested, from when she was a little girl. Her long face with cheekbones too high, and round, puffy cheeks and a flat nose, and always too tall, taller than the other girls in the climbing clubs, and now at five-ten, taller by an inch than her husband. *Yes, she had put on weight in the last year, but she had always been bigger than the other female climbers. Training for K2 would reduce her size a little, possibly.*

Suek Yen was relieved when Young Kim stood to signal the end of the meeting, but there was one more thing, one more issue at the back of her mind that she needed to know about. Reluctantly, she raised her hand once more, causing a sigh of exasperation from her husband. The other men, mostly standing now, stopped and looked at her.

"Director Shin, sir, I am curious about... I was wondering why there has been no mention of my friend, Sophie Janot and the French expedition that will also be..."

Shin cut her off. "Well, in fact, there are conflicting reports of whether or not your friend is still alive on mount Cho Oyu as we speak." He picked up his folders. "Either way, the French, and Miss Janot, will not be a factor for us to consider on K2." He flashed a brief, knowing smile around the table. "The French expedition has been assigned the Northeast Ridge route on the mountain – no doubt, more political intrigue by the Americans, but good for us also. It is an unclimbable route in the fashion the French girl adheres to, plus, she has no funds with which to do anything else. I doubt that she will even enter the contest."

Suek Yen sat still at the table while the men packed up their folders and shook hands again. Her thoughts drifted back many years to the all-women, commemorative expedition to Annapurna, where she first met and climbed with Sophie Janot. She had to smile when she recalled the grace and skill and power of the diminutive French woman, and how friendly and compatible and helpful she was to this lonely, language-challenged Korean girl. They carried loads together and shared a tent, and on summit day Sophie, the expedition's *superstar,* insisted that it would be Suek Yen accompanying her in the lead pair. Then Sophie led all the difficult pitches, fixing rope that Suek Yen couldn't have climbed without, and then encouraging, pushing, and cheering her up the last interminable snow slope, through the unbearable cold and unrelenting wind, one step every thirty seconds in the thin air. And finally they were at the top, with nothing left to climb, where Sophie hugged her tightly while crying like a baby, mumbling in French through her sobs, then planting a French flag and saying a prayer for her heroes, Herzog, and Lachenal, who on June 3rd, 1950, had stood where Sophie and Suek were standing. Suek Yen knew she wouldn't have made it to the summit that day without Sophie, but when they got back down, it was Suek Yen who received all the credit from Sophie, for getting them both to the top with her *determination, incredible strength and endurance,* Sophie had told the Korean press. Suek Yen had a tear in her eye when her husband tapped her shoulder impatiently.

The Mercedes sped north on the highway towards Seoul. The snow had stopped and the late afternoon sun was shining off the Taebaek Mountains far to the east. Suek Yen sat close to the door and gazed out at the mountains that she had been climbing since she was a little girl, and then as a talented teenager with Mong as her instructor. They hadn't spoken since they'd driven back through the *Snow Leopard* gates, Mong's face set in his usual hard scowl to show his disapproval of her conduct at the meeting. Suek Yen didn't care. The meeting had made it clear how little she mattered to everyone involved with the expedition, including her husband. She was simply a vehicle to make *Snow Leopard* equipment and clothing famous beyond Korea, Japan and Indonesia. She would do her part. For *Snow Leopard* and herself. She would lose twenty pounds and look trim in the beautiful red outfits, and be fit, to climb aggressively up the West Ridge and be the first woman to the top, and become the most famous woman climber in the world. Then, she would be a celebrity, the American agent had said, a world-wide *brand* ... and she would be free.

Chapter 6

A familiar noise awakened Sophie with a start. Her eyes flashed open and she sat up to hear more clearly. It was another avalanche, roaring down the mountain toward their tent. She leaned over to warn Victor and heard the sound again. It was Victor coughing. A low rumbling cough from deep in his sleeping bag. "Victor," she said softly, "Victor are you all right?"

The Russian rolled slightly to his right. "Yes Sophie, I am okay. It is nothing." He coughed again, but contained it. "I will be fine. Go to sleep, you need to sleep."

Sophie was concerned about Victor because of the exhausting day he'd had, but a cough in the mountains was too common an affliction to worry too much about. The "Khumbu cough" came with the altitude, dry air, and over-exertion. She lay back down and looked at her watch. In another hour, she would start getting ready. The wind was buffeting the tent walls, but thankfully it wasn't snowing. Sophie took the glove liner off of her right hand to test the temperature of the air inside the tent, knowing that it would be thirty degrees colder outside with the chill factor. In the illumination from the small battery light against the tent wall, she could see the depth of the cloud her breath made. The air was cold, very cold. She wished she had more clothing to add but they'd had to sleep in their parkas to make it through the night, and there was nothing else.

Sophie snuggled down a little deeper into the warm sleeping bag. She wouldn't sleep too soundly – she was never able to sleep well in the thin air before going for a summit – but another hour of rest would be valuable. It would be eight hours to the top, much of that time at over 8,000 meters, with 65% less oxygen in the air. *Her first time above 8,000 meters in three years. As always, without supplemental oxygen. Alone.* She closed her eyes and saw her daughters and longed to hold them in her arms. *Why was she doing this? Why not just pack up and head down with the first light and go home? Would her parents and daughters and friends be asking that question in the weeks and months to come – 'why didn't she just walk down after the avalanche and come home, instead of going up, alone, in winter, to disappear on a mountain called Cho Oyu?'*

She knew the danger, even though Cho was considered a benign mountain, an easy climb, even for the amateurs climbing with oxygen in the spring. Surrounded by guides and Sherpas, dozens of them made it to the top each year. But, Sophie knew it was still an 8,000 meter mountain, and 44 climbers had perished on it – nowhere near the fatality rates of Annapurna, K2, and Nanga Parbat, or the 235 deaths on Everest – but now it was winter, when only fools and Poles climbed in the Himalaya.

"Sophie, you need to sleep." Victor was up on an elbow looking down at her open eyes, staring into the darkness at the top of the tent.

Sophie could feel her pensive scowl, and relaxed her face. "Yes Victor, I know. I feel good."

Victor dropped back down into his sleeping bag. "When you are ready, I will make you breakfast." He coughed softly.

"Merci Victor. I will have a cheese omelet and ham please. And a fresh orange."

"Yes, and I will also brew a pot of coffee."

"And a copy of *Le Monde*, on the patio please."

"Yes Sophie. I think the newspapers will arrive soon."

A few moments of silence passed before Sophie spoke again. "Victor, I do need to ask you a serious question."

Victor rolled toward her, his eyes still closed. "Yes Sophie, what it is?"

"Victor, I need to know – you need to be honest with me... do you think that France can win the World Cup this summer? I think that this will be our year, no?"

Victor smiled, opened his eyes to better consider the question and rolled onto his back. "Well, no Sophie. I am sorry, but I don't think that France will do it this time. I think that probably the Netherlands and Germany are stronger than your side. And Brazil of course can always win every game if they are not so lazy and stupid. Portugal and Argentina have the superstars, Ronaldo and Messi, and can always play well. The Italians are the defenders, with quality players at every position. But Spain... *La Roja*, a magical team with Xavi and Iniesta and David Villa – *ah, such a player!* They are also too much for your side, and for everyone else I think. And France... well, Thierry, is maybe too old, and Ribbery not enough in the midfield, and the coach... he doesn't know who to play and... "

"Okay, okay Victor. Thank you." Sophie was perturbed. "I didn't know you were such an expert. But, you are wrong. You will see. *Les Bleus* will be victorious this year, and I will plant their flag at the top of K2 in July to celebrate!"

Victor chuckled and coughed once more as he rolled away from her. "I hope so Sophie. That would be nice for you."

"Actually Victor, there *is* something that I need to know." Victor rolled back toward her without speaking. "I wanted to ask you Victor..." She hesitated. "I wanted to know if you will be coming with me to K2 this summer."

After a moment of silence, Victor rose up on one elbow to look at Sophie. "I'm surprised that you ask that Sophie. You should know that I will be with you on K2, if you invite me to go. I will be very proud to climb K2 with you."

"Well, I know that Logan... the Americans, have been recruiting many of the best climbers, and paying large stipends, so... I thought..."

"Yes, the Americans called me," said Victor. He shrugged. "I told them I would let them know. They invited me to New York – at their expense." He chuckled. "I should go, just to see New York one time."

"So, will you go to New York? To talk to them?"

"No Sophie," he said softly. "Now that you have finally invited me, I will be on K2 with you this summer. We will go to the summit together."

In the dark tent, Sophie glanced over to see if Victor was looking at her, but saw that he'd turned away. She put a hand gently on his sleeping bag. "Merci Victor."

A few minutes past 3:00am, Sophie stood in the snow while Victor pulled the straps of her crampons tight across the tops of her boots. She felt foolish letting Victor help her as if she were a child, but he'd wanted to come out of the tent to see her off. She hoisted the coil of rope over her head, diagonally across her chest, pulled her balaclava up over her mouth, and turned on the Petzl headlamp strapped across her forehead. The yellow beam was weak beyond a few feet in front of her, but it would keep her on the right track until the sun delivered a hint of light in a few hours. She faced down the mountain, toward where she thought base camp might be, and moved her head back and forth, to signal Dr. Clement, who would surely be up and scouring the dark mountain with his binoculars.

Victor rose to his feet and examined the few ice screws, pitons and slings hanging from Sophie's harness. Satisfied, he reached down and pulled her ice axe out of the snow and handed it to her. She wished she had ski poles, but they were all lost in the avalanche. She would have to use her ax as a pole. Two hours up the ridge, she knew, the route would become too steep for ski poles anyway. Victor went around behind her and lashed the two willow wands he'd found in the tent, to her pack. "Put a wand in the snow at the top of the ice cliff, next to the ice screw so you can find the rope. You don't know how the weather will be when you get back there."

"Yes, Victor. You know, this is not my first mountain."

"Okay, okay Sophie," Victor said firmly. "Now listen, this is important."

"Victor, I've worked out the time. I know where I have to be."

"Yes, Sophie, but I know how much you need to get to the top, and sometimes good judgment can be ignored in such situations."

Sophie smiled under her balaclava and shrugged. "Okay, aller de l'avant et être mon papa Victor."

Victor ignored her gibe. "You need to reach the summit by eleven o'clock, no later, in order to be back here by six at the latest. It will be dark then but I will shine a light for you. You will be okay as long as you are down the ice cliff."

"I will be back before then."

He raised his voice impatiently. "Sophie, listen to me. If you don't make it to the top of the ice cliff by eight o'clock, you need to turn back. Do you understand? It is three hours at least to the top from there. And..." Victor stopped and looked up into the darkness to where the summit was, testing the breeze with his cheeks and his eyelids. "The weather concerns me. You will be at the end of the 36-hour window that Clement predicted."

Sophie nodded. She'd already figured out her turn-around time, as all climbers do. There was nothing she could do about the weather now, and didn't need a lecture, although she appreciated Victor's concern. He took a step toward her. She could see the worry across his face, and still, the exhaustion. They were closer now than two mountain climbers normally would be, and she could see in his eyes how Victor's feelings for her had changed since the start of the expedition. After a moment, Sophie reached up and patted his chest. "Merci Victor," she said softly. "Rest and drink fluids today. I will wave to you from the summit."

She turned and started up the slope at a good pace to ward off the intense cold. The thinner air above would soon limit her to excruciating slowness so she needed to make good time to the base of the ice cliff. She felt good, was well acclimatized, and well hydrated – Victor had made her eat and drink more than she'd wanted – and in spite of the ordeal of the avalanche, she felt well rested and was in surprisingly good spirits. *Eight hours to the summit, then seven hours back, rappelling quickly down the ice cliff. Steady, safe, uneventful climbing. And when she reached camp again, Victor would have hot soup and food ready for her and she would drink fluids, eat and get warm while Victor massaged her cold toes. And when they turned off the stove and the battery lantern, ready for sleep, she would slip out of her parka and her thermal suit, wool socks and her panties, and slide into Victor's sleeping bag and press her naked body against his and they would keep each other warm through the night.*

Sophie stopped to breathe deeply and to check the time. She fumbled with her long glove and the sleeve of her parka trying to get to her watch. Every physical movement was less coordinated at altitude, as was mental concentration and focus, and it would all get worse the higher she went. She filled her lungs as best she could and forced herself to concentrate. She wasn't clipped on to a fixed rope with a dozen other climbers all watching out for each other -- she was alone and she needed to be careful. In the dark, relying only on her sense of direction and memory of the route maps and pictures she had studied, it would be easy to wander off in the wrong direction and get lost, and that would be fatal.

She'd been climbing for two hours, making decent time on the crusty layer of snow left by the avalanches. Having to break trail by herself through two feet of powder in the thin air would have ended the climb after ten minutes. The avalanches that almost killed her and Victor, had made the summit bid possible. Another hour and she would be at the base of the ice cliff. Then two hours on the difficult, sixty degree pitch up the ice to the base of the summit snow slope, and three more hours to the top.

Sophie trudged up through the snow that in some spots was still up to her knees where the avalanches hadn't touched it. Her fingers were cold and her toes were starting to feel numb, which alarmed her because she had so far yet to go. The problem was the slow pace caused by the thin air. She needed to go faster and to keep wiggling her extremities. Suddenly her headlamp faded out, extinguishing the yellow swath of light in the snow in front of her. She pulled her hood back, feeling the sting of the icy breeze going through her wool hat, and took off the headlamp. She looked at it for a few moments, then tossed it into the snow. The length of the expedition had taken its toll on the batteries, as well as the climbers.

Looking up the mountain, Sophie was surprised to see that the sky had cleared and the three-quarter moon, low in the sky, was casting sufficient light to distinguish the features of the mountain. She could see stars in the clear sky – rare for the Himalaya in winter. With her headlamp gone, it was almost too good to be true. But, it would make the air colder, and there was something ominous about a clear sky in the mountains. Like a vacuum pulling in the winds off the Tibetan plains and the moisture from the great river basins of India, clear sky in the Himalaya never lasted for long.

Above her she could make out the imposing wall of the ice cliff that looked to be another two hundred meters up the slope. She looked down toward Camp 3 where Victor would be resting, and then to the base of the mountain where Clement and the others would be waiting for news. They were all far below her now. Looking off into the distance she gazed at the dim outlines of so many other mountains, with no light or sign of life to be seen. Sophie knew there was only one other winter climb scheduled – on Broad Peak in the Karakorums – and that expedition had already given up and gone home. She smiled at the thought that at that moment, she was the highest person in the entire world not in an airplane.

At the base of the ice cliff, Sophie checked her time and was encouraged that she was a little ahead of schedule. The feeling had returned to her toes, and her fingers also felt warm from exertion. And now she was about to undertake the kind of climbing she loved and excelled at, certain that she could make it to the top of the ice cliff in less than two hours.

Examining the wall above her in the dim light, Sophie traversed the base of the cliff and picked out a route that would avoid several near-vertical pitches, but it was still the most technical section of the upper mountain, and climbing most of it un-roped, she needed to be careful and concentrate on every step. With her ice hammer in her left hand, ax in the other, Sophie started up the icy slope, kicking the front points of her crampons into the firm mix of ice and snow. Making slow but steady progress up the cliff, the pace allowed her to catch her breath after every step. This was her kind of climbing – physically and mentally challenging – not nearly as difficult as the north face of the Eiger, or Changabang, or Ama Dablam, but still, an invigorating short stretch of mountain.

Sophie moved efficiently up the ice cliff, and began to feel again, the satisfaction and elation of so many past expeditions, when she climbed for the right reasons, with the right people, loving the adventure and the camaraderie. Now the expedition felt right, and she smiled at the thought of Victor waiting for her in the tent below. It was like the old days, climbing with friends, and with lovers.

She came to a shelf of snow, a good place to stop, where she could stand with her hands free and put in an ice screw. It was about halfway up the ice cliff – time to stop tempting fate and put in some protection and rope up. Sophie was certain that she could make it to the top without difficulty, but she would need the mid-point anchor anyway, when she rappelled down the cliff in the afternoon. The rope trailing below her through a carabiner clipped to her harness, slowed her down a bit, but it was the trade-off for safety.

The top half of the cliff was less vertical than the first half, more of a steep snow slope. Sophie pushed herself to go faster up the easier grade, but the thin air defeated her aggressiveness. Every two steps, she had to stop and draw in large breaths of the icy air through her balaclava to get enough oxygen. She'd been there before and knew that the rest of the way to the summit would be a lonely endurance test, taking the largest strides she could, and the shortest stops for air. She would need to find a comfortable pace, and stick with it.

At the top of the cliff she dropped to the snow to rest and put in an ice screw for the rope. She took off her pack and brought out a package of energy gel, her last two Fig Newtons, and her half-empty water bottle, which had frozen. Though she had no appetite, she forced down the Fig Newtons and the energy gel, then tucked the water bottle inside her parka.

A freshening wind beat against Sophie as she labored to drive in the ice screw. Finally satisfied, she clipped a carabiner onto the screw and tied off the rope. She took off her harness and stuffed it into her pack with the bivy sack, spare gloves and the few packets of energy gel she had left. Sophie clipped the pack onto the ice screw. She wouldn't need any of it until she got back to this spot, and shedding even ounces of weight would make a great difference.

Sophie again checked her watch, and was shocked to see that it was eight-twenty. She was twenty minutes behind schedule. *How had she lost track? How had she been going so much slower than she thought?* Sophie knew, it was the effect on the body and the mind of spending hours at the edge of hypoxia. She hadn't even noticed the dull, milky sun rising far to the east, or the swirling mist of the clouds far below her.

Resolved to make up the lost time, she pulled her ax from the snow and started up the summit slope. She'd gone ten meters when she had to stop to catch her breath. Bending over to fill her lungs while leaning on the ax, she looked back toward her pack, lying in the snow and had a flash of a thought, something she needed to do but couldn't remember. *Like her body, her mind was fuzzy and slow.* Then she saw the two willow wands lying in the snow where she'd left them when she'd taken off her pack. She stared at them for a second, debating whether the effort to go back the short distance was worth the effort. Finally, she retraced her steps and pushed one of the green willow sticks into the snow at the ice screw. She took the second wand with her and headed back up the slope.

The summit slope was wide at the bottom, gradually narrowing as it funneled up to the top of the mountain. The footing was good, and even with a brief stop every two steps for air, Sophie figured she was making good time. After an hour, she came to a point where she needed to take a half-turn to the right to stay in the middle of the slope, she pushed the second willow wand into the snow. Missing the turn on the way back would send her down the west ridge where she could very conceivably never be found.

Sophie looked up the slope to the summit. It looked so close and so easy – a short jog up the hill and she'd be done, and then she could go home. But, like the final leg of every 8,000er she'd climbed, the deception was a cruel hoax the mountain played, luring determined, exhausted, oxygen-starved climbers into a test that was much more grueling than it appeared. This was the point, she knew, where many exhausted climbers, excited by *summit fever,* had lost their way by underestimating the extreme rigor and length of the final push, and refusing to turn around while they still had the strength and mental capacity to get themselves back down the mountain. Sophie knew the statistics – about twenty-five percent of the fatalities on the 8,000 meter mountains came on the way down, and on some mountains – like K2 – the percentage was much higher. Summiting K2, doubled your chances of dying on the mountain.

Sophie did a quick evaluation of her physical condition. She was very cold, but not yet shivering; her fingers and toes were cold, but not near frostbite stage. She pulled the water bottle from inside her parka and drank the bit of water that had melted, then started up the summit slope.

After another hour of slow but steady climbing, the wind started to gust harder. Icy snow flew across her path, pelting her down suit. Sophie put her head down to shield her face, staring only at the snow in front of her, occasionally glancing up to check her bearings, thinking about nothing but the next step. The frigid air became colder and the feeling started to leave her toes, and then her fingers. She trudged on slowly – two steps and a stop to breathe – never considering giving up, knowing she would make it, because she had no place else to go. She had no other options.

Sophie looked up to check the route and was shocked at the vision in front of her. Five meters up the slope, her daughters, Wanda and Chantal, wearing short summer dresses and barefoot, were hopping and skipping up the slope. Giggling with broad grins that highlighted their dimples, both girls half-turned back toward Sophie and waved her towards them. "Venez sur maman!" They called out to her.

Sophie couldn't understand why they were in black and white, but she laughed, with tears in her eyes, and rushed up the slope, trying to catch their small hands reaching out to her. But the girls stayed ahead of her, laughing, having a game, teasing Sophie. Then Sophie had to drop to her knees to breathe as deeply as she could, to gain some oxygen in the thin air. She raised her goggles up to find the girls again but they were gone, and she was alone again. Then Sophie saw that there was no slope left, only a few steps up through some powder snow to a small level platform. She was at the summit. Sophie breathed deeply and shook her head, knowing that she needed to go lower, very quickly.

Only after she walked the final few yards to the top of the mountain, did Sophie look around her and see how dramatically the weather had changed. A gray blanket of thick clouds surrounded her, rising up from the valleys and glaciers below, concealing all but the peaks of the dozens of mountains spread out for miles around Cho Oyu. It would be snowing on the mountain below her.

She took her camera out from its warm pouch inside her parka to document her achievement. Without photos and without a witness, Sophie knew that Miss Hawley, as warm as their relationship was, could never certify her Cho summit. Fortunately, fifteen miles to the east, the unmistakable crown of the king, Everest, was still visible through the growing mass of clouds. It was incontrovertible proof of being at the top of Cho Oyu. She quickly took several pictures of the summit platform with Everest in the background, some shots of the other mountains surrounding her, then clipped the camera to her ice ax and took several pictures of herself holding her unfurled flag of the French national soccer team. The wind caused several pictures of Sophie with the flag covering her face.

She was desperate to sit down and rest for a while and enjoy her short, exclusive stay at the summit, but from deep inside a voice was shouting at her to *get off the summit and get down the mountain!* She remained standing, turning slowly to take in the complete panorama of the summit, oblivious to the frigid wind that was blowing the cold right through her body. She turned three complete circles, and then caught herself, knowing she needed to be thinking about something, doing something. She saw the ice ax standing up in the snow and suddenly everything clicked into her consciousness – *Camp 3, Victor, Base Camp, Wanda and Chantal waiting for her at home, and it was snowing on the mountain below. She needed to get moving down the mountain, or she was going to die on Cho Oyu, as so many other climbers had.* She looked at her watch and saw that it was noontime. *An hour behind schedule.* She pulled the ax from the snow and started down.

An hour down from the summit, she ran into light snow, pinging her sideways on the wind that was now constant. Sophie was making good progress – she'd gotten her second wind that always came to her after several hours of exertion at extreme altitude – and knew the snowstorm wouldn't be a problem as long as she could find the rope at the top of the ice cliff. Where the slope was steep enough, Sophie saved considerable time by glissading down the hill on the heels of her boots or her backside. It was a technique that Sophie was an expert at – because Poppi Janot insisted on it – from the hours and hours spent racing her brothers and cousins down so many slopes around Argentiere in their early teens. The danger, she knew, would come from losing her balance and tumbling forward, rolling and bouncing, out of control down the mountain. With no chance to flatten out and arrest her fall, she would tumble several thousand feet down the west face of the mountain.

Using her ax as a ski pole, Sophie skied down a long, fairly gentle slope on the soles of her boots, flexing her knees, zigzagging down the hill, enjoying herself as much as she had since being on the mountain. She wished the girls were with her, following behind on their little skis, as they had done on that glorious sunny day at Chamonix last spring.

At the base of the slope, Sophie let herself slip to a seat on the snow and struggled to catch her breath. Then she realized how hard it was snowing. She couldn't see anything on the slope at her feet or down the mountain. She was in a whiteout. The end of Clément's thirty-six hour window of good weather had slammed shut on her.

Sophie quickly got to her feet to try and set her bearings. She knew she had to be getting close, within a few hundred meters of the turn leading down to the top of the ice cliff. But if she missed it, she would be wandering around for hours on the slope with the temperature dropping and no shelter. And then it would be dark. She was tempted to stay where she was and wait for the snow to stop to gain some visibility. It was probably the prudent thing to do, but it was too cold, she was too far away from the ice cliff, and it could snow for hours. And this wasn't the place where she wanted to die. She closed her eyes and drew a mental picture of the mountain and where she thought she was on it, and started down again.

Head down and shoulders hunched against the cold and the blowing snow, Sophie fought her way down the slope. After about two hundred meters, she wiped the snow from her goggles, stopped to look around her through the blizzard, and could see nothing. She was hopelessly lost, exhausted, and dehydrated. It was foolish to continue down the line she was on until she could see some sort of landmark, so she dropped down onto the snow. She wished she'd brought the bivy sack with her, although she knew that in this cold, it would only prolong the inevitable for a few hours. She sat with her knees pulled up in front of her, head down to avoid the blowing snow, resisting the strong impulse to roll onto her side, curl up and let the snow cover her.

Sophie was convinced now that she would never get off Cho Oyu. She had stopped shivering, which was a bad sign, and had no feeling in her feet or hands. Memories of all the close calls she'd had in the mountains came flooding back – snapped ropes, loose pitons, the storms, avalanches, acute mountain sickness, exhaustion, injured companions – but nothing was ever this bad, nothing this cold. She wished she'd taken the satellite phone, to call the girls, instead of leaving it with Victor at Camp 3, where it belonged. *But what would she say to them anyway? Did she really want to tell them that their selfish, egotistical, financially desperate mother was trapped, freezing to death, seven thousand meters high on a mountain most people had never heard of?* Sophie's tears fell into her ice-coated goggles. She sat in the snow with her arms covering her head, her face against her drawn-up knees, and went to sleep. She dreamed of the beach at Saint-Jean-Cap-Ferrat, topless on a blanket, the sun baking her while the girls played in the sand by the water. A bead of sweat rolled off her forehead. Then she was awakened. Someone was pulling on her hand. Someone was pushing on her shoulder. Sophie opened her eyes and painfully raised up her head and saw Wanda and Chantal, still in black and white, trying to pull her up off her towel on the warm beach. *Levez-vous de Mama! Venir et se lever Mama. Vous avez besoin de se mettre debout!* Sophie laughed and tried to pull the girls to her, but then they were gone

Suddenly, Sophie saw the snow around her and realized where she was. The snow had stopped and there was no wind. Sophie pushed up her goggles to see, and had to blink her eyes at the apparition in front of her – another joke of the mind, it must be – not ten meters down the slope, sticking straight up out of the fresh blanket of powder snow was the green willow wand she'd put up what now seemed like days ago. Sophie looked off to her left, down the slope beyond the wand. Yes, now the way was clear to the ice cliff. She could make it there easily now, find the first wand, then down the rope and back to the tent. She pushed herself up painfully, pulled the ax from the snow and started down. The storm had threatened to kill her, then it let her go.

It was eight o'clock by the time Sophie reached the top of the last slope leading down to the tent at Camp 3. After the storm, the sky had cleared once again and, miraculously, the small moon provided just enough illumination to distinguish the broad features of the slope. And now she was back, successful, and alive, and very lucky.

The barrel-shaped tent came into view, filling Sophie with relief, and excitement. But, something wasn't right. There was no light in the tent. No lantern, no candle, no Primus stove melting snow for her chicken soup. And no Victor flashing a beacon of light for her to navigate her way home by. *No, this wasn't right. Victor would have come far up the slope to meet her in the dark. He probably would have come up to the base of the ice cliff looking for her.*

The inside of the tent was cold and damp. The battery lamp offered only a dim light – its frigid batteries were almost done. Victor's sleeping bag was laid out neatly on top of Sophie's to make for more room in the tent. The two Primus stoves stood just inside the flap, both pans stuffed with snow ready to be melted, the matches sitting between them next to the wide candle. Packages of soup and noodles were laid out beside the stoves. Sophie lit the candle and both of the stoves. Then she found the note, sitting on top of a pair of her socks on Victor's sleeping bag. She grabbed the note and felt something hard in the socks. It was the satellite phone. The light on the phone was dim and she got only static trying to call Clement at Base Camp. She brought the note over to the candle.

> *S – So sorry. Have to go down now – 2pm. Headache is strong, getting worse. Feeling dizzy also. Cannot wait. I will rest at camp 2, then come back up for you - V*

The letters were ragged and messy, as though written by a small child. Sophie sat and stared at the note and tried to think. Then she realized that she hadn't even taken her goggles off. She didn't know what to do. Her body was frozen and her mind was stuck, on some thought she'd had but then forgotten. She wondered if she should take off her goggles. *But I'll need them if I go out to look for Victor.* She read the note again – *headache... getting worse... dizzy.* Sophie grimaced, and a tear dropped onto the lens of her goggles. She knew it would have been much worse than Victor described – for him to leave her, to leave her coming down alone from the summit. *Much worse.* Yes, Victor would know the symptoms of HACE as well as anyone. He'd seen it take climbers before.

Sophie pushed her hood back, pulled off her goggles, wool hat and balaclava and felt the cold of the tent. She tossed the note down and tried the sat-phone again. It was completely dead. *Victor had left at two o'clock. He would be at Camp 2 by now, or dead in the snow somewhere in between.* She made some tea and soup but wasn't very hungry. She took off her boots and rubbed her toes for a long time, put dry socks on and zipped herself into her sleeping bag with Victor's bag on top of her and went to sleep.

The day was clear, and windless, and Sophie was grateful for the easy passage down the main slope of the mountain, scoured by the avalanches of two days ago. Her pack was light. She took her personal things, the sat-phone and the coil of rope, but left the equipment and the two tents where they were. Everything had taken a good beating in the five weeks they'd been on the mountain, and wasn't worth the trouble to her anymore, and today she would be going all the way down to base camp and wouldn't need any of it. Word would go out about the bounty left at Camp 3, and in the spring some enterprising Sherpas would go up and bring it all down. The tents and the stoves would be worth a month's pay.

Halfway to Camp 2, Sophie looked down the slope and saw the colorful outfits of three climbers standing together in the snow. From three hundred meters away she instantly knew what was happening and had to choke back a sob. The purple suit would be Ang Phu; the orange parka was Toby Houle, the twenty-four year old Canadian; and the red was Carlos Medina, the young Spaniard. Sophie knew that the more experienced Ang would be in charge, in communication with Dr. Clement. The closer she got to the group the slower she walked, suddenly feeling the cumulative effects of one of the hardest expeditions of her career, and now, another tragic one.

As she reached them, Carlos came toward her, his eyes wide with concern. "My God Sophie, are you all right?" He hugged her.

Sophie pushed back her hood and put her goggles up. "Yes, Carlos, I am okay. I am alive." She could tell from the expression on Carlos' face and the looks from Toby and Ang Phu, that she must be a scary sight to them. She knew she had lost fifteen pounds, at least; all her clothing seemed to be two sizes too large. And her eyes would be sunken and glassy.

She took a few steps closer, and saw that they had wrapped Victor in a bivy sack and were tying a rope around it. After she left, they would find a deep crevasse to lower Victor into. His old leather pouch with his personal papers sat in the snow next to his body. Clement would make sure that it was returned to Victor's wife in Stavropol. Clement was good at things like that.

"Did you make it to the top Sophie?" asked Toby.

She nodded. "Yes," she said softly. Sophie looked over at Victor's lifeless form in the nylon sack, knowing that it was her fault he was dead. If she'd insisted they go down after surviving the avalanche, like they should have, he would still be alive. "Yes, I went to the top." Sophie pulled her goggles back down, turned away from the others, and walked down the mountain.

Chapter 7

It was a rare winter day in New York, sunny and warm; a beautiful day to hike through the concrete canyons of the world's most walkable city. Jack Finley was enjoying himself, walking up Lexington Avenue, taking in the early afternoon sights... the bumper-to-bumper traffic, pedestrians by the thousands – always in a hurry – and of course, the beautiful women that go nearly unnoticed on the sidewalks of New York; the women you never see in Burlington.

Jack could tolerate New York for a few days at a time, and since Zermatt Sports was footing the bill for everything, he didn't mind that the trip was all a waste of time. If Logan Healy hadn't pleaded with him to come to New York to learn what he could about the *Team Logan-K2* expedition, he'd be back at the dealership in Burlington trying to sell used Buicks and rust-proofing treatments. As Logan had promised, the call from Phil Masters, the Zermatt VP, came a week after Jack had spoken to her – the day of the erroneous report about Sophie on Cho Oyu. To Jack, Masters sounded a lot like his sales manager in Burlington.

"Jack, Phil Masters here. A huge honor to talk to you, a living legend of mountain climbing."

"Hi Phil, Logan told me you were going to call."

"Recommended you highly, first on her list, even though you've been a bit inactive."

"I'm active enough. Just haven't been to Asia for a while."

"Want you to come down to New York, consult with us about the expedition. We'll fly you down, put you up at a hotel for a couple of nights. Everything on us."

"Are you the expedition leader Phil?"

"I'm Director of Special Ops for Zermatt, and this is my full-time project this year, making sure the expedition is a huge success. Big project, as you'll see."

"So, you're a climber then. You'll be the climb leader on the mountain."

Masters snickered. "No Jack. I'm the CEO of Team Logan-K2. Never been on a mountain in my life. But the climbing part, that's only one component of this project. There's logistics, human resources, recruiting, training, team-building, finance, accounting, marketing, global communications, brand integration, corporate partnerships... there's a hell of a lot more to this than getting up a mountain."

Jack had to smile to himself at the phrase, "a mountain," in reference to K2.

"But of course," Masters continued, "We're bringing in one of the most famous expedition leaders in the world, Morris O'Dell, to run things at the mountain. I'm sure you've heard of him. Maybe even know him."

"Yeah, we've met," said Jack. "Did Logan tell you I'm not going to K2 this summer?"

"Well, we'll see what we can do about that Jack. You're the superstar everyone wants on this expedition. Logan wants you. OSN wants you. And most of all, Rudi Joost wants you, and Rudi has a way of..."

"Alright Phil, I can take New York for a couple of days, so you can take your best shot, but I'll repeat it for you – I'm not going to K2. I've been there... three times."

"Fair enough Jack. We'll email you the plane and hotel confirmations. Looking forward to meeting you in person."

"Hey Masters," said Jack, before they hung up, "Will you be going to K2 with the expedition?"

"Yeah, course I will. I'm in charge," replied Masters.

"Oh," said Jack. "Well, I'm sure you'll have a great time."

Jack looked at his watch and saw that he still had an hour until the two o'clock meeting, and was only six blocks from 46th Street. Two blocks east on 46th, was the world headquarters of Zermatt Sports. He had to consciously slow his walk down to a normal pace. Jack was accustomed to always moving quickly, with long strides, but this was one meeting he didn't want to be early for. He had no desire to be sitting around for a half hour in a Zermatt waiting room with a bunch of other itinerant climbers, as if they were all applying for a job on the Zermatt maintenance crew.

Crossing 41st Street with a crowd of pedestrians, Jack nearly knocked over an elderly woman in front of him when he was distracted by the sight of a familiar figure on the sidewalk ahead. The man was leaning back against a marble slab of the next building, arms crossed, staring up at the sky with rapt attention on something. He wore a tan, corduroy sport jacket, a black flannel shirt, blue jeans and well-worn hiking shoes. Long brown hair flowed out from under a gray, wool skull cap. A three or four day growth of dark whiskers covered his long, thin face beneath dark sunglasses. At his feet on the sidewalk sat a very new looking, black leather travel bag with the unmistakable slashed silver- Z logo of Zermatt Sports.

Jack stood still on the sidewalk and had to grin as he watched his old friend Rob Page, staring into space without moving a muscle. Page was six feet tall, slender almost to the point of gauntness, with broad bony shoulders. Anyone else watching him might think he was a rock star, an actor, or a dancer on Broadway, but not an English travel writer and one of the world's most accomplished mountain climbers. Jack moved to within two yards of him but Page's concentration never wavered.

After a few moments, Jack followed Page's line of sight, looking up, across the street and a block north. He almost laughed when he figured out the object of Page's attention, reaching high into the sky, towering over all the other buildings – the magnificent Chrysler Building with its stainless steel fan of sunbursts gleaming high in the afternoon sun. He knew right away what Page was doing. He'd done it himself on a few buildings in New York

"Find the route yet?" asked Jack.

His friend grinned at the sound of Jack's voice, without averting his gaze. "Finding a proper route's not the difficult part mate, except for getting over those bloody fantails or whatever they are at the top. It's all that nasty eighty year old brick coming apart on you all the way up that's the dodgy part."

"How do you think Tasker and Boardman would have gone about it?"

Page pushed his sunglasses up on his head and turned to Jack with a broad grin. "Still your heroes aye Jack?" he said, almost reverently.

"Always."

Rob Page glanced back at the top of the Chrysler Building. "Well I should think that Joe Tasker would have insisted on climbing in a snowstorm, and Peter would have required that they have a race up it side by side."

The two men laughed, then embraced, then shook hands. "How are you my old friend?" said Page.

"I'm fine," said Jack. "Five years since Manaslu."

"Been a while. Miss you at the pubs in Kat.

"Yeah, don't get out much anymore. Family, you know."

"I heard. But you're going on *this* one?" Page gestured up the street, in the direction of the Zermatt building.

"No, I don't think so. Just doing Logan a favor." said Jack. He looked down at the Zermatt bag at Page's feet. "So you've been up to see them?"

"Just got out. Funny, *they* seem to think you're going. *'Got Jack Finley, the living legend. Going to the top with Logan.'* That's the pitch Morris O'Dell's making."

Jack shook his head. "Pushy bunch, it seems. Just like Logan."

"When's your appointment?" asked Page.

"On my way up now."

"You know O'Dell?"

"Mostly by reputation. Met him once, on Everest."

"Figures. That's where he's made his living for a lot of years now. Good living too. Taking sods up the back way, from Tibet. Plus the odd trip to Broad Peak and the Gasherbrums in the summer, and selling Russian oxygen to the lot of them." Page shouldered the Zermatt bag. "C'mon, I'll walk a bit with you."

"Tough route, going up the North Ridge from Tibet," said Jack resuming the walk up Lexington.

Page chuckled. "Not that O'Dell would know anything about it. Hasn't been above base camp in ten years, and never did much before that. Climbed Everest twice; Cho once; that's it."

"So who does his climbing for him?"

Page smiled. "Our old pal, Mathias. Runs everything on the mountain for O'Dell."

Jack also smiled at the mention of their friend, the South African climber, Alby Mathias. "Yeah... *Mathias*, good man to be with on Everest."

"Good man to be with on any mountain," said Page. "He's the best. May not get everyone to the top, but he'll get 'em all down. Best thing O'Dell brings to this whole bloody expedition is Mathias."

"Doesn't sound like you're too keen on O'Dell," said Jack.

"Bugger couldn't find Annapurna on a map. Lead from the rear, with his walkie-talkies, a big, long spyglass and a cup of tea. Not my style, yeah? Thinks he's the new Bonington, except Bonington was one of the great climbers in the world for a long time before he settled in to organizing trips and writing his books. Went up a lot of difficult routes, always at the front," Page grinned. "Lest Tasker and Boardman were along."

"Still *your* hero, aye?" said Jack.

A black boy of about twelve was walking toward them. Page dropped the Zermatt bag from his shoulder and held out a hand to stop the boy. "Hey there mate. Here's a nice bag o' stuff for you." He put the bag in the boy's hands, and started walking again.

"Anything good?" asked Jack, nodding back toward the boy.

"Nah – T-shirt, warm-up suit, some fleece, water bottle – typical Zermatt logo shit. Rubbish. Leather bag's worth more than the rest of it, but I'd never use it. Been looking for a kid to give it to since I came out."

They came to the corner of 46th Street. Looking across Lexington Avenue to the east, Jack could see the forty story Zermatt headquarters with a huge slashed- Z logo high up on the west side of the building. He turned to Page. "Stick around for a couple of beers after I'm done here?"

"Wish I could mate. Plane to Vancouver leaves at four. Meeting some of the lads for a bit of heli-skiing in Banff."

Jack rolled his eyes. "Must be nice." He turned to face his friend. "So, Rob, you in or out?"

Page shrugged, and squinted toward the Zermatt building. "Don't know. Like to get back, have another go at K2 … might be my last chance, the way climbing is going these days. Pay's good too – ten grand American is a lot of money for a guide job. But," he nodded toward the Zermatt building, "this is fucked. You'll see. All these young kids going, and flying everything in on giant helicopters. Racing the Koreans to the top. It's a bleedin' circus, with Morris O'Dell the ringleader. Plus no guarantees about being on a summit party. Mainly they're looking for pack mules to get Logan and her video crew up the mountain ahead of Sukey." Page glanced at his watch. "Thinking I was probably going to go 'cause they said you were locked in, along with Mathias, but now as I learn that's not the case, I'm going to have to mull it over."

"Well, I'll let you know if anything changes," said Jack, shaking Page's hand. "It was great seeing you again Rob. Wish we could spend more time together." Jack took a step away but saw that Page didn't move.

"Jack, uhm, what about Sophie?" said Page, studying Jack's face. "She's going to be on K2 as well."

"Yeah, I know," said Jack with a scowl.

"Had a bit of a scrape on Cho. Made it to the top by herself – *fucking incredible* – lost another toe and a couple of finger tips." Page's dark eyes bore in on Jack. "Heard she took it hard, losing the Russian."

"You know him?"

"No. A lot younger than us, but everyone says he was a strong climber. And a good guy, which you don't hear so often about the Russians."

Jack shrugged, trying to evade the subject. "Haven't talked to Sophie in ten years, so... I'll let you know how the meeting goes."

Page had a serious look on his face as he gazed up 46th Street. "Jack, thing is, these people up there, they have no idea of what they're in for. Get the feeling this could all end in one of those bloody messes that everybody on the mountain will have a book about out in time for Christmas. Maybe you can warn them." He smiled. "Maybe they'll listen to a living legend." The two men hugged one more time, then parted.

The expansive lobby of the Zermatt building was consumed by an exhibit of a dozen, twelve-foot high photographs of Logan Healy modeling various pieces of Zermatt clothing – winter parkas, casual wear, skin-tight spandex, warm-up suits, Zermatt footwear and sunglasses – all with a reverse band along the bottom of the pictures promoting *"Team Logan- K2, July on the Outdoor Sports Network. Sponsored Exclusively by Zermatt Sports."* At a counter against one wall, a very attractive young woman in a black Zermatt warm-up suit was selling posters of the photographs to a line of enthusiastic German school girls. Jack Finley stood for a moment examining a photo of Logan, stylishly posed in a short Zermatt winter jacket, jeans and high leather boots. She wore purple-tinted sunglasses and a pouting, sultry expression on her face. It was the look of international chic. Jack smiled to himself at the image they were creating for Logan. He knew who she really was.

The whisper quiet elevator opened on the 37th floor to reveal another high-ceiling lobby. On a wall, directly facing the elevator was another huge picture of Logan Healy in full Zermatt-branded Himalayan climbing gear, frosted goggles up on her forehead, oxygen mask pulled down away from her mouth, leaning on an ice ax and holding a small American flag in the air. Her beautiful white teeth gleamed through the posed smile. Jack examined the background of the picture and from the long horizon and brown hills, guessed that it was taken on Shisha Pangma, the only eight-thousand meter mountain located entirely in China. Completely filling the wall space of the lobby were similar huge blowups of photos of Logan at the summit of other 8,000 meter mountains. Some were slightly blurry – from camera movement or snow flurries – and several pictures showed other climbers with her. There were thirteen photos in all.

There was no reception desk in the lobby, just a small stand with two directional signs. To the left was THE MATTERHORN ROOM; to the right, THE MONT BLANC ROOM. In the wall under the Shisha Pangma picture, Jack could see the lens of a security camera. Immediately, a trim young woman with long blond hair tied in a ponytail, came from the Mont Blanc Room. She was wearing a black warm-up suit, accented by thin bands of teal blue, a *Z logo* on the breast of the jacket, and pink tennis shoes. High on the right sleeve of her warm-up jacket was a printed image of the pink *breast cancer awareness* ribbon.

"Good afternoon Mr. Finley," she said warmly, advancing toward him with her hand out. "I'm Monica. I'll take you in to meet the team." Monica had a beautiful smile and the carriage of a fashion model.

Jack followed Monica into a conference room the size of a small gymnasium. The far wall of the two-story room was completely covered with a brilliantly lighted photo of K2 from the air. Jack had seen the photo before, but never so impressively displayed. The center of the room was occupied by a forty foot long, polished mahogany conference table, surrounded by a group of very attractive young men and women standing next to their chairs. They were all attired in the ubiquitous black and teal Zermatt warm-up suits. At the end of the table nearest to Jack, stood two older men wearing black blazers with the Zermatt Z on the left breast.

After entering the room, Monica abruptly left Jack to take her place at the table as a new picture faded in to replace K2 on the wall. While Jack was still marveling at the fact that the entire wall was a giant LCD screen, a new picture came into focus. It was Jack at the summit of Kangchenjunga, his fourteenth and last 8,000 meter mountain. He had both arms raised in triumph, an ice ax held aloft in one hand, his trademark New England Patriots flag in the other. Except for the white circles around his eyes from the goggles, and the sunscreen smeared over his nose, his entire face was bright red. His smile seemed to stretch from ear to ear.

As Jack took a step into the room, everyone standing around the table began clapping their hands. Jack smiled sheepishly but his eyes couldn't leave the larger than life image of himself on the far wall. He looked at his face, smiling with unabashed happiness and triumph, and remembered clearly that moment at the summit – what he thought then was the beginning of a great new chapter in his life, without realizing that his time in the spotlight would only last for a few weeks and a quick succession of unnoticed appearances on the Today Show, the CBS Evening News and Conan O'Brien. A few months later, he was back in Vermont, interviewing for a position as a sales associate at Champlain Buick-GMC.

Jack looked toward the table and held his hand up to stem the applause as one of the older men approached him. The man was tall and distinguished looking with short gray hair and the air of importance about him. He smiled broadly and held out his hand. "Welcome Jack. I'm Phil Masters." Before Jack could respond, Masters held Jack's arm in the air like a winning prize fighter, turned back to the room and bellowed in a deep voice, "Mister Jack Finley, only the second American to summit *all fourteen of the highest mountains in the world!"* Again, the room erupted in applause, this time, more energetically. Jack smiled and was embarrassed. He held his palm up once more and shook his head, but inside he felt the warm stirring of pride over this acknowledgement of his accomplishment. It felt good, and different, after the last three years.

The second man at the head of the table moved over and squeezed Jack's hand with an iron grip. "Morris O'Dell. A great pleasure to meet you Jack." O'Dell was tall and trim with the chiseled good looks of film star. He had bright blue eyes and blond hair curling over his ears. To Jack, he appeared closer to forty than his actual age of fifty-five.

"Nice to meet you Morris. I've heard a lot about you over the years," said Jack. Obviously O'Dell didn't remember meeting Jack on Everest, so he wouldn't bother to bring it up. O'Dell motioned Jack to an empty seat at the middle of the table. Everyone around the table took their seats.

When Jack was settled into his chair, Phil Masters, standing, with a remote control in his hand, began the program. "Jack, as you will see in the next few minutes, *Team Logan - K2*, will be unlike any expedition to the Himalayas that you have ever been on. Totally financed by Zermatt Sports, it will be the most modern, the most experienced, diverse, well-equipped, well-supplied, and environmentally-sensitive expedition to ever assault an eight thousand meter mountain. It will also be the most watched and most followed climb in history, with live TV, on the Outdoor Sports Network, originating right from the mountain." Masters smiled around the table. "To meet the challenge of this grand opportunity, we've assembled an exceptional group of climbers and staffers to represent Zermatt Sports on this international stage."

The picture of Jack faded from the far wall, replaced by a larger-than-life photo of Logan Healy in full climbing gear, smiling down at the conference table. Jack surmised from all the tents and oxygen bottles scattered in the background, that the picture was taken on Everest at the South Col.

"The singular goal of this expedition of course, will be to enable Logan Healy, the international spokesperson and icon of Zermatt Sports, to reach the summit of K2 and become the first woman in history to conquer all fourteen of the eight thousand meter mountains." The *team* around the table once again burst into applause. Jack wondered if clapping was mandatory at every performance of Masters' presentation.

"Now Jack, let me show you the heart of the expedition and the future of Himalayan mountaineering." A picture of a giant black helicopter with the Zermatt Z emblazoned on the tall rear rotor tower filled the wall screen. "A U.S. Army, Chinook CH-47, one of the largest, most powerful and dependable helicopters in the world. Having done its duty in the Afghanistan theater, it has now become *Zermatt Air One* and is currently being retrofitted at our private staging area in Rawalpindi. With two brand new, fifty percent more powerful engines, along with reengineered, longer, lighter and wider rotor blades, and stripped of its heavy armor plating and military hardware, it can now operate at previously unimagined altitudes. We will now be able to fly straight up from Skardu to base camp on the Godwin-Austen glacier. Of course, the Koreans are doing the same thing, so this part of the race will be a draw."

Masters droned on about the capabilities of the great helicopter and the elimination of all the problems and hardships of the eight to twelve day trek in to the mountain, plus the enormous benefit of avoiding the hiring of the thousand porters that would be needed to transport the expedition's gear and food to the mountain. Jack's attention wandered and his eyes left the picture of the helicopter. Aside from the obvious acclimatization problem, he couldn't argue with the idea of flying in to base camp and avoiding the exhausting trek and hassling with an army of porters and their endless issues, or avoiding the squalid camp sites at villages like Paiju and Urdukas. Flying in to the mountains wasn't a new idea, but until now, nobody was willing to spend the money to equip a large helicopter to conquer the thin air. But, now, the economics were right.

Jack looked around the table at the healthy, eager, enthusiastic, and beautiful young faces of *Team Logan K2.* There were four men and three women – three more women than you would usually find on an expedition to the big mountains – probably in deference to Logan Healy's longtime distain for the male dominated "old boys" club of high-altitude mountaineering that made it so difficult for her to secure a spot on Himalayan expeditions early in her career. Now that she was *the* international face of climbing, she would do all she could to promote opportunities for women. But Jack was puzzled as to what roles all these obviously inexperienced climbers would be playing in the expedition. When his eyes came to Monica, directly across the table from him, he found that she had been watching him. She smiled a smile that went beyond friendly, then turned away, toward Morris O'Dell who had risen from his seat to take over the presentation.

"Now Jack, let me show you the incredible line-up of experienced guides you'll be joining," O'Dell began. "Er, that is, we sincerely *hope* you'll be joining." There were chuckles and numerous smiles from around the table directed at Jack. "First, of course, is Alby Mathias from South Africa." The picture of the helicopter on the wall dissolved into a photo of Mathias at a high camp surrounded by deep snow. "One of the best in the world, and an old friend of yours." Jack gazed up at the picture of Mathias, tall and rugged, grinning at the camera, always upbeat, confident, strong, ready to go up, carrying a heavier load than anyone else on the mountain and happy to do it. Jack thought about the many mountains he'd been on with Mathias, and Rob Page – a few back in the old days, with Sophie.

Then a picture of Rob appeared. "Rob Page from England, another chum of yours," continued O'Dell. "Plus three outstanding young climbers you may not know." A picture of three men in like Zermatt parkas came up on the wall. "The blonde haired fellow on the left is Fred Terry, from Oregon – lot of experience, guided for several years on Denali, and five eight thousanders under his belt. Middle is Timmy Burns, very experienced climber from New Zealand; and last is Gordie Yorke from British Columbia. Yorke has ten eight thousanders, and will be taking a crack at Annapurna in May. With K2 this summer, good bet to be the first Canadian to get all fourteen." Jack had heard of Yorke, and had met him briefly on a mountain he couldn't recall.

The next slide on the wall showed head shots of Jack, Mathias, Page, and the other three climbers. "There you have it," said O'Dell loudly. "You couldn't find a stronger team of experienced climbers to be the backbone of our expedition. All handpicked by Logan Healy for the most important climb of her career." The table again applauded. O'Dell pressed a button on the remote. "And to complete the roster of professionals..." A slide showing head shots and names of eight Sherpas lit up the wall. "We'll be bringing over eight of the finest climbing Sherpas in Nepal to join us in the Karakorums. In addition, we've contracted with ten Hunza high altitude porters, for the general unloading and setup work at the lower camps."

Jack recognized several of the faces and names of the Sherpas and was certain that they would all be extremely strong climbers, even on K2, which had proven in the past to be too technical for some Sherpas. He was impressed... *six professional climbers and eight Sherpas, plus ten HAPs.* Team Logan K2 was undoubtedly, the most formidable team he'd ever been invited on. Even K2 might submit to this level of firepower. With the helicopter ride replacing the eight day trek, the expedition was beginning to look like a Himalayan Club Med. *And, of course, there was the money... ten thousand, Rob mentioned. A lot of clear- coats and rust-proofings.*

O'Dell continued, his voice loud with pride, "We'll be bringing in thirty tons of equipment, including two high-capacity generators to power base camp activities, 30,000 feet of rope, and 600 bottles of oxygen. We'll have a first-class Ops and communications tent, mess tent with, I might add, an outstanding wine selection and several kegs of fine ales, and a complete infirmary." O'Dell clicked the remote and the picture of K2 reappeared. "Jack, this will be an historic climb of K2, which the entire world of mountaineering will be watching. You don't want to miss it." The table gave O'Dell a polite round of applause as he handed the remote to Phil Masters.

"Great job Morris, wonderfully done. Going to be a fabulous expedition," said Masters coming to his feet. "Now Jack I want you to meet the Zermatt support staff that will also be climbing K2 in July. We've got some wonderful, talented, very accomplished, very driven young people with us whom I am very proud of. So let's go around the table and let each person introduce themself, tell you about the role they play, and a little about their physical activities and climbing experience. And, Jack, I need to tell you that every one of these young people seated at the table attended Alby Mathias's climbing school in Switzerland, and summited Mount Everest last May, and Denali in the summer, as part of their training for the expedition." Collectively, Masters and the table seemed to beam with pride.

Immediately to Masters right, two young men kicked off the introductions. "I'm Arnie, and he's Bert," said the first man, nodding to his partner next to him.

"Bert 'n Arnie," said the second man, returning the grins from around the table. We're the video crew. We'll be doing all the video of the climb, plus B-roll shots and interviews at base camp."

"And then, putting it all together afterward," said Arnie. "We both graduated from Hampshire College; life-long skiers, runners. I've climbed Denali, Rainier, Everest. We owned our own video company before going to work in-house for Zermatt two years ago."

"I've climbed in the Alps, Denali, Everest," said Bert. He grinned, "Mount Washington, but that probably doesn't count." The table laughed. Jack wondered if Bert and Arnie were a couple.

Jack smiled at the videographers. "Why do you bother?" he said. Bert and Arnie were obviously too puzzled to respond. "Haven't you ever watched any mountain climbing video?" Jack continued. "It's *boring*. Nothing happens. Climbing is a slow motion activity. All you get are people panting and standing in the snow looking up the slope, or making small talk at basecamp. It's horrible stuff. Nothing exciting happens unless somebody... well..."

Arnie tried to explain. "But you need to *document* the... "

Jack cut him off. "So, you and Bert will be at the summit, looking down, waiting for Logan to get up there."

"Why yes, hopefully," said Arnie.

Jack grinned, then turned to the next person at the table, a beautiful girl in her late twenties, with shoulder-length dark hair and a pale complexion. Irish, Jack guessed.

"Hi, I'm Samantha Ryan, the *Director of Social Media*, from Kenilworth, Illinois. I'll be at base camp and on the mountain, managing the Twitter and Facebook posts for all of the climbers and support staff, as well as the daily video posts to YouTube. I'll also be managing Logan's twice-daily blog and providing on-site updates to the expedition website." She smiled. "It all goes through me." It sounded to Jack like a warning to everyone in the room. Samantha was a graduate of Northwestern, where she played lacrosse; a runner, with three marathons; and proud climber of Everest and Denali.

Next came Monica. She hunched her shoulders and leaned in closer to the table, as if a more serious topic was at hand. She smiled. "Monica DeForrest, from Wilbraham, Massachusetts. First of all, Jack, thank you for coming here today. We're all honored to have you at the table and hopefully, as part of the team when we go to Pakistan." As she leaned in to the table, Jack couldn't help but notice how her very ample breasts filled out the top of her warm-up suit. He tried to keep his eyes on her face, but her beauty was intimidating. "I'm the *Director of Sustainability* for the expedition. My job is multifaceted and complex. To simplify, I'll be working to minimize our carbon footprint, as well as the physical, social, and geo-political impact of the expedition on all of the areas and publics we will come in contact with. We will leave Pakistan and the Karakorums, as we found them, and, with hopefully, a higher level understanding of, and appreciation for, the global ethos of the Zermatt brand."

Jack had to bite the inside of his cheek to not laugh. He thought about the carbon footprint of the monstrous black helicopter Monica would be riding in, but remained silent. Monica was a graduate of the University of Massachusetts, and held combined Masters degrees in economics and sustainability from Western New England University. She had been a Yoga instructor before joining Zermatt Sports. When she was done, Monica smiled at Jack as if they were the only people in the room, then leaned back slowly into her chair.

Next to Monica was Dr. Eric Chen, the expedition doctor, a handsome and very fit looking Asian man in his late thirties. He was a Dartmouth Medical grad and a specialist in high-altitude medicine who had been on several Himalayan expeditions. The doctor just smiled at Jack, who winked back at him. "I know the fine doctor from two expeditions we were on together," said Jack. "Nice to see you again Eric."

"I really hope you'll be going with us," said Dr. Chen. He sat back and glanced at the very attractive woman seated next to him.

"Hello Jack, I'm Lisa Greenway, from Aurora, Colorado." She was slim and fragile looking, with a long, delicate neck, a narrow face with sparkling blue eyes. Her light brown hair was piled haphazardly on top of her head. "I'm the Zermatt *Director of Brand Integration*." She was small, but had a strong, confident voice. "My job is to promote the exposure of the Zermatt logo, and maximize opportunities for brand integration and product placement in the worldwide coverage of the expedition, *and* to protect the trademark." She paused. "It all goes through me." Lisa glanced very briefly toward Samantha and Monica. "My MBA is from Stanford, and I have been at Zermatt for six years, since the company started." She smiled broadly, and suddenly she looked stunning. Turning away from Lisa, Jack noticed that Monica didn't look as happy as she had before.

The last person at the table was a short, slightly overweight black man wearing large, wire-rimmed glasses. He smiled at Jack. "Hello, I'm Jay Hamilton, the Communications Officer, in charge of all electronics for the expedition. We will be using the most sophisticated and expensive communications systems ever brought to the Himalayas." Hamilton was from San Diego, held a Masters in Electrical Engineering from Cal Tech, and had climbed Everest and Denali. "But I hate cold weather," he added with a big grin.

Jack laughed. "Well it shouldn't be too cold on K2, but I'd bring some mittens just in case." The table laughed along with Hamilton.

"And there you have it Jack." Phil Masters was standing with his arms spread wide. "Team Logan - K2," he said loudly with pride. "I'm sure you'll agree, the finest expedition ever put together to tackle K2."

Before Jack could say anything, the wall lit up with bright light and a dark figure in the center began to come into focus. Phil Masters pointed to the screen. "Now, we have a very special surprise guest for you Jack. Live and in real time, from Mount Chimborazo in Ecuador."

Logan Healy came into focus. She was dressed in a lightweight, teal blue Zermatt climbing suit and full harness. She pulled off a wool hat, fluffed out her long blond hair, then put her sunglasses up on her head. Someone off camera said something to her, and Logan smiled and moved in closer to the camera, peering inquiringly into the lens. "Hey, I can't see shit in this thing," she said, eliciting chuckles from the conference table. She pulled back and looked away from the camera. "It's too fucking sunny here. I can't see shit. Are they there, in New York?" Someone said something to her. She got in closer to the lens. "Hey Finn, you there? They tell me you can hear me, so I want you to get up on the conference table and take your shirt off so the girls can see your abs, okay?" Logan Healy laughed. "Finn, I'm on one of our favorite mountains – Chimborazo – doing some conditioning. Love this mountain. Wish you were here. We could get some skis and race down." She laughed, as the reception on the screen started to go fuzzy, the audio garbled. "Finn, go see Rudi, and tell him you're coming, okay? Don't be a pig Finn. I want you there on K2 with us." Then the screen went blank.

Everyone in the conference room was grinning over Logan's performance. Jack shook his head in amazement. Even from a mountain on another continent, Logan could command a room.

"Sorry for the reception problem Jack," said Masters. He held his arms apart. "So there you have it Jack." He put his hands together and took his seat. "Now, I think everyone would appreciate hearing a few of your thoughts on the expedition."

Then the room was silent. Everyone was looking at Jack. The dog and pony show was over; the pretty girls had done their thing. Now it was his turn to speak. He looked up at the wall where the beautiful picture of K2 had reappeared, trying to organize his thoughts, without sounding too negative.

Rob Page was right. The whole thing was fucked, and these people had no idea of what they were getting into. Flying in to base camp – everyone was going to be sick as a dog for a week, some much worse – a case of HAPE or HACE for sure halfway up the mountain. You're just not ready for this. It's too steep, too cold... too much history. You're all going to die if you try to climb K2.

"Well," said Jack. He cleared his throat. "It certainly is going to be an exciting expedition." He looked around at the bright, beautiful, smiling faces staring back at him. *Need to warn them.* "But..." He smiled. "There are some things you need to think about. I know you've all climbed Mount Everest – and that's truly, a great accomplishment – but, K2 is not Mount Everest. Climbing Everest would be like going up to the fortieth floor of this building we're in, using the stairs. K2, would be like climbing up the outside of the building." Jack saw some smirks and heard a few chuckles. He leaned forward onto the table and spoke a little louder. "Last May when you all went up Everest, 260 climbers made it to the top. A new record for Everest, by far. Perfect weather. Perfect conditions." He looked around the table. "Do you know how many made it to the summit of K2 last year?" He waited a few seconds for an answer. The smirks had disappeared. Making a circle with his thumb and forefinger, he held up his hand. "Zero," he said. "Not one climber made it to the top of K2 last year, and there were plenty of professional climbers trying – even with a much longer climbing season than Everest."

Jack paused to let it sink in, then looked at Samantha. "Samantha, last summer when you were on Everest, did you see any bodies up there? Or parts of bodies, tattered climbing suits?"

Samantha shrugged. "Yeah, I guess we saw a few things," she said softly.

"Of course you did," said Jack. "They're all over the place. And that's where they'll stay." He turned away from Samantha. "But you'll never see any bodies on K2, even though plenty of climbers have died up there over the years. Anybody know why?" Jack looked around again. The table was silent. "Gravity." He smiled. "K2 is too steep for bodies to stay on. The avalanches and the wind, they scour the mountain and all the bodies end up down in the glaciers. Sometimes, years later, they make an appearance. K2 is steep, and it's huge. You don't hike up it. You climb, all the way. And it's a *long* way."

The faces around the table were more somber now. Jack felt like a great kill joy. "Listen, the only point I'm trying to make is that K2 is the hardest mountain in the world to climb, believe me... I almost died up there myself. So, don't think you're ready because you climbed Everest or Denali." He smiled trying to lighten up the mood. "So, go to K2, and enjoy yourself. Do a little climbing. Go up House's Chimney." He shook his head. "But don't go any higher – leave that to the professionals and Logan and the Sherpas."

Arnie raised his hand. "What about the video crew?"

Jack looked over at him, and then at Bert. "Especially the video crew."

Then Masters was on his feet. "Well thank you for that, um, opinion, Jack. And now, Ashlene will take you up to meet with Mr. Joost." A slender red head was suddenly at Jack's elbow.

Jack shook hands with Masters and O'Dell, and then the *team*, made their way around the table to shake hands. The last was Monica, who shook hands and then gave Jack a hug and another dazzling smile. "It wouldn't be nearly as much fun without you Jack," she said softly.

Chapter 8

After graduation from the prestigious Universite de Geneve in 1978, Rudi Joost earned an MBA in finance at the Harvard Business School, and set about making his fortune on Wall Street at the best moment in history to begin making a fortune on Wall Street. Four years of trading bonds at UBS-New York made him a wealthy young man. His portfolio grew dramatically during a three year tenure at Merrill Lynch, where he specialized in the exotic new derivatives markets. But, the pot of gold came when he moved on to Bear Stearns to manage the arcane craft of packaging what eventually became known as *collateralized debt obligations.* Joost became very rich during his ten years at Bear Stearns, before his entrepreneurial spirit and corporate politics forced him to leave to create of a family of extremely successful private hedge funds. Within a few years, Rudi Joost was being included on the lower rungs of various lists of the world's wealthiest people.

At the age of forty, Rudi Joost was just a little short of a billionaire, married to his college sweetheart, a loving but dull woman, with two pleasant, obedient children, a penthouse apartment on Central Park West, and homes in St. Moritz and Palm Springs. But, what he craved the most, and didn't have, was fame. Every day he'd read the Wall Street Journal, envious of the notoriety of successful business people like Bill Gates, Donald Trump, and Warren Buffet, but what he really aspired to was the style and bravado image of business celebrities like Richard Branson, Phil Knight, and Young Kim, the emerging Asian business superstar founder of *Snow Leopard Industries.*

When the opportunity was presented to take over a fashionable but debt-ridden Italian shoe and sportswear company for a fire sale price of $100million, he jumped at it, not as an investment, but as the vehicle to the new image and lifestyle he coveted. This was his path to international fame – as a marketer of leisure high-fashion sportswear and athletics equipment to the burgeoning new upper-middle class that came to rule the world's economy in the eighties and nineties. He would be the European Phil Knight.

The company's assets included a world-class design department, cutting edge clothing lines, several contracts with second-level European soccer teams, and dozens of endorsement deals with promising young golfers, skiers, footballers, and tennis players. What it lacked was a marketing vision and the financial horsepower to compete with the global brands and gain distribution beyond Europe. Rudi Joost would immediately solve both problems.

He renamed his company *Zermatt Sports* with a stylish *slashed-Z* logo, moved the headquarters to New York, and embarked on a marketing strategy, described in a *Fortune Magazine* cover story as *"Rudy Joost Bets The Ranch."* Joost sold his hedge fund business, adding another $600million to his portfolio, and turned all of his attention to Zermatt Sports and the challenge of making the *Zermatt Z,* an international icon.

Rudi was unconcerned with the enormous personal financial risk the international business press obsessed over. Rather, he reveled in it. Suddenly his picture was in all the newspapers, including a coveted dot-matrix portrait in the Wall Street Journal. The magazines all wanted interviews, and the cable news channels couldn't get enough of him. He went on a diet, got a personal trainer, and let his hair grow over his ears for the first time in his life. His confidence wasn't a façade. Joost knew that he could exhaust his entire fortune on Zermatt, go broke and start over, and soon be as rich as he ever was. Rudi Joost knew how to make money in the financial markets. And he planned on making a lot more, betting big on the certainty of the coming implosion of the housing bubble that he had done so much to create. The mid-2000's was when he projected the massive credit gap that would bring down the high-flying investment banks with their huge portfolios of CDOs and worthless *credit default swaps.* Rudi would take no pleasure in, nor shed a tear over, the nearly instantaneous and complete destruction of his former employer, Bear Stearns. They should have seen it coming. Everyone on the street should have seen it coming. It had always been just a question of *when.* His timing was a few years off, but by the end of 2008, Rudi Joost had made another billion, and his face was back on the covers of *Forbes, Fortune* and *Inc.*

Life appeared seemingly perfect for Rudi Joost, but he knew there was a piece missing, without knowing what it was... until the day scheduled for interviews with the Zermatt stable of athlete-endorsers, and Logan Healy walked into his office, smiling, confident, brash, and so beautiful she made Rudi's heart pound and his palms sweat. Logan had been a moderately successful ski racer for a number of years. Tall, strong and fast, her only failing was her inability to resist the need to go all out at every moment, at every turn on even the most treacherous courses. Too often, she would extricate herself from a retaining fence, grinning and waving to the cameras, with more broken bones and torn cartilage. She was a media darling though, and as she continued to mix the conquest of high mountains with ski racing, her value to Zermatt far exceeded her meager endorsement contract. Climbing and trekking were rapidly growing sports, particularly in the huge Asian markets, and it seemed, that Asian men in particular were enthralled with tall, blonde American women. Logan Healy would be the next international sports icon, Rudi Joost was certain. And, she would be the next Mrs. Rudi Joost, he was just as certain, the perfect complement to his new life in the international lens. Their affair began soon after. Rudi's wife returned to Switzerland, a divorced woman, and the richest person in Zug.

A white phone on Rudi Joost's enormous glass coffee table buzzed softly. He looked at his watch with irritation, and pressed a button on the phone.

"Glenda Craft is here sir," said one of his secretaries. "And Mr. Finley is on his way up."

"Yes, okay, send her in please. And Mr. Finley, when he arrives." Joost closed out of a file, and shut the laptop in front of him. He furrowed his brow in frustration. He couldn't understand Logan's obsession with having this *used car salesman* on the expedition to K2. He was providing the expedition with unlimited resources and the best climbing talent in the world, surely sufficient to reach the top of one more mountain. But he understood why Glenda Craft wanted Finley on the team. And Glenda 's Outdoor Sports Network was a critical component of the entire endeavor.

Joost rose from the white leather chair to greet his first guest. "Glenda, wonderful to see you again."

Glenda Craft, Senior Vice President of Programming for the Outdoor Sports Network, was slim, tanned and elegant in a charcoal gray wool pant suit, as she strode across the expansive office. She carried only a thin leather portfolio tucked under her right arm, and a white I-phone in her left hand. "Hello Rudi, how are you, and how is our show progressing?" She reached out a hand to her host. At five foot ten, Glenda was two inches taller than Joost. He quickly offered her a chair.

"I'm wonderful Glenda, and everything is going well with the expedition. Jack Finley is on his way in."

"Splendid Rudi. So Finley is on board?"

"Well, no, not officially. But, we haven't talked money yet. I eavesdropped on some of the meeting downstairs with Masters and O'Dell, and it seems Mr. Finley has some... uh, reservations about..."

"Reservations? About what? He's a goddamn mountain climber. This is a mountain climbing expedition. This is what these guys *do*. All the other climbers have jumped at the opportunity."

"All but Page, Rob Page, he's thinking about it."

"I don't give a shit about Page. He's nobody. But we *need* Finley. *He's* the one who had the long affair with the French girl. He grew up with Logan. He's drop dead handsome – all the girls love him. Plus, he's got the frumpy wife back home and he can't keep his dick in his pocket for more than a day. He's *perfect.*"

"Don't forget, he's also climbed all fourteen of the 8,000 meter mountains."

"Oh yeah, that too."

"So, we'll just have to make Mr. Finley an offer he can't refuse."

"Listen Rudi, my ass is on the line here. We're spending a fortune to produce this show, and we're going to put Logan Healy and Zermatt Sports in the primetime spotlight for a solid month, all around the world, but if we don't get the hormones flowing on that mountain, this whole thing turns into a National Geographic snooze-fuck and nobody's going to care who gets to the top first."

Rudi laughed. "Okay, calm down Glenda. Finley will have his price. Everyone does. Plus, we have some other incentives to, ah, put in play."

The white phone buzzed softly. "Mr. Finley is here sir."

"Excellent. Please, show him in," said Joost coming to his feet. He moved toward the door to greet Jack.

The sun had dropped behind the buildings to the west by the time Jack Finley left Zermatt headquarters. Even in his light windbreaker, the cooler temperature felt refreshing as he walked west on 46th Street. Jack had a natural affinity for cold weather, and a disdain for heat. He visited Florida once, in September, and couldn't understand how so many people could stand living in hell. Vermont was fine for him – Alaska would be perfect, he'd always thought.

The leather Zermatt bag bounced on its shoulder strap as he took his normal long strides, eating up the sidewalk in front of him, dodging the rush hour pedestrian traffic. He had to chuckle when he thought about the bag and about Rob Page giving his away to the black kid. After the meeting with Rudi Joost and the woman from OSN, Joost's secretary met Jack coming out of the office. She handed him his Zermatt bag. "A small gift from Zermatt Sports, Mr. Finley."

Jack smiled at her. "Anything good in it?" he asked.

The woman raised her eyebrows. *"Well, there are some very nice clothing pieces, and a few logo items, but, in the side pocket you'll also find an exquisite gold and diamond Zermatt chronograph wristwatch worth a little over nine thousand dollars. So, you don't want to miss that."* Jack laughed, picturing the boy strutting down the street wearing his flashy new Zermatt warm-up suit and his nine thousand dollar watch. He wanted to be able to see Rob Page's face when he told him.

Jack was ready for a few beers, and getting hungry, but he wanted to walk for a while to clear his head and think about everything that had happened that afternoon. He had come to New York at Logan's request – only to give her his opinion of the expedition – convinced that there was no way he would be going back to K2 in the summer. He was even more certain after he talked to Rob Page. *Page was right – as he always was concerning anything about climbing – 'These people have no idea of what they're getting into.' Jesus, was he right about that.*

But Jack knew it was worse than Rob had thought. Phil Masters' *Zermatt* staff – the company's expression of diversity for a worldwide audience – was a disaster in the making: three beautiful, territorial young women, ready for a cat fight before the expedition even leaves New York; a delusional gay video crew; a black communications director who hates cold weather; and Masters himself, masquerading as an adventurer, a fish out of water in the mountains who would likely come apart at the seams at the first hardship. Then there would be Morris O'Dell, sitting around base camp, sampling the wine list, staring into his laptop, while he tried to over-manage every movement on the mountain through his telescope – Jack had seen that act before. The professional guides were also a problem, no matter what O'Dell thought. Good chemistry among the lead climbers is paramount on an expedition and he hadn't climbed with any of them except Mathias, and Page, who was probably not even going. The others, and their abilities, were strangers, and the Canadian, Gordie Yorke, climbing Annapurna in the spring and closing in on being the first Canadian to bag all fourteen, would be a troublesome, unpredictable quantity. Jack had seen that before too – he'd seen it in himself – when the big prize is within reach, climbers tend to put themselves first, the team a distant second. And that was dangerous. Then there was Rudi Joost and his marketing goals, and the ambitious Glenda Craft, a living cliché of a TV exec, going to the Himalaya to produce a reality show. Jack shook his head. It was a complete circus. "*Survivor*" goes to the mountains. But this was K2 and it was only a question of how high the body count would go.

Jack turned down Broadway towards Times Square, walking quickly, excited. He'd find a saloon and have a few beers, and then a nice dinner, and think it all over before calling Rudi Joost with his decision. But as ill-fated and poorly conceived as the expedition was, Jack knew that he'd already made up his mind. Even before Joost and Glenda Craft had made him the offer – *thirty thousand dollars*, half from Zermatt, and half from

OSN – he knew that he would be going. It wasn't the money. It wasn't any one thing that had changed his mind. It was the experience of the whole day, from meeting his old friend Rob Page on the street, and the genuine applause from the Zermatt staff around the table; seeing the picture of K2 on the wall, and then Alby Mathias and the Sherpas; and Logan Healy, reveling in the sunshine and deep snow, high on Chimborazo. It was the planning of an expedition to the Himalaya – something he had gone through so many times in the last twenty years, and loved. And this wasn't an expedition to just any mountain; it was K2, the toughest eight thousand meter mountain in the world. The excitement of it all gripped him like nothing had in the last three years and he suddenly realized how much he missed it, ached for it, and how boring his life had become. The thought of standing by his cube at Champlain Buick - GMC, in July, waiting for a good "up" to stroll in, while *Team Logan-K2* attacked the greatest mountain in the world, knotted his stomach.

Jack knew, probably better than anyone, the problems, challenges and perils of the Zermatt *Team Logan-K2* expedition, but, as Morris O'Dell had said, *"Jack, this will be an historic climb of K2, which the entire world of mountaineering will be watching. You don't want to miss it."* That would be true, no doubt. He hoped it would be for the right reasons. At least he wouldn't have a burning case of *summit fever* – he'd been to the top – and he and Mathias, could devote themselves to making sure that Logan Healy and the *Zermatt girls, Bert and Arnie,* and the black communications guy, were still alive at the end of it all. That would be accomplishment enough.

At a cozy booth next to the window at a tavern near Times Square, Jack tucked his Zermatt travel bag in the opposite seat and ordered a tall draft *Long Trail Ale.* He would do what he could for the economy of central Vermont.

He took out his cell phone, ignoring the texts and phone messages, and called Rob Page. Rob would have to start making his plans too, if he was going to K2. Jack was surprised when Page answered – he'd thought Rob would be in the air, on his way to Vancouver – and he'd just leave a message.

"Hey mate. All done at the *big-Z*?"

"Thought you'd be in the air by now," said Jack.

"Bloody airlines. All the same. Always a delay. But I'm easy, you know. Been chatting up a pretty, young lawyer going on holiday, so, may be for the best."

Jack laughed. Same old Rob. "Well good luck with that mate," said Jack. "Wanted to let you know..."

"Don't have to even say it Jack. I knew you'd be going before you did. No way you could resist this much action, even if it is a bloody mess."

Jack laughed. "You know me too well, Rob. I've missed it all too much. And the money's..."

"You don't have to tell me Jack. I know they offered you a lot more. You're the superstar, I'm a mule. Anyway, yeah it's a good payday mate, for a free ride to the big mountain. Hard to pass up."

"So you'll be going?"

"I don't know Jack, I..."

"Rob, come on, it might be the last chance for us to climb together. It's going to be an adventure."

Page laughed, and then went silent for a moment. "Jack, you know, I still need K2. I need the summit."

"Then it will be you and Logan on summit day," Jack said, more seriously. He knew what Page was saying. "Mathias knows you need the summit. He'll take care of you. You'll be part of history."

There was a long pause. "Okay Jack, but not for the money, not for Zermatt, and not for that silly TV network. I'll go for Logan, and for K2, and for you, Mathias, and a safe climb, hey mate?"

"See you in Rawalpindi my friend."

Jack called Rudi Joost and told him he was in. "Wonderful Jack." said Joost. "Our expedition is complete. Logan will be overjoyed! Thank you Jack, for making my life easier." Masters would be in touch with all the arrangements and the financial details, and a package of *Team Logan K2* clothing would be sent to Burlington.

Jack clicked off, and thought about Rudi Joost. He smiled to himself and shook his head. He didn't get it. Logan had to be three inches taller than her future husband, and probably outweighed him. She was outgoing to an extreme; he, reserved and guarded, even a little squirrely. The wedding was scheduled for October in Brookline, Massachusetts, where Logan's parents lived. Was there ever a more mismatched couple headed to the altar? Without his money, Jack knew, Rudi Joost wouldn't get a second glance from Logan Healy. *Being a billionaire certainly has its perks,* thought Jack, as he drained his beer.

He ordered another Long Trail, and a shot of Jack Daniels. He'd have a private toast to his friend, Rene Charest, who would give anything to be going to K2 in July. Then, he'd call home, to check in and remind Peggy to pick him up at the Burlington airport the next day. He'd avoid any talk of substance about the day's activities. He wouldn't talk about leaving for Pakistan in June, or the thirty thousand dollars he would be getting paid. That wasn't a discussion he wanted to start on the phone. It wouldn't be that easy with Peggy. It would be months of arguing and silence, and slamming of doors and drawers, and irrational outbursts. This would be the big one, and he'd have to pay for it. And, he knew, there would be only one way to avoid Armageddon and the complete meltdown of his marriage.

Jack held his small glass of Jack Daniels in the air. "To you Rene, my friend. Wish you were going to be with us on K2." He took a sip of the whiskey and held the glass up for another toast. He chuckled. "And here's to selling *personal fucking lines* insurance for my asshole father-in-law, and moving to Charlotte." He finished the Jack Daniels. "I hope it's worth it."

Jack had a steak dinner before heading back to his hotel. He walked down Broadway into the cacophony of lights, advertising and promotional mayhem of Times Square, feeling exuberant, excited, enjoying the rhythm of the city. It was early and he didn't want to go back to the hotel, but he didn't know what he wanted to do, or where to go. Plus, he still had the large black Zermatt bag on his shoulder.

He walked slowly, through the always moving throng of pedestrians, enjoying the sight of so many beautiful women in their twenties, thirties, forties – New York was alive with attractive women, and Jack could feel the familiar pangs of desire growling inside him. He looked at the discount admission card to a *gentleman's club* one of the street hawkers had pressed into his hand. Jack thought about it for a second, then tossed it into a waste receptacle. *No, that wouldn't do it for him.* He'd go back to the hotel, drop the Zermatt bag off, then see what was happening around the hotel, then go up and have a nightcap and get to bed early.

Stepping off the curb to cross Broadway, an image high above him caught Jack's eye. It was on one of the huge electronic billboards that cast Times Square in perpetual daylight... an ad for the Outdoor Sports Network. And there was Logan Healy, beautiful, stylish, smiling down at New York, from under a headline of lights in full color – *Only on OSN! This Summer! The Race To The Top! K2, The Savage Mountain!* Beneath the picture, an electronic band of type ran rapidly across the screen. *Who Will Win? Logan?* and then the picture changed as the copy ran by, *Sukey?* Jack had to chuckle as a picture of Chun Suek Yen appeared – her grin making her eyes disappear into slits and her plump cheeks look like apples. And then, a kick in the gut, as Sophie's picture lit up Times Square. *Sophie?* asked the copy. Her black hair, thick and straight seemed to flow around her face without a plan; a hint of a smile but not a grin; eyes squinting slightly in sunlight. It was Sophie's look – Jack knew it well; loved it for a long time – not pretty, not cute, but incredibly beautiful. Then Logan was back. Around and around they went.

Jack went back to his hotel room, tossed the Zermatt bag in the corner, unlocked the mini-bar and took out a small bottle of Jack Daniels. He sat in the chair by the window, looking down at Manhattan, the Hudson River and New Jersey beyond, sipping the whiskey, and thinking, finally, about what it would be like see Sophie again at K2. Seeing her picture above Times Square had jarred lose the memories of being in the mountains with Sophie – wonderful, glorious, warm memories of experiences that would never be repeated. Jack felt disgusted with himself, for never having gotten over the feeling of loss, for never being able to mend the hole in his stomach.

He kicked off his shoes, resigned to being in for the night, and took another Jack Daniels from the mini-bar, even though they were twelve dollars apiece – *fuck it!* – Zermatt was paying. He took a long swig, then his cell phone rang.

"Hey Finn! You did it man. You made my day, yahooo!" Logan Healy's voice drifted away from the phone while she celebrated. Then she was back. "Rudi just called with the good news. That's great Finn... fucking excellent! I am *so* glad you're going."

Jack was laughing, as it seemed he always did when he talked to Logan. "Hi Logan. How's Chimborazo?"

"Aw, it's great Finn. My favorite mountain. I'm sitting outside the tent at base camp having a bottle of wine with Mathias. It's still light here. Mathias says hi."

"Tell him hi, and to make sure he gets you in good shape for K2." Jack heard Mathias laugh.

"So K2, the expedition, it's not too screwed up right?" Logan's voice had taken on more somber tone. "It'll be okay, huh Finn?"

Jack took in a deep breath, wondering how much he should tell her. He didn't want to spoil her good mood or her enthusiasm for the expedition. There was no point in that. "Yeah, it'll be fine Logan. A little unconventional, with all the Zermatt stuff, and the TV show, but, we'll manage. We'll get you to the top Logan, and keep everyone alive."

"Okay Jack, thanks. That's exactly what I needed to hear." Then the fun was back in her voice again. "Hey Finn, so you told the kids at the meeting that they were all going to die, huh? Love that! Scared the shit out of 'em Masters said."

Jack chuckled. "No, it wasn't that bad. I just..."

"So Finn, which one did you pick?" Logan laughed.

"What do you...?"

Logan interrupted him. "Gotta go Finn. See you in Islamabad in June. The Serena. Rudi took a whole floor. Perfect timing, the World Cup will be on." She clicked off.

Jack finished the nip of Jack Daniels and smiled. *The Serena! No more sleeping on the floor at the Best Western in Pindi with eight guys sharing a room.* He glanced at his watch and thought about going out. Then, he heard a soft rapping on the door. All he could see through the peep hole was someone, back to the door, wearing a baseball cap.

Jack opened the door, and the person turned around slowly to face him. It was Monica, from the Zermatt team. Her hair was tucked up under the cap. She wore a short, tan leather jacket, blue jeans and tall suede boots. Jack smiled. "You're out of uniform," he said.

"Brought these over for you," Monica said, handing him a thick, brown envelope with the Zermatt logo in the corner. "Your contract, and a bunch of other forms, giving up any rights you ever thought you might have, to Zermatt Sports. Some insurance stuff."

Jack took the envelope and just looked at her. Monica smiled at him, then shrugged her shoulders. "So, are you going to invite me in?" she said softly.

Jack backed away, opening the door for her. He put the envelope on the desk, and walked back to her. In the dim light of the room, her eyes and lips sparkled, and the zipped up leather jacket bulged at her breasts. Jack reached over and took her hat off and tossed it on the bed.

Monica reached up and unpinned her hair, letting it flow down to her shoulders. She unzipped her jacket and let if fall to the floor, then moved a step forward, pressing herself against Jack, as her arms went around his neck.

Chapter 9

Islamabad's only five star hotel, the Serena, was bustling with a clientele the hotel had rarely seen before. The elegant lobby was teeming with rugged-looking men with backpacks and trekking boots, trim young women in fashionable warm-ups, and TV technicians and comely young production assistants. Print journalists, paparazzi, and camera crews outfitted for the June heat in college T-shirts and cargo shorts were searching for prey, eventually ending up in the expansive, overly air-conditioned bar. For a hotel that catered to Eastern diplomats, wealthy Arabs, upper class business travelers and war profiteers, a lobby dominated by mountain climbers and media people was a rare occurrence. Stranger yet at the Serena, was an occupancy dominated by Americans.

The hotel wasn't complaining. During the June through October climbing season in the Karakorums, the Serena would usually only get a small, up-scale smattering of the expedition people, most of whom stayed at the cheaper Marriott, or the Best Western in Rawalpindi, for their one or two night stay-overs before heading to Skardu. Plus, business was down in general due to concerns about terrorism and the prickly relationship between Pakistan and the U.S. *Zermatt Sports'* booking of twenty-four of the Serena's best rooms, plus the Presidential Suite for Rudi Joost and Logan Healy, along with the Outdoor Sports Network taking another twelve rooms – all at top-dollar rates – would make it a very profitable week for the Serena. OSN had also leased one of the hotel's larger conference rooms to use as a broadcast center and studio, through the end of August. The general population of Pakistan may not share their sentiments, but the management of the Hotel Serena was beginning to love these Americans with their Platinum American Express cards and disregard for prices.

The crowd milling through the Serena lobby was augmented by a number of climbers of different nationalities from other expeditions also on their way in to the Karakorums for the summer climbing season. By edict of the Pakistani Alpine Club, K2 was off limits to all but the Zermatt expedition, the Koreans of Snow Leopard, and the French team of Sophie Janot – the result of a lucrative stipend from the Outdoor Sports Network. But a generous number of permits had been issued for K2's neighbors – Broad Peak, Gasherbrum I. and Gasherbrum II. – to expeditions from around the world, including a few of the large commercial outfits from the United States and New Zealand. A Russian and a Polish expedition were already working on Nanga Parbat, about seventy miles southwest of K2. Another dozen permits had been sold to the commercial trekking companies, who had no difficulty in selling out all spots at inflated prices. It seemed that the opportunity to witness even some part of the race to the top of K2 by the three women, whom the media had now made into international celebrities, along with the attendant television and tabloid coverage of the event, had made the Karakorums the *in spot* for summer jet-setters and their pretenders. It was rumored that Ben Affleck and Johnny Depp were coming in sometime in July for a little trekking, and that Brad Pitt would be doing an OSN special at Naga Parbat commemorating the wartime adventures of Heinrich Harrer, whom he portrayed in *Seven Years in Tibet.* And word was out that at the end of the week, Logan Healy's favorite band the *Dropkick Murphy's* from Boston, would be in the Serena's grand ballroom for the great sendoff party the night before the expedition would depart for Skardu. It was turning into Super Bowl Week in Islamabad.

The only discordant note in the festive scene at the Serena came in the form of the black-suited security men positioned at each entryway to the hotel and at all the main rooms off the lobby. Outside the broad open-air entrance, a dozen more black suits, wearing dark sun glasses, stood at their posts around the valet-parking circle. At opposite sides of the circle stood black Cadillac Escalades with dark tinted windows, manned by additional security guards with automatic weapons across their laps. American business came with a certain amount of overhead.

The conference room that had been converted into the OSN studio was directly across the lobby from the bar and was in full production mode at 11:00am. At either end of the room, separated by temporary partitions, were small studios with green-screen backdrops, boom microphones, hard and soft quartz lamps, and robotic video cameras. At a console in the center of the room, the director, Marty Gallagher, managed the production at three computer screens.

Sitting on a stool in front of one of the green screens was Samantha Ryan, the Zermatt Director of Social Media. She'd spent an hour in makeup, where they'd teased out her ebony hair, did her eyes and lips, and made her look like a young Ava Gardner. She wore a tight-fitting, teal blue V-neck jersey with the Zermatt Z logo on the left breast, and never looked more beautiful – because this was reality television, and it was all about sex. She looked straight at her interviewer on another stool only five feet away, two feet to the right of the camera lens. Samantha wasn't to look directly into the camera – the camera would be America observing her, getting to know her, sharing her dreams and her apprehensions about climbing K2, and eventually, caring about her, and falling in love with her and with the other *Z – Girls,* as they had been dubbed.

Samantha had been on the stool for an hour. Only one hour more. The producer interviewing her looked down at the notes on her clipboard, then looked up, smiling. *"Samantha, tell us about your last romantic relationship before coming over here to climb K2."* And so it went. *"Miss Ryan, you're aware of how many people have died on K2, tell us how you feel about that. Do you feel intimidated by all the male professional climbers on the expedition?"* The producer continued to probe into Samantha's family, her college life, climbing experiences and her fears, searching for any provocative background information they might be able to meld with video from the mountain when they put the show together. When she was done, the producer turned to look at her boss, Glenda Craft, standing behind her, to see if she was satisfied. The OSN Senior Vice President in charge of reality programming smiled and stepped forward.

"Samantha, now that you've met all of the professional climbers on the expedition," said Glenda, "tell us, which one would you choose to fuck your brains out in a sleeping bag at a high camp?"

Samantha laughed knowing that her interview was finally over. "Tough choice," she answered, sliding off the stool, "but if I were to get my *brains* fucked out, I'd rather get to it this afternoon right after cocktails."

Glenda laughed and clapped her hands together. *Sam had the right stuff.*

In the studio at the opposite end of the conference room, Gordie Yorke, the Canadian climber was being interviewed by another producer. "Okay Don, last question. Climbing K2 will bring you very close to having climbed all of the fourteen eight-thousanders. How do you suppress that goal in order to get Logan Healy to the top?" The OSN crew had done their homework. They would probe, cajole and coax as much personal information out of Team Zermatt to provide as much controversy, titillation and conflict as they could over the four weeks on the mountain that the show would run. They didn't care who won the race to the top, only that some dramatic moments and hopefully, some juicy relationships occurred on the way up.

Glenda Craft smiled. She was having a good day. "Okay," barked the Director at one of the production assistants, "We need Monica and Tim Burns in make-up." Glenda's only problem was time. They needed to produce all of the B-roll interviews that afternoon and the schedule was tight. They would then do Logan Healy and Rudi Joost that evening – they would take longer. Then, a day of location shots around Islamabad with some of the climbers and *Z-Team* members, a day of production meetings, the big Zermatt Fashion Show and send-off party with that *God awful Irish band from Boston*, a day for packing, then flying to some place called Skardu. The following day, the expedition would helicopter in to K2 base camp, and then the real production problems would start. Glenda would stay at base camp for two days, then turn the production over to her director, Marty Gallagher, before flying back to New York to await the first look at the videos, and pray that her career in television was not over.

In the bar, Alby Mathias, Rob Page and Jack Finley, impressed that the hotel had Guinness Stout on draft, stood at a tall table near the entrance, holding court with any and all climbers who wandered through, drawn to the bar by the several flat-screen televisions that would soon be showing the World Cup games. Mathias knew almost everyone, and Page and Jack knew the rest. Mathias and Page were already legends of mountaineering, and Jack was an international climbing celebrity who drew a crowd. Several times he'd had to pose for camera-phone pictures with a group of giddy Korean, or Japanese trekkers. Mathias, a consummate salesman, was having great success cadging rounds of drinks out of their admirers. Soon they had a tableful of dark beers and small glasses of Jack Daniel's.

A young woman wearing an OSN blazer came into the bar. "Monica DeForrest, please, and Mister Burns, please, Timmy Burns," she called out.

Jack knew that Monica wasn't in the bar. He'd been keeping an eye out for her ever since he'd arrived. He hadn't seen or talked to her since his last night in New York, four months earlier.

At a nearby table, Timmy Burns, the professional climber from New Zealand, downed the remains of his beer, reluctantly rose out of his chair and headed for the OSN studio. As he passed by their table, Jack, Mathias and Page raised their beer mugs in a mock toast, as they did for everyone headed for the OSN executioners.

"There's a good lad Timmy," Page called out. "Your turn in the barrel mate."

Burns gave Page a high-five as he passed the table. Then he turned back as he walked. "I'll be back in time to watch Algeria soften up the English side, getting' 'em ready for slaughterin' by da Kiwis, next round."

"Not happening mate," said Page, "and the Kiwis'll be already home in their straw huts when the Lions move on to the knockout round!" he added loudly. Burns turned around again, laughing, and gave Page the finger.

"Rooney, Rooney, Rooney!" Page called out after him. Several 'Rooney, Rooney's' echoed back from the lobby and distant reaches of the bar. Page grinned at Mathias and Jack. "Great time to be out and about on the world, aye mates, during World Cup. Puts all the broodin' and feudin' to rest for a while." He held his glass up for another toast. "To the Cup."

"To the Cup," responded Mathias and Jack, clinking glasses.

"And then, let's have one for Rene also," said Mathias, holding up a small glass of Jack Daniel's. Jack had told them the story of Rene Charest's visit to the auto dealership.

"To our friend Rene," said Page, softly. "Wish he was here with us."

"To Rene," said Jack.

Out in the lobby, several well-dressed Pakistani men, accompanied by Rudi Joost, and Phil Masters, were striding toward the hotel entrance where two long white limousines had just pulled up. Behind them were four Korean men, including Young Kim, the President of Snow Leopard Industries. Following the entourage at a distance was Morris O'Dell. He obviously had not been invited to wherever the group was going. Seeing Mathias, Jack, and Page, O'Dell came into to the bar.

O'Dell also, was very well known among the other climbing people in the bar. Like a politician running for reelection, he smiled broadly, waving and nodding to acquaintances around the room. He moved toward the Zermatt climbers' table, gathering in a white-jacketed waiter on the way, ordering another round for the boys and a Guinness for himself. "Alby, Rob, Jack," he said, shaking hands around the table.

"One for the Chief boys," said Mathias, holding up his glass for another toast, and handing O'Dell a shot of Jack Daniel's.

"Hear, hear," responded Page and Jack, smiling at Morris O'Dell.

O'Dell downed the liquor in one impressive gulp. "Thank you boys," he said, wiping his mouth with his sleeve. "Good to see you fellows doing some early hydrating, getting ready for the climb."

Page laughed. "Gettin' tuned for the Cup game coming up, chief."

O'Dell grinned and gave Page a high-five. "Lions in a walkover today, aye mate. Algeria right?"

"Rooney, Rooney, Rooney," Page chanted loudly. *Rooney, Rooney, Rooney,* came the response again from several tables. Page beamed with pride over the new cheer he'd created for the English side.

Jack grinned and watched Rob Page, whom he knew, wasn't a big fan of Morris O'Dell. Page was right – the World Cup did engender a sense of camaraderie and good will.

The table enjoyed a long drink of Guinness, just as the waiter returned with another tray- full. O'Dell tossed a black Visa card on the tray and pointed out to the waiter, a few nearby tables with climbers from the UK.

"Good way to run up a ten thousand pound tab on your card Morris," said Mathias.

O'Dell laughed. "Zermatt's card, not mine."

"So," said Mathias nodding toward the lobby, "How'd it go with the Pakkis?"

"Well, good for us," said O'Dell, "But not so good for the Koreans." He chuckled. "And not so good for Rudi Joost either. The climbing ministry loves the helicopters, but the buggers are making us pay for the porters whether we use them or not. Five hundred porters, eight days in, eight days out, at twelve dollars a day. Same for the Koreans. Almost a hundred grand."

"Twelve dollars a day? That's robbery," said Mathias. "Going rate's five dollars."

O'Dell smiled and shrugged his shoulders. "Seems that not everyone is so eager to embrace the *new era* of Himalayan expeditions when there's still money to be spread around. Doubt that the Baltis will see much of it, but we still avoid a hard trek each way, plus those bloody awful porter strikes."

"So the meeting with the Alpine Club was good for us?" asked Page.

"Got the ground rules," said O'Dell. "Nobody goes anywhere above base camp before July first, and everyone's done by August fifth." O'Dell shrugged. "That's the deal the PAC made with Outdoor Sports Net. So, we got five weeks to get Logan up the hill."

"Jesus, that's pretty tight Morris," said Mathias. "Weather could make five weeks a fantasy."

"Forecast for July couldn't be better," said O'Dell. "Very little moisture coming out of the basins in India they tell me. But anyway, that's the way OSN wants it, and it's *their* dime so it's a five-week show boys. No dilly dallyin'. Up and down. Good show, there you go!"

"How's that good for *us*?" Asked Page.

O'Dell took a drink of his Guinness, then leaned in over the table. "Cause now it's in the bag for us mate. The Koreans'll never make it up the West Ridge in five weeks. Can't be done, even with the army of climbers they got with them." He leaned back and laughed. "Wait 'til you see the bloody mob they brought over! I went past their staging area down in Pindi two days ago and there must have been fifty, sixty climbers and HAPs, all dressed in those hideous black and silver outfits – you know, all that Snow Leopard crap – all out on the tarmac doing fucking jumping jacks. *Unbelievable!*"

"Didn't the Koreans bitch about the five weeks?" Asked Mathias.

"Little bit," said O'Dell, "But their own TV network, KTV, has a deal with OSN, and it's expensive for them to be here too. So in the end, they just accept their fate, like the Koreans always do." O'Dell laughed. "They just figure they'll go to the whip and climb a little faster." He shook his head. "Shit, they don't know what they're up against. Any of you guys ever gone over and taken a look at the West Ridge?"

"Yeah," said Jack softly, "I went up there one year with some guys wanted to see where Bonington tried to go up it."

"So you know how bad it is," said O'Dell.

Jack put his glass down on the table. "It's murder. If the snow's deep, it might take 'em five weeks just to get to the ridge."

"Exactly," said O'Dell.

"Yeah well, don't underestimate the Roks," said Mathias. "I've climbed with them. They're like machines. They're the Asian version of the Poles. They'll carry Sukey to the top on their backs if they have to."

The men went silent, drinking their beers, looking over at one of the large TV screens over the bar where the preliminaries to the England - Algeria game were starting. Another topic for discussion was hanging over them. Rob Page, sensing that Jack didn't want to be the one to bring it up, put his beer down on the table. "What about the French?" he asked. "Was Sophie represented at the meeting?"

O'Dell nodded. "Yeah, she was. I was surprised to see him, the old man, the great Marcel Janot himself. I'd never met him before. Quiet guy. Didn't say a word. Shook hands with everyone, saying 'bon jour', very softly. Didn't say anything about the five week limit. Probably realized it wasn't going to happen for Sophie anyway – five weeks or five months – she's never going to go up the Northeast Ridge with that tiny crew she's got." O'Dell shrugged. "*Alpine style* and *no oxygen.* I don't know what they're thinking about," he said softly. "This isn't the mountain for it."

"They're all out at Gasherbrum right now," said Mathias. "Sophie's on her way down today. Got to the summit late yesterday afternoon." He smiled at Jack. "Her thirteenth eight-thousander." Mathias shook his head. "Poor kid can't get a break. Another brutal climb I heard. Lot of snow and wind up there the last few weeks. Went to the top with Ang Phu."

"Great climber," said O'Dell. "Ang's one of the best Sherpas in the world. Tried to recruit him for Zermatt."

Jack was curious. "What happened?"

O'Dell shrugged and raised his eyebrows. "Wasn't interested in the money. Said he was committed to Sophie. Imagine... a Sherpa didn't care about making more money."

"So, no chance for Sophie on the Northeast Ridge?" asked Page.

O'Dell laughed. "No, Jesus no. You read Ridgeway's book. We all read it. Incredible climb in '78. First ones to make it up the Northeast Ridge. First Americans to make it to the summit of K2. One of the great climbs in mountaineering history – pure determination and endurance. And look at the *climbers* they had on that expedition – John Roskelly, Lou Reichardt..."

"Wickwire, and Ridgeway, and Whittaker," added Mathias. "*Strong* climbers."

"Some of the best ever," said Page.

"And it took them eight weeks to climb the ridge," said O'Dell, "Probably the strongest team to ever attack K2, and in the end, the porters had to carry Wickwire all the way out to Askole. Lucky to survive it."

O'Dell glanced over at the TV screen where the game was just under way, and finished his beer. "And what does Sophie have?" he said to no one in particular. "The Spaniard, Carlos Medina – good climber I'm told, but young – a Canadian kid, three good Sherpas, and two professional guides from Courmayeur her father recruited after the difficulties on Cho Oyu." He shook his head at looked straight at Jack. "Not enough, I'm afraid.

Not nearly a strong enough team. And Sophie will be exhausted after two hard climbs. The whole team will be exhausted, and short on supplies, I'd think, after too many weeks on Gasherbrum. It would be a mistake for her to even attempt the ridge." O'Dell edged a little closer to Jack and spoke softly. "What she should do Jack, is come out and rest for a month, then go back in August. Climb the Abruzzi – all the ropes will be in place, campsites established – *she's a celebrity* – the Pakistanis won't give a shit about her permit – and then she'll have her fourteenth. She'll have her last mountain." He rapped the table with his knuckles and turned to join Rob Page, standing with a group of Brits at the bar watching the football game.

Jack sat in silence with Mathias, thinking about Sophie and her plight to climb K2. Yes, Jack had read the book, *The Last Step: The America Ascent of K2* by Rick Ridgeway. Every climber has read it. One of the greatest expedition books ever written. Jack read it when he was fifteen, and then two more times after that. What Herzog's *Annapurna* was to a generation of older climbers, *The Last Step* was to Jack Finley. He knew O'Dell was right. The Northeast Ridge would be suicide for Sophie's small, inexperienced team. *But what could he do about it? Sophie didn't need warning – she knew what she was facing – and she certainly wasn't going to listen to anything he had to say, after ten years apart.*

Jack looked out into the lobby, still bustling with expedition and OSN people. He looked over the crowd, wondering if he'd see Marcel Janot. Jack was surprised to hear Janot's name. Surprised that he would be in Pakistan, but it made sense with Sophie and Dr. Clement still on Gasherbrum. Jack wondered if Janot had gotten so old that he wouldn't recognize him after ten years.

Jack felt a body bump him from the side. He looked back to see Lisa Greenway across the table, standing next to Mathias. Next to Jack, Monica was pressing playfully against him, smiling broadly. She'd just come from her OSN video interview and her blond hair was flowing majestically around her shoulders. Her make-up job was perfect, and she wore a fragrance that Jack immediately recognized from New York.

"Hey Jack," she said softly, "Nice to see you again."

"Yeah, hi Monica," Jack replied. He was uncomfortable with their closeness in public. He smiled at Lisa across the table, but she didn't look happy.

"You guys are out of uniform," said Lisa, frowning at Mathias and then Jack. "You know you're supposed to be in Zermatt logo wear at all times in public. It's in your contracts."

Mathias laughed. "Well, Miss Greenway, captain of the logo police, it just so happens that I've got my *Zermatt – Z* right here, tattooed on *little Alby's head*." He started pulling down his zipper, "so, if I can just coax him out of his cave..." Monica and Jack were laughing, and Lisa couldn't maintain her stern look.

"*No, Jesus Alby*," said Lisa, pulling Mathias's hand away from his zipper. She looked around with a grin on her face. "C'mon you guys. I'll be in trouble if Phil Masters comes through here and doesn't see enough logos."

Jack was watching Lisa and couldn't help noticing the way she stood close to Mathias and how she had pulled his hand away – *familiar, not the first time they had touched* – and there was the sound of her voice saying '*Jesus Alby*'- *not with anger, but more like affection*. And Mathias, even with several beers and a Jack Daniel's in him, wasn't prone to crudeness - it was more like familiarity. Jack could recognize the subtle signs and sounds, the words of a hidden relationship. He'd been there. He was the master. Mathias, he knew, had been divorced for many years, but was remarried and had small children.

A commotion in the lobby drew Jack's attention away from Mathias and Lisa. Logan Healy was moving through the lobby like the Queen of England. With her was her long-time best friend, Anja Lindgren, a well-known Swedish ski racer, who had turned her severely spiked blond hair into several shades of green and maroon. Diamond studs adorned Anja's lower lip, left eyebrow and the side of her nose. Both women showed ample amounts of cleavage and leg in their low-cut, abbreviated sun dresses. Bert and Arnie, the Zermatt video crew, were moving backwards in front of them, recording the show. The paparazzi and an OSN video team struggled to keep up.

They breezed into the bar, a passage through the crowd magically opening up in front of them. Logan spied the table of Zermatt climbers and made a detour to greet them. She briefly hugged Page and Mathias. "Hey, *logo Lisa* and *sustainable Monica*," she said, giving the women a high-five. Then she came around to Jack. "Hey Finn," she said, into his ear, hugging him closely. She pulled her head back and kissed him full on the mouth, then hugged him again. "Thanks Finn, thanks for being here. Sorry we haven't been able to spend much time together." She moved her mouth to Jack's ear and lowered her voice. "We'll catch up, up on the mountain, when we get rid of all these assholes." Jack laughed. As Logan stepped back and took Jack's glass of beer, draining half the mug, Jack noticed Anja Lindgren glaring at him from across the table.

"What's going on here Finn?" Logan asked, nodding toward the TV screens and the crowd in front of the bar.

"Football," said Jack. "The World Cup."

Logan shook her head and started off on her rounds. "Not football if the Patriots aren't playing right?" Jack laughed as Logan and her friend disappeared into the crowd. A promo for the upcoming game between the United States and Slovenia appeared on the TV screen, and Jack could hear Logan's unmistakable voice starting a U-S-A, U-S-A chant. Then she emerged from the crowd with a beer bottle in one hand and a small American flag in the other, leading an enthusiastic conga line through the tables, chanting U-S-A, U-S-A, which quickly grew to a riotous roar. Passersby from the lobby crowded in to see what the demonstration was about. The OSN video crew was standing on the bar recording the scene.

Jack couldn't stop laughing as he chanted along with the crowd and watched his childhood friend in action. There wasn't a barroom anywhere in the world that Logan Healy couldn't take over.

"Hey Jack!" someone yelled. Jack looked over to see a man with a camera standing a few feet away, just as the flash went off. Monica was pressed against Jack's arm, smiling, her blonde hair flowing down his sleeve. The photographer took two more quick pictures, then turned his camera on Lisa and Mathias.

"Aw fuck," Jack exclaimed. "Hey!" he called out to the photographer, but he'd moved off into the crowd. Jack could already see the photo of him and the gorgeous Monica in full color on the front page of the sports section in tomorrow's USA Today.

Then, Monica had her hand on Jack's back, turning him to his left. "Smile Jack, like you're having a good time," she said, laughing, pointing toward the Zermatt video team of Bert and Arnie, standing a few feet away with a sophisticated looking video camera and a boom mike. "Wave to the folks back home." said Monica waving to the camera.

Jack turned his head and stared at Monica. She was smiling, relaxed, having fun, a beautiful girl ready to party. *She really didn't know what she was doing. She had no idea.* Jack shook his head and stepped away from the table. "I have to go," he said, to no one in particular. "Going to use the men's room."

Jack went out into the lobby, the beer and liquor making his first steps unsteady. He walked to the back of the hotel and went out through some glass doors into the nearly empty pool area. The afternoon heat felt good after sitting in the frigid bar. He thought about going back to his room and calling home. He looked at his watch. *No, five in the morning in Vermont.* He sat down on a lounge chair to think.

What would he say to her anyway? 'They took some pictures of me in a hotel bar with beer mugs and shot glasses all over the table and a gorgeous young blonde hanging all over me, but don't worry about it Peg, it's harmless, it doesn't mean anything, just part of the job. This is what mountain climbers do.' He pictured Peggy and Ralph and little Beth coming down to breakfast at her parents' house in Charlotte, and finding the Burlington Free Press on the kitchen table, opened to a full color picture of him and Monica, taken at the luxurious Serena Hotel in Islamabad, Pakistan. And then probably seeing the video on *Entertainment Tonight!*

Christ! Peggy doesn't even know where fucking Pakistan is. This isn't fair to her. It's not fair, even after the deal they'd made – Jack going to work for her father's insurance agency when he got back, and then moving to Charlotte – Peg didn't deserve this. Ralph and Beth didn't deserve this. This wasn't part of the bargain.

The sweat was starting to roll down from Jack's forehead. He thought about jumping into the pool. Page was right, he knew, that day back in New York. *'This is fucked'* he'd said *'A bleedin' circus.'* But Jack had known it too, and he came anyway. He should have known better. *What he should do, is pack up that afternoon, head for the airport, and go home.* But he knew he couldn't do that. He was committed. He'd taken half the money. He'd promised Logan. He was part of the show.

Jack was about to get up from the lounge chair when he saw one of the young Pakistani desk clerks walking toward him with a wide grin on his face and a white envelope in his hand.

"Hello, hello, Mister Finley sir. A message for you please." The clerk handed Jack the small invitation size envelope with the Serena logo in the middle, and stood looking down at him. After a few moments, Jack realized what he was waiting for, and gave him two dollars. The young man bowed and left.

Wondering what party he'd been invited to, Jack opened the envelope and took out the folded card. The message was written in almost scribbled text. It took Jack a couple of readings to decipher it...

Hello Jack – Please meet with me, tomorrow in the morning at nine o'clock. Anwar Café, Saddar Bazaar, Rawalpindi. I need to speak with you. Merci. It was signed simply with a large, flourished J – the mark of Marcel Janot.

Jack stared down at the note and laughed. *Just when you thought the day couldn't get any weirder.*

Chapter 10

The Serena Hotel's lobby was still bustling with activity at eight o'clock in the morning. People were leaving the restaurant while others went in for breakfast. OSN technical crews were carrying equipment and pushing dollies loaded with cameras, batteries, and lighting toward the main entrance where a white van was being loaded. Small groups of trekkers were gathered with their guides receiving instructions on the day's activities. Piles of luggage and backpacks announced that some expeditions were heading to the airport for the flight to Skardu.

Walking past the OSN studio/conference room, Jack saw that the green screens and lighting equipment were still in place to record the video interviews with Zermatt team members who had been pushed back a day. On the stool closest to the door was Jay Hamilton, the Zermatt communications officer, his black skin shining with moisture under the heat of the quartz lamps. Hamilton grinned broadly and waved. Jack waved back and gave him a thumbs-up, wondering how the overweight little black man had ever made his way onto a serious mountain climbing expedition to the Himalaya. He liked Hamilton with his friendly, outgoing personality and self-deprecating sense of humor, and while he was certain that Hamilton was a crack electronics man, Jack also knew that he didn't belong anywhere on the slopes and ridges of K2.

A large poster on an easel outside the studio doorway announced the day's schedule of activities. Noon to two o'clock, was the Zermatt Equipment Show, sponsored by North Face; at three o'clock, Dr. Monica DeForrest, Director of Sustainability for Zermatt Industries, would deliver a lecture entitled, "Green Expeditions to the Himalaya: A Template." At eight that evening, Rudi Joost and Logan Healy would engage in a Skype Press Conference with journalists in London, Paris, New York, and Los Angeles.

A voice called out to Jack as he walked past the studio. "Mister Finley, Mister Finley." Jack turned around and walked backwards. It was one of the OSN producers, standing in the doorway with a clipboard in her hands. "We need you in makeup right away. We have to get your interview this morning."

Jack smiled and waved to her. "Be back in a few minutes," he lied. "I'll be in as soon as I get back." He turned around and continued walking toward the front entrance. Jack hoped that by the time he returned, they would have concluded the other interviews and forgotten about him. But that wouldn't happen, he knew. Jack Finley was their marquee name on the OSN show – just the second American to climb all fourteen – they weren't going to let him off the hook. He wondered if Ed Viesturs would have allowed himself to become part of a carney show like this if he was still climbing. *No, no way, not Viesturs. But Ed Viesturs wasn't selling used Buicks for a living.*

The temperature was a perfectly still, seventy degrees outside. Jack looked to the northwest, toward the foothills of the western end of the Hindu Kush. He gazed up into the perfectly blue, cloudless sky, and wondered if the sky was as blue over K2, and the wind so calm. Anything close would make it the most ideal climbing day of the summer on K2. It was a shame to waste it, because ideal climbing days on K2 were rare.

Standing next to the van being loaded with OSN video equipment, Alby Mathias was talking to Marty Gallagher, executive director of the OSN production. Soon the van would be leaving for the beautiful Faisal Mosque with the Zermatt climbers and, of course, the *Z-Girls,* for some outside shots. Mathias saw Jack and cut off his conversation with Gallagher. "Hey Jack," said Mathias, walking over to him. He was studying Jack's basketball shorts, University of Vermont tee-shirt, and New England Patriots baseball cap. Mathias didn't look pleased. "You're supposed to be wearing a Zermatt polo shirt for these outdoor shots, Jack, and the trekking shorts." He shook his head. "Lisa's going to go bullshit when she sees you."

Jack shrugged, put on his sunglasses, and looked around for a cab. "I'll have to catch up with you later," he said, taking a step toward the parking circle.

Mathias put out an arm to block his path. "Whoa there partner. You can't play hooky here. You already skipped the video interview. All this shit's in your contract Jack."

"Yeah, I know," said Jack, holding up a hand to one of the taxi drivers. He turned toward Mathias. "Need to go down to Pindi for a while. I'll be back in about an hour. I'll catch up." He grinned. "And I'll have all my logos in place."

Mathias wasn't amused. "Meeting up with someone?"

Jack ignored the question and climbed into the taxi, an ancient Simca. He liked Mathias, who was obviously becoming more than the climb leader for the expedition, but he didn't feel the need to explain anything to his old friend, especially his reason for going to Rawalpindi.

Jack gave the driver the address of the *Anwar Café,* in *Saddar Bazaar, Rawalpindi.* "Yes, I know the Anwar," the driver said. "Very good. Very good." But Jack sensed a subtle hint of apprehension in his voice.

The cab made its way quickly through the beautiful, tree-lined avenues of the neatly organized capitol and was soon surrounded by heavier traffic on the Murree Road. Ten minutes later, they were immersed in the congestion and confusion of the old city of Rawalpindi that Jack was more familiar with from years past. The financially strapped expeditions of his youth didn't stay in fine hotels in Islamabad.

As they joined the smog-generating traffic of old colorful double-decker buses and ancient lorries lumbering along under the weight of too many passengers, animals and produce, it all started to feel more comfortable to Jack. They passed the small hotel where Jack and Sophie had stayed, years ago, when they climbed Broad Peak, and had their first look at K2. Jack had stayed there again on his way to K2 for an ill-fated climb with a mixed expedition of Americans and Canadians, without Sophie, who was attending to university requirements at the Sorbonne. Jack struggled to recall the exact years, but the nostalgic remembrances of his stays in Rawalpindi brought back the pangs of regret he thought he had gotten out of his system long ago. And now Sophie was only two hundred miles away, and soon they would be much closer. He wondered if there was any way they could both be climbing on the same mountain and not come face-to-face. Jack took in a deep breath, realizing that in a few minutes he would be seeing Sophie's father, once, his friend, teacher and idol, before he became his enemy.

Jack remembered the narrow lanes, traffic and shops of the Saddar Bazaar, but couldn't recall ever visiting the Anwar Cafe. It was small and plain, indistinguishable from dozens of neighborhood restaurants in Rawalpindi, with a tiled floor and a dozen old wooden tables. There was no bar, and like all the other cafes, no alcohol. Just as it was when Jack had first come to the city, outside of the larger hotels, there was no alcohol to be found in Pindi. The ubiquitous neon Pepsi sign glowed in the front window.

Jack took a small table near the window so he could see Janot coming. He ordered a chai and sat watching the traffic on the street and the steady stream of pedestrians walking past the cafe. Just as his tea arrived, Jack noticed a black Cadillac Escalade with dark windows, pull into a spot across the street from the Anwar. The driver's window went down revealing a stern-looking man with a black mustache, wearing dark sunglasses, staring directly at Jack through the cafe window. The Escalade was sticking a little too far out into the street, slowing the traffic and causing drivers to honk their horns. The driver ignored them. Jack gazed back at him for a moment, then turned away and looked around the interior of the cafe as he realized the folly of walking around a busy city in northern Pakistan wearing a New England Patriots hat and a UVM tee-shirt. It had been six years since he'd been to Pakistan. A lot had changed.

Toward the back of the restaurant, two tables were occupied. A middle-aged couple was eating breakfast, and at the other table, a younger man drinking tea, stared into a laptop. Jack watched him for a few seconds, wondering who he might be communicating with. A vision of himself on the internet, sitting on a stool blindfolded while a bearded Taliban cut through his neck with a curved knife jumped into Jack's head. He turned back toward the street to see if the black Escalade was still there, and saw Marcel Janot standing in the doorway, looking at him.

Janot had always been short, but now he looked even shorter to Jack, and much older than the man who had taught him so much climbing technique during that long-ago summer. He was wearing an old tweed jacket and heavy canvas pants, as if he was about to go out for a jaunt through the foothills of the Alps. On his head, Janot wore a rumpled, old fishing hat with the brim pulled down around his head. He nodded to Jack, without smiling, and came over to the table. He looked briefly at Jack's Patriot's hat and seemed to nod to himself, as if confirming an old opinion.

Jack stood up and extended his hand. "Hello Janot." He smiled. "It's been a long time," he said, motioning for Janot to take the seat across the table.

Janot shook hands and nodded. "Yes, Jack," he said softly. "Many years." Janot sat.

"How is mademoiselle Janot?" Jack asked. He had always had great affection for Sophie's mother.

"She is... uhm, a little weary these days, and missing Sophie very much."

The waiter came to the table and Janot just pointed to Jack's cup of tea. He looked around the interior of the café, and remained silent. Finally, he looked at Jack and put his hands up on the table. Jack recognized the short, powerful fingers of the *blacksmith of Argentiere* -- where the incredible strength of his daughter's fingers came from. Jack could see Sophie hanging one handed from a treacherous position on a vertical face of one of the great walls of Yosemite, her feet dangling in space, a thousand feet of air beneath her, taking a short rest, winking at him, smiling, unconcerned, her silken black hair flowing over one eye while her strong fingers, Janot's fingers, held her to the rock.

"Merci, Jack," Janot said softly. "Thank you for coming." Jack remained silent. He'd let Janot run this meeting. Jack was surprised at the instant animosity he still felt for the old man in front of him, the man who was adamant, resolute, that this, *"American ski bum" he'd called him, would never marry his daughter*. The appearance of Janot also stirred the deep well of animosity Jack still felt for himself for abandoning Sophie so easily and so quickly.

"I thought that maybe here was better for you than Islamabad to meet." Janot smiled briefly. "Some in your expedition, maybe they would find it, ah, curious, to see us together."

Jack shrugged noncommittally. Janot was probably right, but what difference would it make? What did he care? He just stared across the table at the old man who had caused him so much heartache.

Janot nodded, understanding that Jack wasn't going to help him get his story out. "Sophie is now down from Gasherbrum I. She has climbed all but K2." Janot stopped talking as the waiter set his tea in front of him. "Merci," he said softly. He looked at his tea without interest. "But now..." Janot looked into his hands trying to find the words. "When we should be going home, now she wants to go up K2, this murderous mountain!" he said more loudly. He shook his head and sat back in his chair as if trying to understand his daughter. His eyes were moist. "She is not well Jack." Janot took in a deep breath and Jack could see again, the intense feelings he'd always had for his daughter. "Cho Oyu was very hard on her. She had surgery, on a finger and a toe, and she lost too much weight." He had to pause. "And... she had grown close to the Russian boy. He was good to her... he saved her life, and... Sophie felt responsible for..." Janot shook his head. "She has lost so many friends..." He put his hands up to wipe his eyes. After a few seconds, he looked back at Jack. "I'm sorry Jack. He breathed deeply. "My Sophie is so sad, and that makes me sad. And now she is so tired, after a difficult climb on Gasherbrum." There was still moisture in his eyes. "You cannot climb great mountains like these, with a heavy heart. You understand this Jack. You must have *joy in your heart*, to climb mountains... as well as strength and energy and enthusiasm."

Janot sat silent for a few moments, leaned back in his chair and threw his hands up. "But now she wants to continue with this *stupid contest,*" he spit out the words, "This... *ignorant* race with the two other girls, all for American television. For money and to be famous!" he nearly shouted. Jack looked around the cafe to see if others were listening.

Janot put his hands in his lap, looked up at Jack and briefly smiled. "This is not why we climb Jack, eh?" he said quietly. "This is not why we come to the mountains... with *helicopters* and *TV cameras*... to *race* to the top, for money and glory! You know this Jack. I know you do. Coming to the mountains like this cannot end well."

Jack crossed his arms in front of him. He wasn't going to help Janot with his misgivings over the bizarre expeditions headed to K2, or the concern he felt for his daughter. That was his problem now. He didn't care. It felt good, after ten years, to bask in the misery and doubts of the great Marcel Janot. He wondered if Janot regretted that day in the barn, on the farm in Argentiere, when he smiled so smugly and told Jack, '*no, do not think about marrying my daughter. It will never happen to you. Jack, you are a good climber, but you will never be a good husband, to any girl, but especially my Sophie.*' Jack recalled the contempt in Janot's voice... and later, the resignation in Sophie's eyes, and the tears when she begged him to wait, '*just another year and things would change; Janot would relent eventually*'. But Jack was too proud, and too cocky, and there were so many other girls around, like the German girl Jack climbed with and had his picture taken with so many times in the year after he'd left Sophie. And then, so quickly came the tabloid courtship of Sophie and the famous Tony Linser... and it was over forever.

Jack looked out to the street and saw that the black Escalade was gone. He glanced at his watch, fished out some bills from his pocket and tossed them on the table. He pushed his chair back and drew his feet under him, to stand up and walk out of the cafe, but he waited. Something held him there, to hear what Janot would say next.

The old man looked up and smiled briefly. He leaned onto the table. "Jack, don't blame me anymore. And don't blame Sophie. She..."

"What do you want Janot? Why did you want to meet with me?" Jack wanted to leave, to be rid of it all, finally, but he needed to hear it from Janot's lips.

Janot shrugged. "Sophie needs your help Jack. She cannot do this thing, the Northeast ridge," he said softly. "With the people she has, if she attempts to reach the top... she will die on K2, Jack. I am certain of that." The old man's eyes were moist again.

Jack's brow furrowed in anger. "Can't *do* it? What do you mean, she can't do it... the Northeast ridge," he said more forcefully. "What happened to your wonderful *Alpine style* of climbing, Janot? You could conquer any mountain, you always said, with four strong climbers, going fast and light, taking everything with them, quickly up to a high camp, and then to the summit, and straight down, leaving the mountain as you found it. The way Messner and Habbeler climbed, you always said. That's how Sophie climbs. You trained her well Janot. Why can't she do this one?" Jack caught himself leaning forward into Janot's face and sounding like a sarcastic punk.

Jack sank back on his chair, embarrassed. Of course Janot knew the difference between K2 and climbing Mont Blanc. Janot knew as much about mountain climbing as anyone alive. He knew the Northeast ridge was a four mile long knife edge, covered with deep snow, continually exposed to the brutal winds raging through Windy Gap, the route blocked by impenetrable buttresses, and offering no safe campsites. Jack thought about the route and about Ridgeway's account of the 1978 climb, the story that he knew almost by heart. Many of the1978 climbers had given up the big mountains after conquering the Northeast ridge of K2. It was an epic, life-changing achievement that nothing else would come close to. And that was a huge, well-funded expedition of *dream team* climbers. It was as far from *Alpine style* climbing as any expedition ever could be.

Janot took in a deep breath and leaned onto the table. "Jack, I know that..."

Jack held a hand up to interrupt Janot. He smiled at him briefly and kept his hand up to silence the old man as he craned his head and looked away, his eyes focused on nothing, trying to recapture his thought. Then, it came to him. *If a team of Whittaker and Roskelly, Wickwire, Reichardt and Ridgeway, Craig Anderson, Chris Chandler, Skip Edmonds, Rob Schaller, and a crew of high-altitude Hunza porters, were just barely able to put four climbers on the summit, using every last ounce of endurance, resolve and incredible bravery...* Jack glanced over at Janot who scowled in puzzlement. *Then, maybe the best way, maybe the only way, to climb the ridge* was *Alpine style... light-weight, lugging no heavy oxygen bottles and tents and food and stoves to sustain a big expedition, but only enough for two climbers to get halfway up, and then sprinting for the top with only one small tent, a bivy sack to sleep in, a stove and a small bag of food, then bivouacking just down from the summit on the way down... as Messner and Habbeler would climb it.*

"Jack, I'm sorry I asked you to come here," said Janot. "I was going to ask you to join our expedition, to... not help Sophie to the summit, but only to keep her alive... for me."

Jack looked away and nodded absently, his thoughts still churning. *It would take two climbers who could go high and move well without oxygen - two superior climbers, two well-rested climbers when they left high camp, two climbers who would climb for the joy of climbing and for the challenge... and for each other. Janot was right about that. That was the only way to get up a mountain like K2. Sophie could do it.* Jack knew better than anyone alive that Sophie Janot was the best climber in the world without oxygen before she retired, and now she would be supremely acclimatized after Cho and Gasherbrum. He also knew, the only other climber in Pakistan who could go to the top of K2 without oxygen...

'Join our expedition.' Jack suddenly focused on Janot's last words. He laughed. "Jesus Janot, what are you talking about? *Go over to your expedition!* I've already taken money from Zermatt. I've paid two months of my mortgage with it. I'm on the Zermatt team." He waved a hand through the air. "That's not going to happen. It's impossible."

"Yes, yes, I know that," said Janot softly. "It was a stupid notion. I'm sorry." He shrugged. "I just don't know what to do."

"Why don't you just *forbid* her to go?" Jack asked, *like you forbid her to marry me,* he wanted to add.

Janot gazed into Jack's eyes as if reading his thoughts. "No, it's not like that. I don't have such influence over my daughter any more. Since the divorce, she is different. She feels like she is nothing now, for herself and for her daughters. All she was ever good at is climbing mountains, she says, so this time she climbs for the money." Janot sighed. "And that is so sad."

Jack leaned forward. "Maybe..." He stopped. He thought about his idea and what he'd almost said. *Jesus, what the fuck was he thinking about! Climbing the Northeast ridge with Sophie. Leave the Zermatt expedition after taking half the money? That would be the end. He'd be bankrupt after Rudi Joost sued the shit out of him, and he'd never climb again, that was for certain. And if he didn't end up dead on K2, Peg would divorce him and he'd never see his kids again. Where was all this coming from? This stupid, nonsensical, romantic notion about climbing with Sophie again.* Jack sat back and chuckled at what he'd almost suggested. *This wasn't Jack Finley. No, Jack Finley would go back to the Serena and get into his Zermatt logos and do his interviews and get his pictures taken, and then, that night he'd call home and tell Peg he loved her and talk to the kids and tell them how much he missed them. Then he'd go down into the bar, find Sustainability Monica and take her up to his room and fuck her until she begged him to stop. That was Jack Finley.* He stood up abruptly and held out his hand to Marcel Janot.

"Good luck, Janot. Say hello to Sophie." He hesitated. "I can't do what you want. "Janot stayed seated and flashed a thin smile up at Jack as they shook hands. "Au revoir Jack. Sois prudent."

Jack left the Anwar Cafe, looked up and down the street for a taxi, and started walking north, toward the center of Rawalpindi. The traffic on the street was heavier now, as was the crowd of pedestrians on the sidewalk. Occasionally he'd get jostled, inadvertently he hoped. He thought about tucking his Patriots cap into the waistband of his shorts, and chuckled, wondering if Tom Brady would hide his Patriots hat if he were walking around Rawalpindi. Jack wondered if Robert Kraft would pay for his ransom if he was kidnapped because he was wearing a Patriots cap.

The black Escalade pulled up roughly to the edge of the street a few yards in front of Jack, as the passenger side window went down. Jack recognized one of the security guards from the Serena leaning out the window. "It would be safer to come with us Mr. Finley, back to the hotel." He nodded toward the backseat and put his window up before Jack could reply.

Jack climbed into the backseat and settled in to the soft leather seat. "Hotel Serena, driver," he called to the front. "Hey, you know any girls in this town?" The security men weren't amused. Between the console and the edge of the front passenger seat, Jack could see the butt of a rifle. He sat back to enjoy the scenery, content to let the men up front do their job, which he knew would also mean a complete report back to the Zermatt and OSN people about his visit to Pindi.

What were they going to do, send him home? Waterboard him for information about his conversation with Janot? No, what they were going to do is dress him up in Zermatt clothing made in Bangladesh, put makeup on him, brush out his hair, take his picture and videotape him saying stupid things about the Z-girls and Logan Healy and then fly him in to basecamp on the Godwin-Austen Glacier, and take more videos and do more interviews, and then send him up the mountain to babysit all the beautiful people of the Z-Team. Then he'd carry tents and oxygen bottles up high so they could all breathe and look happy for the cameras. And when the weather turned bad and the temperature dropped to twenty below zero and they all wanted to go home, he'd be the one to take Logan up through the bottleneck to the saddle and then lead the traverse under the great Serac, fixing rope along one of the steepest, most treacherous stretches of climbing in the Himalaya, and push, drag and cajole Logan Healy to the top of K2. And then, the hard part would begin. Jack swallowed back the sudden wave of fear that enveloped him as he thought about the reality of actually climbing K2. All the glitz and glamour, the fun and games, of the *Team Logan -K2* expedition had obscured the memories of his experiences on K2, where several times he'd conceded to himself that he'd never get down. He took in a deep breath to fight his anxiety. *Jesus, these people have no idea of the ordeal that lies ahead of them.*

The Escalade had passed through the narrow streets of central Rawalpindi and was on a main boulevard headed to the Murree Road back to Islamabad. Jack gazed out the window, absorbed in his thoughts when he spied a figure sitting on a bench at the edge of a small park. There was something familiar about the black warm-up jacket with the teal blue stripes down the sleeves, and the mop of black hair. As they passed by, the figure raised her head, and Jack was sure.

"Hey," he said loudly to the driver. "Pull over, stop right here," he commanded, knowing that it would take the sound of authority to get make them stop. "Pull over, right here. I need to get out," he said tapping the driver's shoulder. Reluctantly, after a long look around, the driver stopped at the edge of the road. "I'll only be a minute," said Jack, escaping from the back seat onto the sidewalk.

He walked quickly back toward the bench. As he came within a few yards of the hunched over figure sitting there, he heard muffled sobs of crying. The woman had her head down, her hands over her face, unmistakably crying. Now, Jack had his doubts. "Sukey? Sukey is that you?" he said coming closer.

Chun Suek Yen lifted her head slowly, not believing she'd heard her familiar name spoken in this city where she knew no one, Koreans were treated with disdain and women were invisible. She squinted into the sun and rubbed her eyes trying to recognize this tall, rugged looking man who was dressed like he was in Southern California.

Jack grinned and tossed his hat on the bench, releasing his long brown hair. "Sukey, it's me, Jack. Jack Finley." He held his arms out to catch her as she sprung from the bench with joy.

She sobbed and laughed at the same time as she pressed herself against him and threw her arms around Jack's neck. "Oh my *god* Jack," she squealed. She jumped up and down as she hugged him, pressing her cheek against his, not letting go. "Oh my god Jack, it really is you. My friend Jack." After several seconds, she loosened her grip and pulled her head back.

Jack laughed and kissed her cheek warmly. "Hello Sukey, my good friend." They hugged again tightly and waltzed on the sidewalk. Finally, they separated and grinned at each other. "So why all this crying on a park bench alone?"

Sukey shrugged and put her hands up to rub the remaining tears from her eyes. She sat down on the bench and patted the seat next to her. Jack sat down and put his arm around her shoulders. Sukey looked at him and laughed. "I can't believe it's you Jack. I'm sitting here alone and so sad, and suddenly... there is Jack Finley who always makes me laugh, and always makes me happy."

Jack smiled at her and rubbed the back of her neck. "So, why the tears Sukey, huh?"

She turned away and shrugged her shoulders. "I am sad because I am scared, and I feel so alone," she said softly. "They put so much pressure on me, and then they treat me like I am nothing. They don't care what I have to say, only that I climb well and be the first to the top. That's all they care about." She turned to look at Jack." And I am afraid of the climb. I don't think I am ready."

"Why Sukey? Why are you afraid? You're a great climber."

"Because they want to go so fast now. Three weeks, they say to get to the top to win. They want me to go up and follow the ropes and not come down, not even one time. Just keep going up, they say." Sukey was scowling with pain. "I can't do that Jack, not even with oxygen the entire climb. You know, you *have* to come down, to acclimatize, to rest."

"That's crazy," said Jack. "You can't climb a mountain as high as K2 like that. Don't they know that?"

"All they know is winning the race Jack. Young Kim and my husband, and the others, they care only about getting *Snow Leopard* to the top first. This expedition Jack, it is very strange, so different. As you Americans would say, it is *all fucked up!*"

Jack laughed heartily and clapped his hands together. "Sukey, all of these expeditions are fucked up. It's not mountain climbing; it's *Dancing With The Stars!*"

Sukey laughed. "So Logan's expedition is the same?"

Jack shook his head. "It's worse. You should see the team we'll be climbing with."

They sat silently together for a few moments. Sukey reached over and clasped Jack's hand. "If I try to climb like this, Jack, I will be sick. Maybe worse. I know my body. I haven't been over six thousand meters in thirteen months."

Jack grinned and shook Sukey's hand. "Think you'll get sick like that night you threw up all over the table in that bar in Kathmandu when we found out they had a case of tequila in the back room?"

Sukey threw back her head laughing. "Oh my *god* Jack. You and Sophie and your friends, you shouldn't have made me drink so much. I was only just a baby then!"

"It was fun though, back in those days, huh? Climbing was better then, when it wasn't so... corporate, huh Sukey?"

Sukey was smiling now, the tears gone, the cherub-faced Korean girl that Jack knew, was back again. "Yes, Jack. More fun," she said softly.

The horn of the Escalade blared from up the street. Jack looked over at it. "Okay Sukey, listen, I've been worried about my own acclimatization too. This flying in on helicopters is great for the supplies and all that, but it's bad for climbers... bad for you. You can't go up that high in a two hour helicopter ride. You'll never recover."

"Yes, I know that Jack, but..."

"So, how about if we walk in? Take the eight days and do it right, get fit and acclimatized, like the old days?"

"Oh *yes* Jack, yes. That would help me a lot. Will you walk in with me?"

Jack stood up. "Yeah, let's do it. We'll fly to Skardu tomorrow and take the Jeeps to Askole and we'll go on a nice trek. I'll get some porters for the tents and stuff - they're already paid for. There will be a lot of trekkers along the route. We'll camp out and get smelly. It'll be fun."

Sukey jumped up from the bench and hugged Jack once more. "Thank you Jack. That will be a wonderful adventure, like the old days and much better for me. I will meet you at the airport tomorrow." She watched Jack jog up to the big black vehicle and get into the back seat, and felt the hole in her stomach she always felt, had felt for many years past, when she'd watched Jack leave with Sophie, or later, other girls. Always her good friend. Just a friend.

Jack walked through the front entryway of the Serena and came face to face with Phil Masters, Morris O'Dell, and Logan Healy having an impromptu conference in the middle of the lobby. There was no avoiding them. They were probably discussing him.

He walked straight up to the group. O'Dell was scowling. "Jack, I hope we're not having a problem here."

Jack ignored him and looked at Masters. "I'll be going to Skardu tomorrow, and then walking in. Need it for the acclimatizing. I'll be at base camp by the first, ready to climb." His voice said it wasn't a negotiable point.

"What the fuck Jack," said O'Dell. "You can't just..."

Masters interrupted him. "Well Jack, that's not in the plan. You can't go off..."

"That's my Jack!" said Logan Healy, clapping her hands together and grinning broadly. "That's why you're here, to fuck things up, and make it all come out better. Have fun Jack. Good idea. We'll see you at base camp." She turned to Masters. "Arrange for some porters and tents and food and shit." She looked back at Jack. "Do me a favor though, Jack, take Hamilton with you. He's fat and out of shape and he'll die if he flies in."

Jack grinned at Logan. "He'll look like a Patriots defensive back when I get him to base camp."

Jack went right into makeup and then to the interview studio. After an hour of the questions he was expecting – about his marriage and kids, his love life, his affair with Sophie, the danger of climbing K2 – the producer surprised him with the old chestnut, the question he'd been asked a hundred times in interviews over the years, always trying to come up with a different answer. *'So, why do you continue to climb such dangerous mountains?'* Jack smiled, and shrugged. "It's the only thing I've ever been good at."

Chapter 11

Jack made sure that he and Jay Hamilton secured seats on the right hand side of the ancient Pakistani Air turbo-prop they flew from Rawalpindi to Skardu. It was a beautiful, blue-sky day and Jack didn't want Hamilton to miss the spectacular view they'd have of Nanga Parbat, the ninth highest mountain in the world. Located just seventy miles southwest of K2, marking the western end of the Himalaya, Nanga Parbat rises precipitously out of nearly level terrain. Flanked by the Indus and Astore rivers, the mountain displays the greatest prominence of any peak in the world, creating a dramatic impression as it comes into view. For the past thirty-five years, since the Karakorums were reopened to climbers, the planes headed to Skardu always passed just north of the Nanga Parbat massif, giving the climbers and trekkers a rare view of the magnificent mountain.

Sukey leaned over the seat in front of her to where Jack and Hamilton were seated. "Mister Jay, quickly, take your camera out. We will be at Nanga Parbat very soon. You will want to get a picture."

Hamilton pulled his cell phone from an inside pocket of his jacket and got it ready. Jack looked at the white iPhone and shook his head. "Geeze Jay, don't you have a real camera?" he said, wondering what ever happened to the Nikons, Minoltas and Canons that climbers always carried in the past.

Hamilton laughed. "Jack, the best camera in the world is the one you have with you."

Sukey slapped Jack on the top of the head. "You're showing your age Jack. Mister Jay can now Tweet his pictures of Nanga Parbat all around the world before we land."

"Better not, or Samantha Ryan will cut his balls off when we get to base camp," said Jack. "All social media goes through *her*." He leaned over to the window as Nanga Parbat came into view.

"Wow," said Hamilton, snapping pictures. "It's incredible. Aren't you guys going to take some pictures?"

Sukey and Jack smiled at each other. Sukey nudged Hamilton lightly on the shoulder. "No Mister Jay, we took our pictures from the top of Parbat."

Hamilton took his last picture and put his camera in his pocket. "Oh yeah," he said sheepishly. "I forget, I'm just a tourist here."

Sukey leaned over Hamilton and pointed out the Rakhiot Face and the ridge she'd climbed years earlier. "But on the south side, that you can't see, is the greatest vertical face in mountaineering."

"The Rupal Face," interjected Jack. "Over fifteen thousand feet, from bottom to top. Almost three miles of brutal, exposed climbing."

"Wow," said Hamilton softly. "Glad we're not climbing that."

Jack and Sukey exchange a knowing glance. Nanga Parbat faded from view, and Sukey dropped back into her seat.

"Jack," said Hamilton, twisting around for a last glimpse of the mountain, "Who was the first to climb Nanga Parbat?"

Jack appreciated Hamilton's curiosity but was surprised at his ignorance, but not greatly. The young climbers of the Zermatt team were not mountaineering historians like the climbers of Jack's generation. They were interested only in their own accomplishments and their collective Facebook, Pinterest and Twitter notoriety that would come from Logan Healy being the first to summit K2 in July. And that was not only sad, but dangerous too. It showed a lack of respect for the mountain. Jack had always climbed every mountain with an appreciation and reverence for the climbers who had come before him, the climbers from so many countries over so many years, who had endured the hardships and sacrifices in establishing the routes, and in too many instances, lost their lives. Because Jack Finley knew better than anyone, that without the established routes, no one would have ever climbed all fourteen of the eight thousand meter mountains. Only a rare handful of climbers like Messner, Kukuczka, and Simon Moro, could forge a career based on pushing new routes up the great mountains.

"In the early years, Parbat was known as the German mountain," Jack began. For the next thirty minutes he had Jay Hamilton's complete attention as he relayed the history of the conquering of Nanga Parbat. He told him about the tragic German assaults on the mountain in the 1930's, including the 1934 expedition led by the famous German climber, Willy Merkl, and backed by the new Nazi government. The climb ended in a violent early July storm, trapping almost the whole team at 7,500 meters. Three of Germany's most heralded climbers, including Merkl, along with six Sherpas, died on the mountain. Then, in 1937, another German expedition of seven climbers and nine Sherpas were all killed instantly by an avalanche on June 14th just below the Rakhiot Peak – still the worst single disaster on an 8,000 meter peak.

"Jesus," said Hamilton softly. "Did anyone ever reach the top alive?"

Jack continued his story, enjoying his recall of the history of Parbat. "Not until after World War Two, when a small German/Austrian team went back in 1953." Jack noticed that in addition to the mesmerized Hamilton, a few trekkers in nearby seats were leaning toward them to hear the story. He continued, a little louder, with the story of the expedition led by the dictatorial Karl Herrligkoffer, whose order to his climbers to turn back from high camp in the face of the oncoming monsoon was obeyed by everyone except the intrepid Austrian climber Hermann Buhl. Buhl continued to ascend on his own, without oxygen, and reached the summit alone on July 3rd – the only solo first-accent of an 8,000 meter mountain. On the descent in darkness, Buhl endured a desperate, seven-hour standing bivouac on a narrow ledge at 26,000 feet, his life spared by a mild, windless night. He returned to the high camp after an incredible forty-one hours of climbing – one of the most heroic and celebrated climbs in mountaineering history. Buhl lost several toes after the climb.

Hermann Buhl was an inspiration to Jack, and to generations of Himalayan climbers, but he knew that Hamilton could never appreciate Buhl's accomplishment. You had to experience the intense cold, loneliness, and the near death of high altitude climbing to revere Hermann Buhl as Jack did. Then, Jack had to tell Jay and his rapt audience of trekkers, about Hermann Buhl's last climb, on a lesser mountain, near K2, called

Chogolisa, in 1957. Following his friend Kurt Diemberger down after being turned away from the summit by bad weather, Buhl disappeared through a benign cornice, a careless, avoidable accident, his body never to be found.

"You know, Jack," said Hamilton pensively, "It seems like almost every mountain climbing story ends with the hero dying at the end."

"Yeah, Jay, a lot of them do," said Jack, as the plane banked to begin its approach to Skardu.

The small airport at Skardu had grown since Jack was last there. There were more buildings, more planes, and definitely more helicopters, most notably the huge black CH-47 at the edge of the runways, with the silver logo of Snow Leopard Industries emblazoned on the large, rear rotor pillar. It sat next to a staging area filled with an assortment of wooden crates, plastic shipping boxes, and large metal conex containers. A yellow Hyundai forklift was busy, carrying boxes up the ramp into the gaping rear entrance of the massive helicopter. A group of Korean men in black and teal outfits were at work on the mountain of cargo headed to K2 base camp.

Two hundred yards up the tarmac, Jack saw the Zermatt compound, surrounded by a high, chain-link fence, adorned with a procession of large, vinyl banners imprinted with the Zermatt logo. *Lisa Greenway would let no opportunity go unexploited.*

Jack, Sukey, Jay Hamilton, and several dozen trekkers, waited on the tarmac for the Pakistani Air crew to unload the baggage from the belly of the plane. Jack was mildly surprised when Sukey lit up a Marlboro Light. "That's not going to help your acclimatization Sukey," he said, trying not to sound like a high school teacher.

Sukey smiled at him. "But it will help me deal with all this bullshit," she said, gazing over toward the *Snow Leopard* compound. Dozens of tightly wrapped rucksacks and duffle bags were being tossed to the tarmac. Jack and Hamilton moved in and shouldered their packs. Sukey stood, enjoying her cigarette, in no hurry.

"Sukey, Jay and I are going to go over to the Zermatt compound to see how much trouble we're in. Want to come?"

Sukey chuckled. "You don't know what trouble is," she said, taking a drag on her cigarette. She looked over again at the Snow Leopard helicopter being loaded, glad that her husband was still in Rawalpindi. She didn't need another screaming match with Monk, who was furious over her decision to trek in to basecamp. His anger wasn't about time, or acclimatization or conditioning. It was about being *independent*. Sukey had shamed him in the eyes of the great businessman, Young Kim, and expedition leader Dong Shin-Soo. They knew he received no obedience or respect from his wife. It was a dark cloud that would be hovering over the remainder of the expedition.

Sukey shook her head. "No, I am going to the hotel to rest. Then, tonight we will go out and get drunk so I can sleep through the horrible jeep ride to Askole tomorrow, okay guys?"

Jack laughed at Sukey's mention of the treacherous drive along the precariously narrow mountainside road along the Braldu Gorge, what many climbers considered the most dangerous part of the trip to K2. "You got it Sukey. Sounds like the best idea I've heard since I came to Pakistan. Okay with you Jay?"

Hamilton grinned. "Hey, I'm with you and Sukey. I'm just a tourist." Hamilton pulled out a thick black cell phone from his jacket. "Let's see who is working over at the compound." Jack looked at Hamilton with raised eyebrows. "Hey, I *am* the communications officer," he said, pushing some buttons on the phone. It became a walkie-talkie. "This is Hamilton, on the runway. Who's working?"

As they began to walk toward the Zermatt staging area, a small blond-haired girl from one of the trekking expeditions ran over and jumped in front of Jack. She was a waif of a girl, in hiking shorts, high wool socks and trekking boots. She wore a large rucksack with a sleeping bag lashed to the top. The pack had to weigh as much as she did. The girl looked to be about eleven or twelve. In her hand she held a much-handled page from an old magazine.

"Excuse me please, mister Finley," she said softly. Nervous, she looked backed toward her group standing a few yards away, and then, up at Jack. "Would you... do you think you could..."

Jack grinned and knelt down to her. "What's your name dear?"

"Je suis... no, no, I mean... I am... Julia-Isabelle Chatelain. And, I would like for you, if you wanted, to autograph my picture... my picture of you and Sophie. Sophie Janot." She smiled briefly, and held out the picture to Jack, along with a Bic pen. "She is my idol. Sophie Janot."

Jack chuckled. "Mine too," he said, taking the picture. It was an old photograph from a magazine with captions in French. Jack and Sophie stood in deep snow, smiling, arms around each other. They were wearing parkas so it must have been taken at a high camp. From the date on the magazine page, Jack thought it might have been at Nanda Devi, but he wasn't sure. He gazed at Sophie, her jet black hair flowing around her face, so small and looking so beautiful, as few women can look in the mountains. He autographed the girl's picture, handed it back, and stood up.

"Where are you from Julia, the mountains?"

She giggled. "Oh no, I am from Paris, but I love the mountains. Someday, I will climb like Sophie." The girl grinned broadly. "I am hoping that I will meet Sophie on this trip," she said, excitedly. "She is at Gasherbrum right now!"

Jack laughed and held up his hand for a high-five from his new friend. "Maybe you will Julia. And I'm sure that Sophie would love to meet you."

Jack caught up with Hamilton, and they walked across the runways to the Zermatt compound. They found Lisa Greenway tossing tight spools of green, red, and yellow rope into plastic shipping containers. Several men in Zermatt work-suits, assisted by a dozen local porters were lifting crates from large wooden shipping pallets.

Lisa had her long brown hair pinned up in a haphazard pile on her head and was sweating through a dark red Stanford t-shirt. Jack couldn't help but notice her slender legs emanating from a pair of skimpy shorts. "That's a lot of rope," said Jack, appreciating the abundance and the quality of the rope they were bringing in. He flashed back to earlier times when he and his climbing buddies had to scrape together enough money to buy used rope in the second-hand shops in Katmandu.

"About five miles worth," said Lisa, stuffing the last spool in a plastic box and closing the lid. She wiped the sweat from her forehead. "So, our walkers appear," she said. "Too good to take the hour and half helicopter ride in with the rest of us. You have to take a week-long hike to the mountain." Lisa smiled at Jack and Hamilton. "The boss says to give you whatever you need."

"Who?" said Jack. "Masters?"

Lisa giggled and waved away the suggestion. "Shit no. Logan called me. Told me you were coming in. Already got your tents, sleeping bags, food and fuel sent on to Askole on the helicopter. Got fifteen porters and a cook waiting for you. Sent them all new Zermatt jackets and hiking boots. Sirdar's name is Azmat." Lisa laughed. "He's all excited to be working for such a *famous* mountaineer as Jack Finley." She put her hands on her slender hips. "Anything *else* you boys might be needing?"

"Could use a light, fifty meter rope for the walk in," said Jack. "You never know what might come up." Hamilton moved off to call in to base camp. "We could use a little company along the trail," Jack added. "Want to walk in with us?"

Lisa smiled, then gazed up at Jack. "I wish I could Jack," she said. "I really wish I could take a long hike to think this all over. I'm not in a real hurry to get to the mountain."

Jack looked at her for a few moments, surprised at her apprehension. "What's the matter Lisa? Having second thoughts?"

Lisa shrugged. "I don't know. I felt great climbing Everest last year, and I've been working out hard the last six months, so, I figured I was ready, you know, but... I've read all the K2 books, and... well, I'm not sure."

Jack gazed down at the attractive woman in front of him, and waited before he spoke. He gathered his thoughts so not to mislead Lisa but also not to insult her. "Lisa," he said softly, "No matter what O'Dell, or Mathias, or Logan says, do *not* go above camp two. No matter what the weather is, no matter how good you feel, don't go any higher than that. Okay?"

Lisa shrugged. "Well, we'll see. We'll see how I'm climbing. You never know. Maybe I really *can* get to the top of K2."

Jack didn't know what to say. He'd given Lisa Greenway the best advice she'd ever gotten in her life and it hadn't gotten through to her. She already had summit fever, and was going to climb as high as she could on K2, and probably a little beyond – encouraged by the whole Zermatt team –

and only then would she realize the difference and the danger between dreams and reality, that so many climbers come face -to-face with on the high mountains. Jack again felt the knot in his stomach he'd had since the beginning of the expedition, since New York, after leaving the Zermatt building. He knew this wasn't the way to climb K2 – with a bunch of beginners and dreamers – but there was nothing he could do to stop it.

"Okay Lisa. Maybe you can," Jack said softly. "But before you go to the top, stop and think about Lillian Bernard, Julie Tullis, and Alison Hargreaves. Okay?" Lisa smiled benignly, and nodded.

"And remember, they were all experienced, professional climbers." He gazed down at Lisa in silence. He knew that if Lisa had read the books, she would know about Bernard, Tullis and Hargreaves, three of the first five women climbers to summit K2. They all died on the way down. The other two, Wanda Rutkiewicz and Chantal Mauduit, died on other mountains a few years after climbing K2. Jack could see from the moisture in her eyes, that Lisa had read the magnificent, heartbreaking book, *Savage Summit* by Jennifer Jordan, and knew the history of the women of K2. He smiled down at her. "Okay Lisa," he said, reaching a hand out to caress her cheek. "You'll be okay. I'll see you at base camp."

"Thanks Jack," said Lisa with a smile. "Make sure you're wearing your logos."

There were seven jeeps and SUVs lined up in front of the Hotel K2 at eight in the morning. Jack threw his light knapsack into the back, and climbed into the front seat next to the driver. Sukey and Hamilton, both hung over from the late night before, squeezed into the rear seat, on each side of one of the adults from the trekking expedition who would be riding with them. In the SUV in front of them, Julia-Isabelle and her girlfriends, were waving to Jack through the rear window. He grinned and waved back.

The trekking group was one of the smaller ones headed into the mountains, explained the man in the backseat, a teacher from Amsterdam. It was made up of ten Dutch and French language teachers, plus a group of middle-school students from each country. They'd changed their itinerary a month ago, from a shorter trek to Nanga Parbat, to the K2 trek in hopes of glimpsing one of the women climbers racing to the top of K2. "And now here I am, sitting next to the great Korean climber, Chun, uh, Chung Yek, uh Suyen," the teacher said, mangling Sukey's name.

Sukey finished taking a long drink from a plastic water bottle and smiled at him. "Close enough," she said, rolling down the window as the caravan began moving. She pulled out a pack of Marlboro Lights and lit one up, much to the obvious disdain of the Dutch school teacher who waved the smoke away from his face. "Part of my weight-loss program," said Sukey. "I need to look good in my new Snow Leopard climbing suits."

Jack turned to look into the back seat and chuckled at the sight of Sukey on one side of the teacher, and Hamilton leaning against the door on the other side. They both looked like hell. Jack had turned in early while Hamilton and Sukey left the hotel to find somewhere to drink. They'd obviously found one. Jack had to drag Hamilton out of bed to get him into the Jeep on time.

Sukey took a final drag on her cigarette and tossed it out the window. "I'm sorry," she said to the teacher. "I won't smoke in the car."

"Thank you," he said. "You speak very good English. Most Koreans do not."

Sukey chuckled. "Most Koreans don't want you to know what they're saying. I spent three years at UCLA."

"Three years only?" asked the teacher.

"I needed to climb mountains," said Sukey. "Not study biology."

"Ah, you must be very happy with the choice you made," said the teacher.

Sukey laughed. "No, I should have stayed in California and worked on my golf game. I was a good golfer. The richest women in Korea are all professional golfers, not mountain climbers."

"But you will certainly be rich, and even more famous, if you win the race on K2," said the teacher. "Do you think you will get to the top first?"

Sukey shrugged and turned to look out the window at the rugged landscape dropping away from the road, down to the Shigar Valley far below. She was silent for a few moments, thinking, as if it was the first time she'd considered her chances. "No," she said softly. "No, I don't think I have a good chance." She continued to gaze out the window. "Logan is a great climber and very strong, and has the easiest route, and the best climbers with her." She glanced toward the front seat. "Professional climbers, like Jack Finley. That's what makes the difference, who you are climbing with, not the number of climbers or the money or the amount of supplies. You need to climb the big mountains with friends, with people you love and trust," she said quietly. She thought about what an outcast she had become on the Korean team. Probably no one on the Snow Leopard expedition would even talk to her on the mountain. It was not the way mountain climbing should be, she knew, and it wasn't safe.

"What about the French woman, Sophie Janot?" asked the teacher.

Sukey smiled. "Sophie is the best woman climber in the world, along with Edurne Pasaban and Gerlinde Kaltenbrunner, and one of the nicest, finest people I have ever known." She glanced at Jack. "Sorry Jack." He shrugged. Sukey looked out the window. "But Sophie is like me, climbing an impossible route. And without the people she... without the right companions." Sukey crossed her arms and leaned against the door, signaling that she was tired of talking. "So, no, it will not be possible for Sophie." Jack turned to look at her just as she closed her eyes.

The teacher from Amsterdam pulled an I-Pad from his bag and turned on the World Cup game between the Netherlands and Cameroon that he had downloaded the previous night. Jack turned in his seat and the teacher held the I-Pad out so they both could watch. "Ah, Robin Van Persie!" said the Dutchman, excitedly, "The best footballer in the world. This will be the year for the Netherlands, I am certain!" Next to him, Jay Hamilton began snoring loudly. He turned up the volume a bit, and for the next few hours, he and Jack passed the time watching World Cup games. The Netherlands was victorious, 2-1 over Cameroon, to advance to the Round of 16. The teacher was ecstatic, happy with the world. A few hours later, they arrived in Askole, the last real settlement they would see before walking into the Karakoram wilderness on their way to K2.

Azmat had their campsite completely set up with a large, multicolored tent for Jack and Jay, and a slightly smaller one for Sukey. Their sleeping bags and air mattresses were neatly laid out inside. A dinner of chicken soup and chapattis simmered on the open fire tended by an elderly man who fussed and took obvious pride in his station as the expedition cook.

As Azmat, the expedition sirdar, led Jack, Sukey and Jay into the campsite, Jack could see that the site was one of the prime spots in the wide expanse of terraced campsites around Askole crowded with trekkers and climbers – mostly headed into the Braldu Valley, some on their way out. Jack could see that Azmat must have negotiated firmly to secure the preferred site, very flat and close to the river. And certainly Azmat would have used the celebrity of his clients – no small matter in the narrow world of Balti porters – in his claim of the site. Their sirdar's pride was evident as he marched his clients into the campsite through the throng of porters waiting for work,.

Standing in a wavering line in front of the tents – as close to a formation of attention as a group of Balti porters could achieve – the expedition's fifteen porters smiled and nodded their greetings to their famous clients. The porters were dressed in the traditional garb of loose-fitting old canvas and muslin rags, Gilgit caps, and well-worn sandals.

Walking next to Jack, Hamilton pointed toward the porters. "Hey Jack," he said, "Where are all the..." Jack pulled his hand down and shook his head at Hamilton to interrupt what he knew he was about to say. Jack knew that they would never see the new Zermatt jackets and hiking boots that Lisa had sent on ahead for the porters. Too valuable to actually wear on an expedition, the gifts were already sent on to the porters' homes throughout the hills around Askole. It was a tradition established long ago, that the porters' contract would include a piece of equipment they could use on the trek – but rarely did – like sunglasses, mittens or boots. To inquire now, about the jackets and shoes would be bad form and an insult to Azmat, in front of his men.

Sitting on straw mats in the center of the campsite, Jack, Sukey, Jay and Azmat enjoyed a dinner of chicken soup, chapattis and apricots. Azmat, who was thirty-five, spoke very good English and was anxious to impress his clients with stories about his father and uncles, who also made long careers as trekking sirdars. They'd led huge expeditions, some of more than

1,000 porters, and been sirdar for some very famous climbers, like Messner and Habbeler, Bonington, and Ed Viesturs and Scott Fischer – climbers as famous as Jack Finley and Miss Sukey, said Azmat grinning broadly. His pride was evident. This would be an expedition for his sons to talk about someday.

As darkness descended over the valley, Sukey and Hamilton, still feeling the effects of their long night in Skardu, turned in early. Jack wandered over to the edge of the campsite and sat on a large brown boulder. Looking around at the rapidly darkening terraced hillsides surrounding Askole, the campfires and battery lanterns of the many expeditions, looked to Jack, what a long-ago civil war encampment by one of the large armies on the eve of a great battle, might look like. Jack closed his eyes and breathed in the nostalgic aroma of the cook fires and reveled in the deja vu of expeditions long past, with the camaraderie of good friends and the many nights on the trail spent with Sophie. It now seemed to Jack like another lifetime.

Suddenly, the serenity of the valley was destroyed by a roaring noise, flashing lights and brilliant spotlights as the huge black helicopter with the silver *Snow Leopard* logo on the side came racing up the valley from the west. It flew only a few hundred feet above the valley floor, already nearing its fully-loaded altitude limit, which it would come precariously close to by the time it reached the Savoia Glacier. K2 base camp, at 5,000 meters high, was at a greater elevation above sea level than the top of Mont Blanc.

Jack listened to the labored thwacking of the helicopter's huge new rotor blades and watched the blinking lights until they disappeared around a bend in the ridgeline far up the valley. A sudden rush of sadness enveloped him as he realized now, for what seemed like the first time, that his career in mountaineering was over and a new generation of climbing had begun. Now, the big mountains were accessible to every climber who could make it to the top of the rock wall at their local gym and could afford a ticket to fly in, strap on an oxygen mask, and jumar up the fixed ropes to the summit. This, he decided, sitting on the boulder in the dark at the head of the trail in Askole, would be his last expedition to the Himalaya.

Chapter 12

The verdant meadows and orchards of Askole were left far behind by noon of the first day. Jack, Sukey and Jay were making very good time, walking just ahead of the French and Dutch teachers' expedition. With only a handful of climbers and porters, everything was simpler and faster, with fewer interruptions, and Jack was enjoying the freedom and rapid progress of the trek. Thirty yards ahead of him, Sukey and Jay Hamilton had been locked together in conversation since they'd started out. Occasionally one or both would laugh and waver in their track, and then recover and continue the conversation. Jack was surprised at how quickly Sukey and Jay had become good friends. Maybe it was the night in Skardu – getting drunk together was always a great bonding experience. Or maybe, it was the role of outcast each felt within their expeditions – Sukey, the only woman on a team that had no respect for women; and Jay, the only minority on a team so awkwardly conscious of equality and political correctness, that he'd become more of a prized asset than a team member. Jack didn't care. He'd been a "Sukey fan" for years, and now he thoroughly enjoyed Jay's intelligence, personality and his sense of humor, and was glad each had found a new friend.

Though very hot and dusty, the first day's hike was fairly easy, on a mostly level plain even though the trek in its entirety would gain almost two thousand meters in altitude by the time they reached Concordia at 5,000 meters high. It was a significant increase at this altitude, and Jack was glad he'd made the decision to walk in. He knew he was in excellent climbing shape, but it had been a long time since he had breathed air this thin, and soon to be much thinner. He was also glad that Logan had made him take Jay Hamilton on the trek. Hamilton was physically capable, but had let himself get a little soft over the last year since he'd climbed Everest. And even though, as communications officer he wouldn't be going high on K2, he needed the acclimatization as much as anyone on the expedition. Living at nearly sea level in Southern California, breathing the fat, heavy air all his life wasn't the best preparation for the Himalaya. To disregard that fact, Jack knew, could be fatal in the mountains. You didn't have to climb beyond 8,000 meters to be struck by Acute Altitude Sickness. Many a climber had been afflicted at much lower altitudes, even at base camp.

Stopping for lunch, on a slope-side clearing on a bank of the Braldu River, Jack, Sukey and Jay sat down amid the French and Dutch trekkers. The cook had prepared large plates of cheese, fruit, and walnuts, for each of the climbers, which they shared with the trekkers around them who in turn shared their bread and cold meats. They drank water until one of the French teachers came around with a bottle of chardonnay, one of the several dozen bottles they had brought along. It seemed that the trekkers, especially the French, would only take the term "roughing it" to a certain point. Jack, Sukey and Jay toasted their new Dutch and French neighbors and friends. Then Julia-Isabelle and some of her friends came through the group with plates of Dutch chocolate for everyone to sample.

Soon after the combined expeditions started out again, they got their first sight of the magnificent silver Zermatt helicopter. It came straight toward them out of the early sun, its dull drone growing continually louder as it bore down upon them. At a distance, the huge helicopter appeared to be flying low enough that they would be able to reach up and touch it. Some of the porters, who had never seen helicopters this large or this loud, edged away from the trail to the safety of some large boulders. As it passed directly over them, they could see the Zermatt – Z painted on the wide belly of the helicopter as well as on the rear rotor pillar. Many of the trekkers waved up to the helicopter with glee as it went by. The whole experience of the trek in to K2 was made even more exciting by the involvement of these monstrous flying machines.

Jay Hamilton followed the flight of the helicopter down the valley to the west. "Headed back to Skardu," he said to Jack and Sukey next to him. "Still bringing in equipment. Be a couple of days before the team comes in."

"Probably going back for more beer," said Jack.

A few minutes later, the deep whap, whap of another helicopter came up behind the trekkers, headed in the other direction, east, into the mountains. They looked up to see the gleaming white, long-bodied, Bell 430 of the Outdoor Sports Network, flash by, flying faster and higher than the lumbering CH-47s. Jack watched it disappear far up the glacier and wondered if he might be participating in one of the last walks from Askole to Concordia by any expedition. He stopped walking and looked far down the trail in front of him and thought about the historic expeditions of the past that had covered this same ground, slept on these same campsites, and reveled in the same spectacular beauty of the landscape as they slowly, laboriously, made their way to the greatest concentration of major mountain peaks anywhere in the world.

Jack pictured the sight of the grand exploration of 1909 by the Duke of the Abruzzi, with its thousand porters, many tons of supplies – including the Duke's iron bed frame – and hundreds of yaks and pack mules, which laid the groundwork for the historic expeditions that came later in the century. It was the expedition that ended with the Duke proclaiming "K2 unclimbable" but established the lower route that became known as the "Abruzzi Spur", which unlocked the upper reaches of the mountain to generations of future expeditions.

Jack thought about the famous 1938 expedition of Charles Houston, the New Hampshire doctor and pioneer in high-altitude medicine – the first "American" expedition. Then, the attempt the following year by Fritz Wiessner, the German-American, the expedition that resulted in the first recorded fatalities on K2, when one of the expedition's prime benefactors, the inexperienced, unfit and totally exhausted, Dudley Wolfe, was inadvertently abandoned at a high camp. A heroic rescue effort by three of the expedition's Darjeeling Sherpas – Pasang Kikuli, Pasang Kitar, and Phinsoo Sherpa – resulted in tragedy, as Wolfe and the three Sherpas were never seen again. Wiessner made it to within 800 feet of the summit, but, the first ascent of K2 would have to wait until after World War II, when the controversial Italian expedition of Ardito Desio put Achille Compagnoni and Lino Lacedelli on the summit on July 31st, 1954.

Later, came the most heroic climb in the history of K2, with Houston's return in 1953. High on the mountain, the climb turned into a legendary rescue effort of fellow climber, Art Gilkey, who had come down with a potentially fatal case of thrombophlebitis. Houston and teammates Bob Bates, George Bell, Bob Craig, Dee Molenaar, Tony Streather, and Pete Schoening, without a second thought, gave up their quest of the summit to attempt a near impossible descent, lowering Gilkey, wrapped in a sleeping bag and tent fragment, from a point high on the famous Black Pyramid at 25,000 feet. A fall by Bell triggered a chain reaction plummet by the entire roped-together team, with the exception of Pete Schoening who had established a belaying point above the other climbers. As his six teammates slid down an icy slope to oblivion, Schoening held fast to the rope wrapped around his ice axe and his waist and saved his companions in what became known in mountaineering history as simply "the belay." Soon after, Art Gilkey was either swept off the mountain by an avalanche, or he cut his anchoring ropes and gave up his life to save his teammates from the grave peril of continuing the improbable rescue attempt. The American climber, Nick Clinch, would immortalize the climb as "the finest moment in the history of American mountaineering was the Homeric retreat of Dr. Houston's party of K2 in 1953."

How many times, Jack thought, on his treks in to K2, Broad Peak and the Gasherbrums, had he stopped to pay his respects at the Gilkey Memorial, a stone cairn erected near the base of K2, memorializing the climbers who had lost their lives on the mountain. Many of the climbers' remains were interred under the rocks; many others remembered on small plaques or tin plates, their names painstakingly hammered out by grieving friends. Jack knew many of the plates; some, he'd climbed with.

Jack looked up to see that most of the trekkers had gone past him. He sensed somebody next to him and looked down to see the girl, Julia-Isabelle gazing up at him. She held out her hand. "May we walk together for a while Mr. Finley?"

Jack smiled and took her hand. "I would enjoy that very much," he said, as they started up the trail.

At three o'clock, the combined expeditions stopped for the night at a place called Paiju. Jack would have preferred continuing for another hour or two, but the spacious campground at Paiju was a standard stop for expeditions heading in to Concordia, or back out to Askole, and Azmat and his porters had already set up the tents and cook stove when Jack, Sukey and Jay arrived. It was also one of the last stops on the trail where the cooks for the two expeditions could barter for some goats and fresh vegetables for the grand feast they planned for that evening's supper. It was also the last spot where there was plentiful wood for a good campfire, which would be a welcome comfort with the temperature dropping rapidly with the falling sun. With the rising altitude and the close proximity of the Biafo glacier, the hikers would be putting away their walking shorts and donning warmer clothing for the remainder of the trek.

While the cooks and their assistants fanned out through the countryside to trade with the local farmers, the porters prepared the tents and sleeping bags, and the children ran off excitedly into the nearby woods to find fuel for the campfire, Jack examined the close-by foothills. Not ready to call it a day, he found Hamilton and pulled him out of their tent. "C'mon, we're going to do some bouldering. Need to get the arms in shape."

Sukey declined their invitation, content to rest and enjoy an early bottle of Chablis and a fresh pack of Gaulois with several of the French teachers. They'd secured good seats, leaning back against small boulders encircling the growing campfire, the teachers excited over the opportunity of spending time with the Korean superstar climber.

Jack and Jay climbed for an hour on some easy rock formations until the sun began to fall, and stopped to rest on a shelf a hundred meters above the campsite. Jay had done well enough, Jack thought, as they sat and rested before heading down. "Not too bad," said Jack. "You're not as helpless as I thought you'd be on the way up."

Hamilton laughed. "Hey, I'm an athlete. I played sports in college."

"Really," said Jack. "What sports?"

"I played flag football, at Cal Tech, and a season of ultimate Frisbee."

Jack laughed, and they exchanged a high-five. They sat for a few moments in silence, looking down at the campsite, the glowing fire and gathering of the trekkers. Hamilton looked over at Jack. "So, what do you think? Think I'm ready for K2?"

Jack gazed off toward the mountains in the east, then back at Hamilton. "No Jay, you're not. And I need you to promise me you won't try to get to the top. You'll be a good climber someday Jay, but you're not nearly ready for K2." Jack looked down at his feet. He spoke softly. "And, I *don't* want to be putting your tin plate on the Gilkey Memorial. Okay? K2 is not for you man, not yet. Okay? Believe me about this. I know."

Hamilton clasped his hands together and nodded to himself in thought. Finally, he spoke. "Yeah, you're right. I've been fooling myself since Everest, thinking I could, you know, do K2 and a bunch of eight-thousanders and be a *real* climber, but, when someone like you tells me it's not going to happen, well... I'm not stupid. I don't want to die here Jack."

Jack closed his eyes briefly and smiled to himself. He patted Hamilton on the knee. "Thank you Jay. I don't want you to die either, not now, not this trip." He stood up to begin their descent. "Someday, after you've climbed Rainier and Denali a few more times, and then Cho Oyu and Broad Peak, and Kanchenjunga, and a few others, without the helicopters and all the rest of this Team-Zermatt baloney, then maybe you'll be ready for K2... on your own, the way it should be climbed. You'll know when you're ready. Okay buddy?"

Hamilton stood up and looked out toward the big mountains to the east. "It's *that* bad, huh?"

"Yeah, it is Jay," said Jack. "It's not for beginners." Jack started down, feeling satisfied that he'd finally accomplished *something* since he'd joined the expedition. It was his job to keep the Zermatt climbers alive, and he'd just saved one of them.

The sun was falling quickly and the campground was alive with long shadows, more crowded than when Jack and Jay went up the hill. Several new camps had been set up, and Jack recognized expeditions on their way out to Askole, after spring assaults on K2, the Gasherbrums and Broad Peak. These were expeditions of climbers – not trekkers and sight-seers – rugged looking young men with their climbing beards and the gaunt, slow manner he'd seen so many times in his past. Climbers, victorious or defeated, it was impossible to tell, all simply ready to get out to Rawalpindi for hot showers, a huge meal, and a flight home to Europe, America, or some to Australia, New Zealand or South Africa. The climbers were glassy-eyed and tired, and if they were lucky, not burdened by the heartbreaking loss of a teammate. Jack had experienced both kinds of treks out of the Karakorums.

When Jack and Jay returned to their campsite, the cooks were in the final stages of preparing the grand meal of the trek. Two goats were being turned slowly over open fires, and several pots were simmering on the cook stoves. As they went to find a spot to sit with Sukey and the trekkers around the large camp fire, Julia-Isabelle came running over to Jack.

"Mr. Finley, sir, do you think we could go over to the other camps," she turned and pointed toward the tents of the climbers headed back to Askole, "and ask if any of the climbers have seen Sophie? To see if she is coming out?"

Jack looked over at the tents. Sophie wasn't a subject he felt like bringing up among a group of veteran climbers, but, he reasoned, these climbers were all probably too young to even know who he was. "Sure we can Julia. Let's go see if anyone's seen Sophie."

They walked into the first camp they came to and found three men sitting around a small fire, on folding camp chairs. The men were all well bearded and thin, and had the tired, underfed look of the end of a long expedition. They rose slowly to their feet to greet their visitors. Jack had to smile when he saw that each man held a can of Pabst Blue Ribbon beer – Logan Healy's preferred drink.

"Ah, P-B-Rs," said Jack, "you must have stopped in at Zermatt."

One of the men laughed and said something in German. Jack just shrugged. Then Julia-Isabelle began speaking fluent German to the man. They had a short conversation.

"He said, that yes, on their way out from Broad Peak they stopped at the Zermatt base camp," said Julia-Isabelle. "It was like a shopping mall, he said. And they gave them a case of beer and some food." Jack smiled down at the girl.

From a nearby tent, a tall bearded man, a little older than the other climbers, pushed his way through the flap. "Thought I heard a familiar voice from the past out here," he said, ambling over to Jack. "How the hell are you Jack?" He stopped in front of Jack. "Jon Golonka."

Jack recognized his old friend. "Wow, Jon!" The two men embraced. They backed off and shook hands. They'd never climbed together but Jack and Golonka, famous in Poland for climbing difficult routes and for several harrowing winter climbs, had run into each other many times over the years.

Jack turned to Julia-Isabelle. "Julia, this is an old friend, Jon Golonka, from Poland." The girl smiled and shook hands with Golonka.

Golonka spoke in German to the other climbers, using Jack's name several times. The climbers nodded and came forward to shake hands with Jack. Golonka reached into a pack on the ground and brought out a Pabst for Jack.

"Thanks Jon." Jack popped open the not-very-cold beer. "My friend Julia here, wanted to ask you fellows a question."

Julia stepped forward and looked at Jon and at the other men. She spoke German – a few sentences in which, Jack could hear the name *Sophie Janot* mentioned several times.

Golonka nodded. "Yes, we saw Sophie, after she'd come down from Gash One. Their porters had come in with fresh supplies, and they were moving base camp down the glacier over to K2. When we were at the Zermatt camp, I'd heard that Sophie's group was having some kind of problem with the porters, that only a few of the Baltis were willing to go through the ice fall to get up to the Northeast Ridge."

"Was she going to stay up there?" asked Jack.

"No, she said she was coming out." Golonka grinned. "Needed a shower, and a bottle of Chardonnay, and to see the French play a World Cup game." He shrugged. "But, she wasn't sure if she had time though, to come out and be back to K2 by the first of July, when everything starts. So, I'm not sure what she's doing."

Jack nodded several times in thought. "How did she look, Jon? How was she doing?"

Golonka shrugged and flashed a brief smile. "Well you know Sophie, she looked fucking great, as always." He quickly glanced toward Julia-

Isabelle. "Sorry," he said. Julia-Isabelle grinned and said something in German that made the other climbers laugh.

Jack was watching her and for an instant, there was something about the girl that reminded him vividly of Sophie. He turned back to Golonka. "No," said Jack. "Not that way."

"Yeah, I know what you're asking," said Golonka. He grimaced. "She looked tired Jack. All used up. Her whole crew looked done. She had a brutal climb on Gasherbrum – lot of snow, horrible winds. Took way too long. They were supposed to be out weeks ago. Sophie was going to fly back to France to rest for a week, see her kids. Now..." Golonka had a pained look on his face. "I don't know how they go and begin climbing K2 in a week." He rolled his eyes. "The Northeast Ridge. It's suicide Jack. They're all going to die up there."

"Yeah, it's a tough route, for sure," said Jack. "Thanks Jon. Nice seeing you again." Jack looked down and saw that Julia-Isabelle had tears in her eyes. He put his hand on her shoulder. "It's okay, Julia. Sophie will be okay. Come on, let's go back."

They walked back to the campsite in silence. The mouth-watering aroma of roasting goat meat filled the air as the combined expeditions lined up in front of the mess tent where the cooks, were dishing out the grand feast. As they entered the camp, Julia-Isabelle stopped and reached up for Jack's hand. He turned back to her. "What is it Julia?"

Her eyes were still moist. "Mister Finley, why did that man say that about Sophie? What is the Northeast Ridge?"

Jack knelt down in front of the girl, which now made her a little taller than himself. "Well, first of all Julia, now that we're such good friends, maybe you could just call me Jack. Okay?" She nodded, then wiped her eyes with her sleeve. "The Northeast Ridge is the route on K2 that Sophie has a permit for. It's a very difficult route up the mountain. It's only been climbed a very few times."

"But why does Sophie have to climb such a hard route?" Julia-Isabelle asked. "Why doesn't she climb the Abruzzi Spur like most expeditions do?"

Jack was impressed with the girl's knowledge of K2. "Well, that's a long story. It's all about the TV show, and the race, and about money." He shrugged. "A lot of stuff."

"But, is Sophie able to climb the Northeast Ridge?"

Jack nodded. "Yes, Sophie can climb anything. Sophie can climb the Northeast Ridge."

"Could you climb the Northeast Ridge, Jack?" Julia-Isabelle stared deep into his eyes.

Jack thought for a few seconds. "Yes, Julia. I could climb it." He stood up but Julia-Isabelle, he could see, was not ready to go.

"Jack, will you climb the Northeast Ridge with Sophie? Will you keep her safe? Please, Jack," she implored.

Jack put his hand on her shoulder. "Come on, let's go eat," he said, starting toward the camp fire.

It was a grand feast that put everyone in a good mood. Bellies were full as they crowded around the massive bonfire, which lit up the dark night and took the chill out of the cold air. Jack, and Jay Hamilton, after changing into their sweatpants and fleece shirts, found seats on a flat rock as one of the Dutch teachers assumed the role of the MC for the night's entertainment.

"Okay, everyone," the teacher announced in English, for the obvious pleasure of the Americans present, "first we have, Azmet and his band of Balti balladeers, to sing... I don't know what, a Baltistan folk song, I think." The crowd laughed and clapped as Azmet and his porters, clapping and dancing, entered the ring around the fire. One of the porters, off to the side, strummed a stringed instrument much like a mandolin, while the porters sang in a language no one else knew, and aggressively danced to a tuneless song. It was an act they obviously had put on before, for countless expeditions, and their joy from the rhythmic hand-clapping and attention of the climbers and trekkers was obvious.

During the porters performance, Julia-Isabelle and two of her friends came scampering around the fire to where Jack and Jay were seated. Julia-Isabelle squeezed in between the two men while her friends sat on the ground in front of them. Julia-Isabelle looked up at Jack with obvious glee. "Wait until you hear our song Jack." The two girls in front of them giggled in anticipation. "We're going to rock this crowd!"

Jack laughed. "Well wait 'til you hear the song Jay and I are going to do," he said, leaning toward the girl and pressing her against Hamilton. Jay looked at Jack with a blank face and his jaw dropped. Jack looked at him. "Don't worry Jay, the crowd's going to love it!" He laughed again and rejoined the rhythmic clapping along with the girls.

As the Balti porters exited to a huge ovation, one of the teachers took center stage juggling three rocks, then reaching down to the ground, added a fourth rock, and then an incredible fifth rock to the rotation, flying through the flame-lit night air. He tossed them behind his back and through his legs, never missing a beat until he finally threw one high into the black night and sent it crashing into the middle of bonfire send sparks and embers, while everyone cheered his magical feats.

Two of the female teachers came forward and performed a seductive and playful rendition of Zou Bisou Bisou, in French that put everyone in a festive mood. Jack was beginning to think that the talent level at this show was a little too high for him to participate in. When the song was over, after a long round of enthusiastic applause, the MC jumped up again. "Now, we have a very special treat from some of our younger members." He pointed over at the three girls. "Julia, Camille and Laure," he shouted.

Camille and Laure bounded to center stage and started clapping and singing out a tune while Julia pulled the elastic from her pony tail and fluffed out her long blonde hair. "And now, live from Paris, France," announced Camille, "it's Lady Julia Gaga!"

Julia pranced and high-stepped her way in between the other two girls as they all launched into a high-energy, rendition of "Poker Face", complete with a techno-pop dance routine they'd obviously perfected back at school. The crowd immediately joined in with rhythmic clapping, and several of the other Dutch and French students jumped up to join the robotic dancing. They were followed by some of the teachers and a few of the deliriously laughing Balti porters. Climbers and trekkers from the other camps had closed in around the encampment to watch the show. At the center of the production, Julia, Camille and Laure, sang and danced themselves to near exhaustion by the time their song ended. They received a huge ovation from the crowd around the bonfire, and from the surrounding camps. It had been a truly spectacular show, as Julia had promised. The girls came back and collapsed to their seats on the ground in front of Jack and Jay.

"And it is time now, I think, for our American friends to join the show." The MC grinned and stretched his hands toward Jack.

Jack jumped up, tapping Jay Hamilton on the shoulder. "Okay Jay, we're on."

Hamilton looked as if he'd seen a ghost. "Wha, what Jack? What are we...?

Jack grinned as he pulled Jay along with him toward center stage next to the fire. "C'mon Jay, every American kid who's ever ridden a team bus in high school knows *American Pie*."

Jay's grin lit up the campsite. "You got that right brother. My favorite song!"

Sukey jumped up and joined the men. "Even Koreans know that one!"

Julia-Isabelle, beaming at her American friends, ran over and handed Jack, Jay and Sukey the three pieces of wood she and her friends had used as prop microphones.

The crowd quieted as Jack, between Jay and Sukey, held up his arms. "And now, an American classic." They waited a few seconds to set the stage, and for Jack to begin in a loud clear voice, doing his best impression of Don McLean.

The crowd surrounding the campfire, erupted in applause at the famous first few words of *American Pie,* which was indeed a long-time classic on both sides of the Atlantic.

With the next stanza, the crowd couldn't resist joining the song in unison, surprising Jack that so many of the Dutch and French trekkers knew the lyrics. Everyone sang louder, sending the song throughout the campsites along the river banks.

Julia-Isabelle and her friends were now up with Jack, Jay and Sukey, singing the lyrics in perfect English, along with many of the campers on the surrounding hill-sides.

When the chorus came, it sounded like the entire Braldu valley had joined in.

Then, Jay Hamilton took over, belting out the up-tempo lyrics, jumping and jive dancing and enjoying his spot in the limelight.

Jack and Sukey were now dancing, hand in hand in a ring with the French girls, singing along with Jay's lead, as everyone around the campfire were on their feet, clapping rhythmically, and immensely enjoying the sing-a-long. The Balti porters were clapping, dancing and enjoying the happiness of their clients. Climbers and trekkers from the surrounding camps had closed in to join in the song.

When the familiar chorus began again, even louder than before, Jack was looking around the campsite, clapping and laughing, enjoying the spectacle of this international ensemble gathered in the wilderness of Pakistan, belting out *American Pie* in several languages. Then, in the darkness at the edge of the gathering, something caught his eye. A dark figure against the black night that sent a chill up his spine. A silhouette, arms crossed, unmoving, not singing, not taking part, just watching the show. He looked away for a moment, losing sight of the figure as his eyes readjusted from the fire. Then he found her again, standing alone in the dark, unmistakably Sophie – as only he would know, even after ten years – from the demure outline, confident stance, and the unmoving grace, the faint glint of the bonfire off her ebony hair. As Jay Hamilton very capably took over the lead, Jack slipped away unnoticed through the ring of onlookers and into the darkness outside the campsite. He stumbled on some lose rocks as he made his way in the dark around the throng. He wondered if he'd been mistaken, or if she'd left, but then, she was there, walking toward him out of the shadows, slowly, arms still crossed against the cool night air. She stopped in front of him and smiled. "Bon soir Jack. As soon as I heard that dreadful song, I knew it would be you."

Chapter 13

Jack had considered this moment many times over the years. What it would be like to stand face-to-face with Sophie again. *What would they say to each other? Would there still be an attraction? Or would they just be old friends, shake hands and behave like the adults they'd become?* But Jack knew the situation had changed the moment Logan Healy had told him that Sophie had been killed on Cho Oyu, instantly tearing open his gut and releasing the years of pent-up remorse he'd always denied himself. Feelings he didn't know he still had.

And now, there she was, standing in front of him in the dim, flickering light of the bonfire, smiling, and even after an arduous climb of an eight-thousand meter mountain and several days' trek, looking as beautiful as Jack had ever remembered her. Ten years suddenly didn't seem like a long time. Jack's heart was pounding. He smiled. "Hey Soph. I'm glad you're not dead."

She laughed and stepped forward and gave Jack a brief hug and kiss on the cheek. The eternal European greeting. "Merci Jack, so am I." Sophie took Jack's hand. "Come and walk me back to my camp. We can talk."

Jack took Sophie's flashlight from her, but they didn't need it. The path through the camps was well-trod and the many campfires and lanterns along the way generated sufficient light.

"Paiju is very crowded this year," said Sophie.

"Yeah, a lot of trekkers, and journalists," Jack replied. "Seems to be some kind of circus going on at K2."

Sophie laughed. "Oui Jack, *circus* is the correct word. Wait 'til you see Logan's base camp." She chuckled again. "It's incredible. I think it is now one of the biggest villages in Pakistan. They have two giant generators, a huge mess tent and a pub with such horrible loud music playing all the time."

"I can imagine," said Jack, laughing.

"They have their own helicopter pad. And Logan has her own tent large enough for twenty people."

"Nice to be marrying one of the world's richest men."

"Well," said Sophie with a long pause. "I wouldn't count on that."

"Why? What do you mean?" Jack was perplexed.

"Oh, let's just say that my intuition tells me that," Sophie giggled, "maybe there is someone besides Mr. Joost in Logan's life."

"*No*, cut it out! Logan is in love, finally."

Sophie giggled again mischievously. "Yes, I think so. But I'm sorry, not with monsieur Joost."

"What? What do you mean?"

"Have you met Logan's friend? The skier, from Sweden?"

"Anja Lindgren, sure," said Jack. "They've been best friends for years."

Sophie giggled. "Yes, and I think, more than friends."

"*No.* Cut it out! The wedding is in October, in Brookline, near Boston where Logan's parents live."

"Believe me Jack. I know about these things." She laughed. "I saw Logan and her friend at the base camp together while mister Joost is still back in Islamabad. And remember, I have also shared a tent with Miss Healy."

"Yeah, me too." Jack laughed and clapped his hands together. "Well that's Logan, always an adventure."

They walked along in silence for a while, at a loss for what might be a suitable subject for casual conversation after ten years. They passed Jon Golonka's campsite, which was dark, with no activity. Jack pointed it out. "Stopped in and saw Jon earlier."

"Oh yes. We met them coming out from Gasherbrum. They'd been turned back on Broad Peak... out of time, out of food and fuel, and money."

"Yeah, we were there a few times, eh Soph?" Sophie nodded in the darkness but didn't reply.

In a few minutes, they reached Sophie's camp. It was set on an incline near the woods -- the price you pay for being one of the last groups into a camp. Three well-worn tents were set up on the uneven ground. Jack recognized the evidence of a tired expedition, too worn out to bother making a level tent platform. He immediately identified Sophie's trademark light blue tent and saw that it had a broken strut in the middle. The tent had Sophie's name printed on it along with several sponsor logos -- *BNP Paribas, Rolex, and Evian*, plus a few others he didn't recognize.

"Got your sponsors back," said Jack.

Sophie sat down on a small camp chair next to a fire that still smoldered with faint embers. She motioned Jack to the other chair next to her. "Yes, for this *event*, the sponsors were eager, especially with the involvement of the American and Korean television companies." She looked over at her sagging tent. "The tent though was for K2, but I needed it on Gasherbrum. I'll have to replace it in Rawalpindi."

"Pindi's a little dangerous these days."

Sophie smiled. "Only for Americans."

"Oh yeah, that's right. Everyone loves the French."

"Because we don't invade countries and drop bombs from little model airplanes."

Jack smiled at the old, familiar needle of America that was for so long a part of their relationship. "Yeah, and if it wasn't for us, you'd be speaking German and drinking beer instead of wine."

Sophie laughed and clapped her hands together softly, enjoying the old joke they'd shared so many times, long ago. Then she jumped up from her seat. "Mon Dieu, Jack, where are my manners!" She rooted through a couple of rucksacks lying in a pile outside the tents. Finally she found what she was looking for and came back with two cans of Pabst Blue Ribbon. She handed Jack one of the warm beers.

Jack laughed again at the sight of the very American beer deep into the Karakorums. "Logan should open up a PBR distributorship in Pakistan."

They opened the beers and Sophie held hers out to Jack. They touched cans. "To a successful climb of K2," said Sophie. "For both of us." Sophie took a drink and made a sour face. "I remember the first time I had one of these. When we were climbing the walls in Colorado. You had a cooler full of them in the back of that awful pickup truck. It was so hot, we drank them all in one night."

Jack remembered the day clearly, but didn't respond. It was a great day, a perfect day, at a great time in his life. It seemed that everything Sophie said, reminded him of those days when they were together, and life was never better. He quietly drew in a deep breath to stem the anxiety in his gut he'd felt from the first moment he'd seen Sophie earlier that night.

"So, have you run into the TV people yet?" he asked, to get away from the past.

"Oh Yes. Two boys from Logan's group climbed up to Camp I on Gash to meet us when we were coming down. I gave them a very short interview – I wasn't in talkative mood."

"That was Bert and Arnie." Jack chuckled. "Part of my job is to keep them alive."

"Good luck. Ang Phu and his nephews had to help them down to basecamp." Sophie took a small sip of beer. "Then when we got down, there was a big crew from your Outdoor Sports Network. They were very insistent on doing another interview. There was a very pushy woman in charge..."

"Glenda Craft," said Jack.

"Oui, very *American*."

Jack chuckled. "That's her."

"But, she did insist on flying us out. At least to Skardu, on their helicopter. That's why we're here. They didn't think it would be appropriate to fly us from Logan's camp, and this is the best landing spot along the way."

"When do they pick you up?"

"Early tomorrow morning. The helicopter will be at the Zermatt basecamp tonight, and is leaving early to go back to Skardu. We have a flight to Rawalpindi from there, and I have to go to Islamabad and give them a long interview in a studio. Then they will fly us back, next week, right to our camp at the base of the ridge. It was the only way to get out and back in time. The boys are tired. Me too."

"That will save you a lot of time."

"And I can rest, finally, and sleep in a bed and wash my hair!" Sophie smiled at the thought.

"Maybe you can watch some World Cup games," said Jack.

Sophie threw her hands in the air. "Oh my *god* Jack, *no!* Have you seen how Les Bleus have embarrassed us? Losing to Mexico, and then to South Africa! I watched some highlights from Logan's pub." Sophie rolled her eyes and laughed. "They have a big, flat screen TV – much bigger than mine at home!"

Jack laughed. "Logan's got to get her Red Sox scores."

"So, no. No World Cup games now. It's over." Sophie looked down at her feet. "Victor was right. He knew about football," Sophie said softly. She looked off into the darkness. "He knew it would not be France's year."

Jack waited for Sophie to turn back. "I'm sorry about your friend. Sorry about Victor." Sophie just stared into the embers of the fire without speaking.

"That was a hard one, huh... Cho Oyu," said Jack.

Sophie sighed and tried to smile. "Yes, Cho was difficult. Very hard. We shouldn't have gone in winter. It was too cold. Too much snow." She took in a deep breath and turned to look at Jack. "I was lucky to make it back down. Lucky and selfish. *I* should have died up there, not Victor. Victor is dead because I didn't make him go down when he should have." She took a long drink of beer, squashed the can and threw it angrily toward a pile of trash. The can bounced noisily across the campsite.

Jack waited a few moments to let her anger subside. "Who's with you now?" he asked.

"We have Carlos and Toby. Carlos Medina from Spain, and Toby Houle is from Canada. They were with me on Cho. Both very strong, good climbers. They have been above eight thousand meters, several times. We have two Alpine guides from Courmayeur that Poppi knows – they just arrived and are back at base camp." Sophie pointed vaguely toward one of the tents, as if trying to remember the names. "And two Americans that Toby recruited after Cho. Ken Wall was a guide with Toby on Denali. He did very well on Gasherbrum. I was pleased with him. The other is Ron Gelinas, from Maine. This was his first mountain in the Himalaya, and he was, I think, a little overmatched. He is on his way home and will not be coming back in for K2."

"Not a very big team for K2." said Jack. "For the Northeast Ridge," he added.

Sophie smiled. "But of course we still have Ang Phu, and now, two of his nephews. They are on their way up to the Northeast Ridge basecamp with Doctor Clement and the porters."

Jack ignored the mention of Clement, whom he knew was never one of Jack's supporters throughout his relationship with Sophie. "And how is the great Ang Phu? Still the king of the Sherpas?"

Sophie nodded. "Yes, he is still the strongest climber in the world, but now he is getting old for this. He is forty – like you Jack." She laughed.

Jack smiled at the friendly jab, but it reminded him that, yes, he was probably the oldest climber in the Karakorum this season. It felt strange to him, after a career in which he was usually one of the younger members of the expedition. "What are Ang's nephews like?"

Sophie shrugged. "They are young and strong, looking to make a name for themselves, like all the young Sherpas now. They went through Ang's climbing school in Nepal, but still learning to climb. They have both climbed Everest several times."

"Who hasn't?" said Jack, tossing his beer can toward the pile of trash.

"Yes, I know. And the Sherpa are the same way. They run up and down Everest, but are not so anxious to go to Annapurna or Makalu, or K2. So this is very big for Ang's nephews. To make it to the summit will greatly increase their fees on future expeditions."

"It's all about the money, for everyone on K2 this year," said Jack softly.

"And me too," said Sophie. "Me too, now."

Neither spoke for a long interval, until Sophie finally broke the silence. "So, you met with Poppi, in Rawalpindi."

"Yeah, he..."

"Jack, I didn't want him to see you... to ask you..."

"It's okay. I didn't mind. It was... nice seeing Janot again. But I was surprised."

"He is very worried," said Sophie.

"With good reason," said Jack, studying Sophie's face carefully.

Sophie shrugged. "The ridge has been climbed before, several times. How hard can it be?" She chuckled.

Jack gazed at her face and thought he discerned a hint of doubt, which he'd never seen in Sophie before any climb they'd been on. "Sophie, it's four miles of knife-edged ridgeline, exposed to the wind all the way, with heavy snow, and no good campsites."

Sophie smiled and then slapped the top of her knees lightly. "Well yes, Jack, I've heard that it can be a handful, as the Brits would say. But what fun would it be if it wasn't?" She shrugged. "We'll manage, somehow. It's the only route we have." She stood up. "Now I need to sleep Jack. It's been a long day, and I need to be up early for my ride."

Jack wanted to stay and talk to her about his ideas for climbing the Northeast Ridge, the ideas that came to him in Rawalpindi when he was talking to her father. He wanted to help her. But now their conversation was over, and he was on the other team. He got up from the uncomfortable little chair and looked down at her in the darkness, only one long step away from him. He wanted to wrap his arms around her and kiss her hard and long on the mouth. "Well, good luck Soph," he managed. "Maybe I'll see you on the mountain."

She smiled. "That would be good, because it would have to be near the top, where the ridge joins the Abruzzi."

"Yes, that's right." Jack had forgotten that the two routes come together very high on the mountain.

They came together for a brief, light hug. Jack started off toward the campsite.

"Hey Jack," Sophie called out softly before he'd gone far. He turned back to her. "How is your wife, and the children?"

"They are all fine. Ralph is four, Beth is one. I miss them. How are your girls?"

"They are wonderful. I miss them terribly."

They looked at each other for a few moments, before Jack turned and disappeared down the path into the darkness.

Jack woke up with a start, and glanced at his watch. Then he heard the drone of the helicopter that had awakened him. As he rolled out of his sleeping bag and pulled on his sweatpants, Jack noticed that Jay Hamilton was not in the tent; his sleeping bag lay zipped up. Jack pulled on a fleece shirt, grinning when he realized where Jay had probably slept last night.

A few of the porters were up, getting ready for breakfast and starting to pack up for an early start in the dim morning light. Jack set off at a trot while searching the sky for the helicopter. He ran around the edge of the campsite, headed for the tents of the trekking group. One of the French teachers was emerging from his tent as Jack approached.

"Julia. Which tent is Julia's?" he asked the bewildered teacher. "I need to find Julia, right away," said Jack, looking up at the helicopter dropping down to land on the flat field a hundred yards up the valley.

The teacher pointed up the line of neatly arranged tents. "She is in the fourth tent, the red one," he said, as Jack trotted away from him toward the small tents.

Jack pushed aside the tent flap and saw only a clutter of sleeping bags and rucksacks. "Julia," Jack said softly. "Julia, are you here?"

Three heads slowly arose from the sleeping bags. Julia brushed aside her long, blond hair and rubbed an eye. "Jack? Quel est le problème?" She sat up.

"Julia," said Jack. "Come quick. And bring your magazine picture." He backed out of the tent.

The girl scrambled instantly out of her sleeping bag. "Is it Sophie!?" she called out excitedly. "Sophie is here?" She clawed through the piles of clothes to find something to wear. Then she went deep into her backpack to find her notebook and the magazine page." She ran out of the tent barefoot.

Jack laughed when he saw her. "Better put some shoes on. We don't have much time." He looked up toward the landing site and saw several figures, laden with full rucksacks, moving up the trail toward the helicopter. Julia darted back into the tent and came out still trying to settle both feet into her hiking boots.

"Is it Sophie?" Julia asked, falling into a trot next to Jack.

"Yes, but we need to move quickly," said Jack.

Julia saw the helicopter landing and the people moving up the trail toward it. Sophie's black ponytail sticking out through the back of a white baseball cap and her diminutive size compared to the other climbers gave her away.

"It's Sophie!" Julia breathed as she pulled away from Jack, at an all-out sprint. Jack had to work hard to stay with her.

The door of the gleaming white OSN helicopter raised up as Sophie's group reached the field. They quickly handed their packs to someone inside the helicopter, and started to climb in. Jack and Julia were still fifty meters away. Julia sprinted away from Jack, waving her hands in the air as the door of the helicopter folded down into place. The twin turbo engines whined at a higher pitch as the rotor picked up speed and the helicopter moved slightly, then rose a foot off the grassy field. Jack and Julia were both waving their arms in the air as they reached the edge of the field. The wind turbulence and the noise brought them to a stop. Then the helicopter seemed to shrug, and dropped softly again to the turf. The whine of the engines immediately decreased as did the turbulence from the slowing rotor.

Jack walked Julia toward the helicopter, stopping as the fuselage door slowly raised up. A stairway folded out and settled firmly on the ground. Sophie appeared in the doorway, smiling at Jack and Julia, and came down the stairs. She was wearing short, brown hiking shorts with cargo pockets and a dark green, long-sleeved T-shirt. As Sophie walked toward them, Jack noticed now the gauntness he hadn't been able to see in the dim light of the previous evening. Her clothes hung loosely on her small frame. Except for the lines around her eyes, Sophie looked like she might be one of Julia's classmates.

Jack moved forward. "Sorry Sophie, but I have a friend here who really wants to meet you. It's why she came to Pakistan." Smiling nervously, Julia came up beside Jack. She had the magazine page with the picture of Jack and Sophie in her hand. "Sophie, this is Julia-Isabelle Chatelain, from Paris." He put his hand on Julia's shoulder urging her forward. "Julia, this is my old friend, Sophie Janot. Sophie is a mountain climber."

Julia giggled as she moved forward, putting her hand out to Sophie and bowing her head briefly. "Bonjour Miss Janot. C'est mon grand plaisir de vous rencontrer enfin."

Sophie smiled at the girl, ignoring her hand as she took a step forward with her arms out and embraced Julia warmly. She kissed her lightly on both cheeks. "Le plaisir est complètement à moi, Julia, et nous devrions parler en français, alors nous pouvons parler de Jack et il ne sait pas ce que nous disons." Both women giggled and glanced at Jack.

"Hey, English only, you two," said Jack.

Sophie took Julia's hand in hers and led her away from the noise and wind of the helicopter. They sat down on a patch of green grass and began speaking French. Jack came over and dropped to his knees next to them. The women laughed, and Julia handed Sophie the magazine page. Sophie spread the page out in her lap. She smiled and looked wistfully at the old picture of her and Jack.

"Nanda Devi, I think," said Jack. "From the date."

Sophie looked up at Jack and smiled. Her eyes were moist. "Yes, Nanda Devi, for sure," she said. "I remember that suit." She giggled. "I loved that suit." She reached out and held Julia's hand. "Nanda Devi is a very special mountain. It is the highest mountain in India and it is sacred. And, it was a very special mountain... for us."

Julia wiped her eyes with her sleeve. "I am sorry Miss Janot, I should not have imposed..."

Sophie laughed as she blinked away her own tears. She shook Julia's hand, "Oh, no, no, my dear. It's fine. It's wonderful to see this picture again." She took Julia's pen. "Jack, I need your back, please."

Jack turned his back to her and felt her hands pressing the magazine page against him as she wrote what seemed to be a long salutation.

"Merci," said Sophie, quickly folding up the page and handing it back to Julia. The girl tucked it carefully into her pocket.

"Merci beaucoup, Sophie," said Julia softly.

Sophie started to get up, then noticed Julia's tears. " Julia, ma chérie, pourquoi tu pleures?"

Jack turned to look at Julia. The girl looked up at him, and then at Sophie. "I cry because I am so worried for you Sophie. Jack tells me that your route on K2 is very hard and dangerous." She let out a sob. "And I don't know why Jack can't go with you to help you and protect you." She wiped her eyes with her sleeve. "K2 is special too, like Nanda Devi, and you should be climbing K2 with Jack."

Sophie came to her knees, reached out and embraced her. "Julia, Julia, everything will be fine. The climb is not so hard. I have climbed many harder routes than this one. I will be successful, and Jack will be also."

They rose to their feet, still embracing. Julia looked at Jack with imploring eyes over Sophie's shoulder. Jack smiled at her and ran a hand over her hair. "C'mon, Julia. Sophie needs to get going."

Sophie and Julia walked hand in hand back to the helicopter speaking French. Jack waited at the edge of the field. He watched them hug tightly, Sophie speaking to her warmly but firmly. Julia smiled and nodded, then turned and trotted back toward Jack. Sophie gazed over at Jack. She flashed a smile, waved, and then climbed into the helicopter.

On the trail back to their campsite, Jack and Julia looked up to watch the helicopter fly past. Julia waved slowly at the dark windows. They watched it disappear quickly up the valley. "She's the nicest person I've ever met," said the girl almost to herself. "I love Sophie,"

Jack put his hand on Julia's shoulder. "Yes, so do I Julia."

When they reached camp, Julia darted into her tent to pack up and get ready for breakfast. Jack was passing by Sukey's tent just as Jay Hamilton came out, bare chested, holding his shoes and a shirt. Jack had to laugh. He threw an arm around Jay's shoulders. "Good for you Jay, and Sukey too." He squeezed Jay in a half headlock, pulling him off balance. "And I mean that buddy."

Chapter 14

The easy trails, bonfires and goat roasts, were now behind them. The next two days showed the trekkers that they were indeed on one of the ruggedest, rockiest, and most formidable passages in Asia. They hiked up and down rocky chasms, across treacherous rope bridges over the surging Braldu river, and camped in desolate, boulder-strewn campsites with no villages in sight. The green pastures and fields gave way to gray and brown, barren hillsides cooled by the constant shade of the mountains rising around them. And in the distance to the west, between the hillsides and rocky crags, when the cloud cover lifted, they would get an occasional glimpse of the majestic, snow covered heights ahead of them and everyone's excitement would build. They were walking into the greatest concentration of high mountains on the earth's surface.

Jack and Sukey knew what to expect. They'd been here before and knew that next to the circuitous trek into the Annapurna basin, the trail to K2 – the only 8,000 meter mountain not visible from any inhabited settlement – was the longest and most difficult approach in mountaineering. Reinhold Messner called it the most difficult part of climbing K2. And, while the trail had been markedly improved upon over the years by the Pakistani Ministry of the Interior to aid tourism, Jack had been concerned about the safety of the students of the trekking group.

His fears were unfounded, he could see, when he dropped back to hike among the trekkers for a while. The students, it was obvious, had been on difficult trails before, in the Alps with their climbing club, and the teachers were all very fit and experienced hikers. Jack enjoyed watching the students stop and assist each other up, or down, some difficult steps, and always, it seemed, Julia-Isabelle was the leader, making sure her mates had a helping hand when needed. Jack watched her for a few minutes at the top step of a short goat path, pulling her friends up and over. Even with her fully-loaded pack, the small girl was strong, agile, and sure-footed. The more he watched her, the more he saw of Sophie in her.

Each day, they watched the helicopters flying up and down the Braldu Valley; the huge Zermatt and Snow Leopard CH-47's – their deafening roar announcing them from a mile away – along with Rudy Joost's sleek, Bell luxury chopper, and the French-made OSN helicopter that had transported Sophie and her team back to Islamabad. With every flyover, Jack and Sukey looked up wistfully as they watched the future of Himalayan mountaineering pass before their eyes. And the Balti porters looked up to see their way of life, and their livelihood, disappearing forever.

When the expeditions approached the campsite at Liligo on their fifth day out, they found the two smaller helicopters parked on the only level patches of ground in the vicinity. Two camera crews were set up on the trail leading into the campsite, as Jack, Sukey and Jay Hamilton walked in, fatigued from a long day of difficult hiking in the ever thinning air. Bert and Arnie were set up on a large flat rock; the OSN crew stood right in the middle of the trail. Marty Gallagher, the OSN director, was talking into his headset. Jack could see that the video cameras, with their long lenses, had been watching them for some time. Fifty yards beyond the video crews, Logan Healy, Morris O'Dell, and Rudi Joost were standing next to Glenda Craft, observing the approach of two of the key players of the grand show.

A handsome, deeply tanned man in his forties appeared next to Gallagher as Jack reached the OSN camera position. The man wore a bright red OSN windbreaker and held a cordless microphone. He stepped into Jack's path with his hand extended and a brilliant white smile on his face. "Hey Jack," he said, shaking hands, "great to see you again. Bruce Kinder, on-air host for OSN, *Quest-K2.*

Jack was certain he'd never met Kinder, but thought he might have seen him on television, announcing some winter X-games kind of events. Jack was tired and hungry and not in the mood for any interviews, but he knew that he'd gone AWOL for the trek in, and needed to do his part for the show.

"So, just a few quick questions," said Kinder, sidling up to Jack. "We already did the lead-in stuff, and got some good long-range footage." He glanced at Gallagher for a microphone check.

"Great," said Jack.

"Now Jack, what made you decide to take an eight day trek into the mountain when you could have taken a two hour helicopter ride?"

"Acclimatization," said Jack. "I needed to acclimate my body to the thin air again."

"But what about all the rest of the Zermatt team, that flew in?"

"Well, some of them may feel sick at basecamp, but more likely, once they start up the mountain. Some will be fine. You never know." Jack smiled for the camera. He looked back at the interviewer. "Plus, since this is probably my last trip to the Karakorums, I wanted to do it right, like so many of the great, historic expeditions of the past did it. Like my idols Messner and Bonington, and Joe Tasker and Peter Boardman did it. Walking in, over the same trails. One last time, before the helicopters turn mountain climbing into an amusement park ride for the rich."

Kinder glanced quickly at Marty Gallagher, and then hurriedly went on to a few more innocuous questions about the walk in, before getting to the main point of the interview. "And Jack, we understand that while on the trail, you met up with your long-time girlfriend, climber Sophie Janot." Kinder grinned at Jack, and added, "What was *that* like after ten years apart?"

Jack was taken by surprise and had no idea of how to answer. He stood mute, as the French and Dutch trekkers, coming into the campsite, started passing by on each side of Jack and his interviewer. The teachers and the students tried to be inconspicuous, but found it hard to resist mugging for the camera. Julia-Isabelle stopped just behind the camera tripod and turned back to Jack with a cross-eyed, goofy face, making him laugh. He relaxed. None of it meant anything anyway.

"Well yes, I ran into Sophie, but I hardly recognized her," said Jack, glancing briefly at Julia. "She'd put on so much weight in the last ten years, and her hair had turned gray, and she was kind of hunched over. And quite frankly, I don't think she remembered me."

Julia-Isabelle covered her mouth with a hand to mute her laughter. Struggling to keep a straight face, Jack turned back toward his interviewer. Unamused, Kinder was waiting for a straight answer. Jack wanted to get the interview over. "Yes, I did run into Sophie on the trail. She was on her way out to Skardu, and we had a very short chat – about the climb ahead. It was nice seeing her again."

Kinder smiled good-naturedly. "Okay Jack, sure. Now, you've been on the trail now for several days with the Korean climber, Chun Suek Yen. What's that been like?"

"Been great. I've known Sukey for a long time. She's a fabulous climber and a wonderful person. We've had a lot of fun on the trek." Jack looked toward the camera and saw that Glenda Craft, arms crossed, was now standing next to Marty Gallagher. She seemed to be paying closer attention to the interview than it warranted.

"Yeah, that's what we've heard Jack," said Kinder. "We also understand that Chun Suek Yen – Sukey, has become, uh, very close to one of the other Zermatt team members walking in with you..."

Jack pulled angrily away from Kinder and started toward Gallagher and Glenda Craft who had an amused smirk on her face. Kinder reached out the microphone toward Jack... "the communications officer, Jay Hamilton. Can you tell us anything about that Jack?"

Jack moved in close between Glenda and Gallagher. "What are you guys trying to do?" he snapped angrily. "You *cannot* even *hint* at something like that!"

Gallagher took a nervous step backward. Glenda Craft just smiled. "So it's true then."

Jack hesitated. "No. No, it's not true, and you can't put anything like that on..."

"Come on Jack... *true love finds its match on the trail to K2...* it's a great story."

Jack shook his head in frustration. "Jesus, you guys don't get it do you. Sukey is a *married* woman... worse, she's a married *Korean* woman.!"

"But not very happily, it seems," said Glenda.

Jack got up as close to her as he could. His jaw muscles were tight with anger. "Glenda," he hissed lowly, "if this story goes on international television, her husband Mong... the Koreans, they'll kill Sukey!"

"Oh *please* Jack. Not so melodramatic." She pulled away from Jack and went to Kinder, and pointed up the trail. "Okay, here comes Sukey."

Jack turned abruptly to get away from the camera crew and almost knocked down Julia-Isabelle who had been listening intently to his exchange with the American woman.

"Is there some trouble for Miss Sukey, Jack?" The girl's brow was furrowed with concern.

"No, everything is okay Julia." He looked over toward the helicopters, then took Julia's hand in his. He needed to get away from Glenda Craft and the OSN crew. "C'mon, there's someone I want you to meet."

Julia's eyes went wide with excitement when she realized who was standing with the two men near the helicopters. She dug into her knapsack for her notebook and a pen.

As they reached Logan, Morris O'Dell, and Rudi Joost, Jack put his hand on Julia's back and urged her forward. "Hey, Logan," said Jack, "Got someone who came all the way from Paris to meet you. This is my friend Julia-Isabelle Chatelain. Julia, this is the world famous Olympic skier and mountain climber, Logan Healy." Jack grinned at his childhood pal.

Logan bent forward and extended her hand to Julia. "Hey Julia," she said, smiling. "C'mon, let's go over here, and we'll let Jack talk to the grownups." She led Julia toward some camp chairs set up near the Zermatt helicopter.

Jack shook hands with Morris O'Dell and Rudi Joost. "Morris, Rudi, everything ready at basecamp?"

O'Dell ignored the question. "Jack, you know you're supposed to be wearing proper Zermatt gear," he gestured back toward the OSN camera crew, "especially for an international TV spot like that."

Jack looked down at his threadbare dark blue New England Patriots, Brady #12 long-sleeve jersey, his longtime favorite trekking shirt, and shrugged. "Yeah, well, you have to change clothes once in a..."

"Jack," Rudi Joost interrupted him, "that was a valuable exposure you missed. Please don't let it happen again." He turned away with a scowl on his face, to watch the OSN crew as they interviewed Sukey.

Jack was reminded again of the real purpose of the Zermatt expedition. He followed Joost's gaze back to the OSN crew just as Sukey raised her voice to Bruce Kinder, then stormed off, obviously not pleased with the interview.

"Fuck!" said Jack angrily. He looked at Rudi Joost. "Joost, you've got to kill that interview. The Koreans will..."

Rudi Joost spun around, glaring at jack. "Kill the interview? Finley, you'd better figure out which side you're on by the time you get to base camp!" Joost strode off toward his helicopter.

Morris O'Dell took a step toward Jack. In his hand, he had a small, black pocket notebook with a Zermatt logo on the front. "Here," he said, holding out the notebook to Jack. "This is your assigned schedule for the entire climb. When you'll climb, with who, what you'll carry, and where you're expected to be every day you're on the mountain. Study it thoroughly and keep it with you at all times." O'Dell turned and started off toward the helicopter.

Jack looked down the trail to where Sukey was walking quickly by herself. Far out in front of her was Jay Hamilton. Jack shook his head. *Kill the interview?* Joost had sounded incredulous. *Of course he wouldn't kill the interview, even if he could. This was exactly what Joost wanted, the implosion of the Snow Leopard expedition – his biggest competition for the lucrative Asian market – live on international television! And it was exactly what Glenda Craft was salivating for, a sex scandal to boost the OSN ratings.*

Jack tucked the notebook into a cargo pocket on his pants, and saw Logan Healy walking toward him. Julia-Isabelle was waiting for him on the trail. "Nice kid," said Logan. "Going to make a good climber someday." She smiled at Jack. "Sorry about all this shit Jack."

"Jesus Logan, can't you do something about OSN?"

Logan shrugged. "It's all way beyond me now Jack. And, believe me, I've got my own problems. Sukey's a big girl. She'll just have to deal with it." The Zermatt helicopter was warming up, the long blades beginning to gain speed.

"Logan, you don't know the Koreans."

"Jack, all they want is to win. To put Sukey on top first. That's all they care about." She looked back at the helicopter. "Gotta go. See you in basecamp."

"Okay Logan. See you in a couple of days. Ready to climb, with all my logos in place."

Logan smiled and gave Jack a high five. "Thanks pal," she said, then walked leisurely back to the helicopter.

The expeditions camped that night in Urdukas, high on a grassy slope overlooking the Baltoro Glacier far below. The campsite, first established by the Duke of Abruzzi nearly one hundred years earlier, yielded one of the most spectacular views of mountain peaks in the world, and signaled to all who stopped there, that they were about to enter a special place – what climber and writer Galen Rowell had dubbed, "The throne room of the mountain Gods." Off in the distance on the south side of the great glacier, they could make out the magnificent peaks of Masherbrum, Trango Towers, the Grand Cathedral and Muztagh Tower, mountains that would dominate any range in the world but the Himalaya. In this place, they were simply warm-up attractions for the great peaks to the east, now shrouded in white sky and snow, indistinguishable on the horizon. It would be another day's march, if the clouds lifted, before they would have their first glimpse of the upper reaches of K2.

To the dismay of the porters, Jack, Sukey and Jay, elected to forgo the day of rest commonly taken at Urdukas, and push on the next day to Goro, their last encampment before reaching the basecamps at Concordia, the confluence of the Baltoro and Godwin-Austen Glaciers. They had been on the trail for six days, and all were anxious to get on to the business of climbing the world's second highest peak. The French and Dutch trekkers concurred with the decision to skip the rest day. After watching the helicopter traffic up and down the Braldu Valley and seeing the TV cameras in action, they too were excited about reaching the epicenter of the world's current obsession with mountaineering.

After dinner, Jack sat for a long time with the teachers from the trekking group, talking about K2, the overcrowding on Everest, the climbing life, and of course, the latest World Cup results. The Dutch teachers were ecstatic over their team's clean slate through the group stage and were confident about the *Oranje's* next game versus Slovakia. The French trekkers preferred to talk about other things. They brought out several bottles of wine, and took many iPhone pictures of themselves with the famous American climber. Their only disappointment came from the lack of an appearance by Sukey and Jay Hamilton, both of whom they had grown very fond of. Many were now quietly rooting for Sukey to be victorious on K2, although they wouldn't voice their preference in the presence of their American friend.

Before heading back to his tent, Jack took a stroll across the campground to see if he knew anyone in the expedition that had arrived earlier in the evening. It was a fairly large Canadian expedition that had just come off of K2, and Jack was never one to pass up an opportunity to glean some intelligence about a mountain from other climbers. Most of the expedition had turned in for the night, but Jack found a Canadian climber, Fred Lafayette, that he had run into a few times in the past, sitting in front of his tent, cooking something in a small pan on a Primus stove.

"We got two climbers to the top, but that's all. I made it as far as the snow dome," Lafayette told Jack. "Then we ran out of time. Had to be off the mountain by the twenty-third of June... no exceptions. Had a Paki liaison officer with us. Kicked us off the mountain to get out of the way of the big show," Lafayette said with a grin, gesturing towards Jack.

"Sorry Fred. That sucks. Pretty high on the mountain to not go all the way."

The Canadian shrugged. "Could have made it too, the way the weather turned." He shook his head disgustedly. "Fought our way up the whole month of June through shitty weather – *Christ*, it snowed every day – then, when the weather improves, we have to go down. Didn't quite get it – could have put a few more on top, easy – but the guys in charge, they just said 'no, that's it'."

Jack left Fred Lafayette to his dinner. At the edge of the encampment, he walked through an area where the expedition's porters were reallocating supplies in several of the ubiquitous light blue drums the porters carried strapped to their backs. The lid was off one of the drums that Jack walked past. He stopped and examined the drum's contents, puzzled by the curious cargo – a dozen or so, coils of climbing rope, of several different colors. The rope was the same brand that filled the sorting bins at the Zermatt staging area at the airport in Skardu. The same brand of rope as the coil that Lisa Greenway gave Jack to carry in his trekking pack. Jack smiled. There was nothing unusual about a drum full of climbing rope in the Karakorums, but it was very strange to see a drum full of *brand new, unused* climbing rope on an expedition headed *away* from the mountains. Jack looked back over the Canadian encampment. *What kind of an expedition can afford to bring so much expensive rope to a mountain – a mountain that requires a lot of rope – and then have so much left unused afterward?* Jack was more accustomed to not having enough rope, and couldn't remember ever trekking out with new rope still in their plastic wrapping.

Passing by Sukey's tent, Jack heard the faint sound of voices inside. The flap was open, so Jack peeked through the opening and saw Sukey and Jay sitting on camp chairs, their heads close together. A candle glowed on the floor between them. They were holding hands, giggling, enjoying each other's company on what was certainly their last night together in Pakistan. Jack backed away, recalling the old saying that all high-altitude mountaineers were familiar with. *What happens in the mountains, stays in the mountains.* But, he knew that on this expedition, that wasn't necessarily true. And, this particular relationship was more problematic than the typical slope-side dalliance. Jack shook his head wearily as he walked to his tent. A screwed up expedition was getting worse, the closer they got to K2. But Logan was right. *Sukey's a big girl.* He hoped she would be able to deal with her new relationship when she was alone again with the Korean expedition, and face-to-face with her husband, Mong.

In his tent, Jack found the satellite-phone in Jay's pack and called home. It was early in the morning in Vermont, and the kids were still sleeping. "Hi Jack," said Peggy. "Saw you on TV in the bar with that blonde girl. Mountain climbing looks like fun."

"That was nothing Peg. Just one of the girls on the expedition. Window dressing for the TV show. How's everything there?"

"Mom and I went looking at houses again yesterday. Found a nice little place in Charlotte; one in Hinesburg." Peggy droned on for a while about house hunting – the only topic she now had any enthusiasm for.

"How's Ralph? Beth?"

"They're fine," said Peggy. "Why wouldn't they be? We've been staying over at mom's a lot. Ralph loves fishing with grandpa. When will you be home?"

"I told you, it will be in August sometime," said Jack, exasperated, knowing that Peggy had not even looked at the itinerary and maps he had left for her.

"Geeze, how long does it take to climb a stupid mountain?"

Jack sighed, discouraged by the typical path their conversations took. "Yeah, well, some take longer than others. I'll talk to you next week."

Chapter 15

The trek to Goro began on the most difficult footing the expeditions had yet encountered. Boulders and large rocks covered the lower end of the Baltoro Glacier, brought down the valley after many years of riding on the thick ice of the slow moving glacier. Where the moraine narrowed, the big rocks would pile up and squeeze together, leaving an ankle-breaking, exhausting hike as the trekkers picked their way carefully through the detritus that long ago rumbled down from high on the steep slopes of the mountains ahead.

Sukey had left early with the porters, to put some distance between herself and Jay Hamilton, and hopefully eliminate any more stories about their relationship. It had been obvious that someone from the French and Dutch trekking group, had tipped off OSN about Sukey and Jay – possibly inadvertently – and although Sukey enjoyed the company of the trekkers, it was simply more prudent to keep her distance from them for the final two days of the walk in. Enough damage had already been done by the OSN interview the previous day. She didn't need to add to the disaster that was waiting for her when she had to face Mong and the other Koreans at base camp.

By late morning, the footing had improved greatly as the rocks became gradually smaller, and the expeditions made good time walking along the gravely moraine or in places, straight up the middle of the glacier. By lunchtime though, after six days of pleasantly benign conditions, the weather finally began to deteriorate.

Jack sat with Jay Hamilton, eating a plate of walnuts, dried fruit and a slice of canned meat, watching the white fog sweep toward them down the glacier. The breeze was picking up and the temperature had dropped ten degrees since they'd stopped to eat. Everyone went into their packs for an extra layer or jacket to ward off the moisture and the cold. They had been lucky on the trek so far, but now the weather was starting to feel more like a trekking day in the Himalaya. It was still nowhere close to the frigid misery they would encounter on the heights of K2, weather that many of the Zermatt climbers had never before experienced, even on Everest. Jack grimaced with the memories of what lay ahead. K2 never disappointed when it came to miserable conditions.

After lunch, Jack, and Jay Hamilton walked up the glacier, enjoying the quiet stillness of the heavy air around them. They were a few hundred meters behind the French and Dutch trekkers who had finished lunch early and hit the trail before them. Sukey would be far ahead with the porters.

Jack took the opportunity to have a frank discussion with Jay. He looked over at his trekking partner. "So Jay, you and Sukey, what's that all about?"

Jay adjusted the straps of his pack as they walked. "She's wonderful Jack. Incredible." He looked over at Jack. "It's not just a roll in the hay, if that's what you're thinking. I think I'm in love with her."

Jack turned away from Jay to hide his involuntary scowl. It was worse than Jack thought – a problem that wouldn't just go away. Love – geeze, was there a more disruptive, problematic emotion to develop on a climb? "What about Sukey? How's she feel?" said Jack.

"The same." Jay shook his head. "Poor kid. She's been unloved and abused for so long, it feels like a totally new emotion to her. After this is all over, she's going to come to San Diego and we'll see what happens."

"Okay," said Jack. "Hope that works out, but when you get to basecamp and the TV cameras and the reporters, you've got to just deny that anything happened between you and Sukey. You're just friends."

"Yeah, I know. Sukey told me about Korean men."

Late in the afternoon, about an hour from Goro, the temperature was colder and a light snow started to fall. Coming toward them in the westerly breeze, the snow stung their faces and quickly coated the dirty, rough surface of the glacier with a thin white blanket. Jack looked toward the gray sky. "Won't be seeing any helicopters for a while," he said to Jay, next to him. "One of the hazards of flying around in the Himalaya."

Jay chuckled. "Yeah, that could be a problem. Joost's helicopter is at basecamp, but the big one is back in Skardu. Supposed to be bringing in the other climbers and the rest of the crew tomorrow."

Jack thought about the black notebook Morris O'Dell had given him, with his schedule laid out in detail as to where he was supposed to be on the mountain every morning, noon and night of the climb. He knew it was ludicrous to expect such a schedule to hold up in the face of such factors as the weather and climbing conditions. O'Dell would be lucky if the schedule held up for more than a day. His seeming amateurism surprised Jack.

In spite of the light snow, Jack and Jay were making good progress. Without the fog, visibility had improved and the glacier was easy walking. The snow wasn't yet deep enough to cover over the crevasses that came along every few hundred meters. Most, they simply jumped or stretched out a leg to step over. A couple of wider ones, they had to detour around. Every few minutes, Jack would gaze off in the distance to see if perhaps the clouds had cleared at all far to the east. He knew there were several spots along the glacier trail, close to Goro, when a clear sky would magically reveal the far-off summit pyramid of K2 glistening in the late afternoon sun. You had to be lucky to experience it.

"Sorry Jay," said Jack. "Looks like you're going to miss out on the long view of K2. It really is an incredible sight, the first time you..." Jack was distracted by a flicker of movement far up the glacier in front of them. He and Jay stopped walking and squinted their eyes to better see what it was. A man, running toward them at a good pace. Then they recognized the orange baseball cap of one of the Dutch teachers. Jack and Jay instinctively started to jog toward the teacher, keeping a wary eye on the snow covered surface in front of them for openings in the ice. Jack hoped the teacher was doing the same.

"What do you think this is about?" Jay exhaled between deep breaths.

"Hope it's not what I think it is," said Jack, picking up the pace.

Thirty meters away from them, the teacher stopped and bent over with his hands on his knees. Then he straightened up and waved an arm to Jack and Jay, motioning to follow him as he started running back in the opposite direction. The two men went into an all-out sprint, sensing the urgency in the teacher's behavior. They quickly caught up to the exhausted teacher. He had stopped, gasping for air and pointing up the glacier.

"A crevasse," he blew out softly. "One of the children has gone down into a..."

Jack didn't wait to hear the final words. He sprinted away from Jay and the teacher as fast as he could run, following the trail of footsteps in the snow. He had his wind now and it felt like Tuesday in Vermont, the final mile of his run down Route 17 and through Bristol, with the oak logs in his pack. Jay and the teacher would be far behind him now, but Jack knew that time was critical. He hoped the crevasse was one of the shallow ones where you could see the bottom down about twenty feet, the kind that climbers occasionally dropped into on a mountain to get away from bad weather. He hoped it wasn't one of the dark, narrow fissures where the walls disappeared into darkness, as did everything that fell into it. With only the fifty meter rope in his pack, and no harness, or crampons, no axe or ice hammer, if he went too far down he wouldn't be able to climb out.

Up ahead, he could see two figures jumping and waving their arms at him. Jack turned back to see that Jay and the teacher were about fifty meters behind him. Slowing to catch his breath as he neared the crevasse, Jack winced with the confirmation of what he had immediately suspected. *Of course, it had to be Julia-Isabelle, always the leader, always out front.* Laure had dropped to her knees on the snow, sobbing. Camille was taking deep breaths to try to talk.

"Nous étions tous chanter et puis, Julia..." Jack shook his head to her as he dropped his pack and unzipped his jacket. Camille started over frantically. "We were all singing and skipping and then Julia turned around for just one moment, and then..." The girl wailed and covered her mouth. Jack gripped her shoulder and smiled at her, then Laure.

"Okay, it's okay," he said firmly, "We'll get her out." He dropped to his knees and peered over the edge of the crevasse. *Jesus, fuck, no!* He couldn't see anything. It was a large crevasse, six feet wide at the top. About thirty feet down the far wall curved under the near wall. "Julia!," he yelled down into the crevasse. "Julia, can you hear me?" He turned an ear downward but heard nothing. He could see where Julia's footsteps went through the snow, and at the top edge of the wall Jack saw a blood stain. She must have hit her face on the edge when she went down.

Jack jumped to his feet, tore open his knapsack and pulled out the coil of green, eight millimeter rope that Lisa Greenway had given him in Skardu. He had to use his pocket knife on the strong plastic wrapping, and quickly started playing the rope out in the snow. He took off his jacket and tossed it to the snow, then wrapped the rope around his waist twice and tied a bowline-on-a-coil knot and pulled it tight at the center of his waist. It was one of the many knots that Marcel Janot insisted he tie over and over again during one of the "rope classes" he and Sophie had to endure during his summer in Argentiere... one of the knots Jack was certain at the time he'd never use. Jack pulled his flashlight out of the pack and stretched the retaining cord over his glove and around his wrist.

Jay and the teacher, breathing hard, finally reached Jack. Jay looked over the edge of the crevasse. "What? Who..."

"Julia," said Jack as he tossed the rope to the teacher. "You'll belay." He turned to Jay. "Get on your phone to Zermatt. Tell them we need Joost's chopper, with two climbers and doctor Chen, here in ten minutes." Jack was glad to see that the teacher had run the rope around his waist, through his legs and over his strong shoulder and had kicked out a small trench in the sand and rocks to brace his heels. The teacher knew how to improvise a belay.

"But Jack, I don't know if they can fly in..."

Jack glared angrily at Jay. "They can fly!" he barked. "You can talk them in by the sound. Burn all the jackets if you need a beacon." Jack moved to the edge of the crevasse and swung his feet over the edge, nodding to the teacher to give him some slack. He turned back to Jay. "Talk to Logan," he said. Jack slid over the edge.

Twenty feet down, the walls converged enough for Jack to be able to press the soles of his hiking boots against the opposite wall and walk himself down the crevasse. Overhead, he could see Jay spotting him and giving instructions to the teacher. "Give me a little slack," Jack called up when he reached the point where the far wall began to angle under the near wall. He would have liked to first bend down and take a look at what he was heading into but he didn't have time to waste. Jack turned around and sat down on the wall and let himself slide down through the narrow passage. Near the bottom of the wall, he saw a blood smear. He had to lean back and pull his head down to get past the first wall.

Then he was in almost complete darkness. The rope went taut but he could feel the narrowness of the fissure with his knees and shoulders. He braced himself between the vertical walls to take the weight off the thin rope and reached for his flashlight. On each side of him there was only blackness beyond the range of the flashlight beam. Directly beneath him, more darkness. *Jesus, how deep can it be?*

He tugged once on the rope to get more slack, and started down. The walls here were about three feet apart, but the deeper he went, the closer they got. He edged himself down another twenty feet but the walls had closed in to a two-foot width and he was having difficulty getting a purchase on the wall with the bottoms of his boots. Suddenly his feet slipped away from the wall and he dropped another four feet until the rope tightened. It felt as if the rope around his waist was on fire. He quickly turned sideways in the chasm and wedged his shoulders between the walls to take his weight off the rope. Jack didn't want his belayers to suddenly give him more slack and send him down to get wedged into a spot he'd never get out of.

Jack turned on the flashlight and scanned the depths beneath him. There was no sign of Julia. About twenty feet farther down, the crevasse took another turn as the wall on his left sloped under the wall on his right. The space between the walls at the bottom looked so narrow that Jack didn't think he could even squeeze into it. He suddenly felt desperation, and heartache, and anger. *How could that little girl have fallen so far down into this ugly place? She didn't deserve to die here. To die like this!*

Jack's neck and jaw muscles tightened with anger as he scanned beneath him, peering out as far on each side of him as the beam would reach. Then, about ten feet off his fall line, at the bottom of the chasm, in the inky darkness he saw a different shade of black. It was something small, that reflected the dim light differently than the dirt encrusted ice of the walls. He tried to edge down a little closer but the rope was taut. He tugged hard on the rope and felt the slack come, lowering him another two feet, but that was all. The flashlight beam danced around the bottom of the chasm until he found the spot again and his heart soared as the outline of the sole of Julia's boot came clearly into view, then next to it, the bottom of the other boot. She'd come down head first, and now she was stuck at the top of another drop-off. Jack was still ten feet above the soles of her shoes, and having trouble maneuvering in the cold, damp and airless wedge of space. He yanked hard on the rope for slack but none came. Suddenly he realized that there must be no more rope left. He'd come down a long ways on the short rope, and with it wrapped several times around his waist, and around the belayer above, they were out of rope.

Jack braced his knees awkwardly between the walls to free up his hands to untie the rope from his waist. He knew how perilous it was for him to unshackle himself from the lifeline, but he had no choice, and time was running out. His flashlight beam was also growing dimmer by the second.

Free of the rope, he worked his way down to the bottom. The wall was cold and slippery with moisture under his feet causing his boots to slip on the angle into the opening below him. Without being able to support his weight on his legs, Jack was close to slipping down the walls and getting wedged helplessly into the narrow chasm. He pushed his upper arms against the walls to gain a new purchase with his feet, and shined the flashlight beam on Julia's boots. They were only a foot away from his own boots, but he didn't know how he was going to reach them with his hands in the cramped space. He would have to go sideways and slide his body all the way down to the bottom to be able to get hold of the girl's feet.

Jack turned off the flashlight to save the weakening batteries and let it hang from his wrist. He wedged a knee against one wall with his foot on the opposite wall to support his weight, and took off his gloves, dropping them into the abyss. He needed a firm grasp when he reached Julia. Then he pulled his soaking wet fleece shirt up over his head to make himself thinner, and tossed the shirt behind him. He pressed his arms against the walls, released his leg hold and started inching his way down as quickly as he dared. He prayed he wouldn't just slide through the slippery chute at the bottom.

Gerry FitzGerald

When Jack felt the opening in the wall with his left foot, he turned sideways and began edging his torso down the narrowing space. Now he could feel the opening with his right hand, bracing himself against the wall with his left arm extended up the surface of the opposite wall. He was down as far as he could go and his muscles began trembling with the effort to keep from sliding through the opening. He flicked on the flashlight. Two feet away from him were Julia's boots. He stretched his right arm out as far as he could, took a hold on Julia's left ankle and gently started to pull. There was no give at all. He pulled harder, with no result. The girl was stuck in the opening leading down to the next chamber of the crevasse.

Jack knew that time was running out. Julia-Isabelle had been in a bad position for too long. He transferred the flashlight to his left hand and, holding on to the edge of the wall with his right, Jack thrust his torso dangerously out into the opening to see why the girl was stuck in the narrow space. He edged up close to Julia's legs and shined the flashlight on her torso. Then he saw what had kept her from sliding all the way down into the darkness below them. Her knapsack was wedged against the slanting wall above her. Jack pulled on the strap around her waist with no movement.

He knew immediately that he would have to go down into the next chamber to be able to cut through the knapsack straps to free the girl – even though he doubted that he'd be able climb out again. He'd worry about that later. Jack pushed himself head first down into the black chasm, searching the walls with his hands and pressing outward, trying to restrain his fall enough to get his legs under him. But his hands started sliding down the slippery walls, slowly, but out of control. He knew he was about to get wedged in, upside down, between the walls, and he was helpless to prevent it. Suddenly, his right hand felt a protrusion coming out of the wall. It was large enough to provide a firm hand-hold to arrest his slide and enable him to pull his legs down under him, knees and feet levered firmly between the walls. Next to his shoulders was Julia's upper torso, her left arm hanging limply. He shined the flashlight trying to find her eyes but her long hair hung straight down, obscuring her face. Jack felt the coldness in her hand

194

and tried to find a pulse in her wrist, but his own fingers were too cold to feel anything.

Then his feet started to slip down the walls. Frantically, his right hand shot up instinctively for the protuberance in the wall that had saved him the first time. In the darkness, he felt the object in the wall with his hand and realized that it was shaped somewhat like a hook. It felt like iron and provided a firm handhold. He regained the leverage between the walls with his feet and moved back up a foot, as close as he could get to Julia and her knapsack. With his left hand, he grasped the flashlight and examined the object in the wall that had saved his life. Jack gasped with surprise when he saw the object he was holding onto – it was a man's leather boot, toe pointing up, solidified into the wall just above the ankle bone. The laces were gone, but the eyelets and lace-lugs were clearly visible. Hobnails came through the sole, where several layers of thin leather were partially rotted away, and the heel was missing. It was a very old boot, Jack could see, from a time long before he began climbing. Jack wondered for a moment about what was inside the shoe, and what it might be attached to inside the wall, but now he had work to do.

Jack reached up and grasped Julia's knapsack strap, and carefully with his cold fingers, opened his knife. He was glad he'd sharpened it before leaving Vermont. The tough strap didn't part easily. Jack had to vigorously saw through the belted fabric while trying to maintain his perch between the walls. Finally the strap parted and Jack was able to pull out the knapsack, at which, Julia immediately started sliding down the wall toward the abyss below. Dropping the knife, Jack reached out with his left arm, across Julia's chest and pulled her toward him. Feeling for her in the darkness, Jack was able to bring Julia down into his lap, while his knees and feet pressed desperately against the walls to keep them both from sliding downward. The girl's knapsack fell against his right arm. Jack knew how dear its contents were to Julia and didn't want to just let it fall. He found a loop in the knapsack's straps and hung it over the toe of the boot in the wall.

Jack repositioned the girl securely, facing him in his lap, brushed her hair aside and shined the flashlight on her face. Her eyes were closed and her face covered with crusted blood. He couldn't tell if she was breathing. Jack thrust his hand up under her jacket and pressed it against her chest, feeling a slow, but distinct heartbeat. Jack pulled Julia's head toward him and squeezed the girl's nostrils closed, pulled her mouth open and covered her bloody lips with his own. He blew warm air into her mouth at short intervals until he had to stop, gasping for air himself. He shined the almost dead flashlight beam on her face and thought he saw her eyelids flutter. "Julia," he cried. "Julia!" He slapped her face lightly, then rubbed her cheeks and her neck roughly trying to massage life back into her. He pulled her mouth to him again and blew air into her. And then she was breathing. He could feel her chest expanding. She let out a groan of pain, but she was alive.

Jack pulled Julia-Isabelle against him, trying to transfer some of his warmth to her, knowing that there was no possible way for him to get her or himself up out of the lower chasm to the rope. He knew now that they both were going to die down in this deep dark crypt. But at least this beautiful, sweet, little girl wouldn't die alone. The flashlight faded out as he reached up for the boot in the wall to hold them both up for just a few minutes more. He let the flashlight go and listened to it in the darkness as it clattered far down the crevasse, bouncing off the walls.

Jack re-braced his legs against the walls and hugged the girl close to him. "Julia," he said softly at her ear. "It's me, Jack. I've got you. I won't let you go."

Julia-Isabelle moved her arms and pressed her face against his cheek. "Jack, J'ai tellement froid." she whispered.

Jack hugged her closer, breathing warm air through her long hair, and waited, holding on to the boot to keep them from sliding down into the void beneath them. Then, they waited, unmoving in the dark silence, Jack's knees pressing against the wall. For ten minutes, then twenty... it seemed like an eternity. Jack's body trembled with exhaustion and he knew he would soon have to let go. Then, he heard something, a faint sound.

He thought it was Julia's voice at first. Then, he heard it again. "Jack!" it echoed from far above them. "Jack, you pig! Where are you Jack?!"

Jack looked up and smiled. It was always comforting to hear the voice of Logan Healy. He heard the sounds of clanging hardware and crampons scraping against the ice walls.

"Down here!" yelled Jack, but it came out weakly. "Here!" he repeated more loudly. "We're down here!"

A strong light shown into his eyes. "Okay, we got you Jack." It was Alby Mathias from the opening just above them. Then Logan Healy coming down the crevasse headfirst. She was fitting a rescue harness over Julia's shoulders. Their helmet lamps lit up the chasm like daylight. Mathias brought ropes and another harness down to Jack.

"Well done mate," said Mathias. "We've got you now." He spoke into a microphone on his shoulder. "Okay, let's bring them out."

Logan was pulled up with Julia in her arms. Jack wrestled the harness on as best he could and immediately felt the rope grow taut. At the last second, he reached down to pull Julia's knapsack from the boot.

When Jack reached the surface, the snow had stopped and the sky was clear. Julia-Isabelle was already lying on a stretcher in the helicopter, wrapped in blankets, an IV tube in her arm. The OSN helicopter was parked nearby, and a video crew was recording it all while Bruce Kinder spoke excitedly into his microphone. Rob Page handed Jack a shirt. "Well done Jack," Page said somberly, shaking his head. "Pretty bad crack, eh?"

"The worst," said Jack.

Logan Healy dropped her harness and hardware roughly to the ice, the ropes still clipped on, and came over to Jack. She had tears in her eyes as she threw her arms around Jack's neck.

"Jack, you scared the shit out of me." she whispered. Her body was trembling. "I've never been down that far."

Jack hugged her tightly. "You're my hero Logan." Bruce Kinder thrust a microphone toward them.

"Jack, can you tell us..." Logan Healy pushed his arm away.

"Take a fucking hike, Kinder!" she said angrily. Kinder retreated as Dr. Eric Chen approached.

"Jack, I need to examine you."

Logan held on to Jack and turned him away from the doctor. She looked into his eyes. "Jack," she said softly, "I want you to know, you can do anything you want here, anything you need to do. Okay? You understand what I'm saying Jack?"

Jack nodded. "Yeah, I do Logan. Thanks. We'll see." Logan turned away, wiping her eyes.

"I'm fine doc," said Jack. "I don't need any..."

"Jack," the doctor insisted. "Just let me..."

"I'm fine," Jack repeated firmly. He nodded toward the helicopter as its engine roared to life, turning the long rotor blades. "How is she?"

Eric Chen shrugged. "I'm not sure. Her vitals are okay, but there may be internal injury. Broken ribs, maybe a punctured lung. We're going to take her to the Army hospital in Skardu and take a look."

"Stay with her doc," said Jack. He picked up Julia-Isabelle's knapsack and handed it to Chen. "Make sure she has this. It's important to her."

The doctor nodded, took the knapsack and trotted back to the helicopter. The door came down and the engines roared, straightening out the rotor blades, as the helicopter lifted, sending a hurricane of powdered snow into the air.

Chapter 16

The final leg of the trek, out of Goro was much leaner and quieter than the caravans of the previous week. Gone were the French and Dutch school teachers and the students, on their way back to Skardu immediately after the incident at the crevasse. The absence of the trekkers' team of porters also contributed to the new feeling of isolation. Jay Hamilton was gone too, opting for transportation on the OSN helicopter from the crevasse site. He needed to be at the Zermatt base camp, setting up the communications center, and better to fly in than to stroll up the glacier past the Snow Leopard camp with video cameras humming and Chun Suek Yen by his side.

Jack and Sukey, carrying only their light personal backpacks, quickly distanced themselves from Azmat and the porters carrying their heavier loads, though lightened now by the absence of a week's worth of food stores. The team of porters was also lighter by several members, already sent home with the depletion of cargo.

Only a fairly benign six-hour walk remained of their journey and Jack and Sukey were anxious to get on to the business at hand. Sukey had heard about the rescue of the girl in the crevasse from the Korean base camp, which was continually monitoring all Zermatt radio traffic. Jack answered her questions succinctly without elaboration, and she quickly dropped the subject. It was clear that Jack was in a less than talkative mood, so they walked in silence at a good pace along the gravelly moraine of the glacier.

It was another damp, gray day, but not cold enough for snow. A good day, Jack thought, for humping along in silence, listening only to your own breaths and footfalls on the gravel, listening only to your own thoughts. And then he was down in the crevasse again, in the darkness, slipping down the lower chamber to oblivion, to a deep, icy grave with Julia in his lap, and he could feel again the hard, smooth leather of the boot that saved them. *How weird was that? A boot sticking out of the wall; a perfect hand-hold, solid and unyielding. From the nineteen thirties, unquestionably.* Jack knew

199

that the skeletal remains of Dudley Wolfe had been discovered by the journalist Jennifer Jordan in 1998. It was in the glacier, where all the corpses ended up sooner or later. K2 was too steep to hold onto its dead. *But the boot was there. Too big for a Sherpa, so it was Dudley Wolfe's right boot, preserved by the ice, after a seventy year journey down the mountain, deep into the glacier, to save Jack and Julia's lives.* He was certain of it. And it would be his secret.

But something else had taken place down in the crevasse besides the discovery of Dudley Wolfe's boot, something that would also be Jack's secret. He tried to avoid it, but he couldn't help thinking again about the feeling, of Julia, frozen and bleeding, sitting in his lap, brushing aside her soft blonde hair and putting his mouth on her bloody lips breathing warm air into her cold lungs, bringing her back to life. She was just a child, but the moment of intimacy brought memories of Sophie racing through his head and made his heart pound and his breathing quicken.

"Jack. Jack, wait up!" Sukey's voice jarred him from his near trance.

Jack looked back, surprised to see Sukey nearly thirty meters behind him. He was breathing hard, moisture crept down from the edge of his wool hat. He stopped to let Sukey catch up.

Sukey touched his arm, breathing deeply after the exertion of trying to keep up.

"Sorry buddy," said Jack, the image of Julia interrupted. "Got kind of lost."

Sukey smiled at him. "Tough being a hero, eh Jack?"

Jack gazed slowly at the mist-shrouded mountain peaks surrounding them. "Yeah, I'm a real hero," he said softly. He put his arm around Sukey's shoulders and squeezed her close to him. "C'mon, let's go climb this mountain."

The Pakistan Institute of Medical Sciences was white, quiet, and antiseptically clean. After a thirty-minute cab ride from her hotel in Rawalpindi, Sophie Janot waited at the main reception desk while a burka covered nurse reached for her telephone. Sophie couldn't remember Julia-

Isabelle's last name and the nurse spoke no French and only spotty English but apparently it was enough.

An hour earlier, Sophie had been awakened by a phone call from Glenda Craft of the Outdoor Sports Network, telling her about Jack Finley's heroic rescue of a French school girl from a deep crevasse on the Baltoro glacier near Goro. The girl's name was Julia, from Paris, and maybe Sophie would like to visit her in the hospital, where OSN could shoot some video of her comforting the girl. *No,* Sophie told her, scrambling out of bed. She would do her interview at the Hotel Serena later in the day, and she would visit the girl at the hospital, but *no bedside video.*

An English speaking nurse arrived to escort Sophie to the Children's Hospital, built by the Japanese in 1992, the nurse said, as a token of friendship between the two countries. The quietude and fresh aromas of the Children's Hospital were a welcome relief from the crowded cacophony and exhaust fumes of Rawalpindi. Sophie was glad she'd had a chance to rest, wash, shave her legs and finally scrub and condition her hair, and feel like an adult again. The nurse stopped at the door of Julia's room and motioned for Sophie to enter.

A small, mustached man in white with a stethoscope around his neck, rose out of a chair as Sophie entered the room. "Hello mademoiselle Janot. It is a great honor to have you here." He held out his hand to Sophie. It was apparent that the doctor had been waiting for her.

Sophie shook the doctor's hand briefly. Obviously, to Sophie's displeasure, someone at OSN had announced her visit to the hospital. She looked over at Julia and winked. The girl's eyes widened. She grinned and gave Sophie a brief wave.

"How is her condition?" Sophie asked softly, turning back to the doctor.

The doctor put his arm around Sophie and turned her away from the bed. "We are glad you are here mademoiselle Janot." He dropped his hand from her back and looked into Sophie's eyes. "We need to do an exploratory surgery, very quickly. She is feverish and we fear internal injury, but... " The doctor hesitated. "The girl's parents insist on taking her

back to Paris for treatment." He shook his head. "There may not be time."
He handed Sophie a white I-phone. "Please talk to the mother."

Sophie took the phone and sat on the edge of Julia's bed. She leaned
forward and hugged the girl. Sophie smiled, but close up, Julia's condition
disturbed her. The girl's face was puffy and severely bruised in several
places, and her eyes were sunken with a yellowish hue. They spoke quietly
in French for several minutes. Julia was lucid and talkative, obviously
elated that Sophie Janot was actually visiting her. Then Sophie pressed the
green button on the phone and spoke with Marie Chatelain, a huge fan of
Sophie's, she told her, and rooting hard for Sophie on K2. She was in St.
Jean Cap Ferrat, at their summer home. Julia's father, an investment banker,
was in New York, but he agreed completely with the decision to bring Julia
back to Paris for treatment. A private jet was on its way to Islamabad.

Sophie and Julia's mother spoke for twenty minutes, about Julia, how
she looked and sounded; about mountain climbing and K2; growing up in
Argentiere, skiing at Chamonix, and Sophie's famous father – the legendary
Marcel Janot – and ultimately, the weakness of Pakistani medical care. And
then, Sophie had to leave for her OSN interview at the Hotel Serena,
agreeing in the end with Julia's mother's decision. Julia would go back to
Paris for treatment. The doctor sighed with disappointment.

The low clouds continued to hinder the view of the magnificent peaks
surrounding them, but Jack and Sukey knew they were getting close when
Concordia widened out at its approach to the Godwin-Austin Glacier, one
of the most famous spots in the history of mountain climbing, where so
many historic climbs had originated. The glacier turned gently to the
northeast, leading to the southeastern face of K2 and the Zermatt base
camp. There was new snow here and Jack insisted they rope together to
walk up the middle of the glacier. The terrain was easy and fast, but there
was always the danger of a hidden crevasse. Sukey brought out a
collapsible ski pole to test the snow, and took the lead.

Two miles up the glacier, Jack watched as Sukey stopped suddenly,
turning her head to the side. Thinking she'd found a crevasse, Jack quickly

caught up to her. Sukey smiled at him. "Do you hear that Jack? What is that?" asked Sukey. "Is it music?"

Jack took his hat off and quieted his breathing to listen. He heard it too, and laughed heartily. "Well, I don't know if you can call it music, but it sure is the Dropkick Murphys, and we're just about home." Jack was amazed that from several miles up the glacier, the music from Logan's base camp was reaching out to them, greeting them to ground zero of *Team Logan - K2*. He could imagine the scene in the pub at the Zermatt base camp.

They followed the sound of the Dropkick Murphys, Katy Perry, and the Dixie Chicks for another hour until they reached the beginning of the Savoia Glacier on their left that went north around Angel Peak to the lower extremities of the Northwest Ridge of K2. As much as Sukey would have preferred to continue on to the music and good fellowship of Logan Healy's base camp, this is where her trek ended.

A half mile up the Savoia Glacier, they could clearly see the massive Korean base camp. There were several large tents, and the huge black Snow Leopard helicopter sitting like a prehistoric bird on the beaten-down snow while a forklift truck brought corrugated metal cargo boxes from its rear opening. Dozens of black-suited Korean soldiers were loading smaller boxes onto a train of snow mobile-pulled trailers that quickly accelerated away, sending tall plumes of powder snow into the air. They were on their way to the Snow Leopard advanced base camp at the foot of the Northwest Ridge, two miles north and five hundred meters higher than the glacier. There was no music coming from the Korean base camp.

"Want me to walk you home little girl? said Jack.

Sukey smiled. "No, it looks like they're coming for me."

Jack looked up the glacier to see a yellow snowcat moving quickly toward them from the basecamp. "Unbelievable," he said softly, amazed once again at the extent of the equipment the big helicopters were capable of bringing in.

Sukey unclipped from the rope and dropped her pack onto the snow. Jack quietly coiled the rope and pulled it over his head and across his chest. He could see that Sukey's eyes were moist. He moved close to her and hugged her tightly. "You can do this Sukey," he whispered into her ear.

"You'll do great. It's just a mountain. Like all the other mountains you've climbed." He pulled back and looked into Sukey's eyes. "You're ready for this. And you're in good hands."

Sukey nodded and smiled. "Yes, I know. I am ready," she said softly. "Thank you Jack, for walking in with me. Thank you for being my friend." She turned her face away from him as they separated. Pulling her pack up over one shoulder, she began walking toward the approaching snowcat.

"Hey buddy," said Jack. Sukey wiped her eyes and turned back to him. "I'll meet you on the summit."

Sukey smiled. "When you see Jay, tell him...tell him I can't wait to see him in San Diego." She turned away quickly as the snowcat drew up next to her. Jack watched her climb into the cabin. He waved as the machine spun effortlessly in the snow and sped off up the Savoia Glacier.

Jack moved to the slower but safer edge of the moraine on the north side of the glacier. He was in no hurry now. It was mid-afternoon and he was enjoying the solitude of walking by himself up the historic trail. This was a good place to be alone. A good place to reflect on the challenge ahead and the mortality and frailty of men trying to conquer the treacherous mountain that was now just another mile ahead. He stopped a short distance beyond Angelus, the secondary peak of the K2 massif, and looked back over his left shoulder toward the Negrotto Saddle, a shortcut to the base of the Northwest Ridge, accessible from the glacier after crossing a wide snow slope. Jack gazed up the snow slope that had killed the British climber, Nick Estcourt in 1978 under a sudden avalanche. One of "Bonington's Boys," Nick Estcourt's death brought about the end of the expedition before it had even started. The members of the small expedition – made up of what would become some of the most legendary English climbers in mountaineering history, including Chris Bonington, Doug Scott, and Jack's idols, Peter Boardman and Joe Tasker – decided to leave for home after Estcourt's death. Jack squinted up at the huge overhanging ice seracs above the snowfield, and wondered if any modern day expedition would pack up and go home after the death of one member. With the expense and difficulty of getting on a permit, he knew it was now a rare occurrence, but

Bonington and Estcourt were best friends and all of the climbers were neighbors, and there would be grieving families to console back in the Lake District of England. Someone would have to make the eight day trek back to Rawalpindi to call Escort's wife anyway, so they all went. It was a different era of mountaineering. On the way out, they ran into the American expedition that would climb the Northeast Ridge, the first American ascent of K2.

Jack started back up the rocky moraine, entertaining himself with thoughts of what it might have been like climbing in the seventies with Tasker and Boardman. He thought he would have hit it off well with the two English climbers. Like Jack in his twenties, they were strong, expert technical climbers, fearless, adventurous, and rebellious, with an independent streak. He could imagine himself climbing together with the young Brits, sharing many an adventure on the high mountains, and in the pubs of Kathmandu and Darjeeling. Jack wondered if he would have been with them, on May 17th, 1982, when Joe Tasker and Peter Boardman went for the summit from their high camp on the Northeast Ridge of Mount Everest and were never seen again.

Two more miles up the glacier, Jack began scanning the rocky slope above him.

He had one more stop to make before he turned himself over to the most over-staffed, over-funded, over-mechanized expedition in the history of mountaineering, and became just another bullet point in the Zermatt public relations campaign.

It took him a while to spot it, up a hundred meters or so, on the slope above the glacier, protected from the rock falls and avalanches. The Gilkey Memorial had grown from a few rocks piled together in 1953 by Charlie Houston and Bob Bates to honor their friend Art Gilkey, to an array of boulders adorned with a cross and a mélange of inscribed plaques and tin plates commemorating the deaths on K2 of dozens of climbers from countries around the world. Jack had made this pilgrimage three times before, each time recognizing new names of men he knew, some he had climbed with. He sat down on a boulder next to the cairn and gazed back across the glacier at the famous Mitre Peak, a rugged, vertical array of seemingly impregnable knife-edge granite peaks. Jack couldn't help visualizing a route and began to fantasize how interesting and satisfying it would be to hike across the glacier and go back to his rock climbing roots and put up an impossibly vertical route on Mitre Peak. But no one cared about an insignificant five thousand meter peak with K2 just up the road. And that was why he was here, to climb K2 one more time. Jack sighed, shouldered his pack and started back down to the glacier, trying to summon up some enthusiasm for the expedition ahead, hoping that he wouldn't be adding any tin plates to the Gilkey Memorial on his way out in a few weeks.

The Zermatt base camp was beyond anything Jack had imagined. The glacier was covered with teal blue tents of all sizes, rows of large plastic shipping containers and dozens of racks of oxygen bottles. The Zermatt logo adorned everything in sight. On the south moraine, the big Zermatt helicopter sat on a landing pad carved out of the rock and gravel. Next to it was Rudi Joost's personal helicopter. A third pad, for the Outdoor Sports Network helicopter, was unoccupied. Next to the landing pads, two large generators hummed, connected to the tent city by thick insulated cables running across the glacier. Near the far edge of the glacier sat a silver Airstream trailer adorned with the colorful OSN logo on the side and an array of satellite dishes sprouting from the top. A large orange tent next to the trailer was illuminated by powerful lighting. Through an open side of the tent, Jack could see the OSN anchor, Bruce Kinder interviewing Phil Masters and Morris O'Dell, sitting at a set that looked like it could be in New York City.

Jack wandered through the tent city, unknown by the dozen or so people he encountered. From their uniforms, most looked like Zermatt service workers, mechanics or security people. They all wore some kind of photo credentials in a plastic sleeve clipped to their clothing. He walked past the largest tent, which would be the mess tent and the pub. From inside, he could hear crowd noises from a television and the unmistakable voice of the English football announcer, Ian Darke, doing play-by-play of a World Cup game. Jack peeked through the open tent door and saw Mathias,

Rob Page, and several other climbers, including a few from the Korean expedition, among the crowd of cheering football fans. Jack was hungry, but he would come back after finding his own tent and stowing his backpack. He also wanted to see Dr. Chen, and check in with Jay Hamilton first.

He walked past the OSN trailer and tent. A professionally printed white poster in front of the tent announced the "The Zermatt High-Altitude Fashion Show and Gear Demonstration" scheduled for the next day at two o'clock. "Participants: Logan Healy, Monica DeForrest, and the professional climbers, Jack Finley, Rob Page and Tim Burns." Jack chuckled and shook his head as he moved on.

Jack found the medical tent and entered to find Dr. Eric Chen administering to the foot of one of the porters. Another dozen porters sat on packing boxes, waiting their turn for the free medical service. Some things never change, thought Jack. He waved to Dr. Chen who interrupted his work and walked over to shake Jack's hand. "You all right Jack?" asked Chen, looking Jack over appraisingly. "Never got a chance to check you out after the crevasse."

"Yeah, I'm fine Doc," said Jack, dismissing the idea. "Have you heard anything about the girl? About Julia?"

Chen shrugged. "Last I heard, she was leaving on a private jet for a hospital in Paris for her recovery. So, she must be stable."

Jack nodded. "Well that's good to hear. She had quite an ordeal down there."

"She'd still be down there if it wasn't for you."

Jack waved off the notion as he looked around the tent to see two of the cots occupied. Samantha Ryan, Zermatt's Director of Social Media was curled up in the fetal position on one. On the cot next to her was Arnie, half of the Zermatt video crew. Jack nodded toward the cots. "What's wrong with them?"

Chen shook his head and shrugged. "The usual. Too high, too fast. There were several others, but these two got it the worst. Gave them some Diamox and sending them down to Askole this afternoon on the chopper. Let them walk in a bit. They'll be okay in a couple of days."

"How about the rest of them?" Jack asked with an involuntary scowl.

Chen sighed. "Well, you never know what will happen higher up, but if they acclimatize gradually – climb high, sleep low – they should be okay."

Jack nodded with the knowledge that he shared with the doctor. It was one thing to have a touch of altitude sickness in base camp; quite another to come down with *high altitude pulmonary or cerebral edema* high on an eight-thousand meter mountain.

In the combined command center/communications tent, Jack found Jay Hamilton staring into three computer screens while talking into a headset microphone. Jack put his hands on Jay's shoulders as he leaned over him to look at what appeared to be weather graphics on the screens. *Weather, the single most critical factor in climbing any eight thousand meter mountain.* Jay looked up at him and grinned. "Gotta go," he said into his microphone. "Talk to you later tonight. Constant updates, okay?"

"Heeey buddy," said Jay, rising out of his camp chair. He and Jack embraced, patting each other on the back. "It's great to see you. How was the hike from Goro?" He waved Jack to a nearby chair.

Jack dropped his pack to the floor and sat down. "I'm fine Jay. Easy walk. Easy weather."

"And how is Sukey?" asked Jay. "Did you walk her up to the Korean base camp?"

"No, they sent a limousine out for her. They were watching for us."

Jay nodded silently. He leaned forward in his chair. "I was over in the pub last night. A bunch of the Koreans came in to watch some soccer. Got the stink-eye from all of them. There're no secrets over there."

Jack shrugged. "Hey, fuck 'em. They're all soldiers, robots, They don't know shit about anything. Sukey's fine. Ready to go. Said she'll meet you in San Diego in a few weeks. So, how are things here?"

Hamilton laughed and clapped his hands together. "Jesus Jack, what a reality show. Mathias is sleeping with Samantha; the Canadian guy..."

"Gordie Yorke," said Jack.

"Yeah, he's an asshole. He's been shacking up with Lisa Greenway." Jay grinned broadly. "But, here's the kicker. Logan and her friend Anja

Lindgren? They're definitely a lot more than just friends. They're staying together and Rudi's pissed. He's gone back to Islamabad... on business, he says."

Jack laughed. "Leave it to Logan to screw up her own expedition."

"OSN's loving it though," said Jay. "Getting great ratings at home and in Europe. Anja can't go anywhere without a camera behind her, and word is they're going to have a video guy follow Mathias and Samantha all the way up. It's like *Bachelorette Of The Mountains*."

"I'm sure Mathias's new wife will enjoy the show," said Jack.

The loud, droning noise of an approaching helicopter quickly descended over the camp before continuing up the glacier to the northeast. Hamilton looked up and smiled. "That would be our third star climber, Miss Sophie Janot, on the OSN chopper, taking her up to their advanced base camp."

Jack shook his head as he stood up. "This just gets weirder all the time. Got to have something to eat, then get some sleep."

Jay grinned at him. "Yeah, you'll need to be well rested for your appearance in the Zermatt High-Altitude Fashion Show tomorrow."

Jack grunted something unintelligible and left the Communications Center.

The sound of a babble of voices, and shoes shuffling through the gravel and stones coating the top of the glacier awakened Jack early. Through the crack in the tent door flap, he could see a brightness that seemed out of place after the week of overcast skies. He arose from his cot and saw that the other three climbers sharing the tent were already outside. After pulling on some hiking shorts and his Patriots shirt, stuffing his bare feet into his trekking shoes, Jack went outside to see what the excitement was about.

As soon as he left the tent and saw the crowd of climbers, the Zermatt crew, and the OSN people gathering on the glacier and on the higher ground of the south moraine, many pointing cameras and cell phones up to the sky, he knew what was going on. After a week of low clouds, the skies had finally cleared and the sun was shining from the east, brilliantly illuminating for the first time, the magnificent mountain they had come to conquer. Jack walked across the glacier, resisting the urge to turn around until he'd gotten to higher ground for the ultimate view. He smiled and waved to the people he knew, but most were too entranced by the view of the mountain to be social.

Jack saw Jay Hamilton gazing skyward with a blank look on his face. He went and stood next to Jay and finally turned around to see the sight that never failed to humble him. Against a dark blue sky, K2 soared to the heavens, the ridgelines and snow slopes they were all so familiar with from photographs were outlined perfectly in the morning light. Two miles above them, around the summit snow slope, a gust of wind blasted a huge cloud of powdery snow into the air, eliciting oohs and ahs from the spectators on the glacier. Even on its best day, K2 couldn't resist a brief show of force.

It was forty degrees on the glacier, in the twenties near the top in clear sun, Jack figured. *An absolutely perfect day for climbing. On a day like this you could make a long run to the summit.* He looked down from the mountain and scanned around the base camp. *So why were they all down here, on the last week in June? Looking up at the mountain from the glacier, when they should have left for the summit eight hours ago from the high camp?* He knew how rare days like this were on K2. Jack turned away from the mountain and saw several OSN video crews recording the sight through long lenses, Bruce Kinder holding a microphone doing commentary on the spectacular view.

"Jesus, it's big, huh Jack?" whispered Jay Hamilton coming out of his reverent trance.

On the other side of Jack, Monica DeForrest was taking pictures with her cell phone. She tucked the phone into a pocket. "I can't believe how much bigger it is in person." She gazed up toward the summit in awe. "It's huge."

Jack chuckled at the reaction of his companions. "Yeah, it's..." He stopped talking as he caught sight of Logan Healy and Dr. Eric Chen staring at him from about twenty meters away. They weren't out on the glacier to enjoy the morning view of K2. When she had Jack's eye, Logan's shoulders shuddered and she sobbed, her hand went up to cover her mouth. Eric Chen put an arm around her back. Jack walked toward them knowing this wouldn't be a happy conversation. He got within a few feet of them before Chen spoke.

"I'm sorry Jack," said the doctor, a painful look across his face. "It's... Julia-Isabelle." He took in a deep breath. "She died on the plane, on the way to Paris." Logan sobbed again. "A ruptured spleen, they think."

Jack just nodded to him, then stepped forward and put his arms around Logan and held her tightly without speaking. He released her, turned around and started walking. He walked past Jay Hamilton and Monica without seeing them. He walked slowly up the moraine, past the helicopters and went another hundred yards up a boulder-strewn slope. Finally he stopped and sat down on a low, flat rock, wrapping his arms around his knees. He closed his eyes, put his forehead down onto his arms, and cried for Julia.

He recalled when he first met her, on the tarmac at the airport in Skardu... Julia in her short walking shorts and knee-high wool socks, with the huge rucksack on her back. Then, walking hand-in-hand on the trail out of Askole, Julia always smiling, always happy, always enjoying every minute of her life. At the campfire show with her friends, doing her incredible Lady Gaga impression, singing and dancing and laughing, throwing her beautiful blonde hair around her perfect, innocent young face. And then, down in the crevasse, in Jack's lap, bloodied, frozen and lifeless, yet still so beautiful. Jack sobbed, then again and again. The tears puddled on the ground between his boots. Finally, the sobbing and the tears subsided. He took in several deep breaths and looked up to see Logan Healy standing a few feet away. He stood and rubbed his eyes with the palms of his hands, and walked over to her. They hugged.

"Hey Finn," said Logan softly, her own tears flowing onto Jack's shoulder.

Jack tried a brief smile. "I loved that girl," he said, squeezing his eyes shut for a moment.

"I know you did Finn."

Jack and Logan hugged in silence for almost a minute. They separated with Jack holding on to each of her shoulders. He smiled at her. "Logan, I have to go. I have to leave you."

Logan nodded. "Yeah, I know you do Jack. I knew it that day at the crevasse, when we brought Julia up."

Jack smiled at her. "You know me pretty well don't you Healy?"

She nodded. "Yeah, I do." She reached her hands up around the back of his neck and pulled him to her. She kissed him hard on the mouth, then stared into his eyes. "I shouldn't have brought you here Jack. I was being selfish. Now, go and keep Sophie safe. Don't let anything happen to her."

"Yeah, I will. I'll take care of her. I promised Julia."

Logan took Jack's hand in hers and turned to start back. "I don't want Sophie dying because of this fucked up TV show contest, making her climb that unclimbable route."

"There are two unclimbable routes in this contest," said Jack.

"Nah, I'm not worried about Sukey. She'll have the whole fucking Korean Army up there, watching out for her. She couldn't get hurt if she wanted to." Logan shook her head and grimaced. "But Sophie, she doesn't have enough. The team's too small. And you know how Sophie is, how competitive she is. She won't give it up."

"No, she'll be pushing hard."

"Oh Jack, you gotta tell her it's over already. I'm going to be up and down in a week and out of here."

"You sound pretty confident," said Jack.

Logan dropped Jack's hand and stopped walking. She turned toward him. "The fix is in Jack. It's over."

"How do you..."

"We've got fixed ropes Jack, top to bottom, all the way up past the bottleneck and on the traverse."

"How'd that happen?"

Logan shrugged. "Masters and O'Dell, they made a deal with that Canadian expedition that went up in June. Fix good ropes all the way up and leave them there, and we'd replace all of their rope, two for one. Brand new stuff, better than what they started with."

Jack scowled with the memory of seeing the new ropes in the porters' barrels in Urdukas where the Canadian expedition had camped on their way out. He shook his head. "Geeze Logan, you've got the only climbable route on the mountain and all the advantages. Do you really need to cheat?"

"Of course I don't Jack." Logan was perturbed. "I didn't know anything about it. But now, I just want to get this over. I'm sick of promoting the logo and all the TV shit, the interviews and prying into everyone's private life." She crossed her arms and sighed. "Anja's going back to Sweden tomorrow." They started walking again. "You knew this was going to be a mess Jack, right from the beginning."

"Yeah, I did. It's not the way to climb mountains."

"I'm sorry Finn," Logan said softly. "I shouldn't have made you come."

Jack chuckled. "Well you didn't exactly *make* me..."

"Oh, of course I did. Ever since we were kids I could bully you and make you do whatever I wanted." They both laughed. "And, I wanted you with me Finn. I always feel safe with you around."

Jack squeezed her hand and they walked back toward the base camp. Logan stopped and looked over the bustling base camp. The smaller helicopter was warming up. "Heading out to Skardu to pick up Rudi," said Logan.

"How you guys doing?" he asked. "Wedding still on?"

Logan chuckled. "Yeah, that's not a problem. I can handle Rudi. Wedding's still on. October in Brookline. The Country Club. And you'd better be there."

"Wouldn't miss it."

They'd reached the edge of the base camp and saw that an OSN video crew had a camera trained on them. Next to the camera operator, Bruce Kinder was talking into a microphone.

Logan sighed. "Kinder. I'd like to drop him down a fucking crevasse before we leave here."

Jack laughed. He looked around the massive camp, and then up at the mountain, toward the distant Northeast Ridge. Lit up by the morning sun, the ridge had a gentle, friendly look to it. Jack knew how much of an illusion that was. "I'll be leaving first thing in the morning," said Jack, turning back to Logan. "Like to get through the ice-fall early in the day."

"Want a ride?" Logan nodded toward the helicopter.

"No. I'll walk. Need to walk up."

"Me too," said Logan. "I'll be leaving early too. We're all going up Broad Peak tomorrow, to get used to the air."

Logan started to walk down the moraine. She turned back to Jack. "Take whatever you need from supply Jack. Take some hardware and a sleeping bag and one of the new small tents... it will be perfect for the Northeast Ridge. And take a barrel of food. Sophie won't have planned on you. And a couple of porters too."

Jack smiled. "Thanks. I will."

"I'll talk to Sophie," said Logan softly. "Tell her what happened, and that you're on your way." Logan squinted into the morning sun. "Be careful Jack. And tell Sophie... tell her... I envy her." Logan turned and started down the moraine toward the camp.

"Hey Logan," Jack stopped her. "Do I still have to do the fashion show?"

Logan laughed and gave Jack the finger over her shoulder.

Jack had dinner in the Zermatt pub tent with Jay Hamilton and Eric Chen, then went around the camp saying his goodbyes, to Mathias, Rob Page, and Timmy Burns, Monica, Lisa Greenway and Samantha Ryan. He knew it was unlikely that he would see any of them again on this climb. In the communications tent, Phil Masters and Morris O'Dell wished him well but seemed glad to be getting rid of him. And now that the word was out about Jack Finley leaving *Team Zermatt* to join Sophie Janot's expedition, an OSN video crew was chasing him around the camp with Bruce Kinder desperate for an interview. Jack enjoyed his new freedom to flatly refuse.

He packed for an early start in the morning, then borrowed Jay Hamilton's sat-phone to make the call he had been dreading all evening. He waited until eleven o'clock so it would at least be eight AM in Vermont and he wouldn't be waking her up. Jack didn't want his wife in too foul a mood for this conversation.

"Saw the latest show Jack. Geeze, looks like all the men got new girl friends," Peggy started right in on him. "Even the black guy, screwing around with the Chinese chick."

"She's Korean."

"It's embarrassing Jack," Peggy said more softly. "Everybody's joking about the show."

"How are the kids?" asked Jack, to change the subject.

"Yeah, well, they're okay. They miss their father. Grandpa took them up to the alpine slide at Stowe last weekend. They're having fun. Saw that show about you saving that girl from the hole in the ice. Ralph was real proud." Peggy paused for a moment. "Sorry Jack, about the girl."

"Yeah, thanks," said Jack. "She was a nice kid."

"Can't wait for you to come home Jack, so you can look at the house in Charlotte... it'll be perfect. And dad has a cubicle at the agency ready for you. He's all set to start training you."

"Yeah, I can't wait. That'll be great."

"Do you mean it Jack? Or are you being sarcastic?"

He chuckled. "'Course I mean it. Can't wait to start selling some *whole life*, and some disability policies."

"Oh Jack, it's a lot better than selling cars. Maybe you can finally make some money."

Jack remained silent. He'd had enough of that topic.

"So, when will you be home Jack?" asked Peggy, sensing the need to change the subject. "On the show, they said everyone starts climbing day after tomorrow – July first."

"Yeah, that's right. It all starts then."

"So, a couple of weeks then, right?"

Jack sighed. He couldn't avoid the reason for his call any longer. "Um, listen, Peg, some things have changed here... "

"Like what?" she said, quickly.

"Well, I'm changing expeditions. I'm leaving the Zermatt team – Logan Healy's team – and I'm, I'm uh, going up to help out the French expedition on the Northeast Ridge. They, uh, need me a little more. They need some help. And Logan's got plenty of climbers. They don't need me."

There was a dangerous silence on the phone. Jack wondered if Peggy understood what he was telling her.

"The French expedition," Peggy stated flatly. "You mean you're joining up with your old girlfriend. You're climbing with that Sophie girl. Is that right?"

"Peg, it's not like that. I'm going up to the Northeast Ridge to help Sophie's team, and try to make sure no one gets hurt. That's all. We're not going to be sharing a tent or anything."

"It's going to be on the show?" she asked.

"Yeah, I'm afraid it..."

"Oh Jack! This is *so fucked!* Don't you know how embarrassing this is going to be? *Dammit Jack!* What's Ralphie going to say? What are my parents going to say?"

"Peg, it doesn't mean anything. It's nothing. I'm just..."

"Jack, I'm going. I have to feed Beth." She hung up the phone.

Chapter 17

It was always a mistake, Jack told himself again, to underestimate the huge scale of anything associated with K2. Distances on the mountain were always longer and more formidable than they looked. Verticality was always more severe than it seemed when looking up a slope, or down. It was a dangerous illusion because everything took longer and was more difficult than expected on K2.

And now the hike up the Godwin-Austen Glacier had become a more arduous trek than Jack had expected. He had made this hike before, one time many years ago, to see where the 1978 American expedition had climbed. He'd gone up to the advance base camp area, camped out one night, and then climbed solo about half way up to the beginning of the North East Ridge, just to see what the route looked like. He remembered how perilous and forbidding it appeared, looking up along the ridge toward the mountain. You climbed in deep snow on an impossibly steep angle, either on the Pakistani side or the Chinese side – four miles of high-altitude exposure to the relentless winds, with several treacherous traverses around impregnable buttresses, the air getting thinner with every step, and no hope of surviving a careless moment. And that's where he was headed again.

Next to Jack, walked Azmat, who had volunteered to make the unexpected last leg of Jack's trek. Ahead of them, two porters selected by Azmat, trundled along under heavy loads of equipment and supplies from the Zermatt stores. Unlike the walk in, Jack now shouldered a full sixty-pound pack that included his sleeping bag, and one of the new high-altitude two-man Zermatt tents. Jack welcomed the exertion and the feeling of finally being on a real Himalayan expedition after the Zermatt carnival. He was starting to feel like a climber again.

After a half-day march, the tents of the French base camp finally came into view. It would be just below the ice fall, Jack knew, and would be used only for the expedition's communication and weather functions, and as a respite for the climbers if they needed to abandon the ridge temporarily. All the climbers, and most of the gear and supplies, would have been moved up to the advance base camp at the base of the ridge, two miles north and several hundred meters higher, to avoid the arduous and dangerous navigation of the ice fall as much as possible. Jack would have preferred to just continue on to the ABC rather than stopping at the base camp where he would have to confront Marcel Janot and Dr. Alain Clement, the manager of Sophie's sponsored expeditions. Jack had met Clement many years ago, when he and Sophie were still a pair, and had run into him again a few times afterward. Clement, Marcel Janot's lifelong best friend, had never attempted to hide his disdain for the American boy who was so undeserving of Sophie's affections. And Jack, after some futile early attempts at conciliation, chose to simply ignore the pompous Frenchman. He didn't expect to have much contact with Clement on this climb.

Both Janot and Clement were standing outside the largest tent waiting for Jack. The tent was adorned with a long banner printed with the logos of the expedition's sponsors – *BNP Paribas, Evian, Rolex, GDF SUEZ,* and a collection of lesser names with smaller logos. The display, to Jack, seemed very minor-league after the multimedia onslaught of the Zermatt expedition.

A table had been set up, covered with charts and notebooks, a laptop, binoculars, and an empty wine bottle. Also standing by was Ang Phu, the expedition's chief Sherpa, no doubt sent down by Sophie to guide Jack and the porters up to the advance base camp. While the ice fall on the Godwin-Austen Glacier was small compared to the massive and perilous Khumbu Ice Fall on Everest, there was always danger in the negotiation of so many crevasses, especially for the heavily laden porters. Jack was glad to see his old friend Ang Phu. He smiled and gave the Sherpa a quick wave, as he moved first toward Janot and Clement.

"Bon jour, Jack," said Janot. They shook hands and hugged briefly. "You of course remember Doctor Clement."

Clement smiled warmly as he took Jack's hand. "Hello Jack. It has been many years."

"Yeah, a long time," said Jack.

"You are looking very fit," said Clement, gesturing for Jack to take a chair.

"I maintain my climbing fitness."

"But, a long time since you have been over eight thousand meters, no?"

"Been a while," said Jack. He ignored Clement's gesture and moved around the table to greet Ang Phu. They embraced warmly. "Good to see you again Ang. I'm glad you are here."

"And I am so happy to now have you with us old friend," said Ang. He glanced quickly toward Clement and Marcel Janot, then back at Jack. "It will be a more safer climb now."

"It is always a safe climb with you on the rope Ang Phu," said Jack moving back around the table as Janot and Clement took their chairs.

The Balti cook delivered plates of ham, bread and cheese to the table, along with a fresh bottle of red wine, then invited Ang Phu, Azmat and the porters into the mess tent to eat.

Jack helped himself to a piece of ham and some bread, and poured a plastic cup full of water, as Janot and Clement began eating. An awkward silence engulfed the table. Jack ate, and waited. Finally, Janot wiped his mouth and cleared his throat.

"Jack, uhm, all of this," said Janot, gesturing with his gnarled hands, "It is unnecessary, your coming up here to join our campaign... it is... while we are very appreciative, Doctor Clement and I," he glanced sideways toward Clement, "and of course Sophie, she is very excited, but..." Jack remained silent. He'd let Janot struggle with whatever message he was trying to convey.

"It is unnecessary Jack," continued Janot. "For our plans," he glanced again at Clement, "to accomplish our goal, you will... ah, not be..."

Clement leaned forward on the table. "Jack, you are not needed here now. There is no need for you to come up here. We have a simple plan, and there is really no role in it for you."

Jack turned toward Janot. "That's not what you were saying when we met in Pindi." He raised his voice for emphasis. "Come and keep Sophie safe, you said. You practically begged me to come and help her. Do you remember that, Janot?"

Janot shrugged. "Things have now changed Jack. The plans are different."

Jack nibbled on a piece of cheese and leaned back, threatening to collapse the flimsy little folding chair. "So, what's changed?" he asked looking to Janot and then at Clement.

Clement took a sip of his wine. "What's changed Jack is that this whole thing," he waved a hand through the air expansively, "this *contest*, this *television show*," he said derisively, "will all be over in ten days... two weeks at most. The American girl will reach the top before Sophie and the Korean girl get half way up these impossible routes. Then, Sophie and Miss Sukey-yen," he said, mangling Sukey's name, "they can come down safely and go up the Abruzzi route if they still want to go to the summit."

"Sophie will be no higher than Camp 3 hopefully, when the contest ends," said Janot. "We do not want her to go any higher, with these boys she has with her."

"Why do you think that Sophie can't win this?" said Jack. He had to admit to himself that everything Clement and Janot had just said made a lot of sense, but he wanted to hear it all.

"Oh Jack," Janot sounded exasperated. "Whoever got the Abruzzi was always going to win a race to the top, but now we learn that your American friend has *fixed ropes*, left in place by the Canadians, all the way from the beginning up through the traverse just below the summit snow slope. A deal was made with the Canadians."

"As well as established campsites all the way up," Clement interjected. "And the weather will remain clear for only another seven days. After that, we don't know. Miss Healy will race to the top to beat the weather."

"And it will be over," said Janot.

Clement poured himself half a glass of wine. "So, there is no need for you to climb with us. Sophie will be no further along than Camp 3, possibly only Camp 2 when the game ends. Then she can abandon the ridge and come down safely, to perhaps climb the Abruzzi..." He shrugged and looked over at Janot before continuing. "If she... still has some enthusiasm for the summit."

Janot grimaced and leaned forward on the table towards Jack. "Sophie, she is now once again, uh, very sad. She grieves for the girl, for..."

"Julia-Isabelle," said Jack.

"Yes, the young girl," said Janot. He shook his head ruefully. "She blames herself. Once again, she blames herself."

"That wasn't her fault."

"And, the Russian boy on Cho," Janot continued. "Sophie, is not of good spirit. Her heart is too heavy for her to climb. It is not good." Janot looked into Jack's eyes imploringly. "You know this Jack, it is not a good disposition to climb in."

Jack took a small chunk of bread and stuffed it into his mouth as he came to his feet. He drained his cup of water. "Well gentlemen," he said looking down at Janot and Clement, "for once, I agree with everything you have said." He glanced at his watch. "That is why I am here... because I promised someone I would keep Sophie safe. I don't care about the contest. And I don't care what you two want. Only about Sophie." He walked over to where his pack stood against a boulder and hoisted it onto his back, then came back near the table. He looked directly at Janot. "So I *am* going up, to climb with Sophie, for however far she goes. But, if Sophie decides she wants to go all the way to the summit, I'll be there next to her, and I won't try to talk her out of it." Jack started to leave the camp.

Janot stood up abruptly. "Finley," he said loudly, stopping Jack. "Sophie is in a very vulnerable state right now."

Jack grinned at Janot. "Don't worry Poppi, I'm a married man now." Jack began walking up the glacier toward the ice fall. Azmat and the porters, and Ang Phu, would have to catch up.

Chun Suek Yen sat on the cot in her tent where she could look out at the Snow Leopard base camp without being seen. It was early in the morning but there was a lot of activity going on around the huge black helicopter. The rear cargo ramp was down and a line of young women, carrying only light, overnight bags, were making their way unsteadily up the ramp under the watchful eye of Nam Jo-min, the expedition's Samsung representative.

The *Snow Leopard* Chairman, Young Kim, had given Jo-min the task of going out and securing the services of at least a dozen prostitutes to service the fifty soldier/climbers of the expedition so that they would be of *serene* mind and body when the climb began. Jo-min had no luck in Rawalpindi and had to take a commercial flight to Karachi to find enough young women willing to spend a night at the K2 base camp. In three days, he returned with fifteen Pakistani, Bangladeshi, and Filipino prostitutes, thrilled to be making a year's income for an overnighter. It was a massive hit on Jo-min's unlimited expense account but a pittance in the financial relationship between Samsung and Snow Leopard Industries. His superiors in Seoul would have no problem with his "entertainment" expenses in Pakistan. They would also have a good chuckle over the grand style of Young Kim.

Sukey watched the last of the young women go up the ramp, and then the closing of the big rear door of the helicopter. She gazed up at the small windows toward the front of the helicopter, where the more important passengers would be seated. That would be where her husband Mong was seated, possibly looking out toward her tent – with bitterness in his heart, she knew. Mong was going home, he'd told her the previous night. She had shamed him once again in the eyes of the other men on the expedition, and most importantly, Young Kim, who now wanted him gone. Snow started flying around the camp as the big rotor blades began to spin. The noise was deafening and the smell of aviation fuel filled the air.

Sukey was glad Mong was leaving. He was no comfort to her and she didn't need another angry shouting session with her husband, as they'd had when she'd arrived at base camp. She continued to deny everything – for her own safety – but the damage had been done – by the American television network, and then the KBS. While the rest of the world cared little about her relationship with the American, she had shamed Young Kim and Snow Leopard Industries, as well as her other sponsors and now her only chance at redemption in their eyes would be to reach the summit of K2 first. Sukey didn't care. She smiled as she took out her phone and looked at the "selfies" of her and Jay Hamilton they'd taken along the trail. She gazed longingly at the picture Jay had sent her of his condominium in San Diego, bathed in bright sun, tall palm trees leaning into a deep blue sky. That's where she would be in a few weeks... to begin the rest of her life.

The light went out in the tent as a dark figure filled the door. Sukey didn't know who it was until he spoke. "Good morning Madame Chun. May I come in please?" asked Yoon Jin Suk, the Climb Leader of the expedition. Jin Suk was one of the few people on the expedition that Sukey knew and had climbed with before. He was the only one in the camp who she would consider a friend. She smiled up at him from her cot. "Yes of course, Jin Suk, please come in."

There were several chairs in Sukey's spacious tent, along with a desk, a lamp, and a small refrigerator, powered by the large generator that was always humming in the background noise of the camp. Jin Suk entered the tent but remained standing where he could be seen through the open door. Sukey noticed that another man appeared to be standing at attention just outside the tent door.

Jin Suk bowed slightly. "Good morning Madame Chun. I wanted to acquaint you with the climbing schedule, now that tomorrow morning, July first, marks the official start of the race to the top of the mountain."

"Yes, thank you Climb Leader Yoon." Sukey was disappointed in Jin Suk's use of the formal address of *Madame*. She thought they were friends.

"You will need to do nothing tomorrow but to continue resting and hydrating. In the afternoon, you will have a final interview with KBS and the American network. On the second day, you will begin to climb, and reach Camp 1. You will carry no load with you except your water bottle and personal items, and will have fixed ropes for your entire climb. Ahead of you will be four teams of soldier-climbers, along with ten of our high-altitude Hunza climbers. Some of them will be pushing on to establish higher camps, while some will be passing you on the way down for a rest night before starting up again with more supplies. You will need to immediately allow them to pass you on the ropes in both directions. The need to quickly establish the high camps is paramount to our success on the mountain."

Sukey halfway held up her hand to interrupt Jin Suk. "Yes, Climb Leader Yoon, I understand all of that. I will climb unburdened on the fixed ropes, with oxygen awaiting me above 7,000 meters. But, you must know Jin Suk, that I will need to come back down one time, to acclimatize. From Camp 3 at least. I will need to go lower than our base camp, and sleep for one night, before returning to the high altitude." She looked up at Jin Suk for his acquiescence.

The Climb Leader shrugged and seemed agitated. He knew that Sukey would be asking for this. She was well known for her embrace of the *Russian method* of acclimatizing, of which Jin Suk and many other climbers were skeptical. He shuffled his feet impatiently. "Yes, well we will see, Madame Chun. We will see how the timing of the climb goes. And you will of course have an unlimited supply of oxygen on the mountain, even to sleep with to make you more comfortable."

Sukey shook her head angrily. "Jin," she said loudly, "I must be able to come down and sleep low for one night." Then, remembering her manners, lowered her voice. "Jin, I know my body. I have climbed above 8,000 meters many times. I know what I need to do." She smiled up at him. "It would not be good public relations for *Snow Leopard* if I were to die from acute altitude sickness on the mountain."

Jin Suk stared down at her, his brow furrowed in thought, without responding. He gazed at her for several seconds before seeming to come out of his trance. "Yes, well we will see what happens and make sure that nothing harms our star climber," he said with a quick fading smile. "But now I need to introduce you to your climbing partner, who will be with you all of the way up the West Ridge. He leaned out of the door to beckon the man inside.

The man had to bend considerably to get his full height through the tent door. He came to attention standing next to Jin Suk. Sukey could see that he was taller than most Korean men, and was powerfully built. He had long arms and large hands. His face was flat, with high cheek bones and thin slits for eyes. From the north, or the mountains, thought Sukey.

"Madame Chun, please let me introduce to you, Major Park Jong-Su." The major bowed slightly to Sukey.

Sukey stood to receive him. "Hello, Major Park. It is good to meet you finally. I'm sure we will have a very enjoyable climb together." While they shook hands, the young soldier bowed his head slightly again and exhibited some strange facial gestures that made Sukey feel that he was trying to smile but didn't know how.

"It is my honor Madame Chun, to accompany such a famous climber on this mountain." His voice was deep and his words sounded genuine, but his hidden eyes and hard countenance gave off a sinister aura.

"The Major is one of our strongest climbers," continued Jin Suk. "He has much experience in the Caucasus, and the Urals, as well as the Taebaeks of course."

Sukey raised her eyebrows with curiosity. "But no 8,000 meter mountains? No Himalayan experience?"

The Climb Leader waved off Sukey's impertinence. "Major Park is an expert, very strong technical climber. You will make a very good climbing team together." With a quick head bow to Sukey, he ushered Park Jong-Su out of the tent.

Sukey watched the two men stride off toward the large headquarters tents. She could tell that Jin Suk was saying something to her new climbing companion. Sukey wished that she could hear what he was saying. *The Caucasus* and *Urals. No 8,000ers. So, not really a climber then.* So what then, would be the Major's actual purpose on the mountain, she wondered.

Music by the Dropkick Murphys blasted throughout the American base camp as the send-off party went into high gear. A keg of Long Trail Ale had been rolled outside to a makeshift bar not far from the pile of wooden packing crates and shipping pallets that would soon make a grand bonfire. At a large, round table at the center of the glacier sat Phil Masters, Morris O'Dell, Dr. Eric Chen, Amanda Ralston, Bruce Kinder, and two of the young, female OSN production assistants. A half dozen other Zermatt and OSN support staffers lingered around the table, joining in on the festive conversations. Much of the talk, and the laughter, was centered around the report of the visit to the Korean camp the night before, of a bevy of definitely non-mountain-climbing women. Several wine bottles and two pitchers of Long Trail Ale sat among platters of chicken wings, sausages, tacos, and a selection of cheese plates. Behind the mess tent, the cooks were heating up the long propane grill for the massive amounts of tenderloins and lamb shanks brought in for the grand celebration dinner.

Doused with a small bucket of aviation fuel, the bonfire erupted instantly into a blazing inferno sending black smoke and flaming embers high into the cold evening air as the crowd cheered. Standing at the edge of the warmth of the roaring fire, Monica DeForrest held her wine glass close to her breast where she could appreciate the subtle bouquet of the excellent cabernet, as she once again pondered vaguely about the expedition's rapidly growing *carbon footprint* that she had long ago given up trying to control. Her degrees and her title had sounded good at the press conferences and seminars in New York and Islamabad, and now it would all be filed away due to the exigencies of the climb. She'd done her job.

Missing from the grand celebration, uncharacteristically, was Logan Healy, secluded in her tent under several lambs-wool blankets in passionate embrace with Anja Lindgren. Logan's great friend would be leaving that evening on the small helicopter once Rudi Joost returned from Islamabad. Anja would be heartbroken... for several days, until she rejoined their European circle of friends, currently summering in Majorca.

Also absent from the festivities was Jay Hamilton. The expedition's communications officer had just completed a final check of the voice-activated radios all the climbers would be equipped with. Now, he sat unmoving, his arms across his chest, staring into the largest of the three computer screens on the table in front of him. He had seen the forecasts for a week of clear weather in the Karakorums from the services in Seattle, Johannesburg, and Stockholm, but still, he stared at the screen, wondering if the rapidly accumulating buildup of moisture in the Bay of Bengal, over a thousand miles away, could have any impact on the mountains of northern Pakistan over the coming weeks.

The sun was dim and falling quickly, along with the temperature, when Jack finally caught sight of the expedition's advance base camp. It was in a small depression, protected from the wind on two sides by small arêtes, and from the back by the steeply rising eastern end of the Northeast Ridge. A mile beyond the camp, the massive cliffs of the ridge were in shadow, casting a blue hue to the snow covered wall. Jack stopped and gazed upward at the ridge and followed its line to the west, continually rising for several miles until it disappeared into the haze. Occasionally, a huge blast of powdered snow would fly off the peak of the ridge, soar and twist in the air before suddenly vanishing in the wind. Jack could feel the cold from where he stood.

As he approached the camp, two men with several weeks' worth of climbing beards came out to meet him. Carlos Medina introduced himself with a broad smile and took Jack's heavy pack from his shoulders. The other was Toby Houle, the Canadian Sophie had mentioned. The climbers shook Jack's hand and welcomed him warmly.

"Well you're a welcome sight," said Medina. "Everyone's been buzzing all day about the news. Like all of a sudden getting Messi to play for our side." He and Jack laughed. Medina shouldered Jack's pack and the two climbers led Jack into the camp. They introduced him to the two new climbers from Courmayeur, Piero and Mario, then the American Ken Wall, and to Ang Phu's nephews, Ringbo and Janbu. The two Sherpas seemed very respectful and almost starry-eyed in Jack's presence. He wondered if Ang Phu hadn't prepped them on his arrival.

The camp was smaller than he'd expected with one larger tent that would be the mess and communications center, and a half dozen smaller tents strewn about a few stacks of equipment and several dozen of the porters' blue transport barrels. Maybe he'd gotten accustomed to the grand scale of the Zermatt base camp and had forgotten what an actual mountaineering camp looked like. Prayer flags were hung between some of the tents, but there were no sponsor banners here.

Carlos Medina showed Jack to his own tent, made ready with a sleeping bag and air mattress. "I'll go and tell Sophie you are here," said Medina.

"No, no," said Jack. "I'll find her."

Medina pointed toward the back of the camp. "She'll be up on the hill, in her reading spot."

Sophie was sitting on a small stool with a notebook in her lap, gazing up at the Northeast Ridge. Jack watched her for nearly a minute, unmoving, her concentration on the ridge unbroken. Finally, he moved closer in the powdered snow to a point a few feet behind her. "I think I know how you can win this," said Jack, jarring Sophie from her trance-like state.

Sophie smiled but kept her eyes up on the mountain. "Yes, I know you do. Like we did it on Annapurna. Do you remember? A straight shot from Camp 4."

"Reaching the summit very late, in the dark," said Jack.

"Oui," said Sophie, rising from her stool and turning toward Jack. "Taking a huge risk. And then somehow surviving the climb down."

Sophie moved to Jack and they hugged warmly. "Oh Jack," she breathed into his ear, "let's do this. Let's do this for Julia."

"For Julia," said Jack.

Chapter 18

A cluster of sky rockets went up from the Zermatt camp at 8:00am, finally – to the relief of all of the expeditions – signaling the start of the great race to the top of K2. The climbers pushed for a 5:00am start, but relented to the OSN's need for more light to shoot the first video footage of the actual race. The fireworks had no explosive charges, only subdued swooshes, to avoid causing avalanches. The temperature was a mild 22°*f* with very little wind. It would be colder higher on the mountain, but for the start, a perfect day for climbing.

Glenda Craft stood just outside the OSN broadcast tent, wrapped in a full-length fur-lined parka to ward off the morning chill – another reason why she couldn't wait to get back to New York, as if she needed one. She was sick of the mountains and tents and climbing people, and the cold dampness in the middle of summer when she should be on her deck in Southampton. And, she had to admit, the show was beginning to sputter and her audiences could see it. The ratings in North America and Europe had dropped for the last two shows and they weren't likely to improve now that all her *stars* were headed up the mountain. She'd gotten as much as she could out of the Zermatt girls and the libidinous mountaineers, and also the married Korean girl and the black communications guy – what a huge break that was! – but none of it had any traction and now nobody cared. The alpha-woman, Logan Healy, and her Swedish girl-toy were off limits, and Jack Finley had been a total flame-out in the sexcapade area before running off to his old girlfriend, where they had no coverage. They'd get some climbing video, but she'd watched enough sleep-inducing mountain climbing footage to know how boring that would be, watching a climber take a step every ten seconds and then listening to him wheezing for air as he stared down at his feet. Glenda could visualize her audience lurching *en masse* for their remote controls. The only real excitement they'd had so far was the French girl falling into the crevasse – now *that* was great TV. Glenda gazed up toward the top of K2 thinking that they may well need a few casualties to save this show. Behind her, the OSN helicopter began to whine in earnest, warming up for her flight to Skardu. She looked at her watch, calculating the number of hours it would be before she was at her table at Café Luxembourg sipping a peach martini.

At the base of the Abruzzi Spur, the Zermatt video crew, Bert and Arnie, were set up in the light snow shooting the climbers as they took their first steps onto the route. A dozen international journalists and free-lance videographers were getting their last look at the expedition before it disappeared up the mountain. Off to the side, Phil Masters and Morris O'Dell were encouraging their troops and checking off the participants on a blue iPad. Albie Mathias was off first, with the team of eight heavily-laden Sherpas carrying the heaviest loads of tents, sleeping bags, and oxygen bottles, destined eventually for the highest camps. They would test the ropes and quickly establish camps one and two. Next came the team of high-altitude Hunza porters, bearing heavy loads of food bags, camp stoves and fuel, that would also be moved high up the mountain. The Hunzas, accompanied by Rob Page to provide communication support, would leave their loads at Camp 1 and return that afternoon to prepare more loads to start up the next day.

A hundred meters up the lower trail, the climbers would all clip onto the fixed ropes to assist them up the demanding, sixty degree walls to Camp 1. Unlike most of the 8,000 meter mountains, the most vertical terrain on K2 was on the lower third of the mountain. All the climbers wore lightweight, Kevlar climbing helmets for protection from the incessant rock falls on the steep, lower walls. Higher up, they would need the helmets to protect from falling chunks of ice.

Mathias and the Sherpas would set up Camp 1, and the following day set out early to establish Camp 2, above House's Chimney, before coming down for more supplies. They would set up the specially designed, battery-powered winch to ferry loads up the chimney named for William P. House who had discovered and pioneered the crucial vertical passage during the first American attempt on the mountain in 1938 led by Charles Houston.

House's Chimney would provide access to the snow slopes above and make the Abruzzi Spur the established route for decades of expeditions to follow.

After the Sherpas and the HAPs had all gone by and were well on their way, Bert and Arnie broke down and packed away the video equipment into their custom- made rucksacks, along with the two dozen extra batteries they would need for the climb. The professional climber, Fred Terry from Oregon, would climb with the video crew and carry the heaviest pack. Their plan was to shoot the video of Logan Healy from above as she climbed, all the way to the top of the mountain.

The next morning, Logan Healy, accompanied by the New Zealander, Timmy Burns, would begin her ascent, documented by one of the OSN crews. She planned on reaching Camp 2. by the end of her first day on the mountain. The "Zermatt Girls", Monica, Samantha and Lisa, wouldn't do any climbing for several days, until the lower camps were well established, and the Sherpas and HAPs had made it back down to pick up new loads. The women were to be accompanied by the final professional climber in camp, Gordie Yorke, from British Columbia, for whom, K2 would be his thirteenth 8,000 meter mountain. The Canadian was not happy about his assignment to bring up the rear with the "brownie troop", and made it known to Phil Masters and Morris O'Dell, that he was not leaving the mountain without gaining the summit. He knew that this might be his only opportunity to add K2 to his list.

The last climber to start up the mountain would be Dr. Eric Chen, who had decided to pack up a rucksack of medical supplies and altitude – sickness meds, and set up for a few days at Camp 2. after Logan and most of the other climbers had moved on to greater heights. Although most of the climbers had done an acclimatization run to around 7,500 meters on Broad Peak, and all would be climbing on supplemental oxygen, he was concerned about what he perceived to be an overall disregard for the hazards inherent when humans climbed to an altitude they were never intended to occupy.

At mid-morning, Sukey commandeered one of the snowmobiles and drove up the rough path the soldiers had carved out of the rugged terrain to ferry supplies to the base of the West Ridge. It took her nearly an hour to cover the three miles to the site of a mountain of wooden and plastic shipping containers sitting at the bottom of a long, snow-covered incline. Better than walking up here under a full pack, thought Sukey. It would take a full day on foot to get to the base of the ridge. She had read that one of the great challenges of the West Ridge was just getting to it, along with the logistical problem of moving supplies up to the ridge. Thereafter, the climbing along the ridge, though precarious, was fairly straight forward, and good progress could be made in a day of mild weather.

Sukey sat on the snowmobile gazing up at the lead climbers using their ice axes and hammers, crampons scraping ice under the snow, trying to find places in the rock to drive in safe anchors for the ropes. Two ropes were being fixed, about twenty yards apart, with at least ten climbers, heavily laden with coils of yellow and green rope, visible at some point below the leaders. The terrain was difficult, but Sukey was still surprised by the lack of progress that had been made in the first few hours of the climb. She looked down to see the expedition leader, Dong Shin-Soo coming toward her down the snowmobile trail. He was choosing his steps carefully on the ice and rock surface.

"Ah, Madame Suek," he said, finally reaching her. "A wonderful day for climbing." He neither offered his hand or smiled.

"Oh yes, expedition leader Shin-Soo," replied Sukey, returning the facetious formality. "A day so fine, I expected the lead climbers to be much further along."

The expedition leader's brow furrowed. "The climbing here is very difficult, and these soldiers work very hard to prepare your route for you." His anger was evident.

"Yes, I know they do," said Sukey. "And that is what they get paid for." She turned her eyes away from Shin-Soo and up toward the climbers above them. She could feel Shin-Soo smoldering in front of her.

When she looked back down at the expedition leader, his face had relaxed and his anger was gone.

"I understand Madame, that you have met your climbing partner, Major Park," he said softly.

"Yes," said Sukey, "A nice young man it seems."

Shin-Soo nodded and gazed at her for a few moments. "So," he said, suddenly, "tomorrow, the West Ridge will be ready for our famous climber." He turned abruptly and started back towards the base of the slope.

Sukey watched the climbers for a few minutes, then pulled out her combined sat/cell phone to see if she might have a message from Jay Hamilton. She knew Jay would be very busy on the first morning of the climb, but she longed for a friendly, encouraging word to help her overcome the growing feeling of dread she now had. There was no message. She squinted up at the ridge and then off toward the higher reaches of K2 far to the east, and wondered if there was any way this could all end well.

Jack Finley could hardly contain his excitement as the starting time approached. It had been three years since he'd been on a Himalayan mountain and now, standing under a fifty pound rucksack with an additional hundred meter coil of rope lashed to the back, gazing up at the arduous route up to the Northeast Ridge, Jack suddenly felt like he was twenty-five again. Strong. Invincible. A little cocky with the knowledge that only a handful of climbers in the world were his equal at the high altitude climbing ahead of them. He suddenly realized how much he missed it all.

The entire expedition was gathered at the starting point, including Marcel Janot and Dr. Clement, who had trekked up early that morning from Base Camp on the glacier. Janot popped the cork out of the large bottle of Champagne they'd brought for the occasion and poured out small plastic cups for the assembled expedition. Sophie brought around the tray of cups to all of the climbers. Ang Phu and his nephews, Ringbo and Janbu, smiled and politely declined the Champagne. Dr. Clement held his cup up for a toast, in English for the sake of the other climbers.

"My friends, as we now begin to climb this magnificent mountain, let us pray for a successful endeavor and let us all leave this place afterward, as we have found it, everyone safe and everyone proud of their efforts. And to the daughter I've always wished was mine," he held his cup out toward Sophie, "we toast Sophie Janot, the finest woman climber in the world."

"Hear, hear. To Sophie," several climbers answered.

Before they could down their Champagne, Sophie held up her hand. "Wait, wait. Another toast please," she said, holding up her cup. She paused for a few moments, looking around at the gathering in front of her. "We all know the hardships that lay ahead of us, so... I need to thank you all for being here, for helping me do this." She held her cup out toward her father and Clement. "To my Poppi. I love you Poppi, and to Doctor Clement."

Janot held his cup to her and nodded. "And especially to my great and wonderful friends who have gotten me to this point," she turned toward Carlos Medina and Toby Houle standing together, "Carlos and Toby, who have been with me since Cho Oyu, and on Gasherbrum. Thank you." Then she turned and looked over the gathering until she found Ang Phu on the outside edge, as he would always be. She smiled. "And thank you, to my uncle of the mountains, my good friend Ang Phu. I would not be here without you." The Sherpa put his hands together and bowed his head in embarrassment. His nephews beamed with pride. The climbers all held their cups up to Ang Phu. "And one more," said Sophie, "I have to add... to our friend," she glanced back at Carlos and Toby, "our friend Victor," she said more softly. "Victor Petrov wanted so much to be here with us," her voice tailed off.

"To Victor," said Carlos Medina. They all downed their few ounces of Champagne.

As Jack and Ang Phu, along with Janbu and Ringbo, hoisted their heavy packs and adjusted their equipment, Sophie went over to Jack. She handed him his ice axe and smiled. They hadn't yet been able to spend any time alone together and Sophie wanted to at least thank him before they started out. Jack studied her closely. He could still see in her eyes the veil of sadness that Janot had referred to, the toll of a hard year and the loss of close friends. He grinned and gently chucked her chin with a gloved hand. "Ready to have to some fun boss?"

She laughed and reached out to touch his arm lightly. "This all feels better now that you're here Jack." She smiled at him. "I'm glad you're here."

Jack nodded and smiled down at Sophie. "Yeah, me too. This is where I belong."

Sophie gazed up at the ridge and the far-off summit cone of K2, and then, back at Jack. "This feels good Jack, yes? This feels right?"

"Yeah, this feels right." He longed to hug her, but spun away abruptly instead. "See you on top boss," he said, turning his head. He slapped the back of Ang Phu's pack and they were off. But he was still thinking about Sophie, and the problems that *love* on an expedition causes – like Jay and Sukey. Climbing, and the terrain, and the snow and the cold and the danger, would keep his mind off of Sophie, he was sure, which is what he needed to do.

They climbed for four hours, Ang Phu and Jack alternating in the lead, finding the route and hammering pitons into the rock beneath the snow and ice layers, and then clipping the rope with carabiners to the pitons. It was arduous labor pushing through the occasional patches of two-feet deep snow, and then the more vertical icy pitches that had to be navigated with judicious placement of ice axes, and the points of the crampons on their boots.

They made good time considering that, unlike the Abruzzi Spur that had been climbed dozens of times, there was no established route up to top of the ridge. They had roughly plotted out a route they thought the 1978 American expedition might have taken, using maps, photos and binoculars, but until you got up onto the terrain you weren't certain of the difficulties. As he always did, Jack tried to climb like a Sherpa, not fast, not slow, but steady, sure footed and careful, always moving, without the many small rest stops that western climbers liked to take. While twenty yards apart, he and Ang Phu moved up the slope virtually in tandem. Occasionally, the lead climber would stop and wait for the other to discuss an option for which way to proceed around a troublesome buttress or up a sheer wall. Several times, Jack unclipped from the rope and went off up the slope to explore, and find the best route. It was the kind of climbing that he, and Ang Phu both reveled in. Mountaineering of the highest order.

Far below them, Ringbo and Janbu, were in no hurry, toting their heavy loads of supplies and coils of rope. They knew their place on this leg of the climb, which was to serve as pack mules simply following the fixed rope and the path set by Ang and Jack, with little climbing skill required. They knew their time would come, at the end of the ridge, after all the heavy loads had been delivered, and they could accomplish what they came here for, to summit K2.

Late in the afternoon, with the entire south slope covered in shadow and the temperature dropping, Jack and Ang came upon a small, protected platform just large enough for two tents. They'd made good progress and now the wind was picking up driving the cold right through their lighter climbing jackets. They were another day's climb away from the top of the ridge and would have liked to put in two more hours of climbing, but were uncertain if they'd find another suitable camp site, so they stopped for the day. A few minutes later Ringbo and Janbu came into the camp, dropped their heavy packs and coils of rope, and set up their tent for the night.

In the first tent, Ang Phu had set up the two camp stoves to melt enough snow to replenish the water bottles, and make supper for the group. Rehydrated, and their bellies full after a day of strenuous climbing, the climbers eagerly zipped themselves into their warm sleeping bags, and zipped shut the tent flaps against the icy wind that buffeted the tents.

In the morning, Jack and Ang Phu would start out early, at first light, leaving the camp set up for the others to follow. They took the loads and coiled ropes from Janbu and Ringbo, up to the ridge and fixed the route to Camp 1. The two young Sherpas headed back down the wall, rappelling down the slope a bit too flamboyantly in their uncle's judgment, all the way to the advance Base Camp. They would pass Carlos Medina and Toby Houle on their way up with full loads, The following day, while Carlos and Toby vacated the halfway camp and climbed up to the ridge, Sophie and the American, Ken Wall, carrying full loads, would head up the rope. They would be followed closely by Piero and Mario, the Courmayeur guides. The expedition was now fully under way.

While Jack and Ang Phu set out along the ridge from Camp 1, breaking trail in the deep snow and fixing rope, the other climbers would deposit their loads at Camp 1. The following morning, they would retreat back down the fixed ropes to the ABC. Over the next few days, they would bring more supplies up to Camp 1. and then back down again. Each climber would make three round trips to Camp 1., before the push to supply Camp 2. would commence. Piero and Mario, by prior agreement with Janot and Dr. Clement, would only go as far as Camp 2. The Italians had never gone higher than the 4,800 meter peak of Mont Blanc and with the expedition not using supplemental oxygen, everyone agreed that they would carry two loads to Camp 2., and then retreat all the way back down to Base Camp, their expedition concluded. But they would have earned their keep, hauling several hundred pounds of food, fuel and other supplies up the wall and all the way to Camp 2. over one of the most unforgiving routes in the Karakorums. Their first and last trip to K2 would be one that they would relive in the cafes of Courmayeur for years to come.

Jack and Ang left Camp 1. at 7:00am, carrying as much rope as they could manage. Their rucksacks were stuffed with coils of rope and their water bottles. They wouldn't need to carry sleeping bags a tent or a stove on this leg as the rope would run out long before they reached the point where they wanted to establish Camp 2. They would fix all the rope they had, hopefully by early afternoon, and then return quickly to Camp 1. in the fading light. The strategy that Sophie, Jack and Ang had decided upon was to make the trek to Camp 2. the longest leg on the ridge, to shorten up the distance from Camp 4., the last camp on the ridge, to the final summit slope. It was from Camp 4. that Jack and Sophie would make their bold dash to the summit.

In the OSN Broadcast Center tent at the Zermatt Base Camp, a video technician was electronically plotting the positions of all three expeditions in preparation for the Day-4 early updates. Bruce Kinder, a clipboard full of notes on his lap, was staring into a video screen watching taped coverage of Sophie Janot and Ken Wall moving up the challenging wall to reach the Northeast Ridge the previous day. The video was shot through a thousand millimeter lens from the OSN camera position halfway up Broad Peak. The camera would also pick up the American climbers on the Abruzzi Spur when they got a little higher up. For progress of the Koreans on the West Ridge, OSN would rely on the scant reports from the Korean Broadcasting Network.

Sitting on a high stool near Kinder, the OSN Broadcast Director, Marty Gallagher, was eying the screen that now showed the position of all three of the expeditions. He folded his arms and smiled. The climb was going better than expected and they would all soon be going back to civilization. He turned toward Kinder. "This is fabulous," he said, pointing at the screen. "The Korean girl is up on the ridge and their climbers are making great progress toward Camp 2." Kinder looked up and nodded. "The French expedition is moving nicely along the ridge, and Logan is just blasting up the Abruzzi – already to Camp 2, with some of the hardest climbing out of the way." He grinned and held up a palm to Bruce Kinder for a high-five. "We'll be out of this fucking place in a week!"

Chapter 19

Logan Healy lay on top of her sleeping bag, tapping out her latest blog entry on an iPad. She'd write as much as she could, fluffing up the mundane climbing prose with passages describing the "treacherous, verticality of the icy terrain", leaving out any reference to the jumars clipped onto the fixed ropes she'd pulled on all the way to Camp3. She'd include a historical reference to Burlington resident Charlie Houston whom she had once met, and to Bob House whose "Chimney" she had fought her way up, a day earlier, on a rickety chain ladder the Canadians had left in place. When she had about five or six hundred words, she'd send the file to Samantha Ryan's laptop somewhere below her on the mountain, probably at Camp 2. by now. The expedition's Social Media Director, would edit and chop up Logan's copy, and add some photos along with plenty of Zermatt logos, for usable Twitter and Facebook entries, and for Logan's daily website blog. Logan didn't bother doing a spell-check, and she didn't need to see the edited entries – they always made more sense and sounded more intelligent when Samantha was done with them. Logan also left out any reference to the expedition's first significant setback. She knew that Rudi, and Phil Masters didn't want any negative information going out on social media. Everything associated with *Zermatt* was to be positive.

Logan strained to listen above the wind for any activity outside. Alby Mathias was on his way down to Camp 3. with their lead Sherpa, Mingma Jumic, who had been hit by a falling boulder and reportedly had a dislocated shoulder. Mingma's expedition was over, and now he would need a great deal of assistance down-climbing the near vertical grades of the lower mountain with one arm strapped tightly to his chest. After spending the night at Camp 3, Mathias and two other Sherpas would be taking Mingma down to Camp 2 to see Dr. Chen, and then to base camp.

It was, Logan calculated, a full-day setback in their schedule and Phil Masters and Morris O'Dell were angry with Mathias. They wanted Mathias and one of the other Sherpas to continue climbing up to establish Camp 4.

while their fourth Sherpa brought Mingma down by himself. O'Dell's carefully crafted climbing schedules had lasted just five days. Mathias didn't even consider complying with their orders. The severity of Mingma's injury and the steepness of the terrain made it a three-man rescue operation, he said, and that was it. Mathias and the Sherpas had cached their loads along the fixed rope and headed down with Mingma, several ropes wrapped around his chest and tethered to his harness.

Logan Healy was in complete agreement with Mathias' decision, which settled the matter for everyone involved. It would now fall upon Logan, Timmy Burns, Rob Page and Fred Terry, to push up to Camp 4. the next day. They would all carry full loads and start out before the sun came up, but now they were behind schedule, and Rudi Joost also wouldn't be pleased when he received the news.

Rudi wasn't pleased about too many things lately, Logan was well aware. She recalled their night together before she had started up the mountain, wondering if she had overplayed her thrall over Rudi. He had taken a day and a half to fly back from London to Islamabad to Skardu, then helicopter in to base camp, to be present in the morning for the OSN cameras and the press when Logan started up the mountain. He wasn't in a good mood. Rudi knew all about Anja Lindgren, and although Logan's occasional sexual escapades were an accepted part of their relationship, maybe she should have been a bit more discreet with Anja around the Zermatt base camp with all the press and video cameras present. The *Anja Affair* though, was further enhancement of Logan's independent, *international rogue* image and the tabloids, sporting press and social media loved it. Vexed as he was, Rudi Joost couldn't hide his elation at seeing the *Zermatt* name and logo seemingly spread across every media platform in Europe. But, they both knew that was why Logan was getting paid so well. It wasn't why Rudi was marrying her. He had been there to hug her and smile for the cameras and promote everything Zermatt when Logan had started up the mountain, but she recalled their final hug and the penetrating, dark look in Rudi's eyes that seemed to be telling her, *don't fuck this up, and don't fuck with me!*

Maybe she had been taking Rudi's blind adoration for granted. After Rudi divorced his wife, Logan had become the embodiment of Zermatt Sports and the obsession of Rudi Joost. She was the princess now, and soon to be the *Queen of Zermatt* upon their wedding in October. It was everything she'd ever wanted – fame, international celebrity, luxurious homes around the globe, the penthouse on Central Park West, and more money than even she could spend. It was a fairy-tale-come-true for a Vermont girl whose only real talents in life were the ability to ski fast, and to endure the physical punishment of climbing tall mountains. But, she was beautiful, she knew, the object of lust and love of boys and men and many women since she was an adolescent. And now she'd chosen the winner, and she would enjoy her new life to the fullest. Even with the prenuptial agreement Rudi was insisting on, Logan would be well taken care of if the marriage didn't work out. *She just had to be careful not to screw it all up before the wedding, which was something, she knew, she was more than capable of.*

It was after eight o'clock, dark, windy and bitter cold, by the time Mathias and the Sherpas made it down to Camp 3. Logan and Rob Page hiked a little way above the camp to greet the wounded Sherpa, while Timmy Burns and Fred Terry had two stoves going in the main tent melting water and brewing chicken soup, noodles, and tea for the team that had now spent thirteen straight hours on the rope. The ever-present video team of Burt and Arnie were set up with a spotlight illuminating the climbers. Mingma Jumic was wrapped up tightly with his arm across his chest, with what appeared to be long pieces of a sleeping bag. Several ropes, clipped to his harness, now trailed in the snow as he limped into camp. The grimace on his face showed how much pain he was in.

Logan was surprised to see that all four of the climbers had been using supplemental oxygen, their regulators still strapped around their necks. As she approached Mathias, Logan was also surprised to see how totally exhausted he seemed to be.

"You needed the gas?" Logan inquired.

Mathias nodded affirmatively as he pulled off his oxygen regulator. "Yeah, the climbing is so steep, every step is an exertion. It's a lot of work in the thin air. You go too slow without the gas, even at 6,700 meters. It's very steep," he exhaled softly.

With Mathias' goggles now up on his head, Logan could see the strain and exhaustion in his eyes. "Jesus Alby, you look worn out."

"Yeah, it's been a tough few days." Mathias smiled. "Tough mountain," he said softly. "When we get Mingma down to base camp, I'm going to take a rest day."

Logan nodded affirmatively. "How is Mingma? How bad was it?"

Mathias grimaced. "It's bad. It's not a dislocation. His shoulder is all smashed up. Broken bones, and a lot of pain. We shot him up and gave him some pills. He was lucky though. A few inches to the left and he gets it on the head, boulder would have gone right through his helmet. He'd still be up there. Needs to get out to the Army hospital in Skardu right away."

"Rudi's helicopter will be standing by," said Logan.

Mathias smiled. "In the old days, I would be walking Mingma all the way out to Askole."

The next day, their sixth on the mountain, Mathias and Mingma with the other Sherpas, started down early in order to reach Base Camp in daylight, while Logan, Rob Page, Timmy Burns and Fred Terry started up for Camp 4. Two hundred meters up the mountain, Logan and Page agreed that they should all go to the supplemental oxygen. They were just beyond the halfway point on the mountain, but as Mathias had said, the steepness of the climbing exacerbated the diminished oxygen content of the air. Logan was glad now that they'd brought so much oxygen to the mountain. They were going to need it.

It was their toughest day on the mountain and Logan and the other climbers were exhausted when they finally reached the spot on a narrow shelf where the Canadians had carved out several usable tent platforms. After passing the packs left by Mathias' team, Logan and Rob Page agreed that a section of rope leading up through several rocky passages, had been worn too thin in spots by the Canadians and needed to be replaced. Logan knew that there was too much traffic coming up behind them to leave a frayed rope in place. Hampered by the bone-chilling wind that had been growing all afternoon, the rope replacement project added another two hours of work to their day. In the morning, they would go down and retrieve the loads left by Mathias and the Sherpas, and then start to ferry supplies up the route to begin the campaign to establish Camp5 just below the base of the *bottleneck,* the last camp before a summit bid.

As darkness descended, the climbers finally had their tents secure and sleeping bags in place at Camp 4. Logan chose Fred Terry to share a tent with because, as she laughingly explained, Fred was a happily married Mormon and Rudi would rest easier. She and Fred made dinner for the group and then they all squeezed in together to watch a replay of the Spain-Paraguay, World Cup game from two days earlier that Logan had loaded onto her iPad. Rob Page, disgusted with the World Cup after England's 4-1 pummeling by Germany in the Round of 16, left at halftime, still grumbling about Frankie Lampard's disallowed goal.

Knowing the final score already, they turned off the game midway through the second half. Timmy Burns went back to his tent. Logan and Fred zipped up the tent flap and settled into their sleeping bags for a well-deserved night of sleep. Just as Logan switched off the battery lantern, her private walkie-talkie to base camp buzzed lightly. It was Morris O'Dell. Logan was immediately concerned that something had happened to Mathias and Mingma and the other Sherpas, that maybe they hadn't arrived at base camp.

"No, no, nothing like that," O'Dell reassured her. "They arrived in good form. Mingma left for Skardu straight away. Something else though has come up."

"What is it Morris?" asked Logan. Fred Terry was now sitting up anxiously.

"Well lass, it appears we've got a speck of weather on the way."

Well accustomed to the English penchant for understatement, Logan didn't need any clarification of the word *speck.* "I thought we had another four or five days."

"That window, I'm afraid, is closing a little more quickly than we'd planned on. Been a bit of moisture sneaking up through the India basin, the services couldn't quite put a finger on."

"When?" asked Logan sharply.

"Tomorrow afternoon, most likely. Maybe tomorrow night. Some wind too. Going to be a nasty few days coming up." There was a pause in the conversation. "Thinking that maybe you shouldn't be going any higher tomorrow. Might be best for you and the boys to come all the way down and take your rest day down here."

Logan thought about what O'Dell was recommending. They'd planned on heading up tomorrow, taking as much gear as they could carry, part of the way to Camp 5. The camp, she knew would be a serious milestone – in sight of the summit cone – the jumping off point for the final push, and she was anxious to get there.

"No Morris. We're already a day behind. We'll head up tomorrow, see how far we can get and cache the packs on the rope and then retreat back here to Camp 4. If the snow gets bad, we can make it down to Camp 2 the next day if we have to."

"Well okay lass," said O'Dell, knowing he wasn't going to talk the real boss of the expedition out of whatever she wanted to do. To himself, he had to admit that he was glad that they would be going up. Camp 5. would be the start of the last chapter, he knew, and with the setback of the Sherpa's injury, they were behind schedule, and in this game there would be no stoppage time added on. Good weather or bad, O'Dell badly needed to win this race and get Logan Healy to the top first. If not, he knew he would most likely never lead another expedition to a big mountain or get any future employment out of Zermatt Sports.

The West Ridge of K2 had only been attempted a handful of times over the years, and successfully climbed by just a few of those expeditions. The history, well researched by the Snow Leopard Expedition leader, Dong Shin-Soo, made him wonder why they were making such excellent progress on the route. His soldier/climbers were performing very admirably, and now, just six days into the climb, the team had pushed up the ridge, successfully negotiating one of the daunting rock buttresses guarding the route and were now just beyond the midway point.

Several of the climbers had shown signs of altitude sickness and had to come down, but there were plenty of replacements and very little time had been lost. They were also consuming their supplemental oxygen supply faster than projected – the lead climbers were on the gas even while sleeping – but, they had brought plenty of oxygen and had moved a great deal of it up the ridge in preparation for their star climber, Madame Chun Suek Yen. Sukey and her escort, Major Park Jong-Su, were making excellent progress as well, gaining steadily on the leaders, as was the plan. In another two days, they would be just one encampment behind the crew fixing the ropes and carrying the supplies up the ridge. In another five or six days, Shin-Soo calculated, they would be at the high camp, ready to make a sprint for the top. While it was difficult to compare the different routes up the mountain, from the reports of the Outdoor Sports Network, Shin-Soo estimated that Suek Yen was ahead of the American girl by several hundred meters, which he considered quite astounding as well as encouraging. The injured Sherpa, he knew, had helped to slow Ms Healy's progress a bit. He'd received no report on the progress of the French expedition, which, he'd always assumed would make it no farther than about halfway up the Northeast Ridge. Sophie Janot, he was certain, didn't have anywhere near the manpower required to make it up such a formidable route, even with the assistance now of the legendary American climber, Jack Finley. One additional climber would have no impact on such a long, difficult route.

Sukey was also aware that she and Major Park were making good progress when they reached their third campsite at three o'clock in the afternoon. She had expected to hike along the now well-traveled trail until at least five o'clock before reaching the tent site, which was completely set up for them by the soldiers ahead. The climbing was simply much easier than she'd expected, clipped to the rope and following the long-striding Major Park whose large boots provided an additional tamping down of the snow. Climbing with just her light-weight personal pack, containing only a water bottle, some snacks, extra gloves, and her new Samsung Galaxy 4 notebook, it felt, to Sukey, much like a leisurely weekend trek on Hallasan Mountain with her father when she was a little girl.

The path they followed, undulated along the steep, northern face of the ridge. In places they walked only a few meters from the top of the ridge and could edge up for a view of the magnificent landscape of China stretching off to the horizon, but most of the trail was ten to twenty meters down from the top, protecting the climbers from the incessant wind blowing over the ridge from the south. There were two spots farther on, Sukey had been told, where the rope would lead them up and over the ridge to easier footing on the Chinese side for short stretches. Several times during the day, when the angle of the trail was right, Sukey could see the stream of lead climbers far ahead, forging their way along the steep face of the ridge, putting in pitons and ice screws to secure the rope. And when the low clouds lifted off the ridge, she could see the spot far in the distance where the ridge began rising at a much steeper angle in its climb to the summit cone. That's where the climbing would become much more rigorous.

Though it was early and they weren't especially tired, Sukey and Major Park were forced to stop for the night because this was where the campsite had been established, probably because it was the only suitable spot in view to hang a tent off the side of the steep ridge.

The orange, barrel-shaped tent was specially made for this purpose, with strong, aluminum struts supporting the tent from the bottom. The deep snow on the ridge had been compacted by the soldiers into as wide a platform as possible in which to nestle the tent into. A network of ropes secured the tent to pitons driven into the rock ten meters above, with additional belaying ropes going into the tent for the climbers to clip onto, independently of the tent. Everyone knew that the snow platform supporting the tent, could at any moment, give way and avalanche its way down the side of the ridge into the impenetrable gorges below. Hopefully, the redundant belaying ropes would keep the tent and the climbers from a similar fate.

By now, Sukey was comfortable with sharing a tent with Major Park. Originally intimidated by Park's size, strength and cold demeanor, Sukey had been able to get to know her companion a little better during the climb and the sharing of two campsites, and could now relax in his presence and also take comfort from the Major's professionalism and physical capabilities. The Major, she learned from conversation made possible only by the intimacy of a small tent, was a member of an elite Korean Army Special Mission Battalion known as the "White Tigers", a quick-strike, counter-terrorism force. He was married with two small children, a boy and a girl. Sukey was surprised when Park showed her his family pictures on his phone. She was certain he smiled when he looked at the pictures. Sukey was also impressed that Major Park insisted on doing all of the cooking, the melting of snow, and all of the cleanup – three of the chores Sukey most detested about mountain climbing.

Sukey nestled down into a seat in the snow to rest and to get away from the icy wind. She reached into an inside pocket of her parka and pulled out a nearly full pack of Marlboro Lights and a small Bic lighter. She struggled in the wind to light a cigarette as she looked down at the tent, debating in her mind whether she should have the conversation with Park tonight, or if she should wait until morning. Either way, she knew, it was going to create a serious problem for Major Park. Sukey was clipped to the fixed rope, but, as she found a piton just over her head, she clipped a sling onto it for additional protection. The seat of snow, she knew, could disappear from under her in an instant. She was waiting for Major Park to finish arranging the sleeping bags, packs, the food bag and the stove in the tent. This also was his job because he was simply much better at it than Sukey. It was also a one-person job because of the precarious position of the tent and difficulty of getting into it.

When the tent was ready, Park looked out of the small opening and waved Sukey down. He scowled, as always, when he saw her smoking. She smiled and waved back weakly. Reluctant to leave her now comfortable and warm seat in the snow, Sukey took a few final drags on her cigarette and tossed it away. She stood slowly, unclipped from the piton and made her way carefully into the tent. The sleeping bags were arranged as in the previous camps, with Sukey in the more secure, up-hill position, while Park took the outside spot where the snow beneath the tent tended to compress and fall away more easily. By morning, Park, at two hundred pounds, would be a half a foot lower in the tent than Sukey.

At the center of the tent, near the open flap facing the ridge, Major Park set up the stove and was melting snow in preparation of their dinner. He searched through the amply supplied food bag and took out a rice packet as well as a freeze-dried beef and noodle dish that he knew Sukey liked. He held up the packages to her for her approval. She smiled and nodded.

As Sukey took off her parka, she felt the satellite phone in one of the inside pockets. She was dying to call Jay Hamilton at the Zermatt base camp just to hear his voice and assure him that everything was going well for her, but she wouldn't dare within earshot of Major Park. She probably wouldn't have a chance to call Jay until she reached base camp tomorrow and was free of Park for the day. And now she needed to bring up with Park, the idea that she would be retreating down the ridge all the way to base camp in the morning. She needed it for her acclimatization, and she'd informed the expedition leader, Dong Jin-Soo, of her intentions several times, but now, she knew, it would create a major firestorm at base camp.

Sukey ate slowly, pushing back the discussion about going down, until after they'd enjoyed the excellent meal Major Park had prepared. "Another wonderful dinner you have prepared Major Park," Sukey said, as she was almost finished. She had become more comfortable addressing him as Major Park, rather than using his familiar name of Jong-Su, and the major seemed to prefer it as well. Park grunted with a quick head nod, as was his customary response to a compliment.

As Park began melting more snow to refill their water bottles, Sukey decided that she couldn't postpone the issue any longer. She cleared her throat. "Major Park, uhm, tomorrow, early, when I wake up, I will be starting down the mountain, down the ridge, back to base camp."

Park turned to listen more intently. "I need to get down to fuller air for my acclimatization, and so do you Major. We need to get down and then take the helicopter out to at least Paiju – Askole would be better, for one night's rest."

Park stuffed another handful of snow into the pot and turned toward Sukey as he sat on his folded sleeping bag. Sukey tried to continue. "Expedition Leader Dong Shin-Soo, is aware of my..."

Park slashed a hand horizontally through the air, an angry look suddenly coming over his face. "No! The Expedition Leader has warned me that this may be your plan. It is something we cannot allow."

Sukey stared at her companion, wondering if, finally, the Major's real purpose on the expedition had revealed itself. She could see that Major Park was firmly in Shin-Soo's corner. It would be useless to debate the issue. "Well Major, tomorrow morning, you may continue going up if you want to, I'm going down."

Park stared at her angrily for a few moments before his face seemed to relax. He nodded several times and took in a deep breath. He reached inside his parka, took out the expedition Walkie-Talkie and pressed two buttons. "We will see what Shin-Soo recommends." He turned away from Sukey and backed away toward the end of the tent, speaking softly to shield his words before realizing that would be impossible in the small tent. He explained Sukey's plans to the Expedition Leader, then listened. Shin-Soo was speaking loudly enough that Sukey could hear his voice crackling through the phone but not discern his words. After what seemed like a long tirade, Major Park dropped the phone to his lap without clicking off.

"Shin-Soo says to make you understand, that, if you retreat to base camp tomorrow morning, then the expedition will be over. He will recall all of the climbers on the ridge and they will bring down with them, all of the rope that had been fixed, along with the campsites, food and oxygen supplies."

Sukey shook her head angrily. "I don't believe him. He couldn't do that without Chairman Kim's permission."

"The Chairman is already back in Busan. He left two days ago," Park said calmly. "Expedition Leader Dong has complete authority."

"But there would be no need," protested Sukey. "We can afford two days for acclimatizing, and still win the race. There is much more climbing left for all of the teams, and we have shown that we can proceed up this ridge very quickly Major, faster than was planned on."

Park lifted the phone and began to speak. He was apparently cut off by Shin-Soo who was able to hear Sukey's words. After another minute of listening, Park clicked off the Walkie-Talkie, the conversation with Shin-

Soo apparently concluded. "He said to tell you that bad weather is coming, tomorrow afternoon and evening. Heavy snow and high winds. The helicopter will not be able to fly, and you would be trapped at base camp for several days possibly. And also, that the Americans are approaching their Camp5. at the base of the Bottleneck. There will be no way to catch them if you go down now."

Park went silent and stared intently at Sukey. She got the feeling that he was hoping she would make the right decision. She wondered what he would do if she said she was still going down in the morning. *This must be why he is here. To provide the final solution if it became apparent that Sukey was not going to win the race, and to avoid the additional shame to Snow Leopard of Sukey's affair with the black American. She would instead die a hero on the most treacherous mountain in the world. That would be Major Park's job.* Sukey's thoughts were interrupted by a noise outside the tent. Some climbers were on the trail, ten meters above the tent, headed down the ridge.

Major Park called out and talked to the climber in charge. There were four in all. Two were very sick – one was coughing up pink fluids, the other suffering from a severe headache. The other two climbers were assisting them down. Park asked them if they wanted to spend the night in the tent. The lead climber declined, saying they needed to get down to base camp before the bad weather arrived tomorrow. Then they continued trudging their way down the path, tethered to the fixed rope.

Park zipped up the flap against the quickening wind and flying snow, and found Sukey peering across the tent at him. She shrugged resignedly. "Okay Major," she said, "we will continue up tomorrow as quickly as we can, to get to the top of this mountain, which is a mountain not to be trifled with something as silly as a race up it. Maybe we can win. I hope we can survive."

Chapter 20

The sun was a dull circle on the horizon behind them when Jack, Ang Phu and Ang's nephews, Ringbo and Janbu, left to finish the job of establishing Camp 2 almost two miles to the west. In the dim light of dawn, they could just barely make out the shape of the huge stone buttress rising out of the ridge, which marked the spot where, ideally, they wanted to site Camp2. Jack and Ang Phu had made it to within two hundred yards of the buttress the previous day before tying off the rope and caching their packs in the snow. Without tarrying, they had turned around and headed back to Camp 1, moving quickly to beat the failing light, growing wind and falling temperature of late afternoon. Even traveling light, without packs or coils of rope, it still took them four hours to get back to Camp 1.

Now, they were trying to beat the bad weather coming in the afternoon to get Camp 2. set up to relieve the traffic jam building up at Camp 1. Jack, Ang and the nephews had had to share two tents with Piero and Mario the previous night, and Sophie and Carlos were on their way up from the halfway camp on the ridge wall. Toby and Ken Wall were also on their way back up from base camp with more heavy loads. Jack and Ang and the nephews needed to sleep at Camp 2. that night, but Jack was worried about finding suitable tent platforms, even just a few square feet, around the base of the buttress. The buttress should provide some shelter and good anchors for the tent and the ropes but there was always the possibility that there would be no possible tent sites, which was the enduring challenge of the entire length of the Northeast Ridge. Jack could vividly recall Rick Ridgeway's descriptions of the precarious tent sites the 1978 American expedition had been forced to use.

The following day, weather permitting, Jack and Ang would push on, fixing as much rope as they could carry and then retreat to Camp 2. for the night. Ringbo and Janbu would head back to Camp 1. for more rope and supplies, passing the Courmayeur guides on their way to Camp 2. carrying the tents and sleeping bags for Camp 3.

So far, everything had gone according to the plans that Sophie had laid out at the beginning of the climb and reiterated over the radio each night. At base camp, Janot and Dr. Clement would listen in on Sophie's instructions for the coming day – who would be climbing with who; who would be going down; who would be coming up with what supplies – but refrained from interfering. It had become clear to Sophie, early on, that her father and Dr. Clement were skeptical of her chances to climb K2 via the Northeast Ridge and had little enthusiasm for the challenge. At their last meeting at Base Camp, Sophie thought it best to relieve them of any responsibility for the logistics of the climb once it got started. She was in complete control of the expedition's fate on the ridge. Janot and Clement would be involved only in forwarding weather updates and news of the other expeditions. The two Frenchmen would pass their time at base camp playing chess, watching the climbers' progress through the powerful telescope, and enjoying a bottle of wine each afternoon.

Sophie and Carlos slept late at the midway camp on the ridge wall. They had about six hours of strenuous, vertical climbing with heavy loads ahead of them, and wanted to get all the rest they could. Plus, once they reached Camp 1. up on the ridge in mid-afternoon, they would be done for the day. After getting a good night's sleep at Camp 1., they would make the long, arduous trek to Camp 2., carrying an additional tent, their sleeping bags and several coils of rope that would be needed farther up the ridge. It would be an exhausting day, Sophie knew, made more difficult by the certainty of deteriorating weather early in the afternoon. She wasn't overly concerned about the bad weather. Once you made it up to the top of the ridge, the climb was a gradually elevating, four-mile hike along a now-established trail through the snow, securely clipped onto a fixed rope. Only in a few spots, most noticeably the two buttresses standing guard over the ridge, was there any technical climbing to be done. It was the kind of climbing that could be done in even the worst conditions.

What made everything possible, at this point, she knew, was the *fixed rope*. Without it, moving supplies along the ridge would be a much slower and more perilous activity. She thought about Jack and Ang Phu, out front, leading the way, belaying each other and clipped to the rope trailing out behind them through the pitons or ice screws they placed every thirty yards or so. Protection, yes, but still a very dangerous and exhausting job, breaking trail though deep, unstable snow, each carrying several coils of rope. And yet, they were still making very good time. Sophie knew how lucky she was to have the two finest high-altitude mountain climbers in the world leading her expedition. It was a stroke of good fortune, having Jack Finley come over to her expedition, and without whom, she knew there would be very little chance of successfully reaching the summit. Yes, Jack was a stroke of good fortune, Sophie knew, but it came at a heavy price.

In spite of the convenience of traveling along a now, well established trail through the snow, clipped on to fixed ropes, it still took Jack, Ang and the nephews until 1:00pm before they reached the end of the rope and the cached packs from the previous day. They were also still about two hundred yards from the buttress and the site for Camp 2. Sitting in the snow for a short rest, a drink and an energy bar, Jack and Ang Phu were facing due south and could see that the weather forecast for later in the day, had been accurate. Their normally spectacular view of the limitless white peaks to the south was totally obscured by gray clouds seeming to churn their way north. The stiffening breeze in their faces also foretold of a less than comfortable night on the mountain. The temperature on the ridge had been holding at around a fairly comfortable ten degrees during daylight. Jack and Ang knew that would be ending very soon. They just hoped they'd be able to secure their night's shelter before the wind made their lives too miserable. In the Himalaya, they knew, it was always about the wind, not the temperature.

Ringbo and Janbu had been lobbying to be allowed to lead the ridge at some point and fix the rope. The young Sherpas were anxious to impress their uncle and to gain more experience under his watchful eye, so Jack and Ang let the nephews go out ahead and fix the rope for the last leg of the trip to Camp 2. This was a good spot to let the young Sherpas take the lead. There was only about two hundred yards left to the buttress, and Jack and Ang could observe them all the way. Jack and Ang turned over some hardware the nephews might need, and shouldered the additional packs that they had left the previous day. The weight of carrying two heavy rucksacks each, made Jack and Ang chuckle over the idea that the nephews knew what they were doing when they volunteered to fix the rope to the buttress.

Progress was slow through the unbroken, deep snow as Ringbo searched for suitable anchor sites to hammer a piton into the rock or turn in an ice screw in places where they couldn't get through the snow and ice. He was roped to Janbu, and to the fixed rope they pulled along behind them. Hefting their own heavy packs and the weight of the ropes made for a tiring afternoon for the young Sherpas. Jack and Ang could see that they were doing well, and hung back about thirty or forty yards so as not to crowd the nephews.

After an hour of arduous work, breaking trail through the deep snow, Ringbo stopped and stood close to the rope, waiting for Janbu to reach him. Jack was watching them closely as they traded places to let Janbu lead for a while. He cringed as Ringbo unclipped from the fixed rope to allow Janbu to go past him before clipping his carabiner back onto the rope. For several seconds he had been standing in the snow on the steep, seventy-degree slope, without any attachment to the fixed rope. Jack knew how fast the snow under your feet could disappear on a slope this steep, and even though roped to his cousin, the force of a fall would have taken them both a long way down the slope. He was relieved to see Ringbo safely clipped to the fixed rope again and Janbu starting out with a loose coil over his shoulder.

Jack thought about saying something later to Ringbo about the safety lapse but knew it would probably fall on deaf ears. He was smiling to himself, remembering his own youthful recklessness, when, thirty yards ahead, Janbu suddenly disappeared into the snow as if he'd been vaporized. Ringbo instinctively wrapped his right arm around the fixed rope and grabbed with his left hand for the belaying rope tied to Janbu as he ran forward to the spot where he'd last seen his cousin. Janbu's weight, plummeting down into the snow, quickly pulled the belaying rope through Ringbo's gloved hand before pulling tight at his harness belt and jerking him from his feet. The slack in the fixed rope allowed Ringbo to slide several meters down the slope to a terrifying position overlooking a drop of a thousand feet. He immediately tried to get to his feet to go to the aid of Janbu but he was hopelessly entangled in his own rope to the fixed line and the belaying rope. Then Jack was at his side, pulling the ropes apart and helping Ringbo to get to his feet in the snow that was now starting to flow away from under their feet. They pulled themselves up to the fixed rope where the snow was firmer, and started up the broken path toward Janbu.

Ang Phu had already jumped down the slope to where Janbu's rope disappeared into the snow and was digging frantically with his ice axe. Ang was roped to Jack who now pulled the rope tight in case the snow gave way under Ang. He wrapped the slack of the rope around the last ice screw that Janbu had put in. Ringbo came up next to Jack and they both tried to pull on the rope to Janbu but with no effect. Looking over the side, Jack could see that Janbu had fallen into a hollow cavern that had formed in the loose snow, and then collapsed in on Janbu as he went down into it. There would now be twenty feet of snow on top of him. Jack yelled to Ang to go down the slope a ways and burrow into the snow from the side. Ang nodded his agreement and, with Jack belaying his rope, slid down the side of the slope to a point where he thought the end of Janbu's rope might place him, and resumed the furious digging with his ice axe. Then Jack belayed Ringbo as he went down the slope to dig next to his uncle.

The normally soft, powdery snow had become compacted where it fell into the cavern on top of Janbu, and the digging was strenuous. The two Sherpas attacked the snow ferociously to try to get through to Janbu and after about ten minutes, had a ten foot tunnel into the snow before they had to stop and take a brief rest to catch their breath in the thin air. Above them, Jack secured the ropes and held on to Janbu's rope to feel if there was any movement. The rope appeared to be frozen into the snow below him. Jack glanced at his watch, knowing that they were getting close to the critical amount of time to be buried in a snow pack. Below, he could see that Ang and Ringbo had resumed digging. He knew they only had another few minutes at the most to free Janbu.

Suddenly the snow moved beneath Jack's feet. He instinctively moved up closer to the fixed rope as the entire snow mass below him started sliding down the slope. Wrapping his arm around the fixed rope, Jack tried to grab hold of the matrix of ropes at his feet in a futile attempt to provide an interim belay before the weight of the climbers beneath him snapped the ropes taught, possibly pulling out the ice screw and the fixed rope. He fully expected that the weight of tons of snow pushing down on the three climbers would simply snap the ropes off close to their harnesses and in another few seconds, he would be all alone on the side of the ridge and his three companions would be lost forever.

The avalanche sent a cloud of icy powder into the air where the wind blew it up the slope leaving Jack blinded, turning his face in toward the ridge to escape the biting cold of the flying crystals. It took a minute for the snow cloud to finally dissipate allowing Jack to turn to look down the slope. He was afraid of what he might see.

He looked down upon what was now a nearly vertical wall to see Ang Phu and Ringbo, covered with snow, miraculously still holding their ice axes, making their way up the steep slope to where an unmoving Janbu hung on the rope about ten feet above them. He had lost his wool hat and goggles and was similarly covered with snow.

Ang reached Janbu first and wiped the snow away from his nose and mouth and away from his ears. Ang planted his ice axe firmly in the snow and reached his arms around Janbu and began applying chest compressions. He instructed Ringbo to lift Janbu at the legs to relieve the tension on the rope and free the pressure on his harness. After a few anxious moments, his back to the slope, Janbu coughed and began moving his arms and legs, searching for some sort of purchase on the now nearly vertical slope.

Ang Phu took off his wool hat, pulled it tightly over Janbu's head, then pulled up the hood of his own parka. He could see that Janbu's nose and cheeks had taken on the distinctive white shade of the beginning of frost bite. His nephew's body, still covered with snow, felt cold and still in Ang's arms. They needed to get the young Sherpa to shelter and get some warm liquids into him very quickly.

Ang and Ringbo got Janbu turned around, facing the steep wall, and on either side of him, began edging up the wall. Above them, Jack was belaying the confused tangle of ropes as best he could, pulling firmly on the rope to Janbu. Jack had to move up to the crest of the ridge and climb over to the Chinese side in order to acquire a firm belaying position.

Janbu had lost his ice axe in the avalanche and could do little more than dig the front points of his crampons into the ice and pull himself up on the rope while Ang and Ringbo supported him by gripping the belt of his harness as they used their axes to pull themselves up to the fixed rope. Their progress was slow, impeded now by an increasingly buffeting wind that drove the cold deep into their bones.

Jack peeked down over the edge of the ridge, pulling hard on all of the ropes, and could see that the three Sherpas were finally near the top of the slope. Taking a look out at the darkening sky to the south, Jack suddenly felt the stinging pelt of snow crystals against his face and goggles and knew they needed to get Janbu into a shelter very quickly.

When Ang and Ringbo reached the top with Janbu, Jack got up close to the young Sherpa to assess the damage. Immediately, Jack reached into an inside pocket of his parka and pulled out a balaclava he hadn't yet needed. He pulled it down over Janbu's wool hat and put it in place over his nose and mouth and ears, then pulled Janbu's hood over his head and zipped the young Sherpa's parka all the way up over his mouth. Jack could see that the first stage of frostbite had set in and while not a serious problem, it needed to be arrested right away. He could also see that Janbu had been inhaling the ice crystals in the air, and was afraid that his core temperature had dropped. The Sherpa was breathing but his eyes were unfocussed and he was moving very slowly.

Now, they had a decision to make. Push ahead and establish Camp 2., put up the tents and get Janbu into a sleeping bag, and start feeding him warm soup and tea – or, start back with him on the long trek back to Camp 1., in order to get him down to base camp as soon as possible. Ang Phu didn't think Janbu was in condition to make the six or seven hour hike back to Camp 1, with bad weather already beginning to engulf them. Jack reluctantly agreed, suspecting that Janbu was in need of immediate medical care. They would forge ahead, put up Camp 2, and tend to Janbu there. Once they were safely in the tents, Jack would call Sophie and Dr. Clement and get their input.

Logan Healy had a sinking feeling of déjà vu as the wind began to blow harder and the pinging sound of icy snow hitting a nylon parka told her that the bad weather had arrived a few hours ahead of what was predicted. She was at the spot at around 7,200 meters that was close to her high point on her second expedition to K2, three years ago. A week of bad weather had ended that underfunded climb and the snow had started at about the same spot, midway between Camps 4 and 5. She stopped climbing and looked at her watch – twelve noon, and the snow was already coming in sideways. The wind was a steady gale and the temperature was surely now below zero. She looked out at the darkening sky to the south and could see the ominous clouds above and below her. It was time to retreat. They didn't want to get snowed in for a week at an altitude above 7,000 meters, where, with oxygen or not, the body began to systematically deteriorate.

"Okay boys," she said into her collar microphone, "that's it for today. We're going down. We'll leave the packs on that shelf we passed about thirty meters ago. We'll spend the night at four, and if the weather keeps up, we'll make a run for base camp and get some rest and some cold beer."

Thirty meters above Logan, Timmy Burns turned and gave her a thumbs-up and started back down the slope. Ken Wall and Fred Terry below her, had already started back toward Camp 4. Within twenty minutes, they were engulfed in a complete whiteout. Without their tethers to the fixed rope, it would have been impossible to move anywhere on the slope without becoming hopelessly lost. Even on the rope, employing their descenders on the steeper pitches, it was a slow moving, laborious retreat.

Logan was furious with herself as she plodded down the route, pulling on a sling clipped to the jumars on the fixed rope. She knew she was down-climbing a bit recklessly but now, all she wanted to do was get down and out of the bad weather. This was a place she had been before. She was aggravated that they hadn't been able to establish Camp 5. high on the snow slope just below the bottle neck. *Bad luck, with Mingma getting hit.* But, that's what happens on a difficult climb. There is always something that goes wrong. If they had gotten to Camp 5, she would have waited out the storm there, risking three or four days at over 7,500 meters, for a shot at the summit as soon as the weather cleared. Then, it would have been over.

But now, being forced all the way down to base camp, they would be at least an additional three days on the mountain. And now, she would all of a sudden be in third place instead of being the odds-on favorite to reach the summit first. She thought about Sukey and Sophie, up on their ridges, well along on their way to the top, according to reports from base camp. Logan knew she had the advantage of the shortest route with fixed ropes already in place, but her two competitors had no option of retreating to base camp. They would have to remain wherever they were on the ridge and just survive the onslaught of the weather, and when skies cleared, they would be in position to close in on the summit.

"*Dammit,*" Logan said into her oxygen mask, recklessly skiing down a steep pitch on her boots, almost crashing into Ken Wall. "*Who the fuck do you have to blow around here to get some decent weather on this mountain!*" She realized suddenly that her collar microphone was still on, as she received a number of responses from volunteers in her earbuds.

Chapter 21

For the first time in three days, Marty Gallagher ventured out of the OSN trailer and stepped off the short stairway into the snow that had drifted in spots to over three feet. Members of the Zermatt maintenance crew were busy shoveling pathways throughout the tents of the basecamp, but they hadn't yet gotten to the OSN area. He waved to Jay Hamilton and Dr. Eric Chen who were leaning into the wind, headed toward the large Zermatt mess tent, where it sounded like the late afternoon happy hour was under way. The entire Zermatt climbing crew had been down off the mountain for four days now and there was genuine concern that the draft beer would soon run out – a crisis, with all of the helicopters grounded by the continuing bad weather. Crews were continually sweeping snow off of the rotor blades of the big Zermatt CH47 and the smaller OSN helicopter to keep the blades from touching the ground. Rudi Joost's helicopter was grounded in Skardu where it had been since evacuating the injured Sherpa, Mingma Jumic.

Gallagher pulled the hood of his red, OSN parka over his head to ward off the sleet, and reached into an inside pocket for the satellite phone to make his daily call to Glenda Craft in New York. It was 7:00am in New York and Glenda would be in her spacious corner office on the 28th floor of the glass and steel tower on 8th Avenue that housed the Outdoor Sports Network Broadcast Center. She was in the office early every day now, anxiously awaiting the call from her on-site producer of *"K2, The Race To The Top"*– the program that Glenda was now certain would be the end of her programming career in television.

"Marty, give me some good news darling," said Glenda, swiveling her chair around to gaze out at the Hudson River, shimmering in the warm, summer morning sun. It would be a glorious day in the Hamptons, where Glenda would be if it weren't for this dreadful mountain climbing program that Rudi Joost had sucked her into. *A reality show from the Himalayas in*

260

Pakistan. What had she been thinking about! "How's the weather Marty? Have we got *any* new footage?"

"Sorry Glenda," said Gallagher, "weather still sucks. High winds and still snowing up on the mountain. Two, three feet of snow down here and sleeting this afternoon. No outside video today. We did interview Phil Masters and Morris O'Dell inside again for about the tenth time but they had nothing new to say. Nothing's happening on the mountain. O'Dell's half in the bag all the time now anyway. The whole expedition is down here in basecamp now – a lot of them are sick with sore throats and headaches. We got some footage of everyone in sick bay but they're all coughing and complaining about something. Not in a good mood. The mess tent shots aren't much better. Don't know what will happen when the beer runs out."

"How about the other expeditions? Any word about the Korean girl or Sophie Janot?"

"Well both climbers are still up on the ridges, we're told, 'cause they got nowhere to go. The routes are so long that at this point, it's too far to go back down to base camp, so both expeditions are hunkered down in their camps up on the ridges. The Koreans tell us that Suek Yen is continuing to make progress, but nobody believes a word of what they say. The Korean broadcasting guys say she's stuck at around the halfway point and their whole crew is waiting out the weather to make one fast push for the summit."

"What about Sophie, and Jack Finley?"

"We think Finley's holed up out at their camp two, about two miles from camp one where Sophie and the rest of them are. Heard that the head Sherpa was bringing back the injured kid, his nephew, I told you about the other day. No way to confirm that though. You can't see shit in this weather."

"How about from our camera up on Broad Peak? They getting any shots?"

"Well, the thing is, uhm, we had to bring those guys down when the snow got really bad, and they left the camera up there, you know, thinking they would be going back up the next day. They put it in the tent, but..."

"Jesus Marty, that's a twenty-seven thousand dollar camera! And the lens cost just as much."

"Yeah, well, we'll see if we can find it."

"Okay, well I have to tell you, it may not matter."

"What do you mean?"

"The boys upstairs are thinking of pulling the plug in another week."

"But we're supposed to have another two weeks, 'til the end of July. That's the deadline we gave the expeditions."

"I know, but it can't be helped. Even after cutting back to the fifteen-minute updates every night, the ratings are in the toilet. How many times can we replay the video of Finley saving the girl in the crevasse? Or showing Logan Healy's ass going up over some rocks?"

"But what about the race?" Gallagher protested. "As soon as the weather clears, someone is going to get to the top first. There's a lot of drama in that."

"Yeah, we thought. But nobody gives a shit in the US, so the sponsors are diving off like this is the Titanic. I don't think we're going to survive 'til the end of the month. We're running up huge expenses out there every day. Reality shows are supposed to be cheap. This one's getting out of hand. Just letting you know what's going on here."

"Well, we'll stay at it 'til you tell us to pack up," said Gallagher wearily. He looked around at the white landscape, feeling the sleet pelt the back of his parka, and wished they were leaving the next day.

"What's the weather forecast there?" asked Glenda.

"High winds and less snow the next couple of days. Then maybe a couple of days of clearing, no snow, but getting colder – if that's possible."

"Well that sounds encouraging," said Glenda cheerily.

"Yeah, going to feel a lot like Palm Springs around here. Talk to you tomorrow."

Marty Gallagher clicked the off button on the sat phone and slid it back into an inside pocket. He gazed over in the direction of Broad Peak, shrouded by the low clouds, and looked up toward where they had left the camera. He shook his head ruefully wondering if the expensive camera with its thousand millimeter lens would never be seen again.

Major Park Jong-su pulled the hood of his parka up over his balaclava and, noting the harsh buffeting of the tent from the wind outside, pulled the hood strings tight and tied them under his chin. He tested his oxygen mask for tightness, then looked over to see if Sukey was ready.

"Okay," the Major said. "Let's go." He unzipped the tent flap allowing the frigid air to fill the tent and letting in a cloud of crystalline snow powder. They crawled out of the tent and each clipped onto the fixed rope, which was mostly buried in the snow.

Before leaving, Sukey dropped down to her knees and peered back into the bedraggled tent they had just spent the last three days in, to see if she'd missed anything they needed to take with them. She considered taking a food bag and the fuel canisters because she wasn't sure what they would find on the ridge up ahead. But the soldiers would need the tent and its provisions on their way down, unlike Sukey, who wouldn't be passing by this camp site again. Whether she reached the summit or not, she would be leaving the mountain via the much shorter Abruzzi Spur route. If she wasn't the first of the women to reach the top, descending by Zermatt's fixed ropes on the Abruzzi would also be a safer route for her, as she was now completely certain that Major Park's reason for being on the expedition was to cause her accidental death in the event that she didn't win the race. It would be unthinkable for Snow Leopard Industries and Chairman Kim, as well as her husband Mong, to endure a press conference in Busan after she had failed on K2, and have to answer questions about her infidelity with a black American climber on the trek in. No, they would never let that happen. She was also certain that if Major Park decided that he needed to do his job, there would be very little she could do about it. There was probably no place on earth better suited to create an accidental death than high on the West Ridge of K2.

Sukey zipped up the tent, adjusted her oxygen mask and regulator, and started out after Major Park, whose long strides, even in the drifted snow covering the trail, had put him twenty yards out in front of her. The trek along the West Ridge was much more difficult now than before the storm. The snow had filled in most of the established trail that the two dozen soldiers ahead of them had tamped into almost a narrow sidewalk. And now, the wind was relentless, driving the sub-zero cold through their protective clothing – even with extra layers added before they left.

It had been Sukey's decision to leave the tent and start moving again, even in the worst of conditions. She had spoken with Dong Shin-Soo, the expedition leader, at basecamp the previous night, who relayed the news from the other expeditions – that the Americans had all retreated to base camp, and Sophie's undermanned team was stalled out on the ridge with an injured Sherpa.

This was her great opportunity, she told Shin-Soo, and then convinced Major Park. While the other two expeditions were idle, she would forge ahead through the bad weather and in two or three more days would be in position to make her summit bid. This was her chance to win the race to the top! They had an established trail and fixed ropes all the way ahead of them. All they needed to do was withstand the cold, which they knew, the wind would bring down to twenty to thirty degrees below zero. Being on oxygen helped, as did an additional layer of clothing, and keeping active on the trail.

After an hour of plodding heavily through the new snow, Sukey was certain that they'd made a mistake. Her body was aching from the exertion and the cold, and she had lost the feeling in her toes and her finger tips. Their progress was very slow in the deep snow, and in many places, Major Park had to spend valuable minutes freeing the fixed rope from where it was frozen to the ice under the snow.

Carrying the additional weight of two oxygen bottles was also having an effect. She and Major Park had decided to take an extra oxygen bottle each because they weren't certain that they would make it to the next camp on the five-hours of gas in the first bottle. And, once you started on oxygen, suddenly going without it, especially at a higher altitude, would be a debilitating situation. It was the cause of many mountaineering fatalities. Fortunately, they knew, there was a generous supply of oxygen cached in the camps ahead of them.

By mid-morning, Sukey wasn't sure she could continue. He toes and fingers were numb and her body was shivering uncontrollably. The wind was blowing snow at them sideways and her goggles and oxygen mask were frosted over. She continually had to scrape away a tiny spot in one of her goggle lenses to see where she was going.

Head down to shield her face from the wind, peeking through the small opening in her goggles only at the path in the snow directly ahead of her, Sukey suddenly bumped into Major Park. He was standing upright with his frozen goggles up on his forehead, peering up the trail at two black-clad soldiers coming towards them. They were tethered to the fixed rope by slings, and to each other by a very short rope of four or five feet. When they reached Sukey and Major Park, the lead soldier put up his goggles and unsnapped his oxygen mask to talk. The second soldier went to his knees, took off his oxygen mask and was coughing fluids into the snow.

While they talked with the first soldier, Major Park and Sukey unclipped from the fixed rope to allow the two men to pass. The leader was taking the other soldier down as it was certain that he was developing *high altitude pulmonary embolism*, and needed to get to base camp right away. Park told him that two more hours down the ridge, the soldiers would come to the fully-provisioned camp that he and Sukey had departed from that morning. The soldier shook his head. His orders were to take the man straight down without stopping, or the man would be dead by that evening. Sukey looked down at the soldier retching into the snow at their feet and wondered how he could possibly make it all the way to base camp. As they passed by them, Sukey noticed that both of the soldiers carried an extra oxygen bottle in their packs.

The lead soldier told them that they had another two hours or so to the next camp site up the ridge, but that there were three soldiers holed up in the two tents there. The leader looked down at the man behind him and yanked firmly on the rope jerking the man to his feet. Park just pulled his goggles down and snapped his mask in place with no further conversation. He could see that Sukey was shivering and generally not doing well, and needed to get to shelter as soon as possible. Park nodded to her and patted her encouragingly on the shoulder in lieu of conversation, and they started out once more. The trail was now a little more established due to the footfalls of the two soldiers they had passed.

After two more hours of excruciating cold, they reached the next encampment just as Sukey's oxygen gave out. She couldn't feel her toes. There were two tents about ten feet down from the trail, partially covered with snow. Outside the tents, a dozen spent oxygen bottles were piled in the snow. Major Park yelled down to the tents without response. He unclipped from the fixed rope and jumped down to the first tent and unzipped the flap. Sukey followed him and looked into the second tent. There were two soldiers in Sukey's tent, and one in the first tent. The soldiers were sleeping with oxygen masks on, though Sukey could see that the regulators were turned up only to one third of the maximum flow that was used for climbing.

Impatient in the freezing wind and knowing that Sukey was in desperate need of warmth, Park awakened the man in the first tent roughly, and ordered him to move to the other tent... and leave the sleeping bag, which he was not pleased about. An angry look from Park silenced the soldier who obviously knew who Major Park was.

Park zipped up the tent securely and put Sophie on top of the warm sleeping bag the soldier had just vacated. He put the tent's second sleeping bag on top of her, lit the stove and put a pot full of snow on the flame. Rummaging through the food bag, he pulled out a package of chicken and rice soup and several packets of tea. While the snow was melting, he reached under the top sleeping bag and took off Sukey's boots. He took off his parka jacket, dropped his suspenders, and pulled up his fleece shirt and wool undershirt. He stripped off Sukey's socks and pulled her feet up under his shirts against the flesh of his stomach, then reached his hands under the shirts and massaged her ice cold toes. Sukey smiled up at the gentle warrior who was so considerate and kind to her, and wondered how he might possibly do what he had been sent to Pakistan to do. *Yes, the Major had been trained to kill and to obey orders, and he would do both if it became necessary.*

Their stomachs full from several pans of soup and rice bars, thoroughly rehydrated by several cups of tea, and warm in their sleeping bags, Sukey and Major Park settled in for a well-deserved rest. The next morning they would again leave early and fight their way through whatever the conditions were to the next encampment and be that much closer to a final sprint to the summit. Sukey was feeling good about what they had accomplished that day.

Major Park took out his deck of cards and they resumed their on-going game of Chinese Poker, a card game, Sukey was certain that Major Park was unbeatable at. They played for peppermint candies, with which Park would have to frequently replenish Sukey's supply from his winnings.

While they played, they talked quietly... about their families and where they grew up. Sukey was curious about Park's career in such an elite branch of military service and his family, which Park, now seemed to enjoy talking about. Park wanted to know more about Sukey's climbing career and hear stories about climbing other 8,000 meter mountains. Sukey had to admit to herself that in spite of what she was certain was Park's mission on the expedition, she had developed a warm feeling towards him. He may well be a highly-trained military assassin, but apart from his career, she found him to be much more sensitive and caring than most Korean men. And, she was certain that the Major had developed feelings for her as well – she could feel it through his hands rubbing her cold feet – and see it in his eyes.

At a lull in their conversation, Major Park took Sukey by surprise. He put his cards down on his sleeping bag. "Uhm, a Madam Suek Yen, I would like to know," he began hesitantly, "I was, uhm, wondering if the story about the American electronics man, the black man, Hamilton... if that was factual or not."

Sukey was shocked and didn't know how to respond. Her eyes left his face and went down to stare at the cards in her hand to give her time to think. Park's question hadn't sounded accusatory or judgmental, but more like an expression of concern. *No, of course she would have to lie to him and just deny everything, as Jack had told her to do. There was no other alternative – maybe one of his jobs was to confirm the story to be true before he executed his mission – she couldn't possibly confide in this man who was there to kill her if the story was true. But now, at this point, did it really make any difference?*

Sukey stared at her cards a few seconds more, then looked up into Park's waiting eyes. She smiled at him, "Yes Major, the story is true. On the trek in, Jay Hamilton and I fell deeply in love and we slept together several times." She nodded and took in a deep breath, determined to get the entire story out. "We have made plans to be together after the expedition is over. I will be divorcing my husband, whom I have despised for many years, and moving to San Diego to live with Jay." She looked off toward the corner of the tent and smiled, as if she was picturing Hamilton in her mind. "Mr. Hamilton is the kindest, gentlest and most sensitive and loving man I have ever met. You can see Major Park, that I am not a pretty woman or at all sexy, I know that, but with Jay none of that matters – he makes me feel beautiful, and we make each other laugh, and we enjoy each other so much..." She looked back at Park, embarrassed. "I'm sorry, sorry, I know you don't want to hear all that."

Park had his head down, and spoke softly. "I think, Madame Suek, that you, uhm, misrepresent yourself." There was silence between them, before Park looked up with a grim look on his face. "You should know Madam Suek, that Chairman Kim had his intelligence man hire one of the Dutch school teachers trekking with you to keep an eye on you and make reports. They have photographs also." He shrugged. "I just thought you should know."

The major put the playing cards back in the box, rolled over and zipped up his sleeping bag. "Goodnight Madam Suek. We will have a good day on the trail tomorrow."

Sukey watched Major Park for a few minutes before unzipping her sleeping bag and pulling her boots on. On her knees, pulling her parka on, Sukey looked over again at Major Park and saw his dark eyes studying her. "I'm going out for a cigarette," she said zipping up the parka.

Outside the tent, Sukey moved to a spot ten yards away and found some privacy in a shallow snow hole. It was too windy to light a cigarette, but that wasn't why she was there. She brought out the sat-phone from an inside pocket and carefully poked in Jay Hamilton's number. He was in the communications tent, looking at the weather screens on the computers.

"Sukey, are you all right? Where are you?" he asked with concern.

"Yes, yes Jay, I am fine, just very cold. We are on the ridge, around sixty-five hundred meters I think. But, I'm sorry Jay, there is something I need you to know, just in case." She told Hamilton of her theory about Major Park. She was certain, so if something happened to her, Jay would know.

"No, no Sukey," Jay protested, "they wouldn't do that. They couldn't do that."

"Yes, Jay they can, and they would, if I don't get to the top first." She'd been outside far too long for a cigarette. "I love you Jay. I have to go."

"Then I'll be going to the top to find you Sukey."

"No, no, don't..." Sukey responded before they lost connection.

Jack Finley had never heard a Sherpa snore as loudly as Ringbo. They had been stuck in the small tent, literally hanging off the side of the eastern buttress of the Northeast Ridge for two and a half days and Jack hadn't gotten two hours of uninterrupted sleep since they'd been there. He wished they hadn't folded up the second tent after Ang Phu had left after the first night to bring Janbu back to Camp 1. But it would have been wasteful using two tents, two stoves and separate fuel canisters. Several times, during the height of one of Ringbo's snoring fits, Jack had wished that he'd been the one to take Janbu back.

Ang Phu, though, was Janbu's uncle and he felt responsible for him. And it was a long, arduous trek in the miserable weather the day after the accident so Jack knew he was better off in the tent at Camp 2. There was also a possibility, Jack knew, that Janbu wouldn't survive the two mile ordeal back to Camp 1, which would be a difficult situation, better dealt with by a member of Janbu's family.

After the accident, Jack had gone ahead alone to fix the rest of the rope to the buttress and locate and set up a camp site. Fortunately they had only been a short distance to the buttress when Janbu fell through the snow. And Jack was ecstatic at his good fortune in quickly finding a suitable camp site when he reached the buttress. Looking down on the north side of the buttress, Jack saw a fairly flat section of snow between a rocky outcropping and the base of the buttress. When he climbed down to it, he was shocked to find a series of old, stainless steel pitons hammered into the rock of the buttress wall. The pitons were pitted and discolored, but they withstood several hard blows from his ice hammer. Jack could hardly believe their luck. They had stumbled across one of the campsites of the 1978 Expedition. Jack smiled to himself and took a moment to look around the campsite and revel in the realization that he was standing on a spot once inhabited by John Roskelly and Lou Reichardt, two of his long-time heroes after multiple readings of *The Last Step.*

Jack set up the one tent he carried, and had the stove going, melting snow, when Ang Phu arrived with his two nephews. Janbu was in bad condition, and it had been very slow going bringing him into the campsite. After they got a bottle of hot tea into the young Sherpa, and bundled him up as warmly as they could in a sleeping bag, Jack went onto the walkie-talkie and spoke with Sophie and Dr. Clement simultaneously.

To Clement, it sounded like Janbu had developed severe bronchitis, possibly frozen sinuses from inhaling so much powdered snow, and very likely was coming down with pneumonia. He probably had some broken ribs and maybe a severely strained diaphragm, and maybe other internal injuries from the snow pack that went down on him. It was imperative to get him all the way down to base camp right away, in the next twenty-four hours, said Clement. His condition was only going to deteriorate in the thin air high on the ridge.

After Clement signed off, Sophie came on. "Sounds like you had and adventure out there Jack."

"Yeah, could easily have been me if I'd been out front fixing the rope. Hope the kid makes it but he doesn't look too good. Ang is going to take him back tomorrow, leaving early to beat the light."

"That's good," said Sophie, "Carlos and I will go out and meet them halfway with some warm bottles of tea, and take over for Ang. He's going to need a rest day himself."

"Yeah, Ang's pretty worn out already. He worked hard to get Janbu out of the snow. Whole thing's taken a lot out of him."

"We'll send him down to base camp with Janbu. Ang will probably want to escort his nephew out to Skardu, so I doubt if you'll see him again this trip. I'll see if we can get him on one of the Zermatt helicopters, if they can fly."

"That's a big loss," said Jack, "Losing Ang and Janbu. Going to make it hard on everyone else." He thought about what Janot and Clement had said to him when he arrived at their base camp. Maybe they were right about the expedition being too short-handed. And *now* would be the time for Sophie to pull the plug, before too many climbers got overextended so far out on the ridge that pushing on or retreating became equally perilous.

"Yeah, I know that Jack. This changes things a lot," Sophie said wearily. "Well, after we get Ang and Jan back here safely, I'm going to talk to the boys and see what they want to do. I'll see what Carlos and Toby, and Ken Wall want to do. We've got a long way to go to Camp 4."

"And then it'll be just you and I boss," Jack said with a chuckle. "A quick little jog up to the summit."

Sophie laughed. "Jesus Jack, what have I gotten us into here?"

"Hey, beats the hell out of selling Buicks in Burlington. Call me tomorrow after you make contact with Ang. If the wind isn't horrible, Ringbo and I will be starting out for Camp 3. See you in a few days."

Jack clicked off, leaving Sophie suddenly alone with her thoughts about the state of the expedition. She was depressed. *Maybe it was just a horrible idea to begin with, to try the Northeast Ridge with an Alpine sized team. And now, losing Ang and Janbu, two of her best climbers, wouldn't she be asking too much of everyone else? And there was Jack, far out on the ridge getting ready push on, because that's what he always does, always optimistic, always ready to laugh, whatever the circumstances. What right did she have to ask Jack to risk his life for her?*

Sophie flopped back onto her sleeping bag, and allowed herself to think about Jack and relive the feeling that tingled through her the moment she saw him at the campfire in Paiju, when she'd heard him singing that awful *American Pie* song. He was singing and laughing and dancing with the kids, having a wonderful time, as he always did, always a child. Sophie flashed back to their years together and ached to go back to the way it once was.

Chapter 22

After four days of snow and high winds on K2, the weather forecast was finally calling for several days of better, if not clear, weather ahead. The three expeditions were looking forward to an early restart of their assaults on the mountain. Two days of windless conditions without snow, even at sub-zero temperatures, was an opportunity to be taken full advantage of.

On the Northeast Ridge, Sophie, Carlos, Toby, and Ken Wall huddled together in the largest of the four tents at Camp 1. The climbers all had an idea of what was on Sophie's mind when she'd called for a meeting. It was a decision, involving all of them, that Sophie wouldn't make on her own. She asked them to decide whether they should continue the climb, because with Janbu's injury, things had changed. The next morning, she told them, Ang Phu would be taking Janbu down to base camp, assisted by the Courmayeur guides, Piero and Mario, and none of them would be coming back up. Their expeditions would be over. Ang Phu would accompany his nephew out to the Pakistani army hospital at Skardu, and then, back to Nepal. Those who remained would be alone on the ridge, along with Jack and Ringbo, now two miles to the west at Camp2. There was a lot of work to be done by only a few climbers to establish Camp 4., the jumping off point that Sophie and Jack would be using as their final stop before heading for the summit. Camp 4. was a long way out – and back – and each man would have to carry heavier loads than normal.

The three climbers shrugged off the idea of quitting. They all knew how much the climb meant to Sophie – that she had invested all of the money she had in the expedition, and had worked tirelessly to secure the corporate sponsorships that had made the climb possible for all of them. To leave K2 without at least one attempt at the summit, would likely destroy her. They would go on.

The next morning, Sophie and Carlos Medina, followed by Toby Houle, sharing a rope with Ken Wall, set out early under full packs to make

Camp 2, hopefully, by mid-afternoon, and then get a good night's rest. The following day, Toby and Ken would push on, to meet up with Jack and Ringbo, at Camp 3. while Sophie and Carlos rested. Then, Sophie and Carlos, on their way to Camp 3. the next day, would pass Toby, Ken and Ringbo on their way back to Camp 2. where they would stay the night before dismantling the camp and starting back to Camp 1. Their expedition drawing to a close. Carlos would go on to Camp 4 with Sophie and Jack, and then to the terminus of the Northeast Ridge where it joined the Abruzzi Spur just above the bottleneck. While Sophie and Jack started up on the difficult final leg of the journey, Carlos would head down the Abruzzi via the fixed ropes of the Zermatt expedition and set up a tent at the Zermatt high camp for Sophie and Jack to use on their descent. While they already had an agreement with Zermatt about leaving the mountain via the Abruzzi Spur, Sophie would call Logan to let her know about Carlos putting a tent up at the Zermatt camp. She knew Logan would be looking forward to possibly meeting up with Carlos. They had climbed together and were good friends.

Ken Wall, in full awareness of his limitations, had signed onto the climb with no expectations of making a bid for the summit. He knew from experience that the altitude of Camp 4 was beyond his endurance. Toby Houle had designs on the summit but had decided to wait until the race was over, retreat to the bottom of the mountain, and after the Zermatt expedition had flown away, give the Abruzzi Spur a shot on his own. Carlos had entertained thoughts of going to the top, but, he quickly realized the logistical challenges left by Sophie's plan for her and Jack to make the near suicidal dash to the summit from Camp 4, and knew there was no place for him in the summit party. Any disappointment Carlos harbored from being denied a summit bid was assuaged by the rapturous joy he felt from the Spanish victory in the World Cup final over the Netherlands. He couldn't wait to get all the way down to the Zermatt base camp to watch the replay and get drunk in celebration. Perhaps, he would join up with Toby for an assault on the Abruzzi if the weather held promise and they could scrounge together enough food and fuel.

Ringbo and Janbu had planned to follow Jack and Sophie, set up a camp above the bottleneck, and after all the contestants in the race had made their summit runs, go for the top themselves. Without his cousin, Ringbo had lost any desire to go to the summit on this trip. There would be other opportunities for he and Janbu to return to K2, especially with the resultant publicity that would come from being on the *Sophie Janot expedition.* Someday, probably next summer, he and Janbu would stand at the summit together.

Two days earlier, Sophie and Carlos had gone out in the driving wind and stinging snow to meet Ang Phu and the injured Janbu. Without the fixed ropes, they knew they wouldn't have gotten fifty meters from Camp 1. They'd gone well beyond the halfway point before they finally met up with the slower-moving Sherpas on their way back. Janbu's condition was worse than Sophie had assumed. He was coughing steadily, complained of a bad headache, and was having difficulty breathing. Sophie made him drink nearly an entire bottle of water, then gave him a dose of Nifedipine, along with the oxygen bottle and a mask she had thought to bring from the emergency kit at Camp 1. The gas had an immediate positive effect on Janbu and allowed him to walk most of the way back, leaning on his uncle for support. Ang Phu was exhausted and clearly needed a day or two of rest. The two Sherpas spent the night at Camp 1, Janbu on light oxygen throughout the night, before heading down to Base Camp the next day, assisted by the Courmayeur guides, Piero and Mario. The Italians were challenged by the thin air of the Karakorums, but they had no equal on the mountain when it came to rescue operations and bringing an incapacitated climber down a mountain. It's what they did in the Alps and the Dolomites, and their expertise with belaying ropes, along with the strength of Ang Phu, was the only chance Janbu had of making it down to Base Camp alive.

Jack and Ringbo left Camp 2 as soon as the weak sun came up over the far end of the ridge behind them to the east. After three days in the small tent, holed up against the brutal winds and frigid cold, it was a welcome relief to once again plod through the snow and exercise their legs. Their first challenge came right away – getting up the western side of the buttress to the top of the ridge. It would require some of the first technical climbing they'd had to do. Fortunately, they again found several pitons put in place by the 1978 expedition, making the job of fixing rope back up to the ridge much easier.

Jack and Ringbo collapsed the two tents to save them from the wind and clipped them to the rope to make it easier for Sophie to find the camp site if more snow fell. They had no choice but to leave much of the equipment and supplies brought up by Ang Phu and Janbu. They overloaded their packs and took as much as they could, and Sophie and Carlos would have to do the same when they were leaving Camp 2. As Jack and Ringbo shouldered their heavy packs, they came face-to-face with the reality of an understaffed expedition. In another few days, everyone would be stressed and exhausted from carrying too much weight and moving too slowly. Losing Ang Phu and Janbu from the climb was a serious setback.

The route along the ridge became much easier beyond the Camp 2. buttress. The edge of the ridge was much less pronounced and the new snow had consolidated well, providing a well-defined path right along the top of the ridge. Jack welcomed the easier footing as, while he and Ringbo each carried several long coils of rope, he knew they would run out of rope before getting to where they wanted to establish Camp 4. If they'd had to fix rope to Camp 3., then Sophie and her crew behind them would have to be pulling up sections of the rope as they went along. It would make the retreat of Toby, Ken and Ringbo, much slower and more precarious.

The condition of the snow was better than Jack had expected. If they had sunk down to their knees with every step, progress would be excruciatingly slow and they would never reach their expected Camp 3. site before it became too dark and too cold to continue. They would have to cache their loads at their farthest point and return to Camp 2, which would be the equal of losing a half day in the race to the top. But the snow had consolidated in the wind-whipped sub-zero temperature to a point where their boots only had to kick through about a foot of snow. Still arduous in the rapidly thinning air, but manageable.

Jack would break trail for about an hour before stopping to let Ringbo take the lead for a while. The always smiling Sherpa welcomed his turn to break trail for Jack. "Okay boss," he liked to say with a laugh. "I take over. Now we go faster!"

Jack and Ringbo used a long, very light, eight millimeter rope between them. The length would provide more security if one of them was caught in a sudden snow slide or slipped on some treacherous footing. Watching the strong, durable Ringbo out in the lead position, Jack could see more and more of Ang Phu in the young Sherpa, physically and in temperament. Ringbo was becoming a professional climber on this expedition, and with the exception of his dreadful snoring, he was turning into an excellent climbing companion. Jack could also see that Ringbo was right – they did go faster when he was in the lead. Jack also found himself, several times, falling too far in back of the industrious Sherpa, causing an exhausting quickening of his pace to catch up. Jack was feeling the effects of the continually thinning air.

At noontime, they stopped for water, food and a brief rest. Jack pounded his ice axe into the snow and secured the heavy packs to it. They sat in the snow, Jack facing off to the north toward China, Ringbo to the south. The day was too overcast to enjoy any scenery of the Tibetan plain or the dozens of magnificent peaks surrounding K2, but with no snow falling and only a gentle breeze, it had turned out to be an excellent day for climbing. Just what they needed, Jack figured, to make up some ground on the other two expeditions. After being trapped at Camp 2. for three days, he assumed that they were now far behind. Logan's group would have gone all the way down to base camp when the storm hit and would now be well rested, well fed, well acclimatized, and fully hydrated, and today, scrambling up the fixed ropes, traveling light with four of their camps already in place, shooting for a summit bid in another two days. Mathias wouldn't be wasting any more time at base camp. On the West Ridge, who knows how far Sukey's army of climbers had gotten. They would be clearing the way, fixing ropes, carrying all the tents, food and oxygen bottles for Sukey who would be following closely behind. They probably never missed a beat because of the weather and now, Sukey was probably gazing up at the summit cone that very second.

Jack turned his eyes toward the mountain, shrouded in clouds, out at the end of what seemed to be the interminable ridge they'd been on for so long now. The intense quiet of the scene was broken only by the far-off sound of avalanches combing the peaks around them, and by the always present breeze whistling past their clothing. His view of the mountain was spotty through the mist, but he could feel it, how big it was and how high it was and how much more elevation they had to overcome. He knew how cold and windy and steep it would be, and he suddenly flashed back to his previous attempts on K2, and felt again the pain of exhaustion and dehydration, frozen fingers and toes, the inability to breathe or to take one more step, and the terror of knowing you were going to die. He took a long drink from his water bottle and breathed deeply, to fight off the fear. He wished Sophie was there next to him, fearless, courageous Sophie, so he could look into her eyes, as he had so many times in the past, at the most dangerous points of their climbs and see her smile and give him a wink, and soak up her confidence, and know that they were going to be all right.

The wind had been kind to them, but it was still too cold to sit idle for too long, and Jack knew they had some difficult climbing ahead of them. Ringbo took the lead and they made good time on the flattened out ridge for another hour before coming to a short, vertical drop on which they would have to fix rope for their own protection and for the other climbers coming behind them. They had another two to three hours of daylight before they would have to locate a suitable site for Camp 3.

The beer taps had been removed and the Samsung flat screen turned off. This was a mandatory attendance meeting for the entire Zermatt expedition. Standing at the front of the room was Morris O'Dell and Alby Mathias. Logan Healy sat up on the bar behind them and the look on her face told everyone that she wasn't in a pleasant mood. Phil Masters was noticeably absent.

"Okay then, lads," began Morris O'Dell, "Tomorrow, early, everyone's heading up. If you're too sick, tired or injured to start up tomorrow morning, your expedition is *over*. We'll probably have just one crack at this – we've got at least two days of clear weather coming to get into position for a summit bid. After that, we don't know for sure, but if we do get some agreeable weather, you'll need to be ready to go."

"So," Alby Mathias took over, "we don't want people spread out up and down the mountain sightseeing and taking random shots at the summit. We're going to maintain order up there, because if the weather turns bad again, I want to know where everyone is and what they're doing." Mathias stepped out into the crowded room. "First and only goal we have this week," he pointed back at Logan Healy seated on the bar, "is to get Logan Healy to the top, quick as possible – in three days hopefully. The other expeditions are on the move and have been making progress during the bad weather, so we've got some catching up to do.

"Okay, first off tomorrow morning will be Logan and myself with the Sherpas bringing up what we'll need for Camp 5. The good news is, we fully stocked Camp 4. before we had to get off the mountain, so you guys will be traveling light – that is if Camp 4 is still there after all the wind we've had," he said, smiling, eliciting some chuckles from the room. "You'll be assigned just a food bag and one more oxygen bottle each, so you should be in good shape when you do reach Camp 5." He glanced over at the "Zermatt girls" Monica, Lisa and Samantha, looking thinner and a little more haggard than they had when they'd arrived at base camp nearly three weeks earlier. "Now, some of you have expressed a desire to make a summit bid. That's fine. That's why we're here and you'll never have a better opportunity – having fixed ropes all the way up through the bottleneck and across the traverse." Mathias found Rob Page and Gordie Yorke in the crowd. "But, *nobody* goes beyond Camp 5. 'til I say *go,* and *nobody* goes for the top before Logan." He waited for Page and Yorke to nod in agreement.

"Okay, if that's clear, here's the order of the summit parties, out of Camp 5., for those who have said they want to give it a shot. Logan and Rob Page are number one; two is Yorke and Timmy Burns; everything goes right there, next will be myself and Lisa," heads turned toward the smiling Lisa Greenway, "followed by Fred Terry and," Mathias looked toward the back of the room, "our intrepid electronics director, Mr. Jay Hamilton, who wants to give it a go." The unexpected mention of his name, brought applause and some whistles for the popular Hamilton. He held up his hands to quiet the crowd and smiled to mask his true thoughts.

Logan Healy jumped down off the bar, quieting the crowd. She looked down at Lisa Greenway, and then over at Jay Hamilton. "Yeah, well it's great, Lisa and Jay, that you're willing to give the top a try, but I gotta tell you, it scares the shit out of me." Logan suddenly had a drawn and serious look on her face. "I know we've been over it all, but... she looked into Lisa's eyes. "Don't die up there because of your pride. Know when to turn around." She turned to Mathias. "You take care of them Alby," she said, then walked quickly to the tent's entrance and left.

Mathias watched Logan leave the tent. He was hoping she would contribute a bit of good-feeling, motivational talk, but clearly, he could see all was not right with the expedition's star and he had an idea why. He turned back to the room. "Alright mates, a word about going to the summit. This is important stuff, so make sure you get it. *You have to arrive at Camp 5. in late-afternoon, early evening.* Then you rest, eat and hydrate, and leave for the summit at 1:00am, no later. It's a twelve-hour round trip – seven hours up and five down, putting you back at Camp 5. in early afternoon, no later. The absolute latest turnaround time is 9:00am. If you haven't made the summit by *nine in the morning, I turn you around.* Has everyone got that?

"And when you get back to Camp 5 you rest for three hours at most and rehydrate – very important – then you get down to Camp 4 or lower. *You don't hang around at Camp 5 no matter how tired you are.* Even though everyone should be well acclimatized – doesn't matter – the altitude up there will be steadily killing your body. Even on oxygen, you can't stay at that altitude for more than two days. Okay?" Mathias looked around the room and received only nods and silence. He hoped there was more enthusiasm for the climb than he was seeing in front of him. He clapped his hands. "Right then. Pasta dinner tonight – eat good – and get hydrated. Recharge all your pods and pads and batteries. Check your headlamps and regulators. Tomorrow we'll get back to the fun."

Logan Healy pulled up the hood of her threadbare University of Vermont sweatshirt as she trudged through the snow back to her tent. The cold wind was sending daggers of ice through the cotton shirt, adding to her discomfort. She was worried about Lisa and Jay. She knew they shouldn't be going high on the mountain but she couldn't veto their summit bids. It's what *Team Zermatt* was all about – *everyone* getting the chance to climb the mountain. *Stupid.* She wished Jack was still there. He'd talk Lisa and Jay out of it. That's why she invited him, no, *begged* him to join the expedition. To be the voice of experience and reason who wasn't beholden to the Zermatt brand.

Logan was also disgusted with herself for letting the rest of her expedition down. She should have been up on the bar, leading the cheers – always up, always happy, ready for a good time, getting everyone in a positive frame of mind for tomorrow's climb. Being herself. But, she didn't have it in her, not today, not after the phone conversation she'd had that afternoon with her loving fiancé.

Rudi Joost was having breakfast in his regular suite at The Ritz in London. Spread out on the table around him were the newspapers and tabloids from the morning and the previous evening. There was no mention in any of them of the happenings on K2 in Pakistan, no mention anywhere of Zermatt Industries, Logan Healy or, most importantly, himself. There hadn't been anything in the media for a least a week, and for the kind of money he was spending on the K2 venture, that was unacceptable.

When the race up the mountain had been interrupted because of the weather, the media and the writers lost interest and moved on, and it seemed there was no way to reignite the buzz that had engulfed the event from the outset. The television audience in the U.S. had plummeted steadily since the first week, and OSN was getting ready to pack up and get out of Pakistan. In Europe, only in France and England was there still a smattering of interest. Of course in Korea, the KTN and the print media were still blasting out news of their *darling climber* Chun Suek Yen, and her benevolent sponsor *Snow Leopard Industries,* and the Asian market couldn't get enough of it. The Korean public was giddy over the possibility that their national hero, Chun Suek Yen, climbing the most difficult route on the mountain, was going to best the heavily favored Americans. The latest reports were putting Sukey very close to the end of the West Ridge, far ahead of the American, Logan Healy, who had been cavorting in her base camp pub during the three days of bad weather. It couldn't be going worse for Rudi Joost. He had never before actually considered the possibility of Logan not getting to the top of K2 first.

Also on the table, next to his placemat, was an over-sized blue file folder that Rudi's in-house chief of security had hand delivered to him a day earlier. It lay open, revealing a small stack of photos and newspaper and magazine clippings. Joost stared down at the photograph at the top of the stack. It was an eight-by-ten, color photo of Logan Healy and Anja Lindgren, squeezing together, their arms around each other's waist. The two women wore bikini bottoms and were topless, their ample breasts pressing against each other. They wore large sunglasses, and smiled broadly into the camera. Behind them a deserted beach ran off into dark blue water. Rudi surmised that it was the Mediterranean, probably on one of the Greek islands.

He reached Logan on her sat-phone, sitting in her tent half-heartedly trying to compose one more worthless blog for her social media posts. "Hello my darling Logan," Joost began, as always. He flipped over the cover to close the folder and pushed it away from him.

"Yeah, hey Rudi. How's London? Any sun there? Tell me what sunshine looks like."

"Yes, I'm sorry darling. Seems you've had a bad spell there."

"Well, if you don't count the snow and the wind and the sleet and the twenty below temperature, it's be been pretty fuckin' balmy here for the last week."

There was a long pause on the phone. "Well, as I understand it," said Joost, "That's what mountain climbing is all about... overcoming adverse conditions."

"Well, that's..."

Joost interrupted her. "Like the Korean and the French girl have been doing. Continuing to climb and making progress." Joost's voice was surprisingly stern. "While you and your friends sit around for three days, swilling beer and watching football games."

The reason for Joost's call was suddenly clear to Logan. "Yeah Rudi, thanks for your concern. Sorry I don't have any toes to send to you. And it's the wine we're swilling. We're just about out of beer."

"Logan, this is serious. I've put too much money into this project to fail, and that's what coming in second is. *Total failure!*" He was close to shouting now. "The two other expeditions are well ahead of you now, so you need to get up that mountain and get up it quickly!"

"We're climbing tomorrow Rudi, and if we finally get some decent weather..."

"I don't want to hear about weather," Joost barked. "Everyone else on the mountain is climbing in bad weather. I don't want to hear about any more excuses."

"Oh, *fuck* Rudi! You don't know *shit* about climbing, so don't talk to me about excuses. You don't know *shit* about frozen ropes, or crampons clogged with ice. And you don't know *shit* about frosted goggles you can't see through, or ice-covered gloves and frozen fingers. And you don't know *shit* about wind that would blow a car off the mountain, or what thirty-below feels like, or frozen toes, or altitude sickness, or dehydration when your water bottle is frozen solid, or trying to light a camp stove in a fifty-mile-an-hour wind..." Now, Logan was yelling.

"Logan, you need to calm down and listen," Joost said firmly. "I've fired Phil Masters because all he gave me was *excuses*. You're in charge now, and I'm holding you responsible for the results. Now, I need to go. Get the job done, and remember, no one will ever remember who came in second in this race, including myself!" Joost clicked off.

Logan had to keep herself from laughing. *The worthless Phil Masters is out and now she's in charge. There's an earth-shaking development.* She took a deep breath, tired and depressed by the whole conversation. *No, 'take care of yourself darling, be careful climbing the world's deadliest mountain, and come back to me safe and sound so we can plan our glorious wedding in October'.* No, it was a clear ultimatum... *you'd better get to the top first, because I'm not marrying some loser!*

Logan was still replaying the disturbing conversation with Rudi in her mind when the sat-phone buzzed again.

"Bon jour mon amie." said Sophie Janot with a giggle.

Logan couldn't suppress a laugh and a broad grin. "Hey, Sophie. You don't know how nice it is to hear your voice."

"You sound a little, ah, deprime? Uh, depressed? Are you okay"

"It shows huh? No, I'm fine. Climb is okay. Tomorrow morning we head back up and then I beat your skinny little ass to the top, for sure."

Sophie laughed. "Oui, that's more like the *Princess of Zermatt* that I read about in all the fashion magazines, and soon, the *Queen!* Eh?"

"Well, between me and you Soph, I'm not sure about the ending of that story."

"Uh oh," said Sophie playfully. "I should maybe send out a little *tweet* tonight."

"I know you won't do that," Logan said somberly.

"No, of course not. You know I wouldn't. Maybe though, I will tell Jack," Sophie said with a giggle. "That will make him happy I think. He doesn't think Mr. Joost is good enough for his childhood friend."

"Yeah, well, Finn had his chance."

"And with me too, you know!" Sophie and Logan laughed together.

"Neither of us was good enough I guess," said Logan. There was a silent pause. "So, how *is* Jack, Sophie? He took it hard, the..."

"Yes, we all did," said Sophie softly. "Julia was a special girl."

"Jack loved her."

"Well, I think the climb has now helped him. Taken his mind off what happened."

"Yeah, I'm glad he went with you," said Logan. "More to do than going up with us. It was a mistake, asking Jack to come with us, but now I'm glad."

"Yes, so am I," said Sophie. "He is now on his way to Camp three. I don't know if we could have done this without him."

"You know, the only reason he came was to be with you again. To see you."

Sophie laughed. "Please stop, Logan. Jack is happily married now, with children."

"It's true. You'll see. There was no other reason for him to come."

"No, no, no, that's not true," said Sophie, "but... the reason I called was to ask you if Carlos could leave a tent at your high camp, for me to use on my way down."

"Yes, of course you can Sophie. And I'll make sure there's a stove and food there, and a sleeping bag for you."

"Oh Logan, you don't have to..."

"So, will you be alone or..."

Sophie giggled. "No, I don't think so. Jack will be with me."

Logan laughed. "I should have known. So, one sleeping bag then."

Sophie laughed. "Or two," she said softly.

Logan smiled and took in a deep breath. "Sophie, take care of yourself. I'll see you at the summit."

"And you my friend."

Chapter 23

Janbu Sherpa died during the night at the midway camp on the Northeast Ridge wall. Marcel Janot and Dr. Clement had climbed up with a bag of medical supplies to meet Ang Phu, Mario, Piero, and the stricken Sherpa at the camp. Clement had wrapped Janbu warmly inside a doubled-up sleeping bag, given him an injection of Frusemide and started a saline-solution drip. In the morning, the young Sherpa was gone, most likely due to internal injuries to his diaphragm and lungs, caused by the massive amount of snow that held him trapped in the avalanche, thought Clement.

Ang Phu and the Courmayeur guides, assisted by Janot, lowered the Sherpa's body down the steep face of the wall, and then carried it the two miles out to the expedition base camp on the Godwin-Austen glacier. Ang Phu would wait a few days for Ringbo to return from Camp 3. and together, they would take Janbu's body back to Nepal. Dr. Clement had gone ahead to make arrangements for a Pakistani Army helicopter to take the Sherpas out to Skardu. Mario and Piero were scheduled to leave the next day when their porters arrived but now, perhaps they would fly out with the Sherpas.

Clement also had to make the call to Sophie who would be on her way to Camp 2. This was not a call Clement was looking forward to. Sophie's capacity for heartache had been surpassed this year, he was certain. Sophie was already settled in at Camp 2 when Clement reached her on the Walkie-talkie. He told her there was nothing anyone could have done after the injuries Janbu had suffered in the accident, and it was a great feat to have gotten the Sherpa down the mountain. Clement also pleaded with her to now abandon the climb. It was too dangerous, without the Sherpas, he told her. The only thing to do was to come back down the ridge. Then, Marcel Janot took his turn at trying to persuade his daughter. Sophie would have none of it and wouldn't discuss it. Carlos went to the other tent to tell Toby and Ken what had happened, and to leave Sophie to herself for a while. By now, Carlos knew that Sophie needed to grieve alone.

Sophie held off her tears in order to call Jack, far out ahead of them on the ridge with Ringbo. They had just found a suitable spot to set up Camp 3. and were building a tent platform into the deep snow when the walkie-talkie buzzed. Jack answered the call and then went silent. He turned toward Ringbo, unable to conceal the look of anguish around his eyes that told Ringbo everything. The Sherpa sunk to his knees in the snow, moaning quietly for his cousin.

Sophie squeezed into a corner of the tent and drew her sleeping bag around her, her tears puddling in the waterproof fabric. She thought about Janbu's gap-toothed smile and his always joyful personality, and about the waste of another young life, lost, for, *what? No good reason at all.* She thought about Victor, and about Julia... *how many more victims would she have on this quest?* Sophie wanted to pack up and start back to Camp 1. *That was the sensible thing to do. Put an end to it all. That's what a sane person would do.* Sophie pulled out her phone and one more time, slowly flipped through the dozens of pictures of Wanda and Chantal.

Word of Janbu's death spread quickly after Clement started making calls to arrange for transportation. Not long after Ang Phu, Janot, Mario and Piero arrived at base camp with Janbu's body, a video crew from OSN came trekking up the glacier to shoot some footage and interview whomever they could get to talk. Marcel Janot faced the camera and Bruce Kinder in his red OSN parka, and his ubiquitous microphone. He gave a brief accounting of what had happened up on the ridge, while Ang Phu sat with his nephew's body, secluded away in the back of the mess tent.

At Camp 2 on the Abruzzi Spur, the six remaining Sherpas of the Zermatt Expedition gathered together in one of their tents to grieve and pray for young Janbu. Then, they took a vote, unanimously deciding to abandon the climb and go down the mountain to join Ang Phu and Ringbo on their journey back to Nepal with Janbu's body. The mountain had become cursed, they were certain, by the use of the helicopters and by the commercial nature of the three expeditions, manifested by the freak injury to Mingma Jumic, the death of the young French girl, and now the loss of their own Janbu Sherpa. There was only death and heartache left in the expedition, and they should be with Ang Phu and Ringbo, they explained to

Mathias. They needed to leave the mountain right away. Mathias, and Morris O'Dell on the walkie-talkie from base camp, were livid. They needed the Sherpas, they pleaded, to establish Camp 5, and threatened to withhold their pay if they left the expedition early. After some loud exchanges between Mathias and the Sherpas, Logan Healy stepped in and the matter was settled. The Sherpas should leave, she said, and they would get their full pay before they left. Logan thanked them for all of their hard work and assured them that the expedition would go on and it would be successful. Logan offered the Sherpas the use of the big Zermatt helicopter to take them out to Skardu, but they declined. The Sherpas packed up their tents and went down the rope in the dark that evening. In the morning, they would trek up the glacier to join Ang Phu and Ringbo, and that afternoon, begin the week-long trek out to Askole.

On the West Ridge, Jack convinced Ringbo to wait until morning to start the return trip to base camp to rejoin Ang Phu. It was late afternoon when they had found a suitable site for Camp 3, and the trip back to Camp 2 was too dangerous in the dark with so much of the route without fixed ropes. In the morning, Jack would accompanying Ringbo back to Camp 2. From there, the Sherpa would have fixed ropes all the way along the ridge and down the ridge wall.

Jack thought about what the departure now of Ringbo meant. The expedition had lost three of its strongest climbers, but Sophie, he knew, would still not abandon the expedition. There would be too much emotion tied up in the climb, and not enough rational thought. And that was dangerous.

The next morning, Jack and Ringbo started out early, heading back to Camp 2. On the difficult sections, they clipped onto the rope they had fixed the previous day. On the easier parts of the trail, along the snow at the crest of the ridge, where they hadn't fixed any rope, they simply roped together for protection. The day was again overcast, but with little wind, the temperature remained around the zero mark, which made for comfortable climbing conditions. They made good progress... *but in the wrong direction.* Jack considered how far along the way to Camp 4. they might have gotten in such ideal conditions, and wondered if Logan and Sukey's expeditions were encountering anything close to the setbacks and bad luck they were experiencing on the Northeast Ridge. It would be a miracle now, he knew, to not come in a distant third in this race.

Around mid-day, Jack and Ringbo met up with Toby and Ken headed for Camp 3. It was a good time for both parties to stop for a water and energy bar break, and they were at a good spot on the wider section of the ridge. They remained roped up while they sat together on the crest of the ridge. They discussed for a moment the idea of Ken Wall escorting Ringbo back to Camp 2 while Jack took up Ken's pack and went on to Camp 3. with Toby, but that would mean Toby would be returning alone the next day. The idea was dismissed.

Jack took a long drink from his water bottle, and then looked at Toby. "So, how is Sophie handling this?"

Toby shrugged. "Not great. You know, too much stuff all piled on. And now she's got Clement and her father begging her to quit, telling her it's crazy to continue."

"What do you guys think?" Jack asked, looking toward Ken Wall. Wall just shrugged and deferred to the more experienced Toby.

Toby squinted up toward the summit cone of K2 still two miles away and a mile higher from where they sat. He turned to Jack. "Well, I'm not the one going for the summit so it'd be easy for me to just say, yeah, let's push on. So, that's up to you and Sophie. But, if I was in charge, I'd say, yeah, it's over. We got too thin. So let's go down and keep everyone else safe. Not going to happen this year, on this route, so, let's live to fight another day." Toby shrugged. "If I were in charge."

Jack smiled. "Yeah, you're probably right, but, I'm sure that's not what Sophie is thinking."

Toby frowned and shook his head. "No, shit, that girl will never quit anything. She's determined to win this thing."

Jack laughed. "Well, maybe she will."

Toby grimaced. "Jack, this plan you've got, a straight shot from Camp 4," he shook his head, "it's *twenty hours* of brutal cold, all of it at over *seventy-eight hundred meters,* without oxygen – you know how slow you'll be moving. With no shelter. And no water except what you carry with you. *Jesus Jack, don't you want to see your wife and kids again?*"

Jack smiled. "Geeze Toby, you make it sound so easy." He reached out and patted Toby affectionately on the shoulder. "Don't worry about us. We'll be okay. As long as the wind isn't too bad. When we get to the Abruzzi, if the weather's bad or the wind too strong, we'll just go down instead of up." He stood and pulled his pack onto his back along with the other men. Toby and Ken said their goodbyes to Ringbo as they exchanged hugs. Jack took a few steps, then stopped. "Hey guys, I almost forgot, when this is all over I'm going to want to talk to you about some *term life*, and maybe your *auto* and *homeowners insurance.* The other men stared blankly while Jack laughed and started back down the trail with Ringbo at his side.

Major Park Jong-Su looked up the trail in front of him and saw that they had a good vantage point to view a long section of the route as it climbed up toward the final reaches of the ridge. He stopped, unbuttoned his oxygen mask, put up his goggles and studied the ridgeline ahead of him. There had to be something wrong, he knew, as he brought out the small pair of binoculars from the breast pocket of his parka. He was scanning the ridge, gradually moving the binoculars higher up the mountain, when Suek Yen caught up to him.

"Is there something wrong Major?" asked Sukey, peering up the ridge, trying to see what Major Park was seeing. "What do you see?"

Park studied the trail for a few more seconds before lowering his binoculars and turning to look down at Sukey. He shrugged. "I don't see anything. That's the problem. We should be seeing Jin Sook's advance party preparing the last mile of the ridge, but I don't see anyone."

"Maybe they are just taking a water and food break."

"Yes, maybe," said Park, skeptically. He pulled down his goggles and they resumed their march. Park was troubled though, by the lack of activity ahead of them. It was finally a good day for climbing, without the high winds. A day when Jin Sook's soldiers should be working on the difficult final mile of the ridge where it makes a sudden upward thrust toward the summit cone. If the advance party was up there now, fixing the ropes on the final section of the ridge, and putting in the last camp, Park thought that it was conceivable that Sukey could get to the top in just two and half more days. From the reports they had received from the expedition leader, Dong Shin-Soo, at base camp, neither of the other expeditions was close to being two days from the top.

After two more hours of kicking through the deep snow, guiding their slings along the fixed rope, they came to a slight bend in the trail where Park's suspicions were confirmed. One hundred meters in front of them, a group of the black-clad soldier-climbers emerged from a bend in the trail, coming toward them. Sukey and Park stood still watching the procession as it approached, mesmerized by the scene of what appeared to be at least six climbers, bearing what looked to be a sleeping bag turned into a stretcher.

The slow progress of the soldiers, made Sukey and Park start forward up the trail, just as it began to snow. Sukey put up her goggles and lifted her face to the sky. It wasn't a heavy snow, but more than just a flurry, and the sky seemed darker now. She reached into her parka for the walkie-talkie, concerned that they had received no report of the coming snow from Dong Shin-Soo at base camp.

"It appeared to us to be only a passing shower," explained Shin-Soo, "Not enough to interrupt your progress today."

"Yes, Expedition Leader Shin-Soo, that is true," responded Sukey, "But, *we must have up-to-date weather reports!*" Her loud voice caused Major Park to smile.

"Yes, yes Madame Suek," the Expedition Leader sounded perturbed, "But we have more urgent news to concern us. You will find that Climb Leader Jin Suk has become ill and is on his way down the mountain."

"We see him coming toward us now," said Sukey.

"It appears to be thrombophlebitis, and he needs to get lower immediately. There are also some other soldiers that are ill."

Now, maybe you believe me Expedition Leader, about the need for proper acclimatization! Sukey shook her head as she watched the soldiers, looking exhausted, coming down the trail toward them.

"We have met up with Jin Suk's party now. I will report in this evening," said Sukey. She returned the Walkie – Talkie to an inside pocket.

The first soldier in the procession reached them. He put up his goggles and unsnapped his oxygen mask. "Climb Leader Jin Suk is very sick," he said, breathing deeply now, trying to extract some oxygen from the thin air. "Cannot walk and in great pain."

Major Park and Sukey pushed past the soldier to where they had laid Jin Suk on the snow. They knelt next to the roped-up sleeping bag where they could see that Jin Suk was conscious. He sat up with great difficulty.

"How are you feeling Yoon?" asked Sukey.

Jin Suk grimaced. "My legs are dead and in great pain." It was plainly a struggle for him to talk. "My expedition is over."

"Yes," said Sukey, "You must get down very quickly.

Jin Suk nodded impatiently. "But Suek Yen, Major Park, you must listen. We have made a very big mistake I am afraid." He reached out and held Sukey's arm. "And now, it may prevent you from getting to the summit."

"What is it Yoon?" asked Sukey. "What has happened?"

Jin Suk shook his head. "We simply brought too many climbers to the mountain. We have too many men that came up the ridge. They all have to eat and use fuel to melt the snow, and, most importantly now, not being properly acclimatized, they have used a great deal of oxygen." He shrugged and contorted his face in pain, as he tried to catch his breath. "Too many mouths to feed. Especially when the weather forces us all into the tents for three and four days at a time."

"What are you saying?" said Major Park loudly. "There are no supplies for us at Camp 4?"

"No, no," said Jin Suk. "There is food for you and the remainder of the oxygen bottles, enough for you to reach the summit, hopefully. You will need to conserve the oxygen though. There are four climbers left, and they will go out tomorrow to fix rope and establish the final camp for you. They are strong young men who will climb with limited oxygen and food. They will establish Camp 5 for you and then come quickly down the mountain." He looked up into Sukey's eyes. "I'm sorry Madame Suek, they will be unable to supply any further support, or" He looked from Sukey to Major Park. "Any sort of rescue operation," he said softly. "They will not have sufficient oxygen or food to linger on the mountain, and will have to get down the mountain quickly, and..." He hesitated. "You will be entirely on your own to get back down." Jin Suk lay back with a groan and motioned with a hand to his men to start out again.

Sukey put her goggles in place and brushed the snow off of them. She turned to watch Jin Suk's party shuffle laboriously down the trail. She shook her head in disbelief. *This was a disaster! How could this happen? Twenty-five soldier climbers and huge supplies of food, fuel and oxygen, reduced now to four climbers trying to establish Camp 5 on limited oxygen and little food! It was because the big helicopter made it so easy to bring in such a large number of climbers – a strategic blunder!* Sukey questioned now whether it would even be possible to reach the summit, let alone be the first. She turned to see Major Park studying her. Park turned his head slightly to watch Jin Suk and the other ailing climbers, then looked back at Sukey.

What was the Major thinking about now? Sukey asked herself.

"Okay, let's go on," said Park. "We need to make good time to get to the next camp before darkness." He started up the trail at a good pace, his size twelve boots tamping down a wide path through the new snow as Sukey fell in behind him.

After another three hours on the trail, Sukey and Major Park arrived at Camp 4. A pile of spent oxygen bottles, covered with a light dusting of snow, sat outside the three tents. A gaunt, tired looking young man, pulling on his parka, emerged from one of the tents to greet them. He was Second Lieutenant Cho, he told them, and he was now in charge of the other three soldiers. His orders were to set out early the next day, no matter what the weather was, and push as far up the trail as they could, fixing the final section of rope and establishing Camp 5 for Sukey to use for her attempt at the summit. The soldiers would use oxygen set at just a twenty-five percent flow, and they would carry two full bottles to Camp 5 for Sukey and Major Park to use on their bid for the summit. There would be only one tent at Camp 5, and not enough space for six climbers, so Sukey and Park should rest for most of the next day, and wait for the soldiers to start down before heading for Camp 5. A tent had been set up here for Sukey and the Major,

Lt. Cho told them, with food and fuel and sleeping bags. He bade them good luck on their mission and disappeared into his tent.

Logan and Albie Mathias needed to take a rest day at Camp 3. They were exhausted. The other climbers were all in agreement. Everything about the climb up from base camp was more difficult than the first time they had come up the ropes two and a half weeks ago. The ropes and the surfaces were all icier, the snow was deeper and without the sunlight, the Abruzzi Spur now seemed to be confined in permanent shadow. And, it was colder, much colder than their first trip up the mountain. They also had the burden of severely overloaded packs, as did the rest of the Zermatt climbers, to make up for the departed Sherpas.

They had divided up the loads that the Sherpas had left at Camp 2. There were the two tents for Camp 5, several more sleeping bags, food bags, an additional camp stove, and ten more oxygen bottles. Logan and Mathias redistributed the equipment between their own already heavy packs, and to Rob Page, Gordie Yorke, Tim Burns, and Fred Terry. Lisa Greenway, and Jay Hamilton only had to carry one oxygen bottle apiece.

"Here you go Mother Theresa," said Albie Mathias, tossing the last oxygen bottle to Logan's feet. "For letting the Sherpas go."

"There was no keeping them," said Logan, stuffing the oxygen tank into her pack, which must be at about sixty pounds, she estimated.

Logan knew it was a good decision to take an extra day at Camp 3, to rest, hydrate and eat as much as they could get down. She wanted everyone in decent shape when they reached Camp 4, because if the weather was good, there would be no more down time. It would be up to Camp 5, the next day for the first two summit parties, and then to the summit that evening. Without the Sherpas, hauling the tents and equipment up to Camp 5 at the base of the bottleneck, would be laborious work for the few climbers left.

Mathias was in agreement about taking a rest day. He had borne the heaviest load up from Camp 2, and he knew how the other climbers were going to feel. Not everyone, however felt the same as Logan and Mathias. Morris O'Dell at base camp was very concerned, he told Mathias. This rest day could conceivably lose the race for Logan. He insisted that Mathias put Logan on the Walkie-talkie.

"My dear," said O'Dell, "I've just gotten off the sat-phone with Mr. Joost, and he is not at all pleased with... "

"Tell Rudi to go fuck himself!" Logan clicked off the phone and tossed it to a far corner of the tent. She zipped up the tent flap for privacy, and pulled out her sat-phone. A few minutes later, she was talking with Anja Lindgren in Majorca.

Chapter 24

Marty Gallagher held a phone to his ear, on hold, waiting for the electronics trader from Karachi to come back on the line with a price he was willing to pay for the OSN editing console. Gallagher watched Bruce Kinder, at the other end of the broadcast trailer as he pulled on his red parka, wool hat, and sheepskin gloves, in preparation for going out onto the glacier to record the only newsworthy event they'd had access to in a week. Gallagher prayed that they would soon get the word from Glenda Craft that he could pull the plug on this moribund K2 show and he would soon be rid of Pakistan, the snow, and the cold, and also be rid of Kinder, the obnoxious asshole he'd been forced to live with for the past month.

"The Sherpas'll be coming up the glacier pretty soon with the kid's body," said Kinder, giving himself one last look in the full-length mirror next to the trailer door. "None of them will give a comment, but should be some good video... carrying the dead kid."

Gallagher smiled and nodded to his anchorman. *Yes, fucking riveting television Bruce, no doubt.* He went back to his call, and began again to record dollar amounts next to dozens of items on a green ledger sheet. He almost laughed when he saw how low some of the offers were, but there would be no negotiation involved in this transaction. OSN would be giving away everything for twenty-five cents on the dollar, and happy to take it. Cameras, microphones, satellite dishes, even the Airstream trailer would be going, FOB the Skardu Airport, and good riddance as far as Gallagher was concerned. After transporting it all half way around the world and two months in the mountains of Pakistan, it was worthless junk now. They would be traveling light on the return trip to New York.

Bruce Kinder and his camera crew went all the way across the glacier and set up on the south moraine in order to shoot the introduction with K2 in the background. The clouds hid most of the mountain but the shot had a nice panoramic effect anyway. They used a collar microphone for this shot so that Kinder could turn and point far up the glacier towards the Sherpas when they came into view. Then, they would pack up and head back across the glacier to get a close-up shot of the Sherpas *carrying out their dead* as Kinder, proud of his penchant for dramatic copywriting, would describe it.

Kinder began his introduction. "We're out here on the Godwin-Austen Glacier at the foot of K2, the second highest mountain..." Suddenly, the giant Zermatt CH-47 helicopter, fifty yards away, let out a high-pitched whistle as the huge blades at the front and rear began to slowly turn. A few seconds later, the multiple engines exploded to life with a deafening roar. Dense, black smoke, the product of ten days of inactivity, belched into the air. Kinder spun around toward the helicopter. "Hey, what the *fuck!*" he yelled, inaudible to the camera crew just a few feet away from him. Kinder shrugged and pointed toward the helicopter. They would at least get some footage of a noisy takeoff. That would be more exciting than anything they'd shot in the past week.

Inside the OSN trailer, Marty Gallagher smiled at the sound of the helicopter coming to life again. It was the sound of his imminent release from this minimum security prison. The pilot must have gotten the *all clear* from the weather service at the Skardu Airport. Visibility through the Braldu Valley had finally lifted to a safe flying altitude for the heavy airship. Gallagher knew that the Zermatt camp was running dangerously low on some vital necessities -- fuel for the two generators, draft beer, wine, bottled water, bar snacks and toilet paper. The helicopter would also be taking out the remnants of the foreign press corps and what remained of the free-lance photographers, eager to finally make their escape. Any drama left in this story would be taking place high on the mountain, far out of their reach, and now, beyond the interest of their media employers.

As difficult as the climb to Camp 4, was proving to be, Logan Healy was in good spirits. The overloaded pack on her back caused the straps to dig into her shoulders and threatened to topple her over backwards if she didn't lean in to the mountain, but she was encouraged and energized by the update she'd received from Morris O'Dell at base camp before they had set out that morning. After assuming that the Zermatt team had fallen behind the other two expeditions when the weather forced them off the mountain, it appeared now from the latest reports that as soon as Logan reached Camp 4, late that afternoon, she would again be ahead of Sukey and Sophie.

The report from the Northeast Ridge, via the OSN update blog, was that the injury and subsequent death of Janbu Sherpa had set Sophie's team back at least two days with Jack Finley having to escort Janbu's cousin, Ringbo, all the way back to Camp 2. And now with the loss of their three Sherpas, the consensus among the Zermatt climbers was that the French expedition would soon be throwing in the towel and retreating from the ridge.

The news from the Korean side of the mountain was nearly as dire. The climb leader, Yoon Jin Suk, was being treated at base camp for a severe case of thrombophlebitis, awaiting evacuation on the Snow Leopard helicopter as soon as the cloud cover lifted. There were also reports of at least a dozen other cases of *acute altitude sickness* among the Koreans, leaving Sukey on her own, still nearly a mile short of the snow slope leading to the summit, and short on oxygen and food. The most difficult route on the mountain was taking its toll.

Logan had forgotten how vertical and technical the climbing was between Camp 3 and Camp 4, made even more strenuous now by the over-loaded rucksack on her back. *Maybe she shouldn't have been so magnanimous toward the Sherpas.* But her spirits were buoyed by the knowledge that she was taking over the lead in the race to the top, and that the following day, she and Rob Page would be heading up to Camp 5. They would eat and hydrate, and try to get a few hours of sleep before starting out for the summit at 1:00am. Hopefully, they would be watching the next morning's sunrise from the top of K2.

At a small, flat shelf carved into the dark rock, Logan unclipped from the fixed rope, dropped her pack and pulled out her water bottle. Just behind her, Alby Mathias gained the shelf and relieved himself of his heavy pack. Logan peeked down the near sixty degree pitch to watch Rob Page and Tim Burns, about thirty meters below them. They had been fortunate on this stretch of the climb, that the weather had been so cold over the last week, consolidating the face and eliminating much of the rock fall that typically menaced this section of the route. Looking farther down the mountain, Logan had to smile when she saw the Zermatt video crew, Bert and Arnie, making their way, tentatively up the rope. "I never thought those video guys would make it even this high," she said to Mathias.

"Yeah, they still plan on being on top to film you arriving there," Mathias said with a grin.

"Well, keep an eye on them," said Logan, "You'll know when to turn them around."

Suddenly, they heard a strange, roaring noise from somewhere down on the glacier far below them. Logan looked puzzled until she realized it was the big Zermatt helicopter coming back to life after being grounded for over a week. She looked up and noticed a section of faint blue sky finally pushing through the gray cloud blanket. A welcome sight, although she knew the forecast was for three days of so-so weather, followed by a question mark in the form of a big front of moist air hovering over central India. Hopefully, she would be well on her way down the ropes or even safely back at basecamp before the weather deteriorated.

Logan and Mathias clipped their ascenders back onto the fixed rope and started up again to allow Page and Burns, who were approaching quickly, to occupy the narrow ledge and enjoy a water break. It was another two hours of difficult, steeply pitched climbing up to Camp 4, and Logan was looking forward to settling in for an evening of rest and rehydration. She planned to be in peak physical condition the following night when she left Camp 5 for the summit.

The climbing soon became easier as the pitches became less steep and more about the legs than the arms. Several snow gullies offered good footing in the crusty snow and some shelter from the wind that lowered the temperature at least ten degrees. Logan and Mathias were making good time now, and she was feeling strong and optimistic about the climb. And, happier than she'd been in days as the climbing took her thoughts off of Rudi Joost.

Finally, they made it over the familiar horizontal ridge that marked the beginning of the snow slope where Camp 4, was sited. Climbing up onto the lower end of the slope, they caught sight of the large, distinctive rock buttress, beneath which was the small, protected plateau where they had situated the tents of Camp 4. They wouldn't be able to see the camp until they'd made their way up the hundred meter snow slope bringing them to the plateau. Even with the help of supplemental oxygen, Logan was winded when she got to the top of the slope. There, catching her breath, she stood, staring, dumbfounded at the sight before her. She put up her goggles, pulled off her oxygen mask, and stood motionless, waiting for Mathias to reach her.

Coming up beside her, Mathias took off his helmet and oxygen mask. "*Jesus, no,*" he said softly. Where the three, bright orange tents, filled with sleeping bags, air mattresses, stoves and food bags, should have been — where they had left them a week earlier – there was nothing.

Logan stood still, shaking her head. "The wind. The wind took it all. Incredible."

They began walking again. Slowly, up the slope through the foot of powder snow, to where Camp 4, once stood. A few pieces of tattered orange nylon fabric were pulled out of the snow, still attached to ropes tied to snow screws. Logan moved over as close as she dared to the edge of the ridge and looked down at the south face of the mountain where the wind had taken the tents and everything in them. Someday, probably decades in the future, bits of orange fabric and pieces of equipment stamped with the Zermatt logo, would begin to emerge from the ice far down the glacier.

"We still have the gas, at least," Mathias called out. He was sweeping the snow off the stack of oxygen bottles at the edge of the camp.

"We should have buried the tents," said Logan, almost to herself, walking back across the camp site. They had, as always, collapsed the tents, but not covered them up. She dropped down into the snow to rest, think and plan their next move, and tried not to cry. Exhaustion, frustration, and the jangle of emotions over Rudi, the wedding, and the loss of Camp 4, were sapping her resolve to stay strong, to be a leader. "Alby," she said wearily, "I need a joint."

It was mid-afternoon and would soon be getting dark and colder, and in another few minutes, Rob Page and Timmy Burns would be arriving at what they thought was Camp 4. Now, they had only the two tents that Logan and Mathias had brought up, destined for Camp 5, one stove, and just two food bags. They would have to make do, somehow, but clearly they couldn't entertain any additional climbers at Camp 4, or higher. She would have to put an end to the summit dreams of several climbers already on their way up.

Logan went on the group radio and gave everyone the bad news. She knew the Koreans and Sophie's crew would be listening in but she didn't care anymore. The sleeping bags and most of the food was gone, but the day after tomorrow, she would be heading to the summit to get this over with. Nothing was going to stop her, and no one was going to beat her to the top.

Bert and Arnie, with their heavy packs of batteries and lighting equipment, could stay one night at Camp 4, while there were two tents to squeeze into, but they would have to head down when Mathias and Timmy Burns started up with one of the tents to set up Camp 5. Gordie Yorke and Lisa Greenway retreated down the rope to Camp 3, where they met up with Fred Terry and Jay Hamilton who had just arrived. They were all instructed to spend the night at Camp 3, and retreat to base camp in the morning.

Dinner that evening was a crowded affair in the largest of the two tents at Camp 3. Fred Terry spooned out the beef stew to Gordie Yorke, Jay Hamilton, and Lisa Greenway. The inside of the tent glowed with the light from a battery lantern as darkness and cold engulfed the mountain. The wind buffeted the tent lightly but without letup.

"Funny, how you get used to the noise up here," said Jay Hamilton, "The noise of the wind. It just never stops... whether you're climbing or sitting in a tent, it's always there."

"This isn't wind," said Yorke. "Wind is what they had up at Camp 4."

"Geeze, I knew it was a bad storm," said Hamilton shaking his head, "but what kind of wind does it take to blow a whole camp site away?"

"One of the characteristics of this mountain," said Fred Terry. "Violent storms; treacherous wind." At 37, Terry was one of the veterans on the expedition.

"It was wind like that, that likely killed the Barrards," said Lisa, quietly, recalling her conversation with Jack Finley on the tarmac at the airport in Skardu. "French husband and wife team, Lilliane and Maurice Barrard. Just after they summited in 1986. Heavy winds on the their way down, then, no one ever saw them again."

"That was a bad season on K2, 1986," said Terry. "Thirteen killed that summer." He looked over at Lisa. "Including two other women; a young Polish climber, and Julie Tullis, a very accomplished English climber. She made the summit, then died on the way down from pulmonary embolism."

Lisa flashed back to her conversation with Jack. *"Do not to go above Camp 2,"* he had told her. She knew he was right, yet, she had been climbing well and felt strong, and she knew she'd never be back here again.

Gordie Yorke brought up what they were all thinking about. "Well, I know Logan wants us off the mountain, but, I've got no intention of getting this close, and then giving up a shot at the summit. This'll be my only chance to climb this mountain, and I'm taking it. I only need two more after K2 to have all fourteen." He went silent for a few seconds, then shrugged. "I'm too close," he said softly.

Then Jay Hamilton spoke. "I'm going with you." All eyes turned toward Hamilton, surprise written across their faces.

"No, no, no, Jay" Fred Terry implored. "On any expedition, you have to be able to recognize when it's falling apart... when it's time to just go down and call it a day. That's where we are now."

"No, I have to go up. I have to get to the top of the West Ridge. It's personal," said Jay.

"What do you mean, the *West Ridge*?" asked Yorke.

Hamilton shifted uncomfortably. He didn't want to get into it, but if he was going to climb with Yorke, he deserved to know. "Yes, I won't be going to the summit. I have no desire to make the top. I'll be going up through the bottle neck, and then making the traverse under the seracs and around to the western summit slope." He looked up toward Yorke. "But, then, I won't be going to the top with you." Jay could see the looks of bewilderment on the faces of his companions. He shrugged. "I need to get to Sukey. She's in danger, and I need to find her."

Having gone this far, Jay felt compelled to tell his companions everything. He recounted his last sat-phone conversation with Sukey, and described for them, Major Park's military background and limited climbing experience. Then he described for them, the intense pressure Sukey was experiencing because of her "immoral" relationship with "a black American climber" on the trek in, and how her husband had been sent home in shame.

Yes, knowing the Korean culture a bit, Fred Terry concluded that Sukey's fears were not without merit.

"Okay," said Yorke. "I'm glad you'll be climbing with me Jay. We'll need to take one of these tents here from Camp 3. We don't know who is going to be at Camp 5 when we get there. Be a tough job lugging everything up the mountain in one pack, even with fixed ropes all the way."

"Yeah, better with the two of us going," said Jay. "Let's get an early start in the morning."

"I'll be going up too," said Lisa Greenway, almost in a whisper. All of the men turned toward her. She shrugged. "I'll never be here again. I'll never have this chance. I feel strong and I'm climbing well, so, I'm going to go higher and see how far I can go."

"Oh, *Christ*," said Fred Terry, shaking his head and falling back against his sleeping bag. *An egotist with summit fever and two complete amateurs, climbing together on K2. This is how disasters happen.*

The weather couldn't have been better on the Northeast Ridge as Carlos Medina, Sophie Janot, and Jack Finley forged their way along the now well-trodden pathway to Camp 3. The trek back to Camp 2 the previous day with Ringbo was Jack's easiest leg yet, carrying a nearly empty pack. Now though, he carried a full load, as did Sophie, twenty meters ahead of him, and Carlos, out in the lead. There would be no resupply of Camp 3, or supplemental loads carried out to Camp 4, by the Sherpas or support climbers. There were no more Sherpas, and all the other climbers were on their way down – they would have by now closed up Camp 2, and started the long trek back to Camp 1. Whatever Sophie, Jack and Carlos had on their backs, plus the supplies already at Camp 3, would be all they would have for their summit bid, and that was a long way off.

They took all the food and most of the fuel canisters. Sophie and Carlos packed their sleeping bags, clothes and personal items, while Jack tied onto his pack the two-person bivouac tent he'd gotten from the Zermatt stores. He hadn't even taken it out of its original packaging, but he had a feeling that it could be a lifesaver on their summit bid if they didn't beat the bad weather that was coming. But they had three days of fine climbing weather, Clement had assured them, before the moisture rolled in. That would be enough. By then, Carlos would be all the way down to the Zermatt base camp watching World Cup Soccer replays, and Sophie and Jack would be clipped to the Americans' fixed rope and on their way down after making the summit.

Halfway to Camp 3, the sun broke through the overcast sky and with little wind, it suddenly felt almost like a spring day. They stopped for a lunch and water break, dropping down into patch of deep snow next to the crown of the ridge. Jack and Carlos sat facing south looking out at Broad Peak, Chogolisa, and the Gasherbrums, while Sophie stood on her knees, her arms draped over the edge of the ridgeline, gazing down at China and the Tibetan Plain. Sophie had broken out one of her prized packages of Fig Newtons and given one each to Jack and Carlos who insisted that Sophie keep the remaining two for herself.

Carlos brought out his Nikon and took advantage of the sunlight to take pictures in every direction. "Okay, now one of you two, please," he said pointing the camera toward Sophie. Jack smiled and moved over beyond Sophie to put her in the foreground of the picture. They both stood in the deep snow, their backs against the ridgeline. "Closer," said Carlos, backing up a step to bring the summit of K2 into the background. Sophie grinned and pushed herself back into Jack while pulling his arm around her. She pushed down the hood of her parka and pulled off her wool hat, releasing her ebony hair to fly into Jack's face. She giggled, tucking her unruly hair into her collar.

Jack smiled for Carlos' camera, but the sudden closeness of Sophie, his arm on her shoulder, and the feel of her always luxuriant, beautiful hair, blowing against his beard and his mouth, produced a spasm of nostalgia that instantly transported him back through the years and left his heart pounding in his chest. They hadn't yet been in such close physical contact on the climb, and now, here they were together in one of the most isolated places on earth, and the feeling of her back against his chest, the sound of her giggle, and the familiar fragrance of her hair, produced a moment of euphoria that Jack didn't want to end. He suddenly felt supremely protective of this woman he had loved for so long. It was his job to see that Sophie made it safely off of this mountain. It was a familiar, comforting feeling.

"Oh my god!, Jack, Carlos, look, look!" exclaimed Sophie pointing at something over the ridge to the north. A small, pale blue butterfly was dancing in the air around her outstretched arm. Then there were several more. One alit on Sophie's glove. Then dozens of the butterflies, followed by thousands more, shining in the sun, swarmed up and over the ridge. They descended down the south slope and in a few seconds, they were gone. Sophie clapped her gloved hands together, applauding the butterflies. "Oh yes, merci peu papilons, a wonderful show!," she said. "I have read about these butterflies that climb the Himalayan peaks, but I have never before seen them." She smiled at Jack. "It must mean good luck for us." She turned to Carlos. "Si, Carlos? Buena suerte, no?"

Carlos laughed and winked at Jack as he rose up out of the snow to get started again. "Oui Sophie, oui. Good luck from the butterflies. Yes, now we need to move." Jack took the lead position on this leg, roped to Sophie behind him, followed by Carlos.

In three more hours, just before they reached the buttress where Jack had sited Camp 3, he showed Sophie and Carlos the spot where Janbu had gone through the snow and then been covered over. Thirty minutes later, they settled in to Camp 3. It was four o'clock, earlier than expected because of the benign hiking conditions on the ridge and the lack of wind. They all agreed it was one of their best days yet on the mountain.

The three climbers left their crampons, ice axes, harnesses and other equipment in a pile outside the one tent at Camp 3, and squeezed inside to eat, drink as much water as they could make, and try to get a night's sleep. The next day's trek to Camp 4, would be more than a mile, on more difficult terrain, continually climbing at an ever steeper pitch, into rapidly thinning air.

Carlos worked at the stove, melting snow to fill and refill their water bottles. They would all drink as fast as Carlos could melt the snow, but no one had an appetite for dinner. It was the effect of the altitude, they all knew – they had experienced it many times before – as much as their bodies needed fuel, the task of eating was a laborious effort in forcing down the food. Carlos brewed up two pots of rehydrated beef barley soup fortified with two packages of Raman noodles, which they ate slowly, unenthusiastically. Jack and Carlos ate most of it; Sophie had very little.

While Carlos melted more water to clean up the cups and utensils, it became clear to Jack that Carlos was accustomed to watching over Sophie, tending to her needs, and that they enjoyed a close relationship. Occasionally, they would share an inside joke or a jibe in French or Spanish, and Jack would feel a twinge of jealousy toward Carlos that was a new and unexpected feeling.

In a corner of the tent, Sophie and taken off the jacket of her parka as the tent warmed up, and was leaning back against one of the sleeping bags. She wore a pure white turtle neck sweater that seemed to glow in contrast to her jet black hair hanging limply around her face. Her breasts pushed firmly against her sweater and when she looked up and found Jack's eyes, she smiled and looked to Jack like the most beautiful woman he had ever seen, as she always had. Ten years and two children had added an inch to her waist and hips, but Jack would be the only person on earth who could tell.

Sophie turned and smiled at Carlos who was handing her a cup of tea. "Drink it all Sophie. You'll need as much fluid as you can take in," said Carlos, turning back to the stove.

"Mercie, mon amie," said Sophie.

Jack smiled to himself. *Yes, of course Carlos would be in love with Sophie. Everyone fell in love with Sophie sooner or later. Who could know her, spend time with her in the mountains, share encampments with her, and not fall in love with Sophie.* Jack thought back to when they had first met, on Everest at a crowded encampment on the South Col when he was

305

twenty-two. It had taken him all of ten minutes to fall madly in love with this beautiful, spunky, little woman with the dark eyes and a voice in English that was like listening to soft music. Carlos, Jack knew, was divorced, as so many climbers are, and owned a very successful climbing school in Switzerland, and an olive grove outside of Barcelona. He had climbed with Sophie on Cho Oyu in the winter, and had summited Gasherbrum II with her in June, two hard, difficult climbs in a small party. *Yes, of course Carlos and Sophie would have a relationship. Good for them.*

That night, before they tried to go to sleep, Sophie called home on the sat-phone and talked to her daughters for a few minutes before clicking off and handing the phone to Jack. He hadn't talked to Peggy in a week. To be honest, he'd been avoiding the always unpleasant gripes his wife had ready for him. But, he knew he should talk to her now, before they started out tomorrow, when things could get more difficult and there may be little opportunity to make a call.

"Hey Jack," said Peggy. It was early morning in Vermont. "Hoping you were going to call. Not getting much information on the TV or in the paper."

"Yeah, things got a little boring here for a few days because of the weather. But, everyone's on the move again. We're getting pretty high on the mountain."

"Still climbing with the French girl?"

"Yeah, uh, that's my job. She's usually a long way behind me though. Having a tough time keeping up." Jack winked at Sophie who grinned and rolled her eyes. Peggy was silent, apparently not wishing to hear any more about the situation.

"How are the kids?" Jack asked.

"Yeah, they're fine," said Peggy. "They miss you. Here, Ralph wants to say hi."

"Hello, hello daddy," said the boy.

"Hey, Ralphie," said Jack. "You taking care of your mama and Beth?"

"Grampa take me to the Alpine Slide," said Ralph, ignoring the question.

"Yeah, that's great," said Jack. "Maybe we can do that when I get home."

"Can we go to Lotsa Balls when you get home daddy?"

Jack chuckled at the mention of the miniature golf course that Ralph loved to go to. "Yeah Ralph, sure, we can go to Lotsa Balls."

"Are you coming home today, daddy?"

"No, but pretty soon Ralph. In a week maybe."

"Okay, bye daddy."

Peggy had taken over the phone. "Jack?" She sounded subdued. "They said on TV that one of your Sherpas died? And they said it was getting very dangerous for your expedition without any Sherpas left, and that you'd probably be giving up soon. Is that true?"

"No," said Jack. "We're okay." He glanced at Sophie who tried to smile. "We'll be on the summit in three days, and then we'll be coming down. Going home."

"Oh Jack," it sounded like Peggy was crying. "Why can't you just go down and come home to us?" She sniffed back her tears. "We miss you Jack. I love you Jack."

Jack had to blink away the moisture in his eyes. He was unprepared for his wife's emotion. It was apparent that it was finally sinking in to Peggy that climbing K2 was not the equivalent of a golf trip to Myrtle Beach with the boys. "Yeah, love you too," he said softly. "Be home in a few days. Have to go, battery's getting weak."

"Okay Jack." Peggy clicked off the phone.

Chapter 25

Sukey strained to hear over the wind buffeting the tent. Major Park was outside suffering another coughing fit, gasping between spasms to catch his breath. It had begun the previous evening and now Sukey was concerned about Park becoming dehydrated from expelling so much moist air from his lungs. He'd also been unable to keep any food down since breakfast that morning. Sukey was certain that the Major was in the early stage of *altitude sickness*, and with all the other climbers gone down the mountain, she feared that she might finally have to call an end to the expedition.

Park zipped up the flap behind him and crawled onto his sleeping bag. He saw the look of concern on Sukey's face. "I'm fine," he said, softly. "I'll be fine in the morning."

Sukey smiled at him in the dim light of the battery lantern. She nodded towards Park's oxygen bottle and mask sitting next to his sleeping bag. He put the mask to his face and breathed deeply for a few seconds, then turned off the regulator.

"No word from Lieutenant Cho? Or from Shin-soo?" Park asked.

Sukey didn't answer him right away. She was watching the Samsung Galaxy notebook in her lap flicker, then fade to black, her second battery now totally spent. She shrugged resignedly and looked over to Park. "No, no word yet. But I'm sure we will hear from Cho very soon. He and his men should be at the Camp 5 site by now." She looked at her watch. It was six o'clock – twelve hours since the lieutenant and his three men had left the encampment to fix the rope up the final section of the ridge and set up the last camp. "We will hear very soon, I'm sure that they are in the tent resting for the night and will be starting down tomorrow morning." But, now it was dark, the temperature below zero, and the wind was relentless. Cho and his men should have reached the end of the ridge several hours ago.

Sukey tossed the dead Note Pad to a corner of the tent. Supposedly, there was a solar charger at one of the camps, but it never revealed itself on the way up. Sukey had searched the other two tents next to theirs for the charger, finding only the squalor of several weeks' worth of food wrappers, used fuel canisters, soiled utensils, dirty clothes, and several more spent oxygen bottles. She'd called the Expedition Leader, Dong Shin-soo at basecamp and ordered him to put together a crew of soldiers to come back up the ridge, clean up the remaining camps and transport all of the excess equipment and trash back down to base camp. She knew if Yoon Jin Suk hadn't gotten sick, he would have had his troops scour the ridge all the way down and left no evidence of them being there. But, Jin Suk was gone, evacuated on the helicopter, and Shin-soo wasn't interested.

Sukey fired up the camp stove to melt more snow to fill the water bottles to keep Major Park hydrated, and to prepare at least a meager dinner of chicken soup and some noodles. At this altitude, it would take over an hour to get a pan of water. Park lay on his sleeping bag trying not to cough, occasionally going back to the oxygen for a few seconds of relief. After their supper, Sukey picked up the paperback book that Park had been reading. It was *Song Of The Sword*, a portrait of the war hero, General Lee Sun-sin, by Park's favorite author Kim Hoon. Sukey read to Park from the page where he had left off, her soft voice soon putting the major to sleep.

After a night of only two hours of fitful sleep, Sukey was up early. She set the stove to work on a pan-full of ice while she left the tent to relieve herself. The wind had died down making the zero degree temperature feel almost pleasant. It would be a good day for climbing, she told herself, if the wind stayed low and the bad weather that was predicted held off for another few days.

Major Park was sitting up putting his boots on when Sukey came back into the tent. He had put on a clean, fleece turtle-neck shirt and looked much better than he had the previous night. Sukey set about making their morning tea and pulling two rice bars from the dwindling food bag. She knew that neither of them could stomach much more for breakfast.

"How are you feeling this morning Major?" asked Sukey. "You look better than last night."

Park flashed a quick smile at her. "Yes, I am feeling much better today, Madam Suek." He looked at his watch. "We will need to leave soon," said Park. "This will be a long day."

Sukey watched him closely for a few moments, then smiled and nodded affirmatively. She reached for the Walkie-talkie. "I will call Expedition Leader Shin Soo." After numerous buzzes on the base-camp phone, Shin Soo finally answered. Sukey could tell that she'd woken him up. She told Shin Soo that they were getting ready to start up the ridge, and then just listened to the Expedition Leader for another minute before speaking again. "Yes, thank you Expedition Leader Dong Shin Soo," Sukey replied. "I will remember that." She clicked off the Walkie-talkie and looked over at Park.

"Shin Soo said that he has not heard from Lieutenant Cho. He doesn't know where they are. He feels that possibly Cho's battery is dead. But, he agrees that we need to start up quickly in order to reach Camp 5 by early evening. The weather will be cold and windy, but without precipitation."

Major Park nodded in agreement, then reached into his personal bag. He brought out a yellow plastic bottle of Bayer Aspirin, poured a dozen pills into his hand and shoveled them into his mouth. He crunched the pills with his teeth and washed them down with a half bottle of water. He tossed the bottle to Sukey who took six pills, one at a time, between bites of her rice bar and mouthfuls of water.

"Shin Soo says that we are in a good position in the race, if we can reach Camp 5 in good time to rest and hydrate. We need to be ready to go for the summit by 2:00am." Sukey recounted for Park, what Shin Soo had told her about Logan Healy's misfortune and the loss of Camp 4. Shin Soo had no news about Sophie Janot's progress but with the three Sherpas quitting the expedition, no one was giving her a chance of getting to the top at all. "But, they are wrong," said Sukey. "Sophie and Jack Finley will reach the end of the Northeast Ridge today, and will be leaving for the summit this evening."

Major Park nodded slowly. "I don't know your friends," he said softly, "But, I believe you."

Sukey looked at him and smiled. "Sophie and Jack are the two finest mountain climbers I have ever known. And, even though they have both found others, they are still very much in love – sometimes a problem, but, always a powerful force on a mountain."

Park watched her for a moment, then turned away, reaching for a food bag behind him. "Yes, I can see how that may be true Madam Suk."

Sukey thought about Expedition Leader Shin Soo's final message, a warning, which she wouldn't relate to Major Park. 'It is imperative Madam Chen Suek Yen, that you are the first to reach the summit tomorrow morning. To come in second to the American will be unacceptable. The Korean nation is depending on you.'

Yes, thank you Expedition Leader, for your kind thoughts and best wishes for a safe attempt at the summit of the world's second highest peak. Sukey shook her head in disgust and shoved the Walkie-talkie into an inside pocket of her parka. Her headache had been throbbing for two days, her knees and ankles hurt, she couldn't get a full breath of air into her lungs and she was so tired she could sleep for a week – and Park was even worse – and here they were, ready to continue up, into the *death zone* because *Korea is depending on you.* Sukey had to chuckle over Shin Soo's warning. Then, she laughed and saw that Major Park was smiling at her. Then he began laughing with her, not caring what was amusing Sukey. It just felt good to laugh, together, and Sukey was glad Major Park was with her.

They started to pack up although both would be traveling very lightly except for a spare oxygen bottle. Park sorted out the meager amount of food they would need at Camp 5 to get them to the top and back down to Camp 4. He tossed two packages of freeze-dried noodles toward Sukey for her to stow in her pack, along with two fuel canisters. He would carry the rest of the food, a coil of rope and some hardware just in case, and his bottle of water. Everything else they would need should be at Camp 5.

Park zipped up, put on his balaclava, wool hat, oxygen mask and goggles, and pulled on his parka hood, gloves and mittens. Sukey was taking her time packing, so Park went outside to put on his crampons and find his ice axe.

Sukey was packing slowly because there were things she would be taking that she didn't want Park to see. She went into her personal bag and took out clean underwear, a pair of socks, and her UCLA sweatshirt –

unnecessary clothing items to take to Camp 5, *if* they were coming back this way. But Sukey knew she wouldn't be returning to Camp 4. She would be meeting up with Jay Hamilton at the American high camp and leaving the mountain via the Abruzzi Spur. In the very likely event that she did not reach the summit before Logan Healy, Sukey knew that she would not survive the down-climb of the West Ridge in the company of Major Park. Park, she was certain, would have no trouble going back down the ridge alone, clipped to the fixed ropes all the way, and the camp sites still intact.

Sukey looked around the tent one last time to make sure she didn't leave anything she would need. She went through her personal bag and debated about a few pieces of clothing before just tossing the bag in a corner. She looked over at Park's sleeping bag and noticed his book, *Song Of The Sword*, and felt a twinge of sadness, realizing that it would be his only company on the way down the mountain.

Outside the tent, the cold air slapped Sukey rudely. She snapped on her oxygen mask, pulled her goggles down, and turned the flow dial on the regulator to fifty percent. She'd wait as long as she could before using it at full flow. Major Park placed her crampons in front of her then knelt down and tightened them onto her boots. Park stood up and looked at her.

"Are you ready Madam Suek?" He held up the palm of a mitten for a high-five.

"Let's do this," she said, pressing a padded mitten into his. She held onto his hand, and looked into his eyes behind the dark goggles. "Thank you Major," she said, releasing his hand. Park hesitated a moment before turning and starting out up the path through the snow.

Rest day at Camp 4 was turning out to be anything but, for Logan Healy. A night of tossing and turning in the thin air and bone-chilling cold, was exacerbated by the totally unexpected donkey-like snoring of Rob Page. Then, her morning sleep was destroyed by the commotion of the video crew, Bert and Arnie, squeezing into her tent. Mathias and Timmy Burns had turned them out of the other tent at first light in order to fold it up and get started on their climb up to Camp 5.

The crush of bodies, foul smells, painful snoring, and the inability to get a full breath of oxygen, was threatening to make this Logan's worst day on the mountain. All night long it had felt like a mistake to take a rest day this high on the mountain, this close to the final leg, but she knew it was the best strategy. Mathias and Timmy Burns were humping everything up to Camp 5 – the tent, sleeping bags, stove, food, and the oxygen tanks – so that she and Page wouldn't be worn out, too tired to leave for the summit at 1:00am the following morning. They would travel light tomorrow moving up to Camp 5, and the difference between carrying a 50-pound pack on your back all day on a steep pitch, and carrying a nearly empty pack, would make a world of difference on the summit push.

Logan thought about the defection of the Sherpas and how different their situation would be now if they were still there. Camp 5 would have been set up the previous day and she would be heading for the summit that evening. She would have been up and down without any exposure to the bad weather coming, and have beaten her rivals to the top by a significant margin. *And all because of the accidental death of a young Sherpa on a different expedition! Sure, Mingma Jumic and Julia-Isabelle were part of the 'curse', but, how can you possibly ignore the pure bad luck of it all?* Logan wondered if anything else could go wrong on this expedition.

Around noontime, Logan was saved from going stir crazy in the crowded tent by Bert & Arnie's suggestion that they go outside and film some *simulated* shots of Logan climbing to Camp 4 and then, discovering that the tents were gone. They sent her down the rope, in full gear, about twenty meters, then filmed her from below, and from above, changing camera positions often to give the illusion that they were filming much more of the route than they were.

Then, they had Logan reenact her discovery of the missing Camp 4 tents. Her attempts at wide-eyed looks of surprise elicited fits of laughter from the video crew and Rob Page, who had come out to direct. For one last cut, Logan craned her head forward, mouth open in shock, bent her knees and threw up her hands and shouted, "*hey, where the fuck did the tents go?*" sending everyone down to the snow in one final spasm of laughter.

313

Logan was on her knees still mugging for the camera when she saw that Bert & Arnie had stopped filming and were looking beyond her, down the snow slope. Then, she heard the footfalls in the snow and the jingle of hardware. She shook her head and rolled her eyes. "*Jesus,* can *anything* get more fucked up around here," she said, turning to see Gordie Yorke and Jay Hamilton plodding up the slope toward her, and then, obscured behind the men, came the tiny figure of Lisa Greenway.

"Going somewhere?" she asked, standing up as Yorke and Hamilton reached her. She looked directly at Jay. "Radio must be all screwed up that you guys didn't get the message about everyone going down."

Hamilton shrugged. "I need to get to Sukey, Logan. She's in trouble." Logan looked at Yorke incredulously. Then, Lisa Greenway was directly in front of her.

"Going to the top chief. This is my only chance."

Logan reached out and pulled Lisa to her in a strong hug. "Lisa, Lisa, why are you doing this to me?"

Lisa pulled back and smiled at Logan. "Not many women have climbed this mountain and survived it. That would be a real accomplishment." She shrugged. "I'm so close."

The three climbers walked past Logan, up to the camp site and dropped their packs heavily onto the snow next to the tent. Logan was glad to see that they had at least arrived with full packs and had brought a tent along.

Logan recognized the resolve in their voices and knew that a high-altitude scream-fest wasn't going to settle anything. She recognized the *summit fever* in Yorke and Lisa, and she'd get Jay alone to get the whole story on Sukey, but for now she'd just let it go. She'd turn Lisa over to Mathias, and Yorke was on his own. But, she did have some leadership duties to attend to. She walked up the slope to where Bert & Arnie were getting some long-lens shots of Mathias and Timmy Burns, who would emerge and disappear in the white haze far above them.

"Time for you guys to pack up and head down," said Logan, thrusting a thumb toward basecamp. This is high enough, and it's getting a little too crowded up here."

Bert & Arnie looked at each other, as if trying to decide who should speak. Bert finally looked up at Logan. "No, I, um, I think we're going to go higher," he said. "We're doing fine, and there's a lot more filming to be done. We'll be okay."

Logan gazed around them at all their equipment, and then she looked up the mountain to where she knew the summit was hidden behind the clouds. She shrugged. Resigned to the situation. "Okay, okay," she said softly. "Just stay out of my way."

The Motorola phone on Marty Gallagher's desk blinked and crackled. "We found it chief! We got the camera."

Gallagher grabbed the Walkie-Talkie and pressed the green button. "You're shitting me! Really? You got it?"

"We found the tent, and everything looks good inside," said the OSN camera man.

"Unbelievable," said Gallagher. "Hold on. Let me see if I can find you."

Gallagher pulled on his parka, grabbed the huge Navy binoculars from a hook on the wall and left the OSN trailer. He trained the long glasses on a spot about a third of the way up Broad Peak standing a half mile due east of the base camp. Gallagher struggled to hold the binoculars steady while still holding the Motorola in one hand. Then he found them – the camera man and the two Hunza high altitude porters who had climbed up with him. They were all waving their arms in the air. Gallagher laughed, then had to lower the heavy binoculars. "That's outstanding! Great job," he said loudly into the phone. "Get the fresh batteries in and when you're ready, we'll test the picture."

Finally, some good news to relay to Glenda! And just in time. Gallagher knew that tomorrow morning was when everyone would be trying for the summit, and there could be some excellent footage to be had from the Broad Peak camera if the clouds stayed off the mountain. The camera position was only about 1,000 meters up from the base camp on the glacier but it offered a perfect shot of the upper reaches of K2 and the end of the Northeast Ridge, if not the summit itself. And they didn't need much of a video – a couple of black dots against the white snow would be gold at this point!

Gallagher tucked the Motorola in his coat pocket and raised the binoculars to try to find the camera position once again when he heard a familiar sound from behind him. It was the dull whap, whap, whap, of the long blades of the Zermatt helicopter from far down the glacier, returning to base camp. *More good news!* The helicopter had been held up in Skardu for several days by intermittent high winds preventing the delivery of the much needed diesel fuel for the generators, and just as important, the draft beer and wine resupply, and most critically, the toilet paper, which the camp was completely out of.

The giant helicopter was still a long way down the glacier, making it hard for Gallagher to pick it out against the gray boulders and overlapping mountainsides. He held up the binoculars with two hands to watch the airship lumbering up the chasm, riding a little lower than usual, he thought. The wind was swirling and gusting, as always, and Gallagher thought he heard a faint change in the pitch of the rotor blades cutting through the thin air. Then, Bruce Kinder was standing next to him, manning a camera himself, trained on the incoming helicopter.

"Finally a shot with some noise and some action," said Kinder. Gallagher nodded with approval. *Sometimes Kinder surprised him.*

The two men stood watching as the huge helicopter lumbered up the glacier toward them, now, about a quarter of a mile out. Suddenly, a plume of gray smoke went up from the forward engine and the CH47 turned slightly sideways revealing the giant Zermatt logo emblazoned along the side. The smoke disappeared in a gust of wind that took the ship out over the south moraine of the glacier, still coming toward them, straightened out now, but riding much lower in the front. Gallagher and Kinder began walking slowly forward, sensing impending disaster, their eyes riveted on the approaching aircraft.

"Keep it rolling Bruce," said Gallagher, just as the front rotor clipped an outcropping of boulders and the scene suddenly changed into a crescendo of mayhem, ungodly noise and the sickening sound and smell of destruction. Smoke, dust and metal shards flew through the air. The men fell defensively to their knees and watched as the nose of the helicopter dug into the crust of the glacier, banging and screeching toward them, plowing through the snow covered boulders, rocks and sediment. Two hundred yards away from them, the smoking wreckage finally came to a stop. The wind quickly cleared away the smoke and dust, revealing that the two rotor blades were gone as was the nose of the ship and all the cockpit windows.

"Holy shit!" said Gallagher, coming to his feet and starting out again toward the wreckage. "Where are the pilots?" He began running up the glacier followed by Kinder trying in vain to hold the camera steady.

Billows of black smoke from the rear of the wreckage slowed Gallagher's advance as he suddenly recalled the thousand gallons of diesel fuel for the generators. Seeing the black smoke, Kinder had already stopped to steady his camera for what he knew would be the *money shot* of this segment. Then, from the side of the fuselage, a figure jumped from the open door, not bothering with the fold-out stairway. The man went back to the opening and helped the other pilot down to the glacier. Marty Gallagher was relieved to see the powder blue uniforms of the Pakistani pilots as they ran toward him. The second pilot out of the ship also wore a red turban and, aided by the first pilot, ran with a limp. The pilots were moving as fast as they could over the boulder-strewn glacier while shouting something that Gallagher couldn't make out. But, from their hand gestures, it was clear that Gallagher and Kinder needed to retreat quickly.

"Get back!" Gallagher yelled to Kinder, then ran forward to help with the second pilot who was limping badly. When he reached the pilots, Gallagher saw that the red turban was actually a white silk scarf, now saturated with blood, wrapped around the man's head.

The first explosion was probably the helicopter's aft fuel tank and nearly blew Gallagher and the pilots off their feet. They all turned to look and saw the rear rotor tower disintegrate in a billowing orange and black ball of flames. The noise was deafening, making Gallagher immediately fear that the explosion would cause avalanches on the mountain.

The men kept scrambling as best they could over the irregular surface, back toward the base camp, encouraged by the alarm in the voices of the pilots telling them to move. The pilots knew what was coming. The explosion of the second fuel tank obliterated the front section of the fuselage and what was left of the nose and cockpit, sending a ball of flame a hundred feet into the air. A few seconds later came the grand finale as the twin five-hundred gallon diesel fuel tanks, bolted temporarily into the ship's midsection, exploded in a thunderous roar that shook the glacier under the fleeing men's feet and sent a wave of hot air rushing past them. Sky rockets of burning metal soared hundreds of feet in the air leaving contrails of white smoke as they rained down upon the glacier. Gallagher and the pilots covered their heads with their arms as they continued to run, while Bruce Kinder had dropped to his knees to hold the camera focused on the incredible show behind them. This, he knew, would be his finest moment of the expedition.

Dozens of people from the base camp were running toward them. Others stood with cell phones held high, recording what was left of the disaster. Eric Chen came with his medical bag and relieved Gallagher of his support of the wounded pilot. Then Morris O'Dell was next to him.

"No one else in the chopper, right?" O'Dell asked of anyone who was listening.

The first Pakistani pilot shook his head. "No. Only us," he said, "and the toilet paper."

Marty Gallagher headed straight for the OSN trailer and his console to check out the footage that Kinder had shot. He saw a download ready from the Broad Peak cameraman who had also captured the whole episode. In spite of the seriousness of the disaster, Gallagher was giddy with excitement when he assembled all of the video. It was incredible stuff. And, only OSN had it. Gallagher got busy on the satellite uplink to New York.

At nine in the morning, Glenda Craft was hosting a party in her office for OSN upper management. A bottle of champagne was opened as they watched, for the third time, the orange and red flames and black smoke of their very own *Hindenburg Disaster* billowing across the huge flat screen on her office wall. The hour-long special that evening would break all OSN ratings records!

And a hundred miles away, another celebration was taking place, in the hills and villages around Askole, Pakistan, where the Balti porters who hadn't worked that summer and didn't know how they were going to make it through the winter, thanked the mountain Gods for destroying the flying bus that had taken away their livelihood.

Chapter 26

Jack, Sophie and Carlos looked down at the red tent collapsed at their feet as if they were saying goodbye to an old friend. Inside the tightly zipped tent were two sleeping bags, the extra camp stove, a battery lantern, some fuel canisters, half a bag of food and a bag of trash they'd generated during their brief stay at Camp 3. All of it expendable weight they couldn't afford to carry any farther. Sophie felt guilty about violating one of the basic tenets of *alpine style climbing* – what you bring up the mountain, you take down the mountain. But, the loss of the Sherpas on the already undermanned expedition mandated some changes they would just have to live with. They also wouldn't be coming back this way. The Northeast Ridge was a one-way trip.

On some mountains, you could count on enterprising porters to come up at the end of the season or the beginning of the next to glean off abandoned equipment, but not here. Not high on the Northeast Ridge. This was a site beyond the reach of the Balti porters who might come to K2 with next year's expeditions. So here it would all remain, undisturbed – for several years probably – until another well-heeled expedition of experienced climbers came along, to be thrilled by the discovery of the third camp site of the *2010 Sophie Janot Expedition.*

They set off at first light, knowing this would be their most difficult day on the ridge so far. They had a long way to go – a mile and a half – to reach the spot at the high end of the ridge where they would establish the final camp. At Camp 4, Jack and Sophie would share the lightweight, two-person tent that Jack had gotten from the Zermatt expedition's stores, while Carlos would continue to climb higher, another two hours on his own, up to the Abruzzi Spur where he would clip onto the Zermatt fixed rope and descend the short distance to the Zermatt high camp. Jack and Sophie would rest, and sleep if they could, rehydrate and eat as much as they could stomach at Camp 4, and then start their twelve-hour climb to the summit at midnight, hoping to reach the summit before noontime. No one was certain when the bad weather would hit, but they needed to be well on their way down the Abruzzi spur when it did.

Sophie paused for a deep breath and watched Carlos, twenty meters out in front of her – methodical, sure footed, determined to set a good pace, as he always did. *Yes, Carlos knew how important it was to get through this leg of the journey as quickly as possible.* The plan was Carlos' idea – the only way, it seemed, for Jack and Sophie to reach Camp 4, without being exhausted from carrying all the equipment they'd abandoned at Camp 3. They needed to be as well-rested as possible for the ordeal they would undertake that night. It wasn't the plan that Sophie had drawn up originally – she, and Jack, were both concerned about Carlos' two hours of additional exposure at the end of the day's climb – but now that they were here, with no Sherpas and no support climbers, it felt like the only plausible way to be able to make a summit bid. Carlos had assured them that he would have no difficulty continuing on to the Zermatt fixed rope. So, they were embarking on a true *Alpine style* assault on an 8,000 meter summit, with deteriorating weather approaching, and no option of turning around. Sophie swallowed back her fears and started out in quick time after Carlos to maintain slack in the rope.

It was a long way to Camp 4, on much more vertical terrain than they had encountered on the ridge so far. With no fixed ropes and a great deal of unstable snow ahead, it would be their most treacherous day on the mountain. They needed to be careful, and above all, alert to the dangers ahead – not all of it underfoot. Today, the altitude would become the biggest hazard of the climb. They would be going much higher, advancing into the dangerously thin supply of oxygen that would slow their legs and arms, their blood flow and thought processes, and their judgement – everything they relied upon for their safety.

Jack was confident because he knew that this was the kind of climbing he and Sophie excelled at. They had been here before, many times, and knew that they could perform at an altitude that would debilitate most of the earth's population. They were special. At a clinic in Switzerland years ago, they'd learned that their heart and lung capacities were far beyond the norm, and their red blood cell count was in the ninety-fifth percentile. And, they had trained their bodies to adapt to the deprivation ahead. They would be fine. But, Jack wasn't as confident in Carlos. While Sophie had vouched for him completely, Carlos had never been as high as they would be going today, and without supplemental oxygen. Jack had seen strong climbers come apart quickly at 8,000 meters – some at much lower heights – and knew that he would have to watch Carlos closely, because today their lives would depend on each other.

The day began in a gray soup of crystalline fog. Not so much a sign of an incoming front as of simply the mountain producing a bit of its own weather – as the Himalaya were famous for and K2 in particular. It would clear up gradually as the sun crept higher, but for another few hours they would see none of the spectacular vista of the Tibetan plain to the north or the neighboring peaks of the Karakorums to the south. They would also see very little of the ridge ahead beyond thirty meters, nor the towering summit cone of K2 looming ominously in the distance.

The first few hours of the climb were uneventful and productive. The temperature stayed close to zero, but with virtually no wind – a blessing they knew they couldn't count on continuing – it was an excellent day for climbing and they made steady progress through the deep snow. On this section of the ridge, they weren't concerned with the lack of fixed ropes, but they did rope together for protection. Carlos was in the lead position – as he preferred to be – followed by Sophie, twenty meters behind him, and then Jack. Jack wanted to be in the rear on this stage of the climb, where he could observe his companions ahead and be vigilant for a fall or for an avalanche off the crest of the ridge, and could quickly establish a belaying position.

They made good progress in the deep, but light powder snow, although, all of the climbers knew that the conditions they were currently encountering would be the easiest of the day. This was where they needed to set their fastest pace, but, it seemed that the pace of Carlos and Sophie was proving to be a bit quicker than Jack's. Several times, the slack on the rope between Sophie and Jack disappeared, ending with a slight tug on Jack's harness. He would wave to Sophie and take a few longer, quicker strides to put the rope at ease again. Sophie would watch for a few seconds, letting some slack build up, before resuming her march. She was concerned about Jack's lack of pace. It wasn't like him. He was always the *fastest* marcher on a trail, not the slowest. Maybe, Jack's three-year layoff from climbing was affecting him more than he let on.

At noontime, they stopped for a rest, food and water break. They'd been climbing steadily for four hours and had done well. They could see, however, that the trail ahead would soon get steeper, and the snow deeper. It would be the next five hours that would determine whether or not Sophie's bid for the summit in a straight shot from Camp 4, starting late that evening, would be possible.

With their ice axes pushed deep into the snow as anchors, the three climbers sat in the snow just down from the crest on the south side of the ridge. It appeared to be a more stable section of snow than the steeper north side, although they had little fear of avalanches this close to the crest. It was the reason climbers had always sought out ridges as the safest routes up a mountain. While the massive drifts of snow could always release and slide away down the mountain, the danger was much less than on the wide faces of the mountain where cliffs of ice and snow could give way without warning, burying everything in its path. Avalanches had long been the primary source of mountain climbing fatalities, and the cause of most of the multiple-death tragedies in the long history of mountaineering.

Sophie sipped steadily at her water bottle until she'd consumed half of it, then pulled out an energy bar. Jack sat a few yards away, resting. Carlos had taken out his camera – never one to miss a photographic opportunity – now that the dull sunlight had dissolved the icy mist they'd been climbing in. No one was in a very talkative mood, which was normal at the higher altitudes.

"You okay Jack?" said Sophie, breaking the silence. Jack just looked over at her and smiled. "You've been pulling at the rope all morning." At this, Carlos looked away from his camera toward Jack, concerned that there might be a problem.

Jack shook his head. "No, I'm fine. Just daydreaming in the back, that's all. A little boring back there." Carlos went back to his photography, and Sophie took a bite of her energy bar.

"Well you're going to lead when we get up to the cliffs," said Sophie. "Your kind of climbing, right Jack?"

Jack grinned and nodded. "That's why I'm here boss." He downed an energy bar in two bites and pulled his water bottle from his pack. He was looking forward to the last two hours of the climb, before they reached the main body of the mountain. It was more vertical terrain up through rock and ice and patches of snow that would require some higher-level technical climbing and route-finding expertise, as well as the judicious placement of the few anchors they'd afforded themselves, along with the fixing of short lengths of rope for Sophie and Carlos to follow. Jack was confident that he would get his second wind, and perform better on the more challenging terrain.

Carlos was on his feet, anxious to get started again. He reached down to help Sophie to her feet. "How are your toes Sophie?" Carlos asked.

Jack couldn't help but take note. The question revealed an intimacy in the knowledge of Sophie's propensity for frostbite.

Sophie smiled at Carlos as she came to her feet and pulled her ice ax from the snow. "They are fine Carlos. My toes are good when I can keep walking. So... on we go. Oui?"

Carlos grinned. "Oui Sophie, nous allons de suite." He pulled his pack onto his back and started out up the ridge. Sophie and Jack prepared to follow.

They had separated by only a few meters when they were stunned by the other-worldly sound of the first explosion of the helicopter down on the glacier. The second explosion came seconds later, and then the full blast of the twin tanks of diesel fuel, which seemed to reverberate throughout the mountains. The three climbers dropped instinctively to their knees.

Jack could see small rivulets of snow begin to run down the sides of the ridge, and immediately raced up the short distance to the top and slid over onto the north side of the ridge. He pushed his axe as far as it would go into the snow and wound the rope tightly around the head of the axe. Jack crawled back up to the crest of the ridge to where he could see that Sophie and Carlos had also belayed the rope around their axes. Then, they waited.

Across the valley, on Broad Peak, a large serac close to the summit cone slowly crumpled and brought down a major avalanche, rumbling noisily through the north face. A snow cloud engulfed the bottom half of the mountain obscuring several more lesser avalanches that could be heard coming down behind it. On K2, a half dozen slides could be seen rolling down the steep slopes visible from the Northeast Ridge, including a good sized one coming down on top of the end of the ridge itself. Ahead of them on the ridge, a large snow mass straddling the ridge, slowly disappeared down each side revealing the sharp crest of the ridge for twenty or thirty meters. This section of the route would now be much safer and quicker to pass through. A plume of black smoke appeared, rising over the southeast flank of K2 that blocked their view of the glacier where the Zermatt base camp would be located. The smoke would come into view and then quickly dissipate in the wind blowing down the glacier.

The three climbers sat still in the snow for another ten minutes waiting and watching – watching the snow on K2 and Broad Peak, and on the ridge ahead and behind them, trying to ascertain the impact of this strange, new occurrence that none of them had ever before experienced in the mountains. The buzz of the Walkie-Talkie in an inside pocket of Sophie's parka suddenly broke the silence.

"Oui, docteur Clement, nous sommes très bien." Sophie conversed in French for several minutes, then tucked the phone back inside her parka.

"The big Zermatt helicopter has crashed, several hundred meters east of the base camp," Sophie said somberly. "The pilots escaped. No one was injured." Sophie stood up and pulled her ax from the snow and unwound the rope. "Clement and Janot, they say we have to now abandon the climb and return, back down the ridge. The snow will be too perilous, they say."

Jack turned and looked back at the seemingly endless ridge behind them, three and a half miles of perilous climbing that they had spent the last two weeks overcoming – a major accomplishment in itself. They could probably make it back to Camp 3, before dark, Jack surmised, but then what? Three more days, minimum, on the ridge with foul weather coming and no Sherpas or support climbers and no fixed ropes, which would have all been taken up by the retreating climbers behind them, and very little food or fuel left. No, retreat was not an option.

Sophie turned and gazed up toward the summit of K2. She concentrated on the huge line of overhanging seracs that reached out from the summit – the signature characteristic of K2 – ominous, frightening, deadly, hanging over the beginning of the infamous *traverse*, the final technical obstacle to overcome before reaching the summit snow field. Every so often – sometimes a year, two, or three years apart, sections of the serac would crumble sending massive blocks of ice and snow, the size of a three-story building, crashing down the mountain destroying everything in its path. As it had two years earlier, resulting in the deaths of eleven climbers in one of the most tragic days of K2's perilous history. Sophie wondered if the blast had weakened the structure of the serac, which they would be passing under tomorrow morning.

She looked back at Carlos and Jack. "Clement also says that Logan is now half-way to their high camp, and will be going to the top tonight. So, on we go boys! Aye?" Sophie's voice sang with optimism. She laughed. "Allez, allez!"

"Si, si. Vamos!" said Carlos starting up the ridge once again.

Jack grinned at Sophie. "Okay boss. On we go."

Logan Healy looked up the rope and watched Gordie Yorke, forty meters above her, pulling himself very ably up and over a steep pitch, followed twenty meters back by Lisa Greenway who was proving to be a much more competent climber than Logan had thought. Somewhere above Yorke and Lisa, Rob Page was leading this leg of the climb. Maybe it wasn't such a bad thing, Logan mused, having more climbers participating on the final push. There was a certain comfort in numbers, and in having more activity above and below her. It felt more like a normal expedition again. She looked down the rope for any sign of Jay Hamilton, who, she knew, would be a long way behind. Logan spoke into the microphone in her collar. "Jay, how are you doing back there?"

It took a worrisome few moments before she heard Hamilton's voice. "Fine Logan. No problems. Making good time."

"Good, Jay," Logan responded. "Just make sure you ..."

The first two explosions, in rapid succession stunned her to silence. The massive one that followed, the loudest sound she'd ever heard in the Himalaya, made her jump causing her to lose her footing on the slope and briefly hang loose on the fixed rope. She quickly regained her footing and spun around to look down toward the glacier where black smoke was billowing into the air far below her. Then, snow was falling on her helmet and shoulders and she was engulfed in a white cloud descending around her. Logan instinctively pulled herself close to the vertical rock wall next to her where she was able to avoid most of the snow coming down. "Pull in close Jay," she said into her collar microphone, "there's some snow coming down."

A minute later the snow stopped running and her radio speaker began crackling with voices. "Everyone okay up there?" Jay Hamilton yelled. "I think the helicopter crashed!"

Logan swung away from the rock face and strained to look up the rope. "Lisa, Lisa, are you okay?" she tried not to sound hysterical. Then she saw Lisa, twenty meters above her, also in a protected position, hugging close to the wall and the fixed rope. Fortunately, they were in a vertical chimney section of a long gulley that offered protection from the falling snow.

"Yes, yes," said Lisa finally. "I'm fine, but I can't see Yorke. Gordie, are you there? He was quite a ways above me."

Logan could see that the gulley above Lisa was still covered by a cloud of snow. "Yorke, Yorke, can you hear me?" Silence. "Lisa, get up there as quick as you can. Find Yorke. I'm right behind you." Logan began scrambling up the slope as fast as she could climb, not even bothering with her ascender, dragging it along the fixed rope next to her.

Rob Page, who was leading the climb and was far above Gordie Yorke came on the radio. "I think Yorke got hit. I'm on my way down."

Logan caught up to Lisa Greenway who was now pulling the fixed rope out of the several feet of new snow that covered the route. They were in a chute on a less vertical section of the gulley where the snow had collected over what looked like a thirty or forty meter length. "Lisa, hurry! We've got to find him." Lisa was moving up the slope as quickly as she could, working hard to pull the fixed rope out of the snow. There was a lot of slack in the fixed rope here because of the less vertical terrain.

Logan couldn't wait. Although she knew it was nearly suicidal, she unclipped her carabiner from the fixed rope and bounded up the snow mass, going around Lisa. If the snow started sliding, Logan would have no protection from riding the avalanche down to the steeper section just below them, before being hurtled on a two mile tumble to her death. She raced up the slope beyond Lisa and plunged her arm deep into the snow, pulling up the fixed rope. She continued another ten meters up the snow mass, where she found Yorke's sling, attached to the rope. "I've got him!," she called out to Lisa right behind her. "I've got his..." Then the end of Yorke's sling, that should have been attached to his climbing harness, came up out of the snow. "Ah, *fuck, no!"* cried Logan, throwing the sling onto the snow. She jumped frantically down the slope, trying to estimate where Yorke would have ended up after being torn from his sling. She began digging madly into the snow with her hands, amazed again at how quickly avalanche snow becomes hard-packed and icy. Lisa was digging into the snow farther down the slope. "Yorke! Yorke! Can you hear me?" Logan cried into her collar microphone. "Can you move anything? Show us where you are!"

"God, I hope his oxygen mask stayed on," said Lisa, pulling snow away with two hands like a dog digging a hole.

"It's his only chance," said Logan, knowing they were well beyond the two minutes normally considered the limit to saving an avalanche victim.

Suddenly there was a movement in the snow mid-way between the two women. A mound pushed up, followed by the ghost-white fingers of a gloveless hand. Logan leapt forward, grabbed the hand and began frantically excavating around it. Then, Rob Page jumped into the snow next to her, wildly pulling snow away from around Yorke's arm and torso, trying to find his head.

It took the three climbers another excruciating two minutes to get Yorke free and sitting up. Page took Yorke's helmet and oxygen mask off to examine him. It took a while before Yorke could talk coherently, but apart from a severely frostbitten left hand and a sore back and neck, he seemed uninjured otherwise. For ten minutes, the climbers all sat unmoving in the snow, breathing deeply and resting after the exertion of the frantic rescue. Logan watched Yorke closely. His face was still contorted and flushed from his exhausting escape. Logan thought about the crashed helicopter down on the glacier, and the avalanche that had come so close to killing one of her climbers. *Maybe the Sherpas were right. Maybe the expedition was cursed.* She gazed up toward where the summit cone was obscured in the clouds, and knew she had to get this climb done with as soon as possible.

After drinking half of his water bottle, Yorke got slowly to his feet, unsteadily at first. Lisa Greenway took off her extra sling and clipped him back onto the fixed rope.

"Thanks guys," said Yorke, "that was a little scary" He took his helmet from Rob Page and looked up the mountain. "So then, let's get cracking here, as you Brits say," said Yorke. "Long way up to Camp 5 still."

Logan stepped in front of Yorke and looked up at his face. It was still bright red from his struggle under the snow. She shook her head. "No, I don't think so Gordie. It's over for you this trip." She tried to smile. "Sorry."

Yorke took a deep breath and grimaced from the pain in his back. He nodded in agreement. "Yeah, I know," he said softly, knowing that he would probably never again get this close to the summit of K2.

Rob Page unclipped a spare mitten from inside his parka and gave it to Yorke. "Sorry mate. You need to get down and see if the good doctor can save a couple of those fingers tips. You're all done here, and, unfortunately, so am I." Page looked at Logan. "I'll take him down. Camp 4 tonight, and then all the way tomorrow."

"Thanks Rob," said Logan. She hugged Page. "Next time," she said softly.

Logan embraced Yorke. "Sorry Gordie, it's the only thing to do."

"Yeah, I know." He gazed up toward the summit once more. "Hate to miss all the fun though. Good luck tonight. Climb safely."

Logan and Lisa said their farewells to Gordie Yorke and Rob Page, and continued up to Camp 5, followed by Jay Hamilton.

Albie Mathias and Timmy Burns had prepared a meager dinner and melted plenty of water by the time Logan, Lisa and Jay reached Camp 5, an hour behind schedule. Logan immediately called down to Morris O'Dell to tell him that Yorke and Page were on their way down. O'Dell gave her the news on the helicopter crash, which she passed on to the group, relieved that there were no casualties.

At dinner, Logan announced the schedule for that night's summit bid. She would be leaving for the summit at 1:00am – by herself – followed an hour later by Jay and Lisa, accompanied part way by Alby Mathias, to just below the *bottleneck.* Bert and Arnie, the video crew, were on their own. Logan would have preferred that Jay and Lisa wait until the following night for their summit climb, but with bad weather coming in, they also had to go up that night. But, Logan didn't want to be burdened or distracted by anyone else climbing with her who wouldn't be able to keep up. She was going to make a fast dash to the summit, and then a fast, one day, run down the mountain to begin to deal with the wreckage at base camp. At seven o'clock, Logan, Jay and Lisa were in their sleeping bags, trying unsuccessfully to get just an hour or two of sleep.

Chapter 27

It was dark and windy and the cold felt like it was freezing Sukey's body from the inside out. Up ahead, Major Park was moving slowly, unsure of where the fixed rope was leading them. They'd been climbing increasingly steeper terrain for the past two hours and now they seemed to have left the ridge and the trail established by the soldiers. The rope had a great deal of slack in it – probably due to Lieutenant Cho running short of anchors – and now they were struggling to follow the route up to the last camp. Sukey had turned her oxygen regulator up to full flow to help combat her shivering, with little relief. It was too late in the day and they needed to find shelter very soon.

Around noontime, Sukey and Major Park had finally run into Lieutenant Cho and his men on their way down from Camp 5. The soldiers were out of supplemental oxygen and looked to be in a bad state. One of the soldiers had taken a fall while leading a steep pitch, putting in the fixed rope, and had a badly damaged shoulder. His arm was wrapped tightly to his body with rope. Their radio batteries were dead, and they informed Sukey and Park, that there was no more fuel or food at the high camp. But, there were two full oxygen bottles, and sleeping bags, waiting for them.

Major Park was furious and screamed at Cho, asking him how they expected Sukey and him to get back down after they'd gone to the summit. Cho was having so much trouble breathing and talking that he paid little mind to Park's rant. He needed to get his men down to Camp 4 as quickly as possible, he said, and Sukey and Park needed to continue up to Camp 5. It was a long and very difficult climb, he warned them. Sukey stepped between Cho and Park and thanked Cho for all his hard work and gave him a brief hug.

When the soldiers resumed their climb down, Sukey reassured Major Park that they would be okay. They had enough food and fuel in their packs. Then, she called Dong Shin-soo at basecamp to let him know that Lt. Cho and his men were on their way down and were going to need assistance very soon. She instructed Shin-soo to borrow oxygen from the Americans and send it up the mountain, along with more fuel and food, as quickly as possible. Cho and his men may not survive the climb down the ridge, she told him, especially if the weather got worse. She was also thinking about Major Park's descent, alone, the following day. Expedition Leader Shin-soo, she could tell, had little interest in anything she was asking for. He did not take orders from women.

Now, Sukey was concerned for her own life. Her fingers and toes had been numb for a dangerously long time; it was four o'clock in the afternoon, and she and Major Park were stumbling along much too slowly in the failing light, unsure of how far they had to go to reach Camp 5. Under any other conditions, they would turn back at this point. This, she knew, was how people died on 8,000 meter mountains. But they had no other option than to go on.

Sukey pulled hard on her ascender, attached to the fixed rope to get over an ice-covered boulder, and bumped into Major Park. He was standing on a small ledge peering straight up, trying to see where the vertically hanging rope disappeared to above them on a formidable granite buttress that looked to rise up at least twenty meters into the dark gray sky.

"Oh, no," said Sukey, following his gaze. "I don't know if I can do this Major."

"Yes, yes, you can, Madam Suek," said Park. "You must."

"My hands and feet are frozen. I'm..."

"We have to continue!" Park said loudly, startling Sukey. Park bent over at the waist and pulled off his oxygen mask to allow him to cough several times and to spit a ball of phlegm into the snow. He affixed his mask and attached a second ascender and sling to the fixed ropes. Park pulled a sling from Sukey's harness and clipped it to the rope. "Once we get over this, we should have only one more hour to the camp," said Park. "Now, we must climb!"

As Park readied himself to go up the rope, Sukey saw that he was breathing hard and that the gauge on the oxygen bottle protruding from his pack showed only ten percent remaining. She chastised herself for complaining. Major Park was sick and in obvious distress but forging on, risking his life, for the sole purpose of getting her to the summit. Sukey put her boot into the stirrup of one of her slings, wrapped one arm around the rope, and pushed upward behind Major Park. She prayed that Lieutenant Cho had put in solid anchors on the buttress above her.

The afternoon weather on the Northeast Ridge had resumed its usual bad disposition, as if to punish the climbers for the benevolent conditions they had enjoyed all morning. *Windy Gap*, a few miles up the glacier to the northeast, was once again living up to its name, sending powerful gusts across the length of the ridge, throwing clouds of icy spindrift a hundred feet in the air, blinding and pelting the climbers with needles of bone chilling cold.

Jack Finley pulled on his ice ax and thrust himself up and over the final rib of the ice cliff that was the last serious obstacle on the Northeast Ridge. He had led the exhausting vertical climb for the last two hours, and now he badly needed to rest. The thin air made every step a major exertion, requiring a complete stop to gain three or four deep breaths before continuing. Before he could drop onto the snow to rest, he needed to secure this section of the rope for Sophie and Carlos coming up behind him. Jack scraped the ice from his goggles, turned his back- pack toward the wind for protection, and put in his last ice screw to anchor the rope. He looked out over the cliff below him and waved to Carlos, who had been waiting patiently in the freezing wind far below him. Jack couldn't see Sophie, but knew that she would be huddled down in a protected spot, trying to avoid the twenty-below-zero temperature that came with the wind, wiggling her fingers and toes as best she could.

With the rope secure and his companions on their way up, Jack sat down on the snow and pulled his legs up toward his chest, trying to breathe. His headache had been pounding all afternoon, his fingers and toes were numb. They needed to find shelter and cook some water. After a few minutes, he got to his feet and looked down the cliff. He didn't want Sophie and Carlos to see how poorly he was doing.

When Sophie and Carlos arrived on the snow slope above the cliff, Jack pulled up and re-coiled the rope over his shoulder. Without any breath-consuming discussion, they moved up the slope fifty meters to a spot they all recognized as the most protected site for their last brief encampment. At the base of a short wall, in deep snow, they carved out a snow cave to protect their small tent from the wind.

Sophie wanted Carlos to wait until they had melted a pan of snow to replenish his water bottle before leaving on the final leg of his climb up to the Abruzzi Spur and the Zermatt fixed rope, but Carlos was anxious to get going with darkness closing in. The route up to the Spur was straight forward, up a fairly benign snow slope, and shouldn't present much of a challenge, but climbing in deep snow, alone, in the dark at this altitude was always cause for worry. The distance wasn't great – only around two hundred meters – but stopping for several seconds after every two steps to gain enough oxygen, would make it a slow, laborious final trek.

Sophie and Jack emptied the meager amounts of water they had left into Carlos's bottle, and then said their goodbyes. Sophie had tears in her eyes as they hugged – she and Carlos had been through a lot together over the last two months, beginning with the trek in to Gasherbrum in June. There wasn't a lot to say now though, and this wasn't the place for long conversations.

"Me encanta a Sophie", said Carlos softly. He released Sophie and embraced Jack. "Take care of her Jack, and yourself."

"Call me when you are on the fixed rope," said Sophie. Carlos had already turned on his head lamp and started out. He raised a hand in acknowledgement.

Sophie laughed when she saw how small the folded out tent was. "My god, Jack, we will have to be married before we get into this together." They both laughed. But the tent fabric was surprisingly resistant to the wind, and in the snow cave, it provided enough protection to allow them the get the stove lit and start melting snow. At this higher altitude, it took an interminably long time to melt just one pan of water, during which they had to leave the tent flap partially open to exhaust the stove.

While Sophie tended to the water, Jack took off her boots and started massaging her numb toes. He could feel through her socks the several toes that were shorter than they should have been. Sophie grimaced from the pain of Jack's strong hands. "That one was from Cho, this year," she said. "It hurt for a long time afterward." She smiled at Jack to hide the pain of his massaging. "I read once, a story about Herzog, that after Annapurna he had lost so many toes he had to have the others amputated to allow him to walk."

"It's true," said Jack.

"Maybe I will have that done also," said Sophie. She chuckled. "I will look funny on the beach with the girls. And maybe I won't swim so fast then."

Jack smiled at her. The tent was in darkness now, illuminated only by the flickering light of the stove flame. "I don't think you'll get to that point."

Sophie poured a pan of water into one of the plastic bottles and secured the top. She reached the pan out of the tent flap, filled it with snow and returned it to the stove. She seemed content to leave the discussion of her toes.

Jack watched her tending to the stove as he massaged. "That was a hard climb, the others told me. You haven't said much about Cho."

Sophie stared into the snow that was slowly melting in the pan, without responding. Finally, she shrugged and pulled off her wool cap, letting her hair fall about her face. "Cho was... it was not a climb I'm very proud of. On Cho, I should have died. I deserved to die there, but... I was more fortunate than..." – her voice tailed off – "than I deserved."

"In the avalanche?" said Jack. "That was a remarkable..."

"No, no, Jack. Not the avalanche. On the way down, after I summited. I had stayed too long at the top... maybe twenty or thirty minutes there, at least, with bad weather arriving. A hypothermic trance, I think. I could have easily died on the summit." She winced as Jack started massaging her other foot, still watching Sophie's face.

"On the way down, the snow came and it was blinding and so cold... and I was lost. I knew then that I would die there. So, I just sat down in the snow... and I went to sleep and dreamed about my girls. I gave up."

Jack slowly massaged her foot, watching her. He didn't know what to say. He'd had no idea how difficult the Cho climb had been.

"Then the storm stopped, and I woke up. A miracle. I was able to get to my feet, and made it down to the ice cliff and found the fixed rope... another miracle."

Sophie went quiet for several minutes and Jack didn't press her. Then she resumed her story. "I made it down to the high camp, but... Victor was gone – he'd left me a note – he knew he needed to get lower. He knew he was suffering from HACE." In the darkness, Sophie sniffed away her tears.

"It happens in the mountains, Sophie," said Jack. "It wasn't your fault."

"Of course it was my fault," said Sophie calmly. We should have gone straight down after the avalanche, but Victor insisted – he was thinking only about me. And then, I was thinking only about me also. Since I began this foolish quest, everything has been only about me."

"Victor did what he came here..."

Sophie ignored him. "And now Victor is dead. And now Janbu is dead, because of me. And Julia is dead also – that sweet little girl – because she came to this place to see me, and then I agreed with her mother against the doctor's wishes, and I killed her too. I killed all of them." Sophie sat up abruptly to fill another bottle of water.

"Sophie, none of that was your..."

"It doesn't matter now Jack." Sophie busied herself with reaching out of the tent for another pan of snow. "We need to make our dinner and eat as much as we can, and then sleep for a while. And then, I need to get to the top of this mountain, so..." She left her sentence in the darkness between them.

After they'd eaten as much of the freeze-dried stew as they could stomach, drained and refilled their water bottles, Jack put the stove and their harnesses and everything else that could survive the night, just outside the tent and zipped up the flap. He put Sophie's boots back on her, laid down next to her and wrapped his arms around her for shared warmth.

Sophie giggled. "Just like the old days, huh Jack?" she said softly.

"No," said Jack. "In the old days I would have had all your clothes off by now." They both laughed.

Jack squeezed Sophie's back in tightly against his chest and brought his knees up into their classic *spoons* position. Sophie's hair tickled his lips, and brought back waves of memories of what seemed like another life. And now, here he was, lying next to Sophie – what he had dreamed about since the day in New York that he had committed to going back to the Himalaya – and now, all he could think about was Peggy in the house in Vermont with Ralphie and Beth. The small back yard would need mowing and Peggy's gardens would be in full bloom with petunias, impatiens, marigolds and sunflowers, and the birdbath would be dry because Peggy never cared to fill it. Jack smiled to himself. He was glad now, that he'd come back to K2. Glad he'd seen Sophie again, and laid next to her alone in a dark tent.

Sophie took her cell phone from an inside pocket. It was at 3% power. She used the last of the phone's energy to pull up a picture of her girls, Wanda and Chantal. Sophie held the phone up briefly over her shoulder for Jack to see. She kissed the screen. "Bonsoir mes chouchous. J'ai va t'embrasser dans mes rêves." She quickly switched off the phone and tucked it away. Maybe she would have enough power to see the picture one more time.

A few minutes later, Carlos called on the Walkie-talkie. He had found the fixed rope and was on his way down to the Zermatt high camp. "Merci Carlos," said Sophie. "Enjoy your World Cup games tomorrow. Save a place at the bar for us."

"Okay Jack, now we need to sleep. Here, take this." Jack could feel Sophie pushing something at him. It was the Sat-phone. "In case we get separated."

Jack pushed the heavy phone into an unused inside pocket of his parka. "You just don't want to carry it anymore."

Sophie giggled. "Goodnight Jack."

It was nearly seven o'clock when Major Park and Sukey finally found the tent at the final camp site set up by Lt. Cho and his men. It was situated in a precarious spot on the smallest of ledges just at the base of the high snow slope that led to the summit. Sukey suddenly realized what an incredible accomplishment Lt. Cho and his soldiers had achieved in setting a fixed rope nearly all the way to the end of the West Ridge and setting up one final encampment for her. The camp was also at least a hundred meters higher on the mountain than the high camps of both Logan and Sophie. Sukey hoped the pain and exertion it took to get this high would be worth it on the final leg to the summit.

The tent was not level but it was anchored securely to the mountain and without it, Sukey knew they would never survive the night. There were two sleeping bags, a stove, and two bottles of oxygen in the tent.

Major Park quickly lit the stove and began melting snow. He wrapped Sukey in one of the sleeping bags, took off her boots and pulled her frozen feet up under his inner shirt, against his stomach. He smiled at Sukey. "Now, we will get warm and have some tea," he said. "Then we will eat some rice and noodles and chicken broth."

"Ugh," Sukey replied, smiling up at Park. "Can't we have a thick, juicy cheeseburger from the grill, covered with onions and avocado, and some French fries? And a large Diet Coke would be nice." They both chuckled.

"Yes, yes, Madam Suek. In a few days, when we return to Islamabad, when you have become the first woman climber to summit all fourteen. Then we will have cheeseburgers."

Sukey began to feel the warmth returning to her toes. She lay back onto the sleeping bags and watched Major Park at work, taking care of her. In the flickering light of the stove flame, his face appeared very handsome, rugged and powerful, and protective. She was lucky, she knew, to have Major Park as her companion. A lesser soldier would have given up this torturous ordeal and abandoned the climb, but not Park. She imagined Park turning towards her and looking into her eyes and then moving over on top of her and kissing her warmly, and then passionately pulling the sleeping bag off of her to get closer.

"Your tea is ready Madam Suek." Park handed her a steaming cup.

Sukey sat up to drink her tea. "Thank you Major." No, she knew, Major Park was happily married, with pictures of his wife and children on his phone. He would never try to take advantage of her – even if she would welcome it. The assassin would be a gentleman to the end.

"Thank you for everything Major. I would not have gotten this far without you."

"No, I don't think that is true Madam Suek. Please, drink your tea."

Sukey reached out and touched Park's hand, and smiled. "And tonight Major, we will have another adventure when we go to the summit together." Park just smiled at her, nodded slightly, and sipped his tea.

As all three teams moved into place for a summit assault that evening, the level of activity around the Zermatt base camp had also increased in anticipation of what was to come. Word came that Rudi Joost would be arriving at base camp the following morning. Immediately upon hearing of the crash of the big helicopter, Joost had recruited an insurance adjuster in London and was now in the air on a private jet, headed straight for Skardu, where his helicopter waited. With the news that Logan was moving into position for a summit assault that evening, he had also recruited journalists from the London Times, Reuters, and USA Today, to cover the historic triumph of the Zermatt team. Rudi was uncertain about his future with Logan, but he knew that the next day would be a great day for the Zermatt brand as the world of outdoor fashion focused on the K2 outcome. He expected his logo to be on the front pages of every newspaper in the world for the next month. That was what he had invested millions of dollars in – just as Snow Leopard's Young Kim had done. The following day, one of them was going to be a colossal loser.

The OSN trailer was bustling with activity, as it had been since the Zermatt generators had run out of fuel the previous day. Only the Zermatt command center with the vital communications and weather computers, still had power, running on a small emergency generator with its own fuel tank. The huge mess tent and pub with its flat screen TV, were dark and cold, as were all of the Zermatt sleep tents. The power would be back on by late afternoon, Morris O'Dell insisted, as soon as the Koreans delivered the five hundred gallons of diesel fuel they had bartered for twenty surplus American oxygen bottles.

In the warmth of the OSN trailer, Samantha Ryan sat on the floor, her crossed legs supporting her lap-top as she expertly hammered out one more of Logan's blogs for the website, dressed up with some video shots of Logan climbing a difficult pitch on her way to Camp 4, that Bert and Arnie had sent down the mountain. This would be Logan's last blog post before her summit bid that night, and Samantha spared no adjectives in building the hype.

Monica DeForrest was similarly engaged with her lap-top, trying to fabricate one more *expedition sustainability* report for which she was obligated, struggling once more with the narrative of trying to somehow minimize the *carbon impact* of an explosion of one thousand gallons of diesel fuel and the complete immolation of one of the world's biggest helicopters, which was still smoldering a short distance down the glacier. It would be a brief report.

The center of activity in the OSN trailer was the small group of journalists and a few Zermatt people all gathered around Bruce Kinder's desk looking at the live video feed from the camera positioned on Broad Peak. The camera and its thousand millimeter lens had narrowly escaped the avalanches brought down by the crash of the Zermatt helicopter. Now, during a brief interlude of clear sky around the peak of K2, the camera was recording some stunningly clear footage of the three climbers of the French team as they advanced on the terminus of the Northeast Ridge. The action was excruciatingly slow – seemingly non-moving, at the distance the climbers were at – but compared to the lack of any *real* video action that they had been used to for the past month, the shots were spectacular.

At the other end of the OSN trailer, Marty Gallagher sat alone at his computer, brow furrowed as he looked at the same screen that Morris O'Dell and Dr. Eric Chen were staring at over in the Zermatt control center forty meters away. It was the same feed – the composite weather projections from the services in Seattle, Edinburgh, and Oslo – that Marcel Janot, Dr. Alain Clement, and Dong Shin-Soo were receiving at their respective base camps.

After six weeks in the mountains, Gallagher was by now an expert at interpreting the long and short-term forecasts for the K2 area and he could clearly see how fast the massive front of moisture from the low-lands of India was moving across the Himalayan foothills on a bearing for the

Karakorums. He studied the time projections on the screen and looked up again at the digital clock on the wall. For the third time, he recalculated in his mind the hours the climbers would need to reach the top and make it back down to the safety of at least the high camp. It was going to be close.

In the early morning darkness in New York, the lights were on in the OSN offices high over 8ᵗʰ Avenue, where Glenda Craft and a team of producers were also looking at the video from the Broad Peak camera. Glenda was giddy with excitement over the turn of events that had put her live, *K2* reality show back at the top of the social media *trending* lists, and would, the following day, be the top story on all of the major network newscasts. The incredible video they had captured of the crash of the Zermatt helicopter had started it, and now, against overwhelming odds, *all three* of the competing expeditions were in position to go for the summit, and only OSN would be bringing it to the world *live,* in real time! Glenda was feeling much better now about her future in the TV business.

Chapter 28

Jack Finley had always had the rare ability to sleep high on an 8,000 meter mountain. Even at a high camp, in bitter cold, where most climbers without supplemental oxygen could only lie still trying to rest their weary bodies for a few precious hours, Jack could close his eyes, slow his breathing and put himself into a deep, rejuvenating sleep. It was a talent that had served him well on his fourteen successful summit attempts on the world's tallest mountains.

Sophie lacked Jack's capacity for sleep, and this night she had too many things on her mind. In a few hours, Logan Healy, one of the strongest and most determined climbers Sophie had ever known, would be leaving her high camp on the Abruzzi Spur and be sprinting for the top on full oxygen, pulling herself up on the fixed rope and hurrying, like everyone else on the mountain, to beat the weather. *Was it all for nothing? All the heartbreak and tragedy that Sophie would be leaving behind on this expedition, only to come in a meaningless second or even third place in this foolish TV reality show?* And she worried about Sukey, softer and more fragile than Logan and herself, distracted now by her love affair with the American, in trouble with the Koreans, her husband, and her sponsor, somewhere high on the awful West Ridge, probably on her own now. Sophie prayed that Sukey had turned around and was on her way down.

Sophie had finally fallen asleep for what seemed like ten or fifteen minutes when she was awakened by the shrill buzz of the Walkie-talkie. It was Dr. Clement, followed by her father, both taking one last attempt at talking Sophie into aborting the final leg of the climb. The bad weather was coming in quickly and it was unpredictable. The intense cold, high winds and the snow, were soon going to make the entire mountain a climbing nightmare. Janot pleaded with Sophie to go only up to the Abruzzi Spur and then head down quickly on the Zermatt fixed ropes. It was, she knew, a very sensible plan – probably the last sensible plan available to her on this expedition.

It was a short conversation, as Janot knew it would be. He'd lived with his daughter's stubbornness for half his life. Sophie and Jack would be leaving soon. They knew from Logan Healy's blog that she would be leaving her high camp at 1:00am – an hour earlier than the typical summit assault would call for, to beat the weather. So Sophie would leave at midnight. At the western end of the Northeast Ridge, she and Jack were higher on the mountain than Logan's Camp 5, but they still had a greater distance to cover. Even with an earlier start, they would have to make excellent time to catch the American who would be climbing on supplemental oxygen.

No one knew where Sukey was, Janot told Sophie. High on the West Ridge somewhere, climbing in high wind and intense cold, was the last report they gotten from the OSN base camp. Sophie shuddered. There was nothing she could do for Sukey now. She looked at her watch. Time to start getting ready anyway. "Good bye Poppi. I love you," Sophie told Janot. "I will call you from the summit." She elbowed Jack awake. "Time to go."

Albie Mathias and Timmy Burns had been up working for an hour before Logan Healy came out of her tent just before one o'clock. Burns had been melting water and filling the bottles that the climbers would have to carry inside their parkas. In their rucksacks, the water would freeze in ten minutes. Mathias had arranged the oxygen tanks – two for Logan, and two each for Jay Hamilton and Lisa Greenway who would be departing after Logan. The last three full tanks would remain at Camp5 for the climbers to use on the way down.

Mathias opened the valve on each tank to check the pressure – sometimes the gauges could be wrong, stuck on the *full* mark when there was much less gas in the tank. He checked the condition of Logan's crampons and the ice-axes that would be so critical on the *traverse,* and laid out three coils of rope, a selection of hardware and slings, and opened a fresh box of batteries for the climbers' Petzl helmet lamps. As always, Mathias was nervous before the final summit assault of climbers in his care. He couldn't do anything about the snow, wind, or weather, but equipment failure was unacceptable.

It was a pitch-black night under overcast skies. No moon. No stars. Only the helmet lamps of Burns and Mathias illuminated the campsite. Logan switched on her lamp and saw that Mathias was talking on the Walkie-talkie they used to communicate with base camp to avoid the voice-activated system that everyone shared. She was anxious to get started, but she was curious about Mathias' conversation. She approached him and could overhear his last words, obviously with Morris O'Dell. "Well, I don't think that's going to happen," Mathias was saying. "Yeah, I'll tell her." Mathias clicked off and frowned at Logan.

Logan shrugged. "So?"

"Weather's bad," said Mathias.

"Yeah, no shit." Logan stuffed an oxygen bottle in her rucksack and clipped another to the outside of the pack.

"O'Dell's worried. Storm's coming faster than we first thought."

Logan straightened up and looked at Mathias. "When?"

Mathias shrugged his shoulders. "There's a window, but it's closing fast."

"How long do I have?"

Mathias used his authoritative voice. "You need to be clipped to that rope and back down through the traverse by eleven. At noontime, it's going to be a blizzard up there."

Logan moved forward and kissed Mathias on the cheek. "I can do that," she said. She moved over to the equipment pile and clipped two slings, a few pitons and an ice screw to her harness and slung the coil of rope over her head and across her chest. "But you'd better get Hamilton and Lisa moving. They can't wait. Tell them to try to catch up to me."

"Hey," Logan looked around the campsite. "Where's Siegfried and Roy?"

Mathias rolled his eyes. "Left an hour ago. Determined to get some video of you heading for the summit."

Logan shook her head. "Should have taken their boots away from them."

"They'll be okay," said Mathias. "They turned out to be pretty useful climbers, and I told them not to go beyond the saddle. The traverse will be too dangerous with all that equipment they're carrying. Get some footage, and come down straight away." Mathias turned toward his tent as a strange figure emerged into the shadows cast by the helmet lamps. "Oh yes, Logan, a friend of yours dropped in for a little stayover last night."

"So, who is this then? Logan said, moving towards the man.

Carlos Medina grinned broadly through a dark beard, his white teeth seeming to light up his face. "Hello Logan," he said reaching out his arms.

"Oh my God, Carlos." Logan embraced her old friend and held him tight. She had completely forgotten the conversation with Sophie about Carlos coming down the Zermatt ropes. She stepped back and looked at Carlos with the experienced mountaineer's eye. He looked gaunt and tired, his parka seemingly two sizes too big.

"Carlos, you look exhausted. "

The Spaniard shrugged and nodded. "Yes, the ridge lived up to its reputation."

"So you won't be going to the top with Sophie." It was more of a statement than a question.

"No. Not this trip. Between Gasherbrum and this one, I have been too long in the mountains. Too high. Now, after I have slept a little more, I will go down to your pub and drink and eat for three days." They both laughed.

"They will take good care of you in the pub, and find you a warm bed too, and we still have some great looking women running around base camp. They're going to go ape-shit over you!"

Carlos laughed, then shook his head. "Oh no. Not necessary. Only cold beer, some real food and the World Cup matches, eh?"

"Yeah, that's right. You won the big one this time. Good for you," said Logan. She paused for a moment. "So, how is Sophie? How is Jack? Are they okay, ready for this?"

Carlos looked into the darkness up the mountain. He nodded. "Yes, Sophie for sure. She is ready. She will climb well." He paused. "Jack, I think Jack will not be going to the summit with her, not this time. He has had to work very hard, like all of us, you know – with the Sherpas gone – everyone carries heavy loads, and the ridge is so long and most of it at very high altitude." He shrugged with finality. "So, no, I think Jack will be coming down."

Logan moved in for a final hug. "Well, don't ever underestimate Jack Finley," she said. "And now, I have to go."

Carlos hugged her tightly. "Be safe Logan. Don't take chances with the weather. You know what's coming."

"I'll be fine my friend. See you in the pub tomorrow night."

Logan took a water bottle from Timmy Burns, and tucked it into a deep pocket inside her parka. Shaking her head without speaking she refused the second bottle as well as a handful of energy bars he held out to her. Logan embraced Timmy briefly. "Climb safely," he told her. Logan pulled on her oxygen mask and tested the flow of gas before turning off the valve completely. Now that she was well acclimated to the altitude, she would wait as long as she could before turning on the gas. She exchanged final *high fives* with Mathias and Burns, and started out up the slope into the darkness, her headlamp casting a dim, yellow cone of light onto the snow ahead of her.

Sukey awoke to find Major Park with the stove going, melting snow. She could feel the wind billowing against the tent and through the flap opening and instantly dreaded the thought of going outside into the dark and the unbearable cold.

Park smiled at her in the flickering light. "We will have hot tea before we leave, but no food now."

"No, no food," Sukey agreed. "I couldn't eat."

Sukey labored to pull off her boots and the thermal socks she had been wearing the last three days. She took her last pair of clean socks and the UCLA sweatshirt from her rucksack. The socks felt thick and comforting inside her boots. She took off her parka jacket, pulled off the sweater she'd been wearing from the beginning of the climb and replaced it with the hooded sweatshirt. She wouldn't need her helmet any longer and tossed it to the corner of the tent with her old socks and sweater. More trash they would be leaving on the mountain.

Sukey and Park drank their tea in silence, each seeming to reflect on the task ahead once they left the relative comfort of the tent and plunged off into the darkness and ten-below-zero cold. After a long, silent interlude, Major Park looked at his watch. It was nearly 2:00am. "Time for us to leave," he said softly.

Sukey nodded slowly. She reached for the Walkie-Talkie and buzzed the base camp. Dong Shin-soo answered right away. Sukey told him they would be leaving for the summit in a few minutes, and asked about the weather. She listened for a few moments, then asked about Lt. Cho and the oxygen from the Americans. She listened for a little while longer, then handed the Walkie-Talkie to Park. "He wants to speak to you."

Almost imperceptibly, Park turned away from Sukey as he spoke into the phone. "Yes, Colonel," Park said very softly. It was the first time Sukey had heard Park use Dong Shin-soo's military title. She watched Park intently as he listened for a long while without speaking. Finally, he spoke again, a bit louder this time. "Yes, yes, Colonel, I know," he said, sounding agitated before abruptly clicking off. He handed the Walkie-Talkie back to Sukey.

Major Park went back to filling their water bottles. "Did our expedition leader have anything important to say to you?" Park asked.

"Yes," said Sukey. "He said to make sure we took many pictures of me at the summit, and also that we need to reach the top by eight o'clock, and then turn around quickly to get back down here before the height of the storm hits this afternoon. Also, he has sent a party up the mountain with food and oxygen to assist Lieutenant Cho and his men." Sukey knew not to ask what Park's conversation with Shin-soo had been about.

Park nodded his approval. "Cho is a good man. I shouldn't have spoken to him as I did."

Then, the time for talk was over. Park pulled on his balaclava, helmet and goggles, then snapped his oxygen mask in place. Sukey wrapped up in her face scarf, pushed her hair back into her wool cap and pulled over her sweatshirt hood and then the fur-lined hood of her parka, the oxygen mask, goggles, and her Petzl lamp. They pulled on their rucksacks, put on the warm gloves they had been sleeping on, and then their mittens.

Outside, the air was frigid in the relentless wind. While Sukey put on her crampons and harness, Park collapsed the tent and tossed a few spent oxygen bottles on top of it. They roped together and Sukey started off, up the long final steps of the ridge leading to the snow slope to the summit. After only twenty meters, Major Park caught up to her and put a hand on her shoulder. He patted his chest, and went ahead of her. Sukey knew this was best. There were no more fixed ropes, and no trail broken by the soldiers. They were truly on their own now with seven hours of climbing in knee-deep snow ahead of them. Sukey was once again thankful to have Major Park and his large boots leading them up the mountain.

Albie Mathias stood in front of Jay Hamilton and Lisa Greenway checking out the equipment on their harnesses with his headlamp. He handed Lisa her ice axe. "If it were up to me, you both would be heading down right now. But, this is Logan's expedition. Everyone gets an opportunity, and all that rubbish."

Lisa clipped onto the fixed rope and looked up the mountain. "Albie, I will never again in my life, be this close to the summit of K2. It's a mountain that not many women have climbed." She shrugged and gave Mathias a brief hug.

"We need to go," said Jay Hamilton. "We'll be fine Albie. We'll keep an eye on the weather."

Mathias turned away with irritation. "Jay, if you wait until you see snow falling, it will already be too late."

Chapter 29

Peggy Finley drove cautiously up Rte. 117, headed for her parents' home in South Burlington. She tentatively passed the spot where two years ago, she'd hit the deer, a large doe that destroyed the front end of her Subaru and smashed the windshield. It was the same time of year, early August, when the deer were active and the full greenery of the forest hid them until the last moment when they leaped out onto the road, usually in pairs. One of the hazards of Vermont in late summer. Ralphie and Beth were safely buckled into their car-seats in the back.

It would have been faster to go up Rte. 100 from Fayston, through Waterbury, to Rte. 89, but then she would have to deal with what her father called "Vermont's *Autobahn*", where *everyone,* it seemed, especially the trailer trucks, traveled at more than eighty miles per hour. Peggy would keep an eye out for the deer, and enjoy the slower and prettier drive through the small towns along Rte. 117.

She and the kids were going to her parents' house for dinner, but mainly to watch the special program coming on the Outdoor Sports Network at 5:00pm, live from the OSN broadcast center at the Zermatt basecamp at K2, in Pakistan. The Finleys didn't get OSN on the their cable system in Fayston and what Peggy had been able to see of it at her parents' house had been boring anyway – they hardly ever mentioned Jack, or Sophie Janot, or the Korean girl, just Logan Healy – and all they ever showed happening was Logan going up a rope or down a rope, and the helicopter exploding, over and over. But this was going to be the night, they said, when everyone was going to the top of the mountain, and then the big contest would be over and Jack would be home in a few days.

Jack had been gone for six weeks and Peggy was anxious for him to get home. Their scratchy little front lawn needed mowing; the screen door in the back had fallen off into the bushes; and the toilet had been running for weeks. Plus, she was getting sick of her parents, and she knew Ralphie had had enough of playing with grandpa – he just wanted to be left alone to play with his Game Boy. Now that Jack had committed to going to work for her father, she had resolved to be less nagging when he got home and had even pledged to lose some weight by cutting out the half-dozen Oreos she had every afternoon watching her shows. Her father was also anxious for Jack to get started on studying for his first insurance brokers exam which he had gone ahead and scheduled for Jack at the beginning of December in Williston. He had assembled all the course study materials Jack would need and everyone at the agency would help him prepare because *you don't want to flunk your first Life and Personal Lines certification exam!* Peggy was certain that Jack would get right into it and would do well on his insurance exams. And he was going to love the little split-level ranch in Charlotte that she and her mother had found. He just had to get this whole mountain-climbing thing out of his system.

Peggy and her parents ate dinner in the kitchen watching the local news on "3 News" the CBS affiliate. Toward the end of the news they ran a feature on the *"Race To The Top of K2"*, which would be culminating that evening as the three expeditions went for the summit. Even the local news talked mostly about Logan Healy... *one of our own*, they said, even though Logan was from Massachusetts. She had gone through the Green Mountain School, and had skied out of Stratton Mountain, during her Olympic and pro skiing career. That was enough to make her a Vermonter. Finally, they mentioned Sophie Janot, accompanied by *another one of our own* – Jack Finley from Fayston – *just the second American to climb all fourteen of the world's 8,000-meter mountains.* They ran a few seconds of a previous interview with a retired Canadian climber, an old friend of Jack's – Rene Charest from Montreal – who called Jack the greatest high-altitude climber in the world. Sophie Janot was in good hands, he said. Peggy's mother beamed with pride. Peggy cringed.

After cleaning up the dinner dishes, Peggy and her parents went into the family room and turned on the big TV over the mantel and tuned in the Outdoor Sports Network. It was just after 5:00pm, which they knew by now, was 3:00am in Pakistan. "Why they want to climb mountains in the dark in the middle of the night is beyond me," Peggy's mother said, not for the first time. They watched through the fuzzy reception as a spotlight suddenly illuminated a man in a red parka with an OSN logo on the front. He held a microphone and wore a huge fur hat. He looked like he was freezing to death.

Marty Gallagher glanced up at the bank of monitors on the wall of the OSN broadcast trailer while two technicians on either side of him manned the electronics board. The pressure was on. Now that the final summit assaults had begun, the whole world was once again taking notice. The live OSN feed was being picked up all over Europe, most of Asia, the mountain-climbing countries of South America, and with great interest in South Africa, Australia, and New Zealand. The entire corporate hierarchy at OSN in New York would also be watching. Gallagher knew his future at the network was on the line. He'd spent the last hour on the phone with Glenda Craft in New York. Her final words to him still rang in his ears – "That lard-ass Kinder better not screw this up!"

Gallagher knew it wasn't fair for them to expect him to produce a live show from his little broadcast trailer. And it wasn't fair to Bruce Kinder to have to do a live intro in zero degree weather in the middle of the night from a mountain in Pakistan. Even though they would be handling most of the switching from New York – Gallagher didn't have the equipment or the people on hand for a multiple-camera live feed. No one anticipated there would be a conclusion to the race with *all three* of the climbers headed for the summit at the same time. Logan Healy, on the easiest route, with fixed ropes already in place, was expected to reach the top days ahead of the other climbers, struggling to get up two of the most difficult routes in the world of mountaineering. But who could foresee the horrible weather they would face, or the abandonment of the climb by the Sherpas, which affected Logan's expedition most of all. And who could predict that Logan's Camp 4 would be blown away by the wind, setting her back a full day? So here they were, and while it might be unfair to Gallagher, it was, as Glenda Craft put it, "a gift from *fucking* heaven – the biggest show in OSN's history, in *prime time*."

Gallagher focused on the large monitor in the middle that showed Bruce Kinder trying to maintain his balance in deep snow, a microphone in one hand, the other trying to keep his stupid fur hat on against the wind. To Gallagher's amazement, earlier in the morning, Kinder, a camera man and a sound technician had trekked south across the glacier and climbed nearly five hundred meters up a neighboring peak to a spot where they had a clear shot at K2's summit cone. They had captured some great footage of the dim glow of Logan Healy's headlamp as she started out from the high camp several hours earlier. Soon after, they saw three more dull cones of light headed up the route behind her. The OSN cameras followed the lights for about twenty minutes, until cloud cover rolled in to obscure everything high on the mountain.

"Ready Bruce, in ten," Gallagher said into the microphone attached to his earphones. He nodded to one of the technicians to cut to Kinder.

"This is Bruce Kinder, coming to you live, from high on a peak on the south side of Pakistan's Godwin-Austen Glacier, where we have a clear view of the upper reaches of the magnificent K2, the second highest mountain in the world." Kinder's timing and delivery were perfect. "After more than four weeks of arduous climbing in horrendous weather and severe avalanche conditions, marked by numerous setbacks, a spectacular helicopter crash, and a tragic fatality on the mountain, the race to the summit has begun. In just a few hours, America's Logan Healy, Sophie Janot from France, or the Korean, Chun Suek Yen, will be the first woman *ever* to have summited all fourteen of the world's eight-thousand meter mountains, a heroic feat that only a few years ago, many said would *never* be accomplished by a woman. Well it's going to happen tonight, and we're bringing it to you *live,* only on OSN, the Outdoor Sports Network."

OSN in New York cut to a pre-recorded, twenty minute biographic video profiling the three climbers. Marty Gallagher couldn't resist a chuckle and a broad grin. He clapped his hands together. "Wow, *fucking* great! He's unbelievable. He even got the Korean girl's name right." With no notes, cue cards or a teleprompter, Kinder had delivered a flawless, dramatic opening that Gallagher knew they were going to love at the OSN building in New York.

A few minutes later, they went back live to Kinder to intro the "dramatic" footage shot earlier showing the headlamps of Logan Healy's team leaving their high camp, headed for the summit.

"Just a few hours ago, we were able to capture the beginning of Logan Healy's run to the top of K2." Viewers saw a tiny, dull cone of light against the totally black background of the mountain. A few minutes later, two more dull glows appeared, followed by the a third light farther back. "Logan Healy was followed out of her high camp by Jay Hamilton, who hails from San Diego, and Lisa Greenway, of Aurora, Colorado, both attempting their second eight thousand meter summit after conquering Mount Everest last May. The fourth lamp on the route belongs to the expedition's climb leader, the South African, Albie Mathias, who is carrying three additional oxygen tanks up the mountain for the climbers to use on their way down. Mathias is doing the job of two Sherpas, carrying a very heavy load of well over sixty pounds up the mountain. Boy, I'll bet he'll be ready for a nice rubdown when he gets back to basecamp."

Gallagher groaned. You could only expect so much from Kinder. "Okay Bruce. Good job. Now, let's intro the Sophie Janot shot, and then we'll close it down and let New York take over until the sun comes up and we can actually see something." Gallagher knew the audience couldn't take too much more of barely moving blips of light that could have been shot in the Catskills.

"Earlier this morning, our thousand millimeter lens, high on Broad Peak," Kinder pointed off to his right, "about a mile to our northeast, was able to record the beginning of the final leg of the summit assault of the French woman, Sophie Janot, and her climbing companion, Vermont native, Jack Finley, as they departed their final encampment high on the Northeast Ridge." Two more blips of light appeared against the total darkness of the mountain. "Earlier in their careers, Janot and Finley were romantically involved for many years before they each married separately."

Gallagher couldn't wait to get away from the blips in the night. "Okay Bruce, back to you for a little on the Korean girl – we have no idea where she is – and then we'll wrap it up here."

Bruce Kinder was still standing in the spotlight battling the wind. "And somewhere on the other side of the mountain, high on the West Ridge, is the Korean climber, Chun Suek Yen, advancing to the summit with her climbing partner, a Korean Army officer. We'll be giving you updates on all of the climbers when the sun rises in a few hours here on K2."

Gallagher assumed that Kinder had more to say. Kinder thought that they were done and assumed his microphone was off. "Okay, let's get the fuck off this hill before my asshole freezes shut."

Gallagher's jaw dropped open just as he heard Glenda Craft crackle into his earphone. "Great finish Marty. Nice touch. Yes, we wanted the whole world to know how cold it is there."

Logan Healy finally found a small, level shelf where she could sit and rest for a minute. She had been climbing for three hours, and even in the dark and bitter cold, she knew she was making good time on a very steep section of the mountain. Her arms and legs were feeling the steepness though, and her fingers and toes felt cold, which alarmed her a little because there was so far to go to reach the summit – and then, the return trip. You were so focused on getting to the top, it was easy to forget about the descent – a fatal lapse made by too many climbers on the big mountains. And, on this descent, the weather was not going to be as pleasant as it was on the way up. She had been caught in storms high on a mountain before and knew the terror and misery they could bring. She needed to keep moving.

Logan pulled the water bottle from inside her parka and took a long, satisfying drink. She unscrewed the top and stuffed a few handfuls of snow into the bottle before pushing it back into an inside pocket. She stood and looked back down the mountain and didn't see any lights. She spoke into her collar microphone. "Jay, Lisa, where are you guys? You okay?"

Hamilton answered first. "Doing fine Lo..." The transmission was breaking up. Then Lisa Greenway's voice came on, sounding like she was breathing hard. "I'm okay. Just... little behind..."

"Jay," shouted Logan, "what's wrong with the radio?"

"Could be ... battery, low ... you've been on the mountain ...est. Battery may... low."

"Oh that's fucking great!" said Logan. "Shitty batteries. Hey, Bert and Arnie, where are you guys? You okay?" She waited in silence. The radio crackled. A weak voice came on.

"This... Bert...okay. Getting... position... ready... video..."

"Bert, wherever you are, don't go any higher," said Logan. "Wait 'til I get there."

The radio crackled with an unintelligible response.

Logan leaned back on the rope and peered up the mountain to see if she could see any lights above her. There was only darkness. "Dammit!" She knew, after several weeks of use on the mountain with everyone chattering like a bunch of teenage girls, in ten below zero temperatures, they should have foreseen the batteries dying out. "Okay, I'm turning off my radio to save the battery. When it's light in a couple of hours, I'll turn it on and we'll see where everyone is. I'm on the Motorola if anyone needs me." Logan reached inside her parka and switched off the radio. She didn't have time to deal with this kind of stuff. She pulled on her ascender and started up the route again.

For four straight hours, Jack had led Sophie up the interminable, never-ending snow slope that would bring them to the high point of the fixed rope on the Abruzzi Spur. They were climbing on a more direct route than Carlos had taken earlier that night. He had joined the fixed rope at a much lower point on the route. Jack and Sophie's direct route would bring them to the Spur just above the *bottleneck*, eliminating a considerable distance of more technical climbing. But, as always, Jack realized once again, *everything* on K2 was bigger and longer and more difficult than it looked.

The trade-off for taking the direct route, was the deeper snow and greater exposure to the wind and avalanche danger. So far, they had been lucky. The wind, while steady, had been fairly benign, and the snow, in long patches, seemed to have been avalanched off recently – probably due to the concussion of the helicopter explosion, or simply high winds over the past few days – leaving them much easier bare rock and ice patches to climb on. There would be no luck involved, however, in finding more oxygen in the air here above 7,000 meters. It was not a variable. Jack's headache had been pounding for the last two days and he had developed a short, painful cough whenever he took in a deep breath of the dry air. When they reached the fixed rope, he told himself, he would take another handful of aspirin and a Dex for the final push.

Jack had tried to maintain a steady pace of three strides and then, a stop for a breath. He could see the dim beam of Sophie's headlamp in the snow beside him and knew that she was having no difficulty maintaining the pace. Soon, they would be one step forward for every breath. The climbing would get a bit easier after they were over the crest ahead of them that was the last vestige of the North East Ridge. Only a hundred meters beyond it, they should find the Zermatt fixed rope, and would actually find themselves on a slight downhill stroll for a short while before they reached the high trail past the menacing seracs leading to the traverse. He felt Sophie pull on the rope that connected them. Jack stopped to let her catch up to him.

"I need a small rest," Sophie said, dropping down to the snow. Jack sat down facing her. Sophie pulled out her water bottle, took a short drink and offered it to Jack. He declined.

"I'm okay."

"Are you? Your cough isn't good. Do you still have your headache?"

Jack shrugged. "It's not too bad. I've had worse at this height."

Sophie turned off her head-lamp so it wouldn't blind Jack as she examined his eyes closely. She nodded. "Okay, okay. But I've been thinking." She tucked the water bottle back into her parka and zipped up. "Soon, we will be at the fixed rope and there will be a decision to make. By then it will be light enough to see what we are faced with. If we can see Logan out in front of us, the race will be over. She will be on oxygen, and we are moving slowly."

Jack could see where Sophie was going. "That doesn't mean we can't catch up..."

Sophie chuckled. *Jack Finley, always the ultimate competitor, always ready for a challenge.* "No Jack, if Logan is already above the bottleneck, the race will be over."

"But you still need the summit, for all *fourteen*. This will be your only chance."

"Yes, yes, I know. But, with the bad weather coming, we can go down the rope to Logan's basecamp and rest, and then, in a few days – the weather always improves after a severe storm – we can come back up and go to the top. It is a much safer plan, Jack. You know it is."

Jack shook his head. He didn't like any plan that encompassed losing. "You came here to be first to the top Sophie, the *first* to summit all fourteen. And I don't care if we see Logan ahead of us or not. We push on. We'll run her down. Things happen up high, you know that. What if she tires, or runs out of oxygen? She still has to pass under the seracs. Still has to manage the traverse – many things can happen there, even with fixed ropes. *We can win this race.*" Jack was pleading now.

Sophie laughed. "Oh Jack, this isn't about you and Logan any more. You're not in the sixth grade now racing her down the mountains in Vermont."

Jack grinned sheepishly, made aware once more of just how well Sophie knew him. "Well, I still think we can win."

Sophie smiled at him. "Yes Jack, but we have a storm coming down upon us, and I have Wanda and Chantal waiting for me at home, and you have your Peggy, and Ralphie and Elizabeth waiting for you, and *none* of them care if I beat Logan to the top."

Jack scowled. "A low blow from la femme Francais."

"So, it's settled," said Sophie.

Jack shrugged. "We'll see," he said, hopping to his feet.

The Walkie-Talkie buzzed inside Sukey's parka. She was grateful for any reason to stop their exhausting trek through the snow, which seemed to be getting deeper with every step. Her legs were burning and she had a throbbing headache. Ahead of her, Major Park felt the pull on the rope between them. He stopped and turned to face back down the hill toward Sukey.

Sukey jammed her ice axe into the snow. Pulling the radio from inside her parka, she dropped a mitten onto the snow at her feet. She stared down at the mitten, realizing that if it chose to slide down the icy snow and off into the darkness behind her, it would be the same as watching several of her fingers slide down the mountain as well. She should have tied it onto her sleeve. Moving slowly, she put her boot on top of the mitten. Everything was happening in slow motion now.

She had to shield the Walkie-Talkie from the wind with her other mitten. "Yes *expedition leader*," said Sukey, turning to find relief from the wind that sent twenty- below- zero cold knifing through her clothing. "Yes, we have made good progress and should be only another two hours from the base of the final summit slope." She clamped a mitten against her hood to cover her ear while she listened. Dong Shin-Soo updated her on the progress of her competitors they had been able to glean from the OSN reports. Logan Healy was approaching the *bottleneck* and by sunrise, would be passing under the great seracs. Sophie Janot and Jack Finley should be getting close to the Zermatt fixed ropes. They appeared to be behind Logan by about an hour.

Sukey looked up the slope and saw that Major Park had his rucksack off and was connecting his second oxygen bottle. He had pushed the depleted tank into the snow, standing it straight up in the middle of the trail. Sukey suddenly realized how difficult it would be to find their way down again if the coming snow storm covered their tracks. They had no willow reeds or anything else to mark the trail. She picked up her mitten, still listening to Dong Shin-Soo. He told her that the relief party had met up with Lt. Cho and his men and were bringing them down. Two of the soldiers were on their way up to Camp 4, where they would leave two full oxygen bottles and food for Sukey and Park to use on the way down. *Camp 4,* it seemed so far away now to Sukey. She wondered if Park would be able to make it all the way down there by himself.

Sukey caught up to Park, hunched over, fighting the wind. He looked at her without speaking. "We need to hurry," said Sukey. Park just nodded and started back up the slope.

Chapter 30

Rudy Joost's helicopter hovered over the wreck of the CH47, just a few hundred meters short of the basecamp landing pad. The pile of charred, twisted metal was still smoldering, the Zermatt logo still legible on the blackened rear rotor pillar lying flat on the glacier. The unmistakable odor of burning rubber hung in the air. As Joost gazed down at the rubble, an angry grimace spread across his face with the realization of the glee that Young Kim would enjoy every time the wreckage was shown on the Korean Television Network. The moment passed.

"Well then, we'll just have to get it into the shop and patch it up it seems," Joost said loudly enough for his passengers to hear. The journalists and the insurance man from London, seated behind him, chuckled politely.

"A total loss for sure Rudy, and no one hurt. Cheers," said the insurance man, resigned to the fact that his company would be paying full value of the policy.

Joost smiled. It wasn't the money. He didn't care about the money. He was thinking now of the agony Young Kim would suffer when Logan Healy reached the top of K2 in a few hours, far ahead of Kim's chubby little climber. Not even the Koreans knew where she was at this point. "So, on we go," said Joost motioning the pilot toward base camp. "We've got an historic day ahead of us."

Joost hadn't talked to Logan since he'd left the mountain a week earlier, but he was certain that by now she would have gotten over the impetuous little triste with her Swedish ski bunny, recalculated her financial future, and would be falling triumphantly into his arms when she came down the mountain tomorrow, *the victor,* and the first woman ever to summit all fourteen 8,000 meter mountains. Logan Healy, the international face of the Zermatt brand!

Morris O'Dell greeted Joost and his guests at the landing pad and accompanied them across the glacier to the base camp. He ushered the journalists and the insurance man into the Pub for breakfast, then walked Joost toward the Communications Center tent.

"So, Morris," said Joost, "where is she at this moment?"

"Come, and I'll show you," said O'Dell, leading Joost into the tent. Eric Chen, Gordie Yorke and Rob Page were gathered in front of a computer monitor showing the live feed from OSN. They made way for O'Dell and the big boss. O'Dell took up a pencil and pointed to a tiny headlamp beam just barely visible on the screen. "This would be Logan, at the moment, just starting up the bottleneck. Doing very well it seems."

Joost glanced at the gold Patek Philippe on his wrist. It was 6:00am. "How long to the top from there?" he asked, looking around from O'Dell to the other climbers. "Another hour or so?"

Rob Page smiled and shook his head. "More like four hours if she pushes it and the bloody wind stays down."

Joost frowned and looked at his watch again. "Any sign of the other women?"

"None," said O'Dell. "Hours behind Logan we think. But, we've got another issue, it seems. Our video crew, Bert Skar and Arnie Turek, they're somewhere above Logan, but we don't seem to know where they are."

Joost looked perturbed. Can't you just call them on the radio?"

O'Dell shrugged. "Another problem. All the radio batteries decided to die off around the same time. Clearly, we underestimated the effect the sub-zero weather would..."

"What about the Walkie-Talkies?" Joost interrupted.

"They're fine," said O'Dell. "We can talk to Logan and to Mathias. But, we also have a couple of other climbers going up the mountain – Jay Hamilton, and Lisa..."

"I don't care about all that," said Joost, clearly annoyed by O'Dell's *other issues.* "When is the bad weather going to hit?"

Eric Chen was looking into a lap-top screen nearby. "It looks like the edge of it will be here about noontime, with the heavier stuff soon to follow. But that could change very quickly."

Joost looked anxiously at his watch again. He looked up at O'Dell. "Well, just make sure you get Logan back down here tomorrow. We've got some important interviews and photo sessions scheduled." He abruptly left the tent to find his insurance adjustor and hike back down the glacier to get a close-up view of his giant helicopter, take photographs, and figure out some way to obscure the Zermatt logos still visible about the wreckage. Over the next few years, the Baltis would cart away the larger pieces of sheet metal, and the glacier would digest the rest of his magnificent helicopter, but in the meantime, he didn't want every expedition coming into Concordia stopping for countless selfies of the wreckage with the Zermatt logo in the background.

Logan Healy stopped for a short rest and a quick drink. She was half way up the *bottleneck*, a notorious landmark on the Abruzzi Spur, aptly named because this was where expeditions slowed to a crawl as climbers struggled in single file to get up the vertical passage that was the only route through the deep snow slopes leading to the summit cone. This was where she was turned back three years earlier on her last attempt at K2, amid the congestion of dozens of climbers from several expeditions all going for the summit in a short window of good weather. She'd run out of time and then oxygen, waiting for her turn up the narrow passage before a sudden windstorm ended any thoughts of trying to continue. She had been lucky. A year later, congestion in the *bottleneck* had led to one of the most tragic days ever seen on K2. But today, she had an exclusive ticket, a free run up the *bottleneck* with no one ahead to slow her down.

Logan tucked the water bottle away then leaned out to scan the darkness above her for any lights that would be Bert and Arnie. She knew from this vantage point she wouldn't see much of the route above but she was still concerned that she had no idea of where they were. It was a good night for climbing, so they were probably okay, but she knew that she should never have allowed them to leave Camp 5. Anxious to get up the *bottleneck* she pulled on her ascender, looked up the mountain, and then stopped. She smiled. Far up the mountain there was a glimmer of shimmering light spreading steadily across the icy curves of the great seracs that guarded the summit cone. Far to the east the sun would be edging over the horizon, bringing dawn to the Karakorums, announcing itself first on the range's highest point. Logan stood, mesmerized by the sight of the crown of the mountain glistening in sunlight while everything around her was still in darkness. She'd seen the morning light come to the top of mountains before, but never quite as spectacularly as this.

Logan pushed her ascender as far up the rope as she could reach, to get started once again, when at the corner of her eye another light flashed. She turned back to look down the mountain and saw it again – a small, extremely bright beam of light off in the darkness of the glacier to the east of base camp. Then she saw that it was actually two specks of brightness she was seeing – the two powerful searchlights at the front of Rudy Joost's personal helicopter. The lights moved steadily up the glacier before she lost sight of them behind the lower reaches of the mountain. *Rudy coming back for the moment of glory, probably with more writers and photographers to document the huge win for the Zermatt brand.* Logan looked back up the route above her and saw again the incredible fire reflecting off the ice coated seracs. *A vision that seemed to make the whole expedition worthwhile no matter how it turned out.* Logan pushed Rudy out of her mind and went back to work.

Jack scanned the upper reaches of the mountain with the small Nikon scope he always carried with him. Sophie kneeled at his side escaping the wind as best she could. They were high on the mountain now where the temperature rarely rose above minus ten degrees and the wind made it truly painful to stop moving. Sophie wiggled her numb toes and fingers, anxious to start climbing again. They were about even with the top of the *bottleneck* and while she couldn't pick out the fixed rope in the snow, she had a clear view of most of the route running under the massive seracs, now lit by the sun rising behind them, and the beginning of the traverse, which to her meant the final lap to the top.

"I don't get it," said Jack, panning back along the route to the top of the *bottleneck* once again. "I don't see anyone. I thought we'd find a bunch of Zermatt climbers up here – Logan, Mathias, Rob Page, some of those new kids. Where is everybody?"

Sophie came to her feet. She turned to look behind her. Directly to the east, the dull, hazy sun was trying to peek over the whiteness that enveloped the Karakorums, and off to the southeast, she could see the dark gray band of the storm clouds spread across the horizon. It seemed to be so far off that it was days away, but Sophie knew how fast weather moved in the mountains.

"We need to get going," she said, starting off again, not waiting for Jack. "When we get to the top of the *bottleneck*, we'll have a better idea of where everyone is."

Jack tucked away his scope. He'd let Sophie take the lead for a while, letting the rope play out between them for about ten meters before he began to follow. The snow here was deep, but so dry and light that it offered almost no resistance to the kick of their boots.

Sukey stood twenty feet away and watched Major Park, on his knees, bent over, vomiting onto the snow. He was retching a clear liquid, specked with red. She moved toward him as he came to his feet. He bent over once again, coughed, and spit out a mouthful of pink phlegm. The wind was whipping around them and blew strands of it onto his boot. He nodded to Sukey. "I'm fine. Let's continue. We're getting close."

Sukey threw her ice axe down on the snow to get his attention as she moved closer to him. Park's oxygen mask hung loose, blowing in the wind as he attempted to spit away the remnants of vomit and saliva that clung to his chin. He wiped his mouth with the back of a mitten. His goggles were up on his helmet and Sukey could see how strained and bloodshot his eyes were. She looked down at the puddle of pink liquid in the snow at their feet.

"No major. It's over now. We got as high as we could, but now we need to get you down the mountain." Sukey knew what pulmonary embolism looked like, and so did Park.

Park shook his head and re-fixed his mask. "No, no, madam Suek, I am fine. We must continue. We are so close, we cannot turn back now." He turned to start up the mountain once again.

Sukey grabbed his arm forcefully. "No Major!" she shouted at him. "We need to turn around right now or you will die up here! We are *not* going *up*!"

"Nonsense madam. I am fine. I feel strong." Park pulled away from her and started up the trail.

"Well I will not be going with you." Sukey picked up her ice axe and started down the trail. She moved down the trail ten meters and turned around to watch him.

Park turned halfway around and looked down at Sukey. Then he looked back up the mountain for several seconds before looking back down at her. Reluctantly, he began walking down to her. When he reached her, Park sank to his knees. His head hung and his shoulders slumped with dejection. Sukey dropped to her knees next to him and put her arm around his back. She could feel his despair.

"I am sorry Madam Suek. I have failed you. You proved to be much stronger than I." He reached out a hand and gripped Sukey's arm. "But, you must continue without me..."

"No, no, major," she interrupted. "We will go down together."

"*No*, you must continue! You are so close now – only a few hours of straightforward climbing in the snow – and you will be victorious. I am sure of it! We have made excellent time to this point."

"But Major, you are sick, and..."

"No, I am easily able to make it down to the last tent, where I will wait for you. We have come so far together." Park wrapped his arm around Sukey's shoulders and pulled her close to him. Their heads touched. "Please madam, go to the top. Win the race, and then our mission will be a success." They both had their goggles up and Park looked closely into Sukey's eyes. "It is very important to me Madam Suek, that you are first to the top. Do you understand what I am saying?"

Sukey took in a deep breath of oxygen and nodded slowly. She suddenly realized what he was telling her. Major Park had a mission, just as she did. And now, she knew she was about to make a horrible decision. She reached an arm around him and tried to hug Major Park as best she could on their knees. "Okay," she said softly. "Okay, I will continue up and be the first to the top, but only if you promise me that you will go *straight down*, all the way down without stopping."

"But Madam Suek," Park protested.

"No, you can't wait for me. You need to continue going down. At Camp 4 you will find oxygen and food, and then, you need to continue down. It is the only way you will survive this expedition. *Promise me.* Promise me that you won't wait for me. If you don't, I will start down, right now." Sukey rose to her feet.

Park looked up at her, not knowing what to say. Finally he pushed himself to his feet and took up his ice axe. He nodded affirmatively. "Yes, Madam Suek, I will go straight down. Yes, it is a sound plan. Soon I will be back on the fixed rope and I will go down. Yes, I need to get much lower very quickly."

"Good. That is best Major Park. I will radio Shin-Soo to have some soldiers meet you halfway. I will stay at Camp 5 tonight after I have been to the top, and go all the way down tomorrow. Now, you need to go. Bad weather is coming."

They stood still in the snow facing each other for several moments while the icy wind blew around them. Finally they embraced. Sukey wrapped her arms around Park, and he squeezed her gently. Park pulled his head away and stared into Sukey's eyes. "It has been my life's greatest honor to come up this mountain with you Chun Suek Yen. I shall never forget you." He abruptly turned, pulled his goggles down and started off down the trail.

Sukey turned, pushed the handle of her ice ax into the snow and started up the steep slope in front of her. Dawn had arrived, surrounding her with gray light, and clearly defining the route. It appeared an easier task than it had in darkness, but now she was alone. For the first time in four weeks Major Park was not by her side. She stopped and looked down the trail. Park was gone. She wondered if she would ever see him again. Sukey put her goggles up for a moment to let the breeze carry her tears away as she pushed upward through the snow.

Logan Healy stood looking up at the huge serac, directly above her, hanging ominously out over the northeast face of the mountain. It was a famous landmark of K2 that only climbers had the privilege of viewing in person. And it was terrifying. The "intimidator" Ed Viesturs had dubbed it. You moved quickly under the serac, praying that it would hold together for another few minutes until you made it past, and reached the beginning of the *traverse.*

Logan lingered under the serac for a minute, studying its features, smiling up at it, daring it to try and get her. Then, it was time to move on. She looked at her watch... 7:30am, a little behind schedule but still okay. She would make up some time on the *traverse* and then on the snow slope to the summit. Logan was feeling very optimistic. The final leg was going well. But now she needed to find the rest of her crew. Just as she reached inside her parka to switch on the voice-activated radio, her Walkie-talkie buzzed. It was Mathias and he was speaking quickly and loudly.

"Logan, we just picked up some bits and pieces from Bert and Arnie on the radio. The transmission is bad, their batteries must be shot too, but it sounds like they're in trouble. I think they're on the *traverse,* but it's difficult to tell."

"Okay, I'm almost at the *traverse.* I'll call you when I find them."

"Let us know. Burnsy and I are on our way up." Mathias clicked off.

Logan turned on her voice-activated radio, hoping she had some battery power left. As soon as it went on, she heard Bert's weak, pleading voice. "... can't breathe... Arnie fell..."

"Bert, hang on! I'm almost there," Logan shouted into her collar mic, doubting if the message got through as she started to jog through the deep powder snow. She was still about two hundred meters from the beginning of the *traverse*, the sixty degree wall of broken ice and snow that you had to climb sideways on the toe-points of your crampons, clinging to the wall with an ice ax and ice hammer. One hundred and twenty meters of arm and leg-burning torture, suspended over a ten thousand foot drop into oblivion. Even with fixed ropes, it was no place for beginners. *Jesus Bert, what the fuck are you doing up here!* Logan knew everything that was happening was entirely her fault because she loved the idea of having video of her all the way up the mountain

At the start of the *traverse,* Logan found several old, rusted pitons that had been driven deep into the rock long ago that held the ends of a dozen ropes of varying ages and condition. Some of the ropes were frayed and frozen into the ice and appeared to have been put up many years earlier. The *traverse* wasn't a spot where you cared about pulling up and recoiling rope on your way out.

Logan had to fall to her knees to rest and catch her breath after her sprint under the seracs. She knew she would need all her strength on the *traverse* if a rescue operation was needed. She would probably need help as well. She came to her feet to scan the trail behind her to see if she could see Jay Hamilton, or Lisa. Shielding her eyes from the dim sun rising in the east, Logan didn't see anyone coming up behind her. Then, far off in the distance, beyond the top of the *bottleneck*, almost obscured by the clouded air, she spied a flash of color. In spite of her predicament, Logan had to chuckle. There was only one climber in the world who wore that color blue, the color of *Les Bleus*, the French national soccer team. Logan raised her arms and waved her ice ax, but she knew Sophie would be concentrating on the snow in front of her. Then she saw another figure, a short way behind Sophie, that would be Jack. But they were probably an hour away and Logan couldn't wait. She pulled out the Walkie-Talkie and got Morris O'Dell at base camp.

"Morris, call over to the French camp and tell Clement to call up to Sophie and Jack and tell them that I may need help on the traverse with Bert and Arnie. Have to go."

"I will, said O'Dell, " but wait, Logan, I have a surprise for you. Rudy is right here..."

"No time," said Logan. She clicked off and stuffed the Motorola back into her parka.

At the start of the *traverse*, Logan unclipped from the green rope they had been using and chose an older but firm-looking white rope to cross the *traverse* on. If Bert and Arnie were having trouble, they would both be on the green rope and there was no telling what sort of predicament they would be in. A separate rope would be safer and allow her more maneuverability.

Logan moved out onto the *traverse*, edging sideways with her ice ax in her stronger left hand, an ice hammer in the right, kicking the points of her crampons firmly into the ice. Mathias had coached her on crossing the *traverse. Not as difficult as it looks, but be patient, go slow, and* never *pull a toe-hold out of the ice without having the ax, hammer, and opposite foot firmly in place.* The *traverse*, she found, wasn't difficult climbing, but it was tedious and exhausting, and with nothing below you for several thousand feet, you *didn't* want to fall and have to depend on the fixed rope to save your life. After she had mastered the technique, Logan began moving more quickly. Ten meters above her, she could see the green rope, which appeared to have almost no slack in it.

Ten minutes into the *traverse*, Logan came to a curve in the wall that obscured her view of anything beyond it. At the edge of the curve, the wall became almost totally vertical, requiring nearly complete reliance on the ax and hammer to support all of her weight. It took her several careful minutes to get around the curve and get a clear view of the rest of the *traverse*. Immediately, she came upon a vertical rope next to her. It was orange, looked very new, and was pulled taut. She looked up. Directly above her, ten feet away, was the face of Bert Skar staring down at her. He was hanging upside down with his back to the mountain, his two feet ensnared in a tangle of ropes. Logan looked down the orange rope and saw Arnie about thirty meters down, clinging to a small icy outcropping looking up at her with a terrified look on his face. He had lost his helmet, and it appeared, his oxygen mask and tank. Arnie released his grip just long enough to wave up at her, then quickly reassumed his hold on the ice.

Logan looked up, and then down again, and shook her head. She wrapped an arm around the fixed rope to gain a secure position, and reach inside her parka for the Walkie-talkie. "Albie, I've found them. They seem to be okay, but it looks like I'm going to be here a while. Better put away the champagne."

Chapter 31

Sophie Janot was an expert at discerning a change in the weather high on a mountain. Poppi had trained her well when she was a teenager, climbing in the Alps and the Dolomites. *Keep your nose to the wind. Smell it, and you'll know when it changes. See the color of the sky and the horizon. Watch the clouds, above and below you. And feel the snow. The snow will tell you a lot.* It was all second nature to Sophie now after so many years in the mountains, so many peaks, so many storms.

And now she smelled the wind, felt the snow with her boots, and watched the clouds drifting out of a darkening horizon, and knew what was coming. At her feet, she reached down and pulled up the green Zermatt rope. She looked down the steep gulley where the rope snaked over hidden boulders, disappearing into the snow and reappearing farther down. The top of the bottleneck. *How easy (and prudent) it would be for her and Jack to clip onto the rope and make their escape down the mountain, which, if this were a normal climb, is exactly what they would be doing.*

Jack pulled up next to her and took out his water bottle. He took a short drink and offered the bottle to Sophie. She took a sip just as she felt the vibration of the Walkie-talkie inside her parka. While Sophie answered the call, Jack looked up the trail toward the traverse through his Nikon scope. He was still perplexed at not seeing anyone ahead of them on the trail.

"Yes, doctor, we are fine. We are now at the top of the bottleneck." Sophie spoke English for Jack's benefit. As Sophie listened to Clement, a grim look came over her face. She quickly looked toward the seracs and the trail leading to the traverse. Jack knew something was wrong somewhere. "Oui doctor, oui. We will try." She clicked off and returned the Walkie-talkie to an inside pocket.

"Logan needs help," she said to Jack. "On the traverse. Her two movie-makers are in trouble."

"I think she has more trouble than that," said Jack. He was peering down the *bottleneck* through the Nikon, fixed on one spot. "Look, halfway down, follow the rope." He handed the glasses to Sophie.

"Oh no," breathed Sophie. She continued to watch the inert figure lying in the snow. The climber was wearing the unmistakable teal and black suit of the Zermatt team, and pink gloves. "I think it is a woman," said Sophie. "She's small, and unmoving."

Jack took the glasses back and studied the figure again, hoping to see some movement. As he tucked the Nikon away, Sophie pulled up the green rope and clipped her descender to it.

"Go help Logan," said Sophie, already climbing over the steep top edge of the *bottleneck.*

Jack knew there wasn't time for a conversation. Things were starting to come apart quickly, and bad weather was on the way. The race to the top was over. The goal now was to avert disaster. He started toward the traverse at as quick a jog as he could manage in the thin air. He looked up at the intimidating seracs overhead and prayed that they would hold fast for another few minutes.

Logan Healy unclipped from her fixed rope and carefully clawed her way up to Bert. She could see that his eyes were blinking and his arms were moving slightly. She clipped onto another fixed rope that ran behind the suspended video man, and moved up close to his head. "Hey Arnie, didn't expect to find you hanging around here."

"I'm Bert. He smiled, then grimaced with pain.

"Oh yeah. Okay."

"My back hurts," said Bert. "I think I strained some muscles. Arnie was moving up to get a good spot to shoot you coming across the traverse, and then he slipped. His sling snapped and he pulled me off. Lost all of our equipment. Having trouble breathing."

"Okay, relax," said Logan, examining his situation. She reached in behind Bert to where his oxygen mask was wedged between his pack and the wall, and pulled it out. She tested it to see that the gas was still flowing and put it over Bert's face. She checked to see that Bert's harness was secure, then clipped him to a fixed rope running behind him. "I'm going to go up and cut your feet loose. Hold tight to the rope."

Logan kicked in the tips of her crampons and swung the ax into the ice as far up the wall as she could reach. She could feel the wind gusting as she slowly edged up to where Bert's feet were entangled in a morass of old ropes. She pulled at the ropes but they were hopelessly tightened around the knee of his left leg and his right boot. Logan looked around her at the wall, trying to figure out how she could anchor herself for the next phase of the operation. She would need both hands free to cut through the maze of ropes while maintaining a secure position on the wall.

The first necessity was to secure her ice ax, which she clipped onto one of the old fixed ropes with a carabiner. If she lost the ax, there was little doubt in her mind that she and Bert would both die trying to get off the traverse. Then, she couldn't believe her good fortune when she spied an old, rusted piton a few feet above her. Whatever rope that had once run through it was now long gone. She ran a sling through the piton, clipped it to her harness and swung herself over to Bert's ensnared boots. Now, came the difficult part. Retrieving her Benchmark locking knife from her lower parka pocket. To be able to open it she would need a bare hand. She carefully pulled off the mitten and glove of her stronger left hand and stuffed them inside her parka.

Her hand was freezing rapidly in the twenty below zero temperature as she began cutting the ropes around Bert's feet. She only had maybe a minute before her hand would be useless and would probably drop the knife. "Okay Bert, hold on tight," she yelled as the razor sharp knife slashed through the ropes. Before she cut what looked to be the last rope around Bert's ankle, she pulled up the end of the rope, ran it through the piton above her, then wrapped it around her right arm to belay his fall as much as she could. Logan glanced down below them to see how Arnie was doing and was surprised to see another climber on the wall next to him.

Jack Finley had come across the traverse, immediately assessed the predicament, and had fixed a rope on a forty-five degree angle, directly to Arnie. There wasn't time or enough equipment for any sophisticated belaying system so Jack had hammered his last piton into the wall and secured Arnie to his own harness and the fixed rope. Imploring Arnie to "kick hard" to sink the points of his crampons into the ice and to hold tight to his shoulder, they were inching their way up the slanted rope. Logan watched them for a few seconds and shook her head in amazement. If it was anyone other than Jack Finley, she knew that Arnie would probably never get off the wall.

Logan cut Bert's legs free and as gently as she could, lowered him to an upright position. Bert groaned and grimaced and clung tightly to the fixed rope as he now tried to get some feeling back into his legs.

"Kick your points into the wall," Logan shouted. She could barely open her frozen left hand and knew she'd never get the knife closed again and back into her pocket so she just tossed it into the air. For a few seconds, she watched the two hundred dollar knife that she had now used once, silently disappear into the wilderness of K2, never to be seen again.

Logan painfully squeezed her frozen hand into her glove and mitten and flexed her fingers as rapidly as she could to get the blood flowing again. She retrieved her ice ax, then edged down next to Bert. "Okay Bert, we need to get out of here. Where's your ax?"

"I don't know. Gone."

"Fuck!" Logan stopped to think. She checked to make sure they were both clipped to the same rope. Then, she dug her ax into the ice above them. "Okay, now when I plant the ax, you grab onto it with your left hand and put your right arm over my shoulder to support yourself while you reposition your feet. We'll share the ax. Got it?"

"Yeah, I think so," said Bert reaching for the ax. He reached his hand across Logan's back and onto her right shoulder.

"Make sure you dig your points in. I don't want you pulling me off this mountain."

With Logan using the ice hammer in her right hand, and sharing the ax with Bert, they began edging their way back across the traverse. Once they got past the treacherous bend in the wall, the steepness of the slope lessened and the task become a little easier. Logan glanced at Bert and saw him looking down at the ten thousand feet of nothingness below them. When he looked up, his eyes were terrified.

"So Bert, I ever tell you about the time I met a mountain climber with no legs? I said to him, 'how you doing'? He says, 'hey, I can't kick.'" They both giggled and she could feel Bert relax a bit. "Doing great Bert. Don't look down. Not far to go now."

Below and to the right of her, Logan could see Jack Finley, with Arnie clinging to his back, making slow but steady progress toward the start of the traverse. Logan shook her head in amazement, wondering how Jack could still have enough strength left to carry Arnie. She wondered if Arnie knew how fortunate he was.

Sophie could see that the girl lying in the snow was breathing deeply and suspected that she had simply fallen asleep from exhaustion, a common malady at high altitude, even on supplemental oxygen. She pulled off a mitten and glove and reached under the girl's balaclava to check for a pulse. Sophie's cold fingers awakened the girl with a start. She sat up and looked around her silently.

Sophie pulled the girl's goggles up onto her helmet and peered into her eyes. Her pupils closed down normally in reaction to the light. Sophie nodded. "Good," she said. Then she unstrapped the girl's oxygen mask and checked inside. As she had suspected, ice had formed over the exit valve. Sophie gently tapped the ice loose, then checked the flow of oxygen.

"What happened? Who are you?" said the girl softly. He voice was raspy.

Sophie pulled out her water bottle and the girl took a long drink.

"Thank you," she said trying to smile. She was coming back to life now. "I'm Lisa Greenway."

Sophie stood up abruptly. "You need to get up now."

"I don't know what happened," said Lisa. "I felt so tired, I sat down to rest for just a minute."

"You fell asleep," said Sophie. "Because you were exhausted and not getting enough oxygen. It's how many people die on the mountains. Now stand up please. How are your fingers and toes?"

The girl stood up and flexed her legs. "Okay, I think." She pulled her ice ax from the snow, and tugged on her ascender clipped to the fixed rope. "Well, thank you, for your help. I need to start up."

Sophie moved in front of her. "No. Your climb is over. You are going down now, as far as you can make it before the storm comes. If you continue up, you will be dead by this evening."

"No, I'm fine." The girl insisted. "I'm going up. I still have time." Lisa tried to take a step past Sophie but Sophie reached out and grasped the fixed rope, blocking her path. The girl gave Sophie a perturbed look. "Hey, let me by, please," said Lisa. "Who are you anyway?"

Sophie reached into a pocket of her parka and took out her gravity knife. "My name is Sophie Janot." With a flick of her wrist, the small knife blade appeared causing a look of sudden fear on Lisa's face. "If you insist on going up, I will cut your oxygen hose." Sophie stared unwaveringly into the girl's confused eyes for several seconds. Then she let go of the rope and reached an arm roughly around behind Lisa and pulled her in close. "Please Lisa," she said softly, "I can't let anyone else die on this expedition." She tightened her hug. "You *have* to go down."

The realization that it was *the* Sophie Janot who was standing here in the snow hugging her, and that Sophie must have come *down* the bottleneck to help her, swept over Lisa, instantly ending her resolve to continue up. "Geeze, I'm so stupid," she said, hugging Sophie. "What am I doing here? Jack told me not to go above Camp 2." The two women separated.

Sophie grinned. "Jack's a smart man."

Lisa nodded and smiled. "I like Jack, a lot."

"Yeah, most girls do," said Sophie. "Now, you need to get moving. There's some horrible weather coming. Stay on the rope."

Lisa took a stride down the mountain, and stopped. "Hey, would you really have cut my air hose?"

Sophie smiled and shrugged. Then she turned and started up the bottleneck.

The sound of Lisa's voice stopped her. "Hey, Sophie?" She turned around.

"Have you seen Jay Hamilton? He was out in front of me."

Sophie shook her head. "Haven't seen anyone."

Lisa hesitated. "Or maybe he was behind me. I'm not sure. Yes, he was behind me I think. He must have gone down."

Sophie nodded and waved, then resumed climbing at an aggressive pace. She knew she was late.

Logan Healy reached the beginning of the traverse, dropped her ice hammer to the snow, and reached back to help Bert off the wall. Jack Finley was coming toward her. Just beyond him, she saw Arnie bending his knees and exercising his legs to get the blood flowing back into his numb toes.

Logan and Jack embraced briefly without speaking. They separated and Jack put his goggles up on his forehead. Logan was shocked at the change in his appearance since she last saw him at the Zermatt base camp. His eyes were glassy, cheeks withered and red over a straggly beard, and he looked as if he had lost twenty pounds. The Northeast Ridge had taken its toll. She smiled. "Hey Finn," she said softly. "Good thing you were here."

"Yeah, you too." Jack nodded back toward the bottleneck. "Sophie went down to help one of your other climbers, a girl. She was lying in the snow."

"Lisa," said Logan. "Jay Hamilton should be down there too."

Jack looked over at Arnie, battling the cold. Jack had given him his spare wool hat. "He's okay. A little banged up. May have a broken rib, but he can climb down. How about your guy?"

Logan glanced at Bert. "You okay Bert? Your legs okay?"

Bert was taking a long drink from his water bottle. He put the cap back on. "Yeah, I'm good. Better than ever. Let's get off this mountain."

Jack pulled his coil of rope up over his head. "I'll take them down." He tossed the end of the rope to Bert who clipped on and handed the end to Arnie. There was no fixed rope between the top of the bottleneck and the traverse because of the relatively easy trail, but Jack wasn't sure about the physical state of the two video men and knew it was best to rope together.

Logan pulled out her Walkie-talkie and buzzed Albie Mathias and told him what was happening then listened for a few seconds before clicking off. "Albie and Tim are an hour below the bottleneck. They'll take these guys off your hands."

Logan picked up her hammer and ax and smiled at Jack. "Thanks Finn."

Jack moved over to her and hugged his old friend. He didn't have to ask the question he already knew the answer to. "Be careful Logan. It's late."

She gave him a brief, hard hug, then turned away. "Have to go." Logan was already ten meters onto the traverse when Jack, Bert and Arnie started down.

Sophie Janot made it to the top of the bottleneck just before Jack, Bert and Arnie. She could see they were all moving slowly with a steady wind blowing against them. Jack was having trouble keeping up with the other two, stopping every few steps to catch his breath. She could see that it had been a strenuous rescue of the video crew.

Bert and Arnie barely nodded to her as they passed, shoulders hunched against the wind, eyes down. They had had enough of the mountain and enough of the bitter cold. Sophie had seen the look before. She began walking up the trail and soon reached Jack. They stopped a few feet apart in silence while Jack took in deep breaths. Jack recoiled the rope as Bert and Arnie clipped onto the fixed rope and headed down the bottleneck.

"How's Logan?" Sophie studied him while she waited for an answer.

Jack put his goggles up. "Better than I am. She's on the traverse. Headed up."

Sophie pressed her lips together knowingly. She pointed down the bottleneck. "The girl in the snow, Lisa, she is fine. She's on her way down. And her companion, Jay... uhm... "

"Hamilton," said Jack.

Sophie nodded. "Oui, yes, she said he is also on his way down."

"Yeah, that's good. Jay is a smart man."

"And so are you Jack. You need to go down, all the way, very quickly now."

Jack nodded slowly. "Yes, I know. How about you?"

"No, I still have some work to do here." Sophie smiled. "I'm going to run her down, right Jack?"

Jack knew there was no point in having a discussion. He moved forward and hugged her. "Okay," he said softly. "Run her down." He looked into her eyes. "Be careful Soph." He turned and started off after Bert and Arnie, wondering if he'd ever see her again. Sophie dug her ax into the snow and started off toward the traverse, grateful for the wind at her back.

From the top of the bottleneck, Jack could see that Bert and Arnie were making good time, going down the long gulley. He looked back at Sophie making her way toward the traverse at a slow, steady pace. He never had to worry about Sophie high on a mountain – the best mountain climber he had ever known. Turning back, to clip his descender onto the fixed rope, Jack saw something he hadn't noticed before – a trail of broken snow leading away from the top of the bottleneck, heading off in a strange direction – to the northeast, up toward a rugged section of deep snow where no K2 climbers would ever be going. He stared, for a few moments, trying to focus his eyes on the trail kicked through the knee-deep snow. Reluctantly, he unclipped from the fixed rope and made his way laboriously up to the strange path. He followed it for about ten meters until he saw, up ahead, the trail dropped off over a steep incline and the footpath disappeared. He knew it would be suicide to continue following the trail in his depleted condition with bad weather approaching. He turned back just as another wave of pain seemed to rumble through his head, as it had been doing for the past hour. At the top of the bottleneck, he clipped onto the fixed rope again, and reached inside his pack for his small kit of medications. With the last of his water, he washed down a handful of aspirins and a dexamethasone. Now, he needed to get lower very quickly. He had been at over seven thousand meters for far too long.

Logan Healy kicked the tips of her crampons securely into the ice and repositioned her ax out as far as she could reliably dig it into the wall above her. She had mastered the technique of crossing the traverse and knew she was moving as quickly as she dared. The wind was gusting now blowing frigid air through her suit and mittens, making it difficult to feel her fingers on the ax and ice hammer. Her toes had gone numb long ago. She had always been fortunate to escape the surgeon's scalpel trimming away pieces of frostbitten toes. Maybe, she wouldn't be so lucky this time.

She'd come a long way across the traverse, passing the spot, thirty meters back, where she had found Bert, yet, the wall seemed endless. She needed desperately to get back on the snow where she could bend her knees, flex her toes and generate some body heat on the arduous hike up the final summit snow slope. And, she couldn't dispel from her mind the agonizing thought that she would have to once again cross the traverse on the way down.

Logan stopped at an anchor to clip her second sling onto the fixed rope to get past the piton. She clipped her first sling directly onto the piton to allow her to rest for a few seconds and check the time. She secured the ax to the rope and took a drink from her water bottle. It took considerable effort with her bulky mittens to expose her watch from under the parka sleeve and the end of her glove. She nearly gasped when she saw the time. It was eleven o'clock. *Oh, my god, how can that be?* She knew she'd lost a lot of time getting Bert down – maybe an hour, she thought – but it must have taken much longer. She looked around and suddenly realized that she couldn't see *anything*. The air was white – above her, below her – blocking out the vast panorama behind her that she had become so accustomed to over the last three weeks. She was in a cloud.

Suddenly, Logan felt all alone – and frightened. The only thing she could see was a few meters of the wall on either side of her. She didn't know what she would be able to see on the summit snow slope, and she knew the fixed ropes would end at the end of the traverse. Plus, the timing was terrible. She still had at least an hour and a half to the top, putting her at the summit when the storm would hit in full force. She had a decision to make.

Logan leaned back on the sling holding her to the piton. She grimaced and closed her eyes, dreading the decision that she knew was the correct one, the one that would send her home to her family and friends and the wonderful life she lived. *But could she live with the decision?*

A sound made Logan snap her eyes open. She'd heard *something. Or was she imagining it?* She strained to hear over the wind, and there it was again. A faint, dull *thunk*. She was sure of it. Logan held her breath to listen for the sound. *Thunk,* followed by two different sounds this time, just barely audible. A few seconds later, it came again. *Thunk, clink, clink.* It sounded a long way off, but Logan knew she had heard the sounds before. *Thunk, clink, clink.* Then, Logan grinned, and she laughed, and she wasn't frightened anymore. *Of course she knew the sound. She'd been making the same sounds for the last hour!* She listened again and heard the *thunk* of an ax digging into the wall, followed by the *clink, clink* of crampons being kicked into the ice. Logan shook her head and laughed again. She wanted to take off her mask and yell into the whiteness all around them... *Sophie! You are incredible!*

Logan's decision had been made for her. She unclipped from the piton, took up her ax, and started out again across the traverse with a smile still on her face and a renewed sense of purpose. Her adrenalin was flowing again. The former ski racer was flying down the Hahnenkamm once more and she could see the finish line.

Sukey could feel the damp warmth of their small kitchen when she was a child, watching her mother cook a steaming pot of bulgogi on the stove, waiting for a warm mandoo dumpling her mother would sneak to her before dinner. Her head was down, fighting the wind in her face, eyes fixed on the snow in front of her. *Thirty below zero with the wind.* She'd never before felt such cold. Moving painfully slowly in the knee deep snow, how she longed for the days with Major Park and his big boots out in front, breaking trail and shielding her from the wind. Now Sukey was alone, tears fogging her goggles, certain that she would be dying on this mountain.

Inside her parka, the vibration of the Walkie-Talkie straightened her up. She could see through the cloudy whiteness in front of her, the vague outline of the summit cone and knew she was still on the correct path. There was no way to tell how far off the summit was. An hour she thought, or maybe two hours with the snow so deep. Sukey was so tired she didn't think she could stay upright for another hour or stand the cold. She debated whether to answer the Walkie-Talkie, or just sit down in the snow and rest and maybe take a nap for a few minutes. The Motorola continued to buzz.

Sukey turned to put her back to the wind and looked down at her broken trail in the snow, and, farther beyond, the long, craggy outline of the Northeast Ridge fading into the clouds. *How far she had come. How far they had come.* She wondered if Major Park had made it down to Camp 4 yet.

Her voice barely made a sound when she clicked on the Walkie-Talkie. She pulled out her water bottle, tore at the Velcro strap of her oxygen mask and tugged the balaclava down under her chin. She drained the final drops of water in her bottle as the frigid air stung her cheeks. She could hear Shin-soo's frantic voice in her ear asking if she was there. There was a great deal of static and the signal was very weak.

Sukey assured the Expedition Leader that she was still making good progress, and asked if his men had met up with Major Park yet. No, he told her, but they were advancing up the ridge at a very fast pace to treat Major Park. And, now he had Chairman Young Kim on the line from Busan to offer her encouragement. Then, the static and the sound in her ear faded away to nothing as the battery power light flickered out. Sukey stared at the dead Walkie-Talkie, relieved that she wouldn't have to listen to the condescending Kim, then tossed it into the snow – twelve less ounces weighing her down. She could feel the heavy sat-phone in an inside pocket and knew she needed to call Jay Hamilton who was on his way up to rescue her from Major Park and take her back down the Abruzzi Spur and all the way to San Diego. She needed to tell him that she was in no danger from Major Park, and he should go back down and wait for her at the Zermatt base camp. She should have called him hours ago. No, she should have called him yesterday. But, again, there was something in her heart that wouldn't let her make the call.

Sukey pulled the balaclava back up over her mouth and nose, and secured her oxygen mask. She edged the zipper of her parka up as far as it would go, then turned back toward the summit once more, forcing her to lean forward to shield her face from the wind. Tiny crystals of snow were starting to ping off of her goggles and mask, but she started forward once more, because she had nowhere else to go.

For ten minutes, Sukey plodded ahead in the deep snow, head down against the wind. But, now she needed to stop and look up to check her bearings. Through the cloud of snow and ice crystals in the air, she could still make out the vague mass of the summit cone directly ahead, but suddenly there was something else in her vision, a distant, hazy dark spot that shouldn't be there. Sukey swept the snow from her goggles, blinked her eyes and focused on the small spot, wondering if she was hallucinating or just allowing her tired mind to imagine something that wasn't there. She endured the icy wind and the snow in her face as she concentrated her focus on the dark spot that couldn't be there... and then, *the spot moved!*

Logan Healy knew now that she would be the first woman ever to climb all fourteen of the 8,000 meter mountains. She'd come through the traverse, taken the hard right turn, and trudged up through twenty meters of deep snow to reach the final summit slope. She stood looking up at the summit, just another forty or fifty meters away, with the snow and the wind in her face, relishing the feeling of conquest. She had done it.

Logan turned away from the wind and took out the Walkie-Talkie. She needed to let base camp know where she was. They deserved that.

Morris O'Dell answered the call. He sounded frantic. "Logan, Logan, we've been waiting to hear. Where are you? Are you all right?"

Logan laughed. "Yes Morris, I'm fine. I'm wonderful! I'm standing on the summit slope about ten minutes from the summit. We did it!" She could hear whooping and cheers in the background.

"That's *wonderful* Logan. Take plenty of pictures. How's the weather?"

"The weather sucks, but I've seen worse. I'll make it down."

"Terrific. Congratulations! Now I've got someone special who wants to talk to you."

Rudy Joost came on the line. "Logan, my darling, I'm so proud of you. The entire *Zermatt* team is so proud of you."

"Thank you Rudy. I'm glad you came back. I'm glad you're there." And Logan knew she meant it. His voice all of a sudden made her feel warm, and secure, and she looked forward to seeing him again. To resuming their life together.

"Of course I'm here darling. I *knew* you would be victorious! Those other girls could never compete with you. You are the best female mountain climber in history!"

"Yeah, okay Rudy. Hey, I gotta get going here. Finish this thing. I'll see you when I get down."

"Yes, yes, get to the top, and I'll see you in the morning. We've got a lot of journalists and photographers waiting for you down here."

"Yeah, great. Love you Rudy." Logan clicked off.

Logan tucked away the Walkie-Talkie and zipped up again. She thought about Rudy. *Yes, this is the way it should be. She wouldn't be an asshole and throw away the greatest life any girl could dream about – who has a birthday party on a monstrous yacht in the Aegean Sea with the fucking Dropkick Murphys playing live on deck?! And, Rudy did love her. Truly. And, she'd still see Anja Lindgren from time to time, and Anja would be fine with that.* Logan had to chuckle at the thought of who's bed Anja might be waking up in at that very moment.

Yes, Rudy loved her. *But he still doesn't know shit about mountain climbing. 'Those other girls could never compete with you.'* Logan turned toward the summit and gripped the head of her ax. She stood for a half a minute gazing up at the top of K2, thinking about what she was about to accomplish. Then, she turned around again and sat down in the snow. *Yes, this is how this should end.*

Logan sat on the slope for ten minutes with the snow and wind pelting her, and began to worry. Finally, at the bottom of the slope, twenty meters down from her, a figure appeared, moving deliberately, one step at a time without oxygen in the thin air, and even in a snow storm, resplendent in her *Azuri Bleu* climbing suit. Logan sat, enjoying the moment, waiting for Sophie to look up at her.

Sophie trudged up the hill, to within five meters of Logan before she sensed something in her path and looked up. Logan had put her goggles up on her helmet and pulled away her oxygen mask. Sophie pulled back, shocked to see anyone on the slope.

Logan laughed. "Hey Soph. What took you so long? I've been up here for two days waiting for you."

Sophie put up her goggles and bent over laughing. "Oh my friend, you weren't, I know, because I heard you on the traverse, just ahead of me. But, I couldn't catch you."

Logan stood up as Sophie reached her. They both squeezed each other tightly. Sophie look up at her. "But why?"

"Because." Logan shrugged. "Because, this is the right way for this to end."

Sophie smiled and kissed Logan on both cheeks. "Okay my friend, but now we need to climb just a bit more."

The two women put their goggles down and started up the slope. They'd only gone a few meters when Sophie stopped. "Can we wait a moment?" she said, turning back and gazing out towards the West Ridge.

Logan knew what she was thinking. "Yes. Sure we can. Let's wait. That would be the *best*."

They stood motionless peering through the driving snow for a minute. Then, another. Then five minutes. "Okay," said Sophie, "we need to go." She pushed her ax into the snow and started up. Logan stood still. Sophie had taken a few steps, then heard Logan's voice.

"Sophie. Sophie! There she is! She's here."

Sophie turned back and saw Logan dashing down the slope. Logan threw her ax down as she jumped through the snow and screamed. *"Sukey! Sukey!"*

Sophie wiped the snow from her goggles and looked down the hill. Then, she saw her. Sukey, in her red suit, hulking against the wind, moving with determination. "Sukey!" she yelled, tears filling her eyes. "We're here!" Sophie ran down the slope not bothering to breathe.

Chapter 32

There were two small flags at the summit. A Canadian flag and a Molson beer flag, flapping straight out in the wind from short metal rods hammered into the ice. They would have been put up by the combined expedition that had summited in June, and had left their fixed ropes in place for the Zermatt team.

The flags were a blessing for Logan, Sophie and Sukey, they knew, because while few people would question the word of three of the most accomplished female climbers in the world, *visual evidence* had always been a crucial factor in the validation of summit claims on the world's tallest mountains. With the snow pelting them sideways and visibility at the summit down to zero, there would be no pictures of the triumphant women with Broad Peak or the Gasherbrums in the background. But, the flags, along with the pictures from the previous expedition, would be all they needed.

Without having to discuss it, the three women knew how they would simultaneously summit K2. With Sukey between them, Logan and Sophie locked arms and prepared for the final step. "Okay," said Logan, pointing to a spot directly in front of the flags. "I say that's the highest point... we all hit it together."

With their cameras set to *video*, the women recorded their final step. Then they hugged, they cried, and they rejoiced in the rare moment of elation that came with the realization that there was no more mountain to climb – they were standing on the highest point of the second tallest mountain in the world. They had done it. "Ladies," said Logan, with a sob in her voice, "I am honored to be standing here with you both."

"Well, if you hadn't..." Sophie started.

"No!" said Logan emphatically. "We never talk about who did what... first, second, third... *none* of that shit, *ever,* to anyone. None of that matters. What matters is that in the history of mountaineering, only *twenty-three* climbers have summited all fourteen, and now, three of them are *women!"*

Logan pulled Sophie and Sukey in close to her and looked into their faces. "We arrived here together! End of the story. Promise me, or I'll push both of you into China." Sophie and Sukey had to laugh, as they always seemed to do around Logan Healy.

"Okay," said Sophie, "but now, we need to take some pictures, and then get off of this mountain. The weather will be getting worse.

They all took pictures of the three of them with their sponsorship banners stretched out tightly against the wind, and the two flags prominently in the foreground. Before she put her camera away, Logan sent the video and several still shots down the mountain to Samantha Ryan's laptop. Logan laughed. "Wow, Rudy's going to shit! Those pictures will be on Facebook and Instagram before we get back through the traverse."

"And in the papers in Seoul and Paris and New York before we get down the mountain," said Sukey

"Yes, and now we need to go," said Sophie impatiently. "My toes are not doing well."

The women made it back down the summit slope much more quickly than it took going up. At the bottom, Logan and Sophie immediately started down the steep left turn that led back to the traverse. Then they noticed that Sukey was hanging back. Sophie took a few strides back toward her. "Sukey, come on. We'll help you through the traverse. You can do it. There are fixed ropes all along it."

Logan, sensing that something else was holding Sukey back, came up the slope to her. "Sukey, what's wrong?"

Sukey shook her head. "I am sorry, my wonderful friends, but I can't go down with you." Sukey turned and looked back toward the West Ridge and saw her trail through the snow rapidly being filled in by the new snow. "I must go back down the ridge. I need to find Major Park. I need to help him down."

"Sukey, *no*," Sophie protested, moving up to her. "You can't *do* this..."

Sukey held her hand up to silence her. She moved quickly to Sophie and hugged her, and then Logan. "I have to. I love you both. Tell Jay I had to do this." With tears in her eyes, Sukey abruptly turned and started down the slope, moving quickly, toward the West Ridge.

Sophie started after her, but Logan held out an arm in front of Sophie. "Come on. We need to go." Both women stood still for a moment, watching Sukey disappear in the driving snow, knowing that there was a very high probability that they would never see their friend again.

A crowd had gathered in the OSN broadcast trailer, not just to get a look at the video and still pictures they had downloaded from Samantha Ryan's laptop, but because it was the warmest spot at the Zermatt basecamp. The weather wasn't nearly as bad as at the top of the mountain, but it was taking its toll with wind and temperatures dropping well below zero. It was not an afternoon to be outside.

Marty Gallagher sat at the console editing the documentation of the simultaneous summiting of K2 by the first three women climbers to have conquered all fourteen of the world's tallest mountains. It was an historic day, and Gallagher knew how valuable the footage was to the OSN network. New York was in a frenzy to get it on the air as soon as possible, and he was working quickly. He glanced up at the big clock on the wall. It was two o'clock, his time – midnight in New York – still prime time for most of the U.S., and soon Glenda Craft would be in his earphones, as she had been for the past hour, imploring him to uplink the live broadcast from K2. On the OSN set in the broadcast tent next to the trailer, Bruce Kinder was standing by, waiting to deliver the climactic video report.

Standing behind Gallagher in the trailer, watching the summiting video again was Rudy Joost, along with the journalists he had brought in with him from London. They had been peppering him with questions about how he felt about the *group summiting* as one of the writers had dubbed it. At first, he had been piqued, wondering what had gotten into Logan Healy, for surely she had been first to the summit slope. But gradually, the more he looked at the video, the more he embraced the outcome. This new development, and Logan's obvious magnanimity to her fellow climbers, may, in the end, prove to be the bigger story of the venture. Already, the writers were talking about Logan's *warm-hearted gesture of sportsmanship. Yes, this could work out very well.* Joost also had to admit to himself that he had been a little surprised – and gratified – by Logan's words of affection from the summit. He wasn't sure where Logan stood on the state of their relationship. But now he had his beautiful fiancé back, and the Zermatt brand would have its international icon on the front pages and talk shows around the world for the next year. It was hard to imagine a better result of the expedition, *as long as everyone on the mountain could now get down safely.*

Across the base camp, in the communications tent, Morris O'Dell was putting the Walkie-Talkie back onto its charging cradle. He'd just talked to Dong Shin-Soo at the Korean camp and relayed the message he'd gotten from Logan Healy that Chun Suek Yen had made the summit and then started back down the West Ridge, alone, to search for Major Park. Shin-Soo told O'Dell that a strong team of Korean climbers had been racing up the ridge all day to reach Park. O'Dell wished him luck.

O'Dell wished himself luck too. Yes, Logan had summited and was on her way down. But now he had climbers strung out all up and down the Abruzzi Spur, with Logan and Sophie Janot somewhere above the bottleneck. He had the two injured videographers on their way to Camp 4 with Timmy Burns, two inexperienced climbers, Lisa Greenway and Jay Hamilton, *somewhere* between four and three, and Mathias somewhere near Camp 5. A brutal storm was raging, communications were limited, and he wasn't certain of exactly where *anyone* was. It was a miracle that Bert and Arnie hadn't perished on the traverse, and now it would be another miracle if everyone made it down. He looked again at the weather map on the laptop in front of him and saw that there would be no break in the weather until early tomorrow morning. Everyone needed to find shelter very soon because the night would not be kind to anyone caught outside.

Albie Mathias was worried too. It was all beginning to look too familiar to him, when things started to go bad and one thing led to another and the lack of communication and bad weather and human frailties all combined to send a well – planned expedition spinning off the rails toward disaster.

Snow and wind were pelting the tent at Camp 5, making it difficult to keep the stove lit. Mathias was trying to melt snow to fill two more water bottles, anticipating the arrival of Jack Finley. After giving Bert and Arnie their fill of water and a few energy bars, Mathias had put them back on the fixed rope, accompanied by Timmy Burns, with instructions to get down to Camp 4 before dark. Bert had told him that Finley was right behind them coming down the bottleneck, but now, a half hour later, Mathias was still waiting for him to arrive.

But it wasn't just Finley. It seemed everything had gone wrong that day. The failure of the *voice-activated radio* was a huge problem, and then the almost miraculous rescue of the video crew had destroyed the timing of the summit bid. Now, everything was late, by several hours, and the only thing that had arrived on time was the storm. It was getting dark, and colder, and he still had two women climbers somewhere high on the mountain. Mathias also had to admit to himself that he too was in a precarious way. He was exhausted after three days of hauling heavy loads that the Sherpas normally would have carried up the mountain, and more critically, he had been at too high an altitude for too long. The body begins to break down quickly above six thousand meters and the mind gradually loses its capacity to concentrate. Mathias knew he needed to go down.

Jack Finley pushed his ax into the drifting snow outside the tent, crawled through the flap, and collapsed onto a sleeping bag at the end of the tent. Mathias extinguished the stove and zipped up the flap.

"Good to see you Jack," he said, handing Finley a full water bottle. "Bit of weather out there." When Jack finally took off his goggles Mathias was stunned at his appearance. Jack's eyes were sunken and glassy and he looked emaciated. He offered Jack his oxygen mask but it was waved away.

"That'll make it worse," said Jack. His voice was weak and scratchy.

Mathias filled Jack in on the excellent news from the summit, then tossed some energy bars onto his lap. "Sorry, no more soup or tea up here. Eat a few of these, then you need to start down again. You need to get lower."

Jack shook his head. "I'll wait for Sophie and Logan." He took a long drink from the water bottle, put the cap on, turned his head to the side and immediately fell asleep. Mathias covered him with a sleeping bag, took the crampons off his boots and put them outside the tent.

Mathias clicked on the Walkie-Talkie and let Morris O'Dell know that Jack had arrived. "He insists on waiting here for Sophie and Logan, so we'll be getting a few hours of sleep."

"Well, when the women do arrive, they shouldn't stay long at Camp 5. They should get down to four, even in the dark. Logan said that Sophie's toes are badly frostbitten, and her own are not good either. I'm sending Dr. Chen up to Camp 3, with his kit to meet them tomorrow morning. Maybe he'll be able to save a few toes. The weather is supposed to clear in the morning so Rudy's helicopter should be able to fly them out to Skardu if necessary."

At Camp 3, Fred Terry had been awaiting the arrival of Lisa Greenway and Jay Hamilton. Morris O'Dell had sent Terry back up from Camp 2, with a bag of food, more fuel canisters and an additional sleeping bag, and told him the novice climbers would probably be in a bad state when they arrived. Neither had ever been so high on an eight thousand meter mountain, enduring prolonged cold and wind like they had today. O'Dell wanted to know the minute they arrived and what condition they were in. He was already thinking about the capacity of Joost's helicopter to ferry stricken climbers out to Skardu the following day.

Terry had been melting snow and had filled three water bottles, and made up a bottle of hot tea. When Lisa and Jay arrived, he would cook up a pan of re-hydrated chicken noodle soup. But now he was getting worried. It was five o'clock and it was dark outside and there was still no sign of the two climbers. He bundled up, put on his head lamp, and carried the battery lantern outside. The fixed rope passed just ten meters from the campsite but in the dark, with the driving snow reducing visibility, it was conceivable that a climber could miss the tent on the way down, which would be disastrous.

Terry picked up the fixed rope to see if he could feel any vibration or change in the tension, then moved up the slope a short distance, struggling against the wind to hold the battery lantern over his head. He waited a few minutes and was encouraged when he felt something in the rope, then he saw the light of a head lamp about fifty meters above him. He continued to wave the lantern as he watched the light get closer. Suddenly a sinking feeling came over him... *there was only one light coming down the slope.* Terry prayed that someone's head lamp had failed, but then the light arrived and he could see it was just one climber, Lisa Greenway, he could tell by her size.

"Hey Fred," said Lisa, unclipping from the rope. "Am I glad to see you. I've never been this cold."

Terry hugged her briefly while still staring up the slope. "Lisa, where's Hamilton?"

Lisa headed for the warmth of the tent. "Oh, Jay went down hours ago."

Terry followed her into the tent where she collapsed on a cushion of sleeping bags. "Lisa, *Lisa! Talk to me!*" He handed her a water bottle then reached over and unsnapped the strap on her helmet. He put her goggles up and pulled the Velcro snap on her oxygen mask. "Lisa, when was the last time you saw him?"

Lisa pulled off her helmet and shook her damp hair out groggily. She looked at Terry. "Saw who?"

"*Hamilton!*" he nearly yelled at her. "*Lisa, focus here.* Where did you last see Hamilton today?"

She took a long drink and shrugged. "This morning, I guess. We left a little after Logan did."

"And where was Hamilton? In front of you or behind you?"

Lisa sat up, seeming to finally grasp the earnestness in Terry's voice. "He was, uhm, behind me. Yeah, I went first and Jay was behind me. We made good time and Jay was right behind me."

"When did you stop Lisa? Where did you turn around?"

Lisa closed her eyes and grimaced. "*Oh God, no.* I remember now. When we were halfway up the bottleneck, I was tired and my legs were burning, and I needed to sit down for a minute. Jay went ahead of me. I told him to go ahead and I'd catch up."

"Then what happened? *Lisa,* did you see him after that?"

Her eyes filled with tears. "*No, no!* I fell asleep, and then Sophie Janot got me up and sent me down. I thought Jay had already gone down."

"Damn it!" said Terry, reaching for the Walkie-Talkie.

Sukey was certain now that she'd made a fatal mistake in trying to find Major Park. The snow was pelting her sideways and the gusting wind was threatening to lift her up and send her off the side of the mountain. She wasn't even sure she was on the same trail she had come up on – nothing looked familiar, and she was struggling to find any remnants of her tracks that the snow had now covered over. If she had just gone down with Sophie and Logan, they'd be through the traverse by now and back on the fixed rope headed down to safety, down to basecamp and to Jay, and she would survive this expedition.

But now, nearly three hours after leaving the summit, she was lost and her fingers and toes had been numb for a dangerously long time, and it was getting dark – very quickly. How foolish she had been to think she could catch up to Park, or to help him if he was in trouble. He was probably down to Camp 4, by now, possibly in the care of the rescue team that Shin-Soo had sent up the ridge. And *she* would probably never even reach the shelter of Camp 5. So she plodded through the deepening snow, stumbling and sliding dangerously down unseen inclines, hoping she was still on the trail. She kept going forward because she was too exhausted to stop, and to sit down in the snow was the end.

Sukey suddenly gasped for air as her oxygen bottle expired. She ripped away the Velcro strap on her mask and breathed in the frigid air that burned her mouth and throat. She had to kneel down and pull off her pack to disconnect the empty oxygen bottle. She'd always railed against the practice of climbers littering the high slopes with spent oxygen bottles, but now she had no choice. As always, the weight of a useless oxygen bottle was too much of a burden. She dropped it in the snow.

As she knelt in the snow breathing deeply, trying to get some oxygen in her lungs, she fought off the strong urge to lie down, curl up in a ball, close her eyes and welcome the warmth that came with freezing to death. She knew it was close. *Why should she fight it?* She eyed the spent oxygen bottle next to her, a layer of new snow already covering it. It would probably be years before anyone climbed this high again on the West

Ridge. The oxygen bottle would be there forever, as would her body if she didn't get up and move. Sukey looked up and saw that complete darkness had engulfed her. She had no idea where the trail was.

Reaching back into her pack, Sukey brought out her headlamp, which magically illuminated the snow far out ahead of her.

Sukey struggled to her feet and immediately saw something just a dozen meters ahead, sticking out of the snow. It was another oxygen bottle, identical to hers. She knew right away it was Major Park's, pushed into the snow as a marker as he had done on the way up, a short distance from Camp 5. Sukey was encouraged by the fact that Park had made it this far, and she knew that he had been carrying the extra oxygen bottle. She estimated that Camp 5, and the beginning of the fixed rope was less than an hour away now and was buoyed by the thought that Park could be there waiting for her.

Sukey's optimism was dashed as soon as she set out again down the trail and found that she need to stop every two steps to try to gain a lung-full of oxygen. She had never been this high before without the gas and doubted that she would ever reach Camp 5 at the rate she was going. She started to shiver, another byproduct of the lack of oxygen. Yet, she could still stand so she continued, head down, shoulders hunched against the wind and the shivering... two steps and a stop to breathe... two steps and a stop.

Sukey had only gone twenty meters beyond where she'd found Park's oxygen bottle when, probing the snow in front of her with her ice ax, she felt something solid. She looked up and was stunned to find an ice ax standing up in the snow. It was Park's. She slowly cast the beam of her headlamp around her, and then she saw him, on the right side of the trail only ten feet away from her. Sukey gasped with fright, then fell to her knees sobbing.

Park was seated as if on a park bench. He'd carved a seat out of the ice to sit and wait for her where she couldn't miss him. His goggles, up on his helmet, glistened in the light from Sukey's headlamp. His eyes were closed and he had a peaceful look on his face. Park's parka jacket was unzipped and his mittens and gloves were gone. Between his knees in front of him, stood an oxygen bottle, the gauge showing it was full. His hands were together on his lap holding something.

Sukey edged up close to him and brushed the snow off his hands. He was holding his old, oversized leather wallet and his cell phone. Sukey wondered if he'd been looking at the pictures of his wife and children. She felt his shoulders, then his face, and knew that he was gone. Sukey took off a mitten and glove, and knelt in front of him. She put her goggles up to let the tears run free and held his cold, hard hand, and even though she was a very lapsed Catholic and Park was a Buddhist, she said the few prayers she could remember. She stood and kissed Park on the forehead then, looked at him for a few moments. She knew she never would have gotten up the West Ridge, and then to the summit without him. And, she surely would have died on the way down if Park hadn't given her this last oxygen bottle. She touched his face one last time. "Thank you Major." She had to fight off the tears. "I will never forget you." Then, it was time to go.

Sukey pushed Park's wallet and phone into her rucksack along with the full oxygen bottle connected to her regulator. With the oxygen flow at the maximum Sukey breathed in the life-giving, rejuvenating gas and felt a surge of energy. She wondered if she should try to do something with Park's body, to get it off the trail so he wouldn't become a landmark to future expeditions, like the famous *green boots* body on the north side of Everest. But, she knew it was a needless concern. Unlike Everest, there wouldn't be any traffic on this trail for years, maybe even a generation of climbing. In time, K2 would inter Park's body like all the others.

Reenergized by the full flow of oxygen, Sukey reached Camp 5, and the beginning of the fixed rope in less than an hour. It was late in the day, and dark, but now that she was tethered to the rope, the storm had become just an annoyance that she was used to. The quicker pace she went down the mountain gave her legs and feet more exercise and feeling had returned to her toes. She decided to skip Camp 5, and continue straight down to the comfort of the larger Camp 4. There, she knew she would be safe. And after she had gotten into a sleeping bag, she would pull out the sat-phone and finally call Jay Hamilton and let him know she had made it and would see him at the Zermatt base camp the following day.

Chapter 33

Sophie grimaced with pain as Jack pulled off her left sock. Her right foot was already under Jack's shirt absorbing the warmth of his chest. Jack massaged her heel and ankle while he assessed the condition of her toes. The dim light of the battery lantern cast shadows around the crowded tent making it difficult to see through the clouds of breath vapor in the air.

"Two black tips Soph. The rest are pretty gray. Probably lose the rest of that second toe, but you don't need that one anyway."

"Yeah, thanks." Sophie sucked in a breath of air between clenched teeth to dull the pain as Jack caressed her toes in the warmth of his hands. The thawing out process was the worst of the pain. She'd been through it before.

Albie Mathias handed Sophie a half-full water bottle he'd just poured. "Here, drink it while it's still warm."

"Thanks," Sophie said, trying to smile at him. She touched his hand. "It's nice to see you again Albie."

"And you Sophie." Mathias turned off the stove, put it outside the tent and zipped up the flap. Sophie and Logan had each already had a full bottle of water. Now it was time to warm up the tent and let the women sleep for a few luxurious minutes.

Sophie leaned back and put her head in Logan's lap. Logan was trying to sleep. Jack had tucked Sophie's left foot under his shirt against his bare skin. Sophie turned toward Mathias. "I need just thirty minutes of sleep Albie, then I will be ready to go down."

"Okay, good," said Mathias. "Can't stay another night this high. We need to start down as soon as you are ready. Dr. Chen will be meeting you at Camp 3, in the morning."

"We plan on reaching Camp 3 tonight," said Sophie, "And to base camp in the morning. Logan has many interviews and television appearances to make." Sophie chuckled. "She is now an international superstar, like Madonna or Lady Gaga."

Logan dug her elbow into Sophie's back. "Yes, so make sure you get all your selfies and autographs before we get down, because I'll be too busy for you people when we get to base camp."

Jack laughed. "We'll try to stay out of..."

He was interrupted by the buzzing of the Walkie-Talkie from under a sleeping bag. It took Mathias a few seconds to find it. "Hello Morris, yes, the ladies are resting and..." Mathias sat up suddenly, causing the others to take notice. *"What? What! How did that happen?!"* Logan and Sophie were fully awake now, sitting up. *"Jesus, what the fuck was she thinking about?"* Mathias listened for a few moments, shaking his head in disbelief. "Okay, okay, I'll do what I can but the weather is brutal up here." He clicked off.

"Albie, what is it?!" Logan knew something bad had happened.

Mathias looked at her. "Hamilton is missing."

Logan and Sophie began talking at once. Logan was angry. "Albie, you told me everyone was on the way down!"

Sophie jumped in. "That girl Lisa, I turned around on the bottleneck, she said Hamilton had already gone down. There was no one above her."

Mathias shrugged. "She got confused. Nobody's seen him since this morning. He was..."

Jack was pulling on his balaclava. "I know where he is," he said calmly. He looked at Mathias. "Let's go get him." He told the others about the strange tracks in the snow he'd noticed at the top of the bottleneck, heading in the opposite direction from the traverse. Jay must have been confused after he unclipped from the fixed rope. Jack stuffed a full water bottle inside his parka, and pulled on his gloves.

"We'll all go," said Sophie pulling on her socks.

"No," said Logan firmly. "Jack and I'll go. Albie, you can't do any more climbing. You stay here until you hear from us. Sophie, you get on the rope and go down, as quickly as you can. Get to Camp 4 and rest, then when you are able, go down to Camp 3 and see the doctor."

Jack unzipped the tent flap letting snow and sub-zero air blow into the tent. Mathias grabbed his arm. "Jack, Logan, wait, this is nuts. If you go up there again... it's a three hour climb to the top of the bottleneck... you'll never find him in the dark and, chances are he's probably already..."

"We'll find him, " said Logan, pushing past Mathias. "I need a full tank and we'll need one for Hamilton. He'll be empty by now. And Jack'll need a tank and mask." She glanced at Jack. "I can't be waiting around for you."

"In the other tent," said Mathias resignedly. "I'll get them."

The snow and the cold wind pelted Mathias as he fought his way to the second tent. He gritted his teeth angrily. He knew this was a fool hardy plan that would most likely end badly. A three-hour climb to the top of the bottleneck, at night, in a storm, to find a lost climber who was probably past saving, was not a sound plan. And he was mad at himself for not being able to go up. But Logan was right, his body was spent from too much work and too much prolonged altitude. He'd be a liability on the search. But, he wasn't sure that Jack Finley was in much better shape.

Jack pushed the extra oxygen tank into his rucksack. He and Logan took fresh headlamps from Mathias, plus two coils of rope and the last battery lantern. Sophie was already clipped to the fixed rope. Jack went over and hugged her and kissed her cheek. "See you at the bottom Soph."

Sophie pulled Jack in tight, her head on his shoulder. "Don't take chances Jack. If you don't find him right away, start down. Don't stay up there too long." Sophie turned and jumped down a snowy incline, her headlamp beam bouncing around the steep trail.

Mathias came up to Jack holding an oxygen mask and regulator already connected to a tank. "Time to make it a little easier on yourself my friend."

Jack didn't like the idea, but he knew it made the most sense. He strapped on the mask and breathed in supplemental oxygen for the first time in over twenty years. Logan was already on the rope and on her way up. They both knew how important it was to find Hamilton quickly. It was eight o'clock – he had been out now for over eighteen hours. The chances of him surviving a twenty-below- zero night at eight thousand meters were very slim.

Morris O'Dell found Rudi Joost in the pub tent having dinner with Marty Gallagher, Monica Deforrest, Samantha Ryan, and the journalists he'd brought in. Several bottles of wine adorned the table in what appeared to be an impromptu celebration of a successful expedition. OSN in New

York had been blasting the summit video around the world and Facebook and Twitter were burning up with the news of the *group summiting.* Pictures of Logan, Sophie and Sukey were on every front page across America and Europe. Rudi was in a celebratory mood.

O'Dell reluctantly took Rudi aside to give him the disturbing news he'd just gotten from Mathias at the high camp. Joost was aghast the latest development. "Going back up to the top? *Tonight?* Logan and Finley! Looking for *who?*" He was yelling at O'Dell, unconcerned with who was listening. "I want to talk to her, right now! Get her on the Walkie-Talkie!" Joost thundered, heading for the door of the tent with O'Dell in pursuit. Marty Gallagher, sensing an emerging story, followed closely behind.

In the communications tent, Joost ripped the Motorola from its cradle and buzzed Logan's phone. Several times he tried with no response. Finally, she clicked on. Joost's receiver was filled with static and noise of the wind. He could barely hear Logan's voice.

"Logan!" Joost was yelling to be heard. "You need to turn around *right now!* This is foolish. You're not going to be able to help that fellow, uh, Washington."

"Hamilton, "O'Dell corrected.

Joost ignored him. "He's probably gone already. Let Finley find him. You need to be down here tomorrow morning for interviews and for..."

Logan had heard enough. "Can't hear anything you're saying Rudi. Gotta go." She clicked off.

Marty Gallagher slipped out of the tent and ran across the glacier to the OSN trailer. He needed to get an update to New York. He also needed to alert his camera crews that as soon as the weather cleared in the morning he wanted the big lenses ready to scour the upper reaches of K2. Finally they had some *real* drama to work with. *Triumph or tragedy*, either one would be a good story.

It was nearly eleven o'clock when Logan and Jack finally made it to the top of the bottleneck. The wind was constant but, fortunately it had stopped snowing. Jack turned on the battery lantern and with the additional light from their headlamps, the area where Jack had seen the tracks was well lit. The tracks in the snow had been filled in by the new snow and obliterated by a day of heavy winds. Jack tried to picture in his mind the tracks that he'd seen that morning. He set off quickly through the deep snow at a forty-five degree angle to the bottleneck, toward the northeast face of the mountain. Logan followed his lead on a parallel track ten meters farther down the slope. It was as cold as it had been all day – twenty-below zero, she estimated. She knew they didn't have a lot of time, for Jay's sake, as well as their own.

They were at the edge of the northeast face of the mountain where the terrain rapidly became steeper. To their left they looked up the slope, their headlamps not illuminating much beyond twenty meters. What they could see was an avalanche-prone face that had been gathering snow all day. They agreed that it would have been improbable for Jay to have gone up the slope, so they headed down toward the more manageable terrain to their right. They could only surmise, and hope, that Jay had gone a short distance, realized his mistake, and had tried to retrace his steps and had gotten lost. His only hope now would have been to find shelter from the storm by digging out a snow cave, and waiting.

After an hour of wading through deep snow, searching for tracks or any sign of Hamilton, Jack suggested that they split up, spend another hour hunting for him, and then meet at the top of the bottleneck. Jack gave Logan the battery lantern which would be a hindrance to him if he had to go down a rope. Logan agreed.

Jack went off toward the steeper terrain of the northeast face, theorizing that Jay may have fallen down an unseen drop-off and was then unable to climb back up. Logan stayed to the right, exploring the deep snow of the flatter terrain, constantly probing with her ax, looking for any sign. Every few moments, she banged her ice hammer against her ax trying to make as much noise as she could. She wasn't far from the end of the trail from the Northeast Ridge that Jack and Sophie had come over early that morning.

After twenty minutes of carefully picking his way down the slope, Jack came to the edge of a steep drop that there was no way around. Coming through here before the storm set in, Jay should have been able to see the cliff, but it was still conceivable that he may have slipped over the edge. Jack reluctantly put in an ice screw, clipped on a carabiner, looped the rope through it and went over the side. The shelf at the bottom of the cliff was only twenty meters down and it was very possible that was where Jay Hamilton was, by now covered with snow.

Logan waded through deep snow, probing with her ax, holding the lantern high overhead on the chance that Jay might spot the light. She estimated that she'd gone about fifty meters down the slope from the spot where she and Jack had split up, but now the terrain was beginning to get steeper. She decided that Jay wouldn't have gone this far off course and turned around. She'd been searching alone now for forty minutes, and needed to get back to the top of the bottleneck and meet up with Jack. She was too cold and too exhausted, and the search felt hopeless.

Mission Beach stretched out before him. The white sand burned his bare feet and the unrelenting sun sent rivers of sweat down his forehead from under his Padres cap. Next to him, Sukey would occasionally race out ahead and laughingly taunt him to try to keep up. Then they reached their blanket and collapsed together on their stomachs, their faces just inches apart, grinning, loving each other with their eyes. It was the kind of day Jay had been dreaming about since returning from the Himalaya, waiting for Sukey to tie up her affairs in Korea and join him in San Diego.

Jay moved in closer to kiss Sukey, when suddenly he felt something crawling under his ribcage. It was under the towel he was laying on and seemed to be vibrating. He tried to reach under himself with his left hand but it wouldn't work. He couldn't move. The vibrating continued but he couldn't move either hand to reach it. Finally, the vibrating stopped. He tried again to move his left arm, and then to roll to his right, but he couldn't move. He knew then that something was desperately wrong.

Jay Hamilton opened his eyes, and saw only darkness. Suddenly, he felt the bitter cold. He wasn't on Mission Beach, he knew, but where was he? In a panic, he used all his strength to move his hand, then his arm, and it came free. He pushed against the snow and was able to roll onto his side. Suddenly, he remembered digging out the snow cave and secluding himself from the wind and the unbearable cold. *Oh jesus! How long had he been there?*

The vibration began again. Jay rolled violently to free his arm and bring his hand up. He ripped off his oxygen mask and gasped for a breath, inhaling the burning cold air. He forced his left hand up to his face and bit the tip of his mitten, then his glove, to free his hand to unzip his parka to get at the SAT phone still buzzing in an inside pocket. It was a struggle to get his thumb onto the green button. He pushed it, but he couldn't talk. He voice wouldn't work. Then he heard Sukey in the ear piece.

"Jay, Jay, are you there? Jay, it's me, Sukey. Are you there?"

He breathed into the mouthpiece, trying to make a sound, afraid she would disconnect. Finally he grunted. From deep in his throat he grunted, then again, louder.

"Jay! Jay, is that you?"

Jay put a small amount of snow in his mouth and swallowed hard, then grunted as loudly as he was able. He forced his voice to work, barely audible, a scratchy whisper. "Sukey, Sukey, it's me."

"*Jay, what's wrong?*" Sukey was yelling now. "*Jay, where are you?*"

"I'm, I'm, in a snow cave."

"Where Jay? Where are you in a snow cave?"

"Snow cave. On the mountain. High up."

"*Jay, how long have you been there? Jay, talk to me!*" Sukey was frantic.

There was a pause as Jay tried to think. "I, I don't know. When the storm hit. All day. Too cold to go on."

Sukey rolled out of the sleeping bag at Camp 4 on the West Ridge, and came to her knees in the small tent she and Park had shared just a few days earlier. "*Jay! You need to listen to me.*" She was shouting into the phone. "*Jay, can you hear me!?*"

There was a short pause, then Jay came on the phone, his voice a little louder now. "Yes. Yes, I hear you."

"Jay! Right now! *You need to kick your way out of that cave!*" Sukey spoke slowly and as loudly as she could. "*Right now! Get out of there!* Push your legs through the snow and get out. Right *now* jay! Get out of there and stand up and walk. They'll be looking for you!" She could hear him trying to get a breath of air and suddenly realized that he would be out of oxygen. She waited, listening.

Hamilton remembered now, how he had dug out the cave with his ax and then backed in as far as he could. And then the small avalanche had covered the opening and blocked the wind, and it became warmer, and he went to sleep. But he knew where the opening was. There wasn't room to bring his foot up to kick away the snow, so he'd have to dig his way out with his ax. But he'd need both hands. He pulled the phone up close to his mouth. "Have to go," he whispered, trying to get some air into his lungs. He heard Sukey shouting as he pressed the red button on the phone. With great effort, he pushed the phone back inside his parka, and with his right hand, he searched for the ax behind him.

Jay's desperation brought on a rush of adrenalin. He pushed the handle of the ax through the snow and felt it give way. When he pulled it back, he could feel the cold air funneling into the cave. He pushed the head of the ax violently into the snow, then again, and again, until there was a hole. He clawed away at the snow and pushed himself out through the opening.

It was pitch dark and the cold was unbearable. Jay pulled his parka hood over his helmet to hide from the wind as he knelt in the snow. He thought about crawling back into the cave, which seemed like a saner option than wandering around, lost in the dark in the coldest temperature he'd ever felt. He looked at the hole into the cave, and then forgot what he'd been thinking about. His mind was moving too slowly, as was his body. He was out of oxygen and he'd finished off his water long ago. Hypoxia was closing in.

Jay's oxygen mask was flapping in the wind. He needed to cover his nose from the stinging cold. He brought up his left hand and noticed calmly that his mitten and glove were gone. He had to think. *Where had he left them?* It was too dark to see around him, but it didn't matter anyway.

Then he saw the light. About twenty meters to his right and moving away from him. He tried to yell but couldn't make a sound. He struggled to get to his feet, pushing hard on the ax. He tried to take a step and fell into the snow, his bare hand buried up to the elbow, the spent oxygen tank sliding out of his pack onto the snow. He looked up quickly. The light was farther away now, his only chance, his last hope fading away. He needed to make a noise.

He grabbed the only thing he had. Making his frozen left hand grip the valve on the oxygen bottle he held it up out of the snow and hit it as hard as he could with the steel head of his ax. In the wind, he couldn't tell if it even made a sound, but he banged it again, and again, each time harder than before. He gasped for air as he brought the ax down as hard as he could. Then, the light stopped moving. Jay struggled to his feet and banged the tank again and again, then dropped into the snow, gasping for air, and watched the light come bouncing toward him.

Then, someone was on top of him, shielding him from the wind. He couldn't tell who it was. The battery lantern in the snow next to them was blinding. Logan pulled off his oxygen mask and put an open water bottle to his mouth. "Drink it all Jay, not too fast," she told him.

While Jay was drinking, Logan pulled the extra oxygen bottle from her pack and connected it to Jay's regulator. She adjusted the valve to full-flow. She put the empty water bottle in her pack and pulled Jay's mask in place. The oxygen and the water had an immediate effect. "Thank you," whispered Jay. "Thank you. Logan?"

"Yeah, it's me. Now we need to get..." She noticed his bare hand. "Jesus Jay, how'd you do that?" She unzipped her parka, pulled out her spare mitten and pushed it onto Jay's stiff hand. "Move your fingers. Keep clenching your hand if you want to save it."

Logan looked at the hole Jay had crawled out of. "You were in there?"

Jay nodded.

"If you hadn't come out when you did, no one would have ever found you." Logan leaned forward and hugged him. "Now, *we need to go!*" She jumped to her feet and pulled Jay up.

By the time they got back to the top of the bottleneck, Jay was moving well enough on his own. The oxygen, water and physical activity had brought him back. Logan made sure his descender was clipped securely to the fixed rope. "Okay, get going, and don't stop. Get down to Camp 5, Mathias will be there. Do what he says"

Jay didn't move. "Aren't you coming?"

Logan took a step backward. "I'll catch up Jay."

"Why? Where are you going?"

She turned and started away from him. "I have to find Jack."

Chapter 34

Jack lay still, afraid to move, afraid to learn how badly he was hurt. He opened his eyes and could see the gray clouds moving across the night sky straight above him, but there was a jagged crack in his vision that shouldn't be there. He tried to take in a breath of air but his nose was blocked forcing him to open his mouth. He gagged and coughed trying to breathe, bringing on a wave of unbearable pain in his face and in his side. His mouth was filled with something, crusty and foreign; a warm liquid ran down the side of his cheek. He tried to turn his head to the side to spit but his neck wouldn't work. Gagging and choking, his panicked stomach muscles shot him to a sitting position. Pain wracked his entire body as he spit and then vomited onto the snow covering his legs.

He brought a hand up and removed his mitten. With his gloved fingers he carefully felt around his face, clenching his teeth to withstand the pain. Nose, broken badly – not for the first time; upper lip split. His goggles were cracked letting in cold air that made his eyes water. Then he realized the oxygen mask was gone along with the hose and regulator. He reached over his shoulder to his pack and felt the empty space where the tank had been. A wave of nausea seized him. He'd probably swallowed a lot of blood. Jack leaned to his side to vomit and spit, the wind blowing everything back into his chest. Taking in a deep breath to gain some oxygen, he felt the sharp pain in his side – surely a broken or cracked rib or two. He tried to pull his balaclava up over his face to ward off the sub-zero wind, but found it caked with congealed, frozen blood.

Jack smiled to himself and chuckled. *Wow, he'd really fucked up now. Time to stop and take inventory of his situation to see if there was any way out of this mess.* He slowly unzipped his parka and reached inside for the water bottle he could feel against his sore ribs. Luckily, it had survived the fall. Desperate for water, he only took a short drink. He'd need the rest for Hamilton, if he found him. The water would probably mean life or death to Jay.

Jack replayed the fall in his mind. Climbing back up the rope to meet up with Logan, his feet in the slings, inching up the doubled-up rope, almost to the top, then, the sickening high-pitched twang of the ice screw snapping out of the ice above. He only vaguely recalled the falling and hitting and bouncing, pin wheeling into the air and hitting snow and ice and rock, then tumbling down a snow slope and going into the air again. He didn't remember landing in the deep snow where he now sat, but he knew he was lucky. Jack had reached fallen climbers who weren't so lucky. He'd seen how an uncontrolled fall of several thousand feet off a mountain could result in an 800-fill down insulated, blood-filled nylon bag of broken bones and oozing organs. *Yes, he had been very lucky.*

His arms and hands worked, but with intense pain in his left shoulder. Legs seemed okay, but a dull pain in his left knee. Then he noticed that the crampon on his left boot was gone. He'd worry about his mobility in the morning when daylight allowed him to figure out where he was. He'd probably fallen fifty meters, but it could have been a hundred. A long, painful climb up to the top to get back to the bottleneck and the fixed rope. But now, Jack needed to focus on getting out of the wind and surviving the night.

He painfully wriggled his backpack off and rolled onto his knees to get at the Zermatt tent he'd been carrying since the beginning of the expedition. It was the tent that he and Sophie had slept in... *when?...yesterday? Last week? It seemed so long ago.* His mind was too fuzzy to remember. He crawled up the slope to a more secure spot where he could carve out a trench in the snow for the tent. He left the backpack where it was. He wouldn't need it, or the tent, in the morning. This, he knew, would be his last night alive on the mountain.

His ice ax was gone forever, so he had to move the snow with his hands. The loss of the ax would be a serious problem in the morning, but he couldn't worry about it now. Jack zipped himself into the tent and set up the staves as best he could from the inside to provide some insulating air that would warm up from his body temperature. Laying on his side, Jack felt the SAT phone Sophie had made him carry in an inside pocket. Tomorrow, maybe, there would be reason to use it. He certainly didn't want anyone coming up the mountain to try to find him. That would be suicide. He hoped Logan had found Jay and gone down right away, or more likely, she had just given up the search for both Jay and he, and then saved herself. Yes, Logan was an experienced, intelligent mountain climber. That's what she would have done.

Jack lay as still as he could in his cocoon. He closed his eyes and tried to feel the late-summer Vermont sun on his face as he hiked up his favorite Sugar Bush ski slope, wading through the tall grass, the wild flowers and fiddleheads waist high at the end of August. Suddenly, he felt an overwhelming need to pee. He knew he wasn't leaving the tent so he just gave in and enjoyed the spread of warmth moving down his legs and hoped he would still be alive in the morning.

The Zermatt base camp was alive with activity at ten o'clock in the morning. The storm had blown through the Karakorums leaving almost spring-like conditions in its wake. It was a calm twenty degrees on the glacier, forecasted to rise into the thirties by mid-afternoon. The cloudless sky was a pale blue that would soon darken to a shade of royal blue and generate hundreds of photographs of a rare view of the summit cone of K2 as the sun rose higher.

Just fifty meters west of the Zermatt camp – as close as they cared to get – a dozen tents of a new Chinese expedition with an August permit for K2 had sprouted on the glacier late the previous afternoon. The expedition's several hundred porters had risen early and already started the long trek back to their villages along the Braldu River. Many of the porters stopped to inspect the wreckage of the big Zermatt helicopter, carrying off pieces of charred sheet metal they would incorporate into the roofs of their huts.

A half a day behind the Chinese, two more expeditions were headed in for late season attempts on Broad Peak and the Gasherbrums. The Zermatt/ Outdoor Sports Network's monopoly of Concordia had ended and the enormous job of packing up had begun in earnest. In two days, the huge Korean CH-47 that Rudi Joost had contracted for at an exorbitant cost, would arrive at the Zermatt camp to swallow as much equipment and supplies that would fit, along with the entire Zermatt team for its exit flight out to Skardu. The two powerful generators would stay where they were just off the glacier, the property now of an enterprising Pakistani interior minister who would be selling electricity to future expeditions.

Behind the pub tent, a large bonfire was consuming the mountain of cardboard shipping boxes and the pile of discarded wooden pallets used to bring in the supplies. Monica DeForrest, the Zermatt *Sustainability Director* had lost all interest in tracking the expedition's carbon footprint and ignored the raging inferno. Over the next few months, the glacier would consume all evidence of the fire.

The Zermatt Pub was already buzzing with activity from curious Chinese and Korean climbers and soldiers, idle Zermatt staff, and the remnants of Sophie Janot's expedition who had closed up their base camp at the end of the Northeast Ridge and had trekked out to the Zermatt camp. The sound system, satellite dish and flat screen TVs, along with the *Drop Kick Murphys, Katy Perry,* and *Dixie Chicks* CDs had all been packed away, and now the pub staff was eagerly serving all comers on a cash basis – origin of currency irrelevant – in an attempt to deplete the remaining stores of food, beer and wine, while supplementing their income from the expedition.

At a corner table, away from the crowd at the bar, Toby Houle and Ken Wall sat by themselves eating Spam sandwiches and draft beer. They had been invited by Morris O'Dell to join the Zermatt group leaving on the Korean helicopter. In Skardu, they would meet up with Dr. Clement, Marcel Janot, and Carlos Medina, who had all flown out the previous day on Rudi Joost's personal helicopter, which was rushing Sophie Janot to the Pakistani Army hospital. Dr. Eric Chen had administered to Sophie's frostbitten toes and fingers at Camp 3, and immediately accompanied her down to base camp. Chen had made arrangements with the surgeons at the hospital to amputate the remaining toes on Sophie's left foot and the ends of three toes on her right. Maybe they could save most of her feet.

In the Outdoor Sports Network's broadcast tent, Rudi Joost was seated on a tall stool in front of Bruce Kinder, to give his last live interview from

K2. When the expedition made it back to Islamabad in a few days, there would be a more extensive press conference at the Serena Hotel.

Joost hardly waited for Kinder to finish his introductory question before he began his pitch. "Complete success is how I'd define it. We came here to put Logan Healy on top of the most difficult mountain in the world, making her the *first* woman to climb all fourteen of the eight thousand-meter mountains."

"But, what about..." Kinder tried to interject.

"And Logan Healy, not only summited K2, she did it *heroically,* risking her life to save *three* of her teammates." Joost shook his head slowly in contemplation, holding up his hand to keep Kinder from interrupting. He continued in a soft, emotional voice. "It was surely one of the most incredible, selfless, rescue missions in mountaineering history, dangerously postponing her summit bid just a few hundred meters from the top to save our video crew members, Bert Skar and Arnie Turek, who had fallen and were hanging upside down on the vertical ice wall of the traverse." Joost shook his head again and grimaced dramatically. "Just an incredible rescue, risking not only her summit bid, but very clearly, risking her life as well."

"But we have reports that Jack Finley..."

In his earphones, Bruce Kinder heard Marty Gallagher from the control room. "Let him go Bruce. This is great stuff."

"And not only did Logan Healy save the lives of Mr. Turek and Mr. Skar," Joost continued, "after reaching the summit of K2 in a blinding snow storm and making it back down to the safety of our high camp, Logan went up again, back up, nearly to the top, a three-hour climb, late in the day, to save the life of another climber, Jay Hamilton, who had secluded himself against the storm in a snow cave, and certainly wouldn't have survived the night.

"There is no doubt, that the Zermatt expedition and the heroism of Logan Healy will go down as one of the greatest chapters in mountaineering history." Joost smiled at Kinder, yielding the floor.

Kinder would let the details of the account go for a different interview. "Yes, thank you Mr. Joost. Now, do we know exactly where Miss Healy is right now and when we can expect her back in base camp?"

"Yes, Logan is on the way down as we speak. After resting at Camp 5, we think she came all the way down to Camp Three to rest and spend the night. And we expect that she started down from there early this morning." Joost grinned as he rose from his chair. "We're preparing a suitable hero's welcome for her that I'm sure your cameras will want to capture for the public."

"Yeah, you bet," replied Kinder. But he wasn't ready to let Joost go. "And what about the other American climber, Jack Finley, who went up with Logan to look for Hamilton..."

Joost was sliding off the stool, his interview done. "Yes, well, we're not sure, but we think Finley is on his way down also. When we know for sure, we'll let you know." He pulled off his collar microphone and handed it to Kinder.

It had been several years since Logan Healy had climbed above six thousand meters without supplemental oxygen. That had been on Gasherbrum I., a small expedition led by a Spanish climber she'd been dating for a while. They had acclimatized extensively, and Logan had made it to the top easily, but hated the torturously slow pace she'd been forced to climb at. She preferred to move quickly on mountains.

Now, she knelt in the snow at the base of the *bottleneck,* holding onto the fixed rope to keep herself upright, knowing something was wrong. She'd been in this spot for twenty minutes, resting, trying to get a lung-full of oxygen, occasionally peering up the rope, hoping to see Jack rappelling his way down, kicking himself far out from the wall in his free and easy style, whooping and laughing like the teenage daredevil she knew so long ago. Logan looked up, but there was nothing, as she knew there wouldn't be. And she knew she wouldn't be going any higher. This was it for her.

After putting Jay Hamilton on the fixed rope the night before, Logan had searched for Jack another two hours before the cold, and the dead lantern batteries forced her back to the *bottleneck* and down the rope. She'd tied the lantern to the fixed rope at the top of the *bottleneck* – she wasn't sure why – maybe, as some sort of beacon to Jack when he got back there. One more piece of junk they'd be leaving on the mountain along with over a hundred oxygen bottles, tents, sleeping bags, discarded clothing and food bag trash.

Mathias had kept Hamilton at Camp 5, only long enough to warm him up in a sleeping bag and get another bottle of water into him. He melted a bottle of water for Logan with the last canister of fuel and left if for her, along with a note. There was no more oxygen at any of the high camps, and he needed to get lower as quickly as possible.

Logan had rested for an hour alone at Camp 5, resisting the powerful urge to fall asleep. She drank half the bottle of water, saving half for Jack, and then started back up to try to get to the top of the *bottleneck* as dawn arrived.

But now, Logan Healy couldn't climb anymore. She could barely move. Exhaustion from three weeks of extreme physical exertion at high altitude, along with nearly 24-hours of continuous climbing, had overtaken her. Logan commanded herself to stand up, but all she could do was lay down in the snow, putting her head in a spot where she could look up the *bottleneck* to see if anyone was coming down it. She held tightly to the rope even though her sling was still clipped on, hoping that she might feel some vibrations in the rope. Tears ran down her cheeks and over her lips and into the snow beneath her face. "I'm sorry Jack," she whispered.

Morris O'Dell stared into his laptop screen at the live feed from the OSN camera high up on Broad Peak. He'd been staring at the scene since dawn when the light finally revealed the features of the summit cone. He could see the shining ice coating on the great seracs and the area around the top of the *bottleneck,* squinting in concentration, hoping to suddenly see a speck of movement or a dot of color that might be Jack Finley's red parka. Occasionally, the camera operator would zoom in or zoom out, changing the context of the scene. Standing behind O'Dell, a crowd had formed. Word had passed along that Jack Finley was missing somewhere high on the mountain. Rob Page stood between Samantha Ryan and Monica

Deforest who couldn't keep the tears from rolling down her cheeks. Timmy Burns, still exhausted after only a short sleep after delivering Bert and Arnie back to base camp, watched the computer screen with an angry grimace on his face. Like the other professional climbers who circumstances had forced to the bottom of the mountain, Burns knew that he should have been high on the mountain available for a rescue team. But all they had now was Logan Healy, somewhere above Camp 5, climbing without oxygen. Fred Terry, who had spent the night at Camp 3, with Lisa Greenway, had wanted to go back up to join the search, but O'Dell had immediately vetoed that idea and ordered them to come down. The last full oxygen bottle was at Camp 3, but it was too far away; and, as he told himself, technically, Finley wasn't part of his expedition. And he now needed to limit the damage. A pall had come over the group. They were all experienced enough to know what a twenty below zero night at the top of the mountain without shelter meant.

On the table next to O'Dell's laptop, sat the Motorola Walkie-talkie in its charging cradle, and the Thuraya Sat-phone. Logan had called in earlier when she was starting up, with instructions not to contact her unless they heard from Jack. O'Dell had gotten the address of Sophie Janot's sat phone from Dr. Clement before he left for Skardu. At first light, O'Dell had tried the number, letting it ring for nearly a minute, without success. If Jack could use the phone, he would see O'Dell's call and would contact them.

Suddenly, the shrill buzz of the Walkie-talkie broke the silence in the tent. O'Dell grabbed the phone. It was Marty Gallagher in the OSN trailer. O'Dell leapt to his feet. "OSN's other camera has picked up something on the *bottleneck*." O'Dell left the tent and raced across the glacier to the OSN trailer, followed closely by Rob Page and Timmy Burns.

Marty Gallagher was on the Walkie-talkie to his camera operator high on the hill on the south side of the glacier. "Go down a little. Farther. See that? Near the bottom of the *bottleneck*."

O'Dell, Page and Burns were all leaning in close to the monitor. "What is that?" asked Gallagher. "Zoom in closer. Focus!" An unmoving figure, lying in the snow, came into view. The lower section of the *bottleneck* was completely shaded by the mountain, making the color of the climber's suit impossible to discern. "Is that Finley?", asked Gallagher. "Is that him?"

Rob Page leaned in closer to the screen, squinting for clarity. "No," he said, pulling back from the monitor, "It's Logan."

"Jesus," said Timmy Burns, "She's not moving."

O'Dell pressed some buttons on the Walkie-talkie just as Rudi Joost burst into the trailer. He shouldered his way to the front of the monitor. "Who's that? Is that Finley?" he asked loudly. They could all hear the Motorola buzzing on speaker.

"No," said Burns, "it's Logan."

"C'mon Logan! Answer it," pleaded O'Dell.

"Logan!?" Joost exploded. "Fuck! Get someone up there to help her! O'Dell! O'Dell get someone up there to help her," screamed Joost.

O'Dell pressed the red button on the Motorola and stood up. He faced Joost. "There isn't anyone," he said softly. "Everyone's down here. Hamilton made it back early this morning and Mathias was going to wait and rest at Camp 3. There isn't anyone." He touched Marty Gallagher's shoulder. "Send that feed to my computer." O'Dell left the OSN trailer and walked slowly, across the glacier.

Jack could feel the sat-phone vibrating inside his parka but there was nothing he could do about it. He'd been crawling up the steep eastern face of the mountain for two hours, barely making any progress. With no ax, no ice hammer, and only one crampon, it was much closer to rock climbing than mountaineering. He held tightly to every icy handhold or bare rock edge he was able to find, pulling his right foot higher and kicking in the toe point of his only crampon to try to push himself up just a little higher. His entire body burned with pain at the exertion it took to gain just a meter of progress, and there was nowhere to rest.

Several times, Jack lost his toehold and slid down the slope several meters before being able to arrest his slide by finding a new handhold. Twice he came to an impassable vertical pitch and had to traverse to his left to find a climbable route. Everything he did seemed to suck the last of his energy and strength out of him and make his body scream from the pain of his injuries. But he kept inching his way up the slope, because, as he kept telling himself, there was only one direction to go.

Finally, after another two hours, he pushed himself up on a solid toehold and found himself reaching into empty air. He crawled up another few meters and looked up and saw in the distance, the great seracs of the top of K2, shimmering in the reflection of the morning sun. He pushed himself up onto a near-level snow surface and rolled onto his back to rest. He had made it.

Morris O'Dell opened his notebook on the personal data of everyone on the expedition, found the home phone number of Jack Finley in Fayston, Vermont, and reached for the SAT phone. It was time to prepare Finley's wife for the worst, which seemed inevitable at this point.

It took several minutes for the call to go through and the connection was poor. It was ten at night in Vermont and Peggy Finley had just gone to bed. The news shocked her, as the last report she had seen on OSN said that Jack, Logan, and Sophie were all on their way down. O'Dell told her about the rescue attempt to find Jay Hamilton and it appeared that Jack was now lost high on the mountain. Peggy was still sobbing when O'Dell told her he'd let her know right away if there was any news and ended the call. It was a call O'Dell had had to make several times in his career; it never got any easier.

In the rare mid-day sunlight, a dozen picture-takers stood around the Zermatt base camp holding up cameras and cell phones to capture the rare view of the summit cone of K2 in all its glory. It was a view that could disappear very quickly in the mountains. The serenity of the scene was broken only by the far-off sound of a green Hyundai snow cat lumbering up the glacier from the west. Where the glacier became impassable with large boulders, the snow cat moved off to the south moraine, tilting at a dangerous angle on the uneven ground but not slowing its advance. Fifty meters from the base camp, the snow cat stopped. *Snow Leopard* logos were visible on its front and side panels. A door opened and Chun Suek Yen climbed out onto the high tread and jumped down to the rocky ground.

Several of the summit photographers recognized who was approaching and turned their cameras toward her. Soon, all the cameras were focused on the famous Korean conqueror of K2.

Sukey tried to smile politely for the cameras but she wasn't in a sociable mood as she strode purposefully toward the Zermatt sleeping tents. She was wearing the red and black *Snow Leopard* warm-up suit that, after losing twenty pounds on the mountain, now clung to her lithe body as snugly as it had to any of the models at Young Kim's house at the meeting when she was insulted by the *Snow Leopard* Chairman.

Sukey entered the tent city and stopped a Zermatt staffer to ask the location of Jay Hamilton's tent. The staffer pointed out a nearby tent. "But" he noted, "Hamilton just made it down a few hours ago and would be sleeping for quite a while." Sukey nodded her thanks.

Hamilton was indeed in a deep sleep, his cot covered by several thick blankets. Sukey got up close and gazed down at her friend, her lover, with a concerned, troubled look on her face, torn by what she was about to do. At the end of the cot, Sukey sat down at a small writing table, took out a piece of Jay's stationery and wrote him a note. This was better, thought Sukey, parting without the personal confrontation, without having to verbalize all her feelings and misgivings, and without having to recount the events of the climb up the West Ridge and her feelings for Major Park, which would now be nearly impossible for her to explain.

She wrote that she had fallen in love on the West Ridge, and even though Park was now gone, she needed to live with that for a while. She needed to remember everything they went through together and cherish the memories of their time on the mountain and the feelings they shared. She couldn't dismiss what she'd come to feel for this gallant soldier who had gotten her to the top of the mountain and then given his life for her. In time... maybe a month, maybe a year... she would be able to move on, and she and Jay could try again.

Sukey ran back to the snow cat with tears in her eyes, never noticing the crowd of people around the entrance to the Communications Tent. She would have liked to stay for a while and see Logan and Jack, but now she was in a hurry. The driver had turned the snow cat around. The *Snow*

Leopard helicopter was waiting for her on the Savoia Glacier and she couldn't miss her flight from Skardu to Rawalpindi, and then, the long KAL flight to Seoul. She needed to be away from K2.

Sukey never noticed Morris O'Dell, Rob Page and Timmy Burns running across the glacier towards the OSN trailer. O'Dell had just gotten off the Walkie-Talkie with an agitated Marty Gallagher. While O'Dell and the others watched the feed of the camera focused on the unmoving Logan Healy, OSN's powerful camera on Broad Peak had suddenly picked up something high on the mountain, at the top of the *bottleneck*. It too was not moving, but it was clearly a climber. A climber in a red parka.

Chapter 35

Jack struggled to get to his feet. His left knee and shoulder were throbbing with pain as was his rib cage. He turned around gingerly in the knee-deep snow to take a look down the slope he had just come up being careful not to lose his balance and fall back over the cliff that he knew he would never survive. Seeing the steepness of the slope, Jack was amazed that he'd been able to make it all the way back up without ropes or an ice ax, and with only one crampon on his boots. He knew he'd been lucky again.

He turned back slowly and gazed up at the great seracs, shining in the afternoon sun, and realized how fortunate he was that the weather was so benign at this altitude. It was a perfect day for climbing; temperature around zero, very light wind. A perfect day for a summit bid. He thought about the storm of the previous day that Sophie and Logan and Sukey had had to climb in. Or was it two days ago? He wasn't sure. But now, he knew he needed to start moving.

Jack took one step and his left knee caved in, sending him face-down into the snow. He lay still for a few moments, breathing deeply to take some oxygen from the dead air, feeling the comfort and warmth of his bed of snow. *How nice it would be to sleep for a while and regain his strength and let his wounds heal.* He closed his eyes and began to drift away, *warm and painless.* A few seconds later Jack's internal alarm went off. He opened his eyes, pushed against the snow and got to his hands and knees. After a few moments of deep breathing, he struggled to his feet. He knew he'd come very close to becoming one of those partially covered, tattered red, orange and green corpses that he'd seen so many times in the mountains.

Jack looked up and focused on the seracs and began trudging through the snow, stopping every three painful strides to try to catch his breath. If he could stay on a bearing toward the seracs, and the summit cone, he knew he'd pass by the top of the bottleneck... and the fixed rope that would save his life.

In the OSN trailer, Morris O'Dell, Marty Gallagher, Rob Page and Tim Burns squeezed in close to the computer screen to watch the image coming in from the camera on Broad Peak. The camera position was two miles away from the summit cone of K2, but through the long lens, they could clearly make out a figure headed toward the top of the bottleneck. In the bright sun, Jack's red parka was easily identifiable. But he was moving very slowly.

"Yes, it's Jack! No question," said Page.

"Looks like he's really struggling," Burns said softly.

"Shit," said Page. "After all that time up there. Overnight."

"Damn miracle he's still alive," said O'Dell. He stood up and bolted for the door of the trailer. "Got to get the SAT phone."

The others stayed glued to the computer screen.

O'Dell raced across the glacier, stumbling on the boulders and loose rocks. He burst into the Zermatt communications tent to find a crowd of babbling, excited voices staring into the computer screen. Rudi Joost, Eric Chen, Samantha Ryan, Monica Deforest and the climbers from Sophie Janot's expedition were riveted on the screen.

"What's happened?" asked O'Dell shouldering his way in front of the computer.

"She's alive!" said Joost, his eyes not leaving the screen. "Logan's alive." The Walkie-Talkie in Joost's hand was buzzing intermittently without reply.

"She moved," said Samantha excitedly. "She sat up."

O'Dell peered in closely to confirm that Logan had changed position. "Yes!" he said as he grabbed the SAT phone from its cradle and bolted for the tent flap. He wanted to be observing Jack when he made the call. "We located Finley," he said on his way out. "On the other camera. He's near the top of the bottleneck!"

Jack shuffled slowly toward the seracs. He'd forgotten what he was looking for and was beginning to feel warm. With every step, he had to stop and take in several deep breaths of the zero-degree air. *He was sweating inside his parka. Too many layers. He needed to sit down for a while and unzip his jacket.* Jack squinted to see and think more clearly. *What had he been searching for?* Suddenly, he felt the vibrations of the SAT phone in an inner pocket. *Yes, the SAT phone! Maybe it was Peggy calling. Peggy and Ralph and Beth calling him from Vermont. He needed to find a place to sit, to be able to open his jacket and get at the phone, and to cool off a bit.*

To the side of the path, Jack spied a flat, iced-over rock that looked almost like a park bench. It took him another minute to make his way to the seat. It was perfect. He felt comfortable and contented sitting on the bench. He forgot about the vibrating phone inside his jacket and then the vibrations ceased. Jack pushed back his snorkel hood and pulled off his wool hat. The frigid air refreshed him. He tugged off his mittens and then his gloves and put them on the bench next to him. He unzipped his parka. Off to his left, from the southeast, a layer of clouds was moving up the mountain. Not a storm, Jack knew, just the mountain making some of its own weather. He closed his eyes and was refreshed by the light tingle of ice crystals in the air.

"Why doesn't he answer the *damn sat-phone?*" Morris O'Dell implored, squinting into the computer screen. "He's just sitting there. What's he doing?"

"Aw fuck," Rob Page said softly, glancing at Timmy Burns.

Burns shook his head. "He's taken his hat and mittens off."

"Hypothermia," said Page softly. "Call him again. We need to reach him quickly!"

O'Dell reached for the SAT Phone, still staring at the screen. "What's he doing now? *What the fuck!* It looks like he's talking to somebody."

"Hallucinating probably," said Page. "He's at that stage."

Jack opened his eyes and sensed someone sitting on the bench next to him. He looked to his right and was shocked to see Tom Brady, dressed in his complete Patriots uniform, with shoulder pads, thigh pads and cleats, but no helmet. He was wearing a red throw-back jersey from the seventies.

Brady's brown hair was long and waving in the breeze, and he had his customary lamp black patches on both cheeks.

"Wow!" said Jack. "Look at you, Tom Brady, mountain climber."

Brady just stared straight ahead.

"How'd you get up here anyway?" asked Jack.

Brady rolled his eyes and shook his head. "Next question."

"Belichick know you're here?" said Jack with a grin.

Brady slowly turned toward Jack with a wry smile and winked.

"Hey Tom," said Jack. "Since you're here, I gotta ask you about that Jets playoff game. What the hell hap..."

"I don't want to talk about it," snapped Brady. "Let it go."

"Yeah, okay," said Jack. "I can understand that. Hey, aren't you supposed to be wearing a helmet?"

Brady gestured towards Jack. "Aren't you supposed to be wearing gloves?

Jack nodded. "Yeah, you're right." He looked down at his hands in his lap. They were white. He flexed his fingers, barely moving them.

The vibration of the SAT phone startled him. Jack grinned. "Probably Bill looking for you."

It took him nearly a minute to get the buzzing SAT phone out of the inside pocket. He pressed the green button with his numbed fingers. O'Dell spoke first.

"Jack! Jack, it's Morris O'Dell, can you hear me?"

Jack pushed the phone up to his ear. "Yeah, hello Morris," said Jack, slowly. "How's everything going?" He glanced to his side. Brady was gone.

"Not good Jack. First, you've got to put your gloves and mittens back on, and then your hat. We can see you from the camera on Broad Peak. We're watching you."

Jack smiled. "No kidding." He held the middle finger of his right hand up toward Broad Peak.

"Yeah, that's a good one Jack," said O'Dell. "Now listen to me. *Right now!* You've got to put your gloves and mittens on. And then you need to stand up. Can you do that Jack?"

"I don't know Morris. I'm tired. It's nice here."

"Jack?" screamed O'Dell, "You're going to die up there if you don't get up, *right now!"*

Jack needed a few moments to catch his breath. "Yeah, I know," he said weakly.

Rob Page took the phone from O'Dell. "Jack, it's me, Rob Page."

"Hey mate."

"Jack, listen to me. You've got to stop fucking around and get moving! Logan is in trouble and she needs help!"

"Logan." Jack said weakly.

"Logan needs help Jack. She's at the bottom of the bottleneck, laying in the snow. She's not moving. Logan's going to *die* if you don't help her Jack!" Page was yelling into the phone.

"Logan," Jack said again, almost to himself. He closed his eyes to think about Logan and put the phone down on his lap. *How nice it would be to sleep for a while to gain some energy.*

"Jack! You need to get up, *right now!"* Page screamed. Jack didn't hear him... he was asleep.

Morris O'Dell stared into the computer screen for another five minutes watching the picture gradually fade away in the cloud that had moved over the top of the mountain. "I guess that's it boys," he said to Page and Timmy Burns, but mostly to himself. He took Marty Gallagher's Walkie-Talkie and called over to the Zermatt tent. Rudi Joost answered. O'Dell filled him in on their conversation with Jack. "Can't see him anymore. It's snowing up there. Last we could see, it looked like he had fallen asleep."

"Logan moved her arm a little while ago," said Joost. "She's definitely alive. But, the picture's fading here too. Clouds are moving in."

"Yeah, okay," said O'Dell softly. "Gotta tell Mathias what's going on." He pressed a few buttons on the Walkie-Talkie. It took a while for Mathias to answer.

"Albie, where are you?" asked O'Dell.

"Still at Camp 3," he said, weakly.

"I thought you were coming down this morning."

"Decided to wait and, uhm, see uhm... found one last full bottle of gas here, so..."

O'Dell could tell that Mathias was in bad shape. He told him about Jack and Logan. "Nothing you can do Albie. Logan's two hours above Camp 5. It'll be getting dark soon. I want you to start down right now. Get to Camp 2, tonight. And down here in the morning."

"Yeah, yeah okay. I'll be down." Mathias clicked off.

Jack was awakened by something hitting his injured knee. He opened his eyes to see the SAT phone that had rolled off his lap. Jack watched it hit the ice on the path in front of him and slide away, disappearing into the deep snow. He shook his head. *That's not good.*

Jack turned slowly to his right to find the seracs, but something caught his eye, across the path, about ten meters away under a light coating of new snow. It was the lantern that he and Logan had brought up the mountain to search for Jay Hamilton. Jack stared at it for a few moments to see if it was another mirage. The events of the previous night came flooding back to him. *Searching for Hamilton with Logan. Why would Logan leave the lantern there?* He put his cracked goggles up on his head and focused on the snow-covered lantern. Then, he saw it. A small piece of rope was looped through the handle at the top of the lantern. *The rope. The fixed rope! Oh Jesus!* Rob Page's words reverberated in his mind... *Logan's in trouble... at the bottom of the bottleneck... she's going to die.*

Jack pushed himself up from the bench. He jumped up and down on his frozen feet and thrust his numb hands into his armpits inside his parka. It took twenty minutes to thaw his fingers to where he could bend them. He painfully zipped up his Jacket and pulled the parka hood tight. He could go without the wool hat. He tried to pull his gloves on over his gray fingers but quickly gave up and went with just his mittens. They were more important anyway. He breathed deeply, to replenish his oxygen supply before taking a step. Suddenly, he was reeling with dizziness and fell to his knees to avoid toppling over. *Water.* He needed water... and his pills, whatever he had left. He unzipped his parka and pulled out the water bottle. He was amazed that it was still half-full... *the water he'd been saving for Hamilton.* Jack took off a mitten and found the small pocket where he kept his stash of pills. He looked over the small palm-full of pills he had left. There were eight or nine aspirins and the four Dexamethasones he was looking for. He shoved four aspirins and two of the Dex's into his mouth and washed them down with one swig of water. The rest of the pills and the water he'd save for Logan. He put the water bottle back inside his parka, zipped up, and crawled toward the lantern. *Hold on Logan. I'm coming.*

Jack got to his knees and pulled the lantern up. He untied the rope and tossed the lantern aside. Reaching down, beyond the last piton, he pulled on the rope as hard as he could. If Logan was on the rope, maybe she would feel the movement and know he was there. The next part would be difficult. He had to take off his mitten to reach into the right leg pocket of his suit to get his knife. He opened it with his teeth, pulled as much slack from the rope as he could, cut off the excess, and retied the fixed rope onto the piton.

With all his slings lost in the fall, and no ice ax, it was going to be a difficult descent down the steep bottleneck. Jack had one carabiner left on his harness, a lifesaver, he knew, as he tied the carabiner to the fixed rope with a very sloppy Prusik hitch and tied one end of the rope to his belt. With his frozen fingers, it was the best he could do. He'd use the carabiner as a handle, pulling on the other end of the rope as a brake.

Jack peered down the steep couloir, now concealed in shadows in the late afternoon. He remembered how difficult a climb it was coming up it – about two hours of strenuous climbing from the bottom. It would be a much quicker, and rougher, trip down with no ax and no descenders. He rechecked the carabiner and the ugly knot he'd tied and edged forward on his seat, scraping his only crampon through the ice as he began sliding down the rope.

Logan Healy opened her eyes and squinted through her snow-covered goggles. She looked down at her boots and her legs splayed out on the snow. *Where are my skis?* Then she remembered the fall, the worst of many – the GS at *Garmisch* – where she'd broken her leg in three places, the jagged end of her shin bone cutting through her G-suit. The end of her Olympic dreams, knowing right away there would be no trip to

Lillehammer. Tears filled her eyes. *I was the best in the world! I would have buried those Austrians.*

She felt the rope move. Behind her head where she was laying against it. Inside her parka, the Walkie-talkie began buzzing. She struggled to raise a hand to her goggles and wiped off the new snow. She could see the steep slope below her and off in the cloudy distance, the glaciers of Concordia, and she was back – to K2. She couldn't unzip her parka to get at the Walkie-talkie. And the rope was still. *Maybe she'd imagined it. How could there be movement in the rope? She was all alone.* Her head was throbbing with pain. She couldn't move and she couldn't breathe, and she knew she was going to die where she lay.

It was pitch dark when Jack reached the bottom of the bottleneck. The descent had taken much longer than he thought it would, and now his rib cage was burning, his left knee wouldn't bend and his fingers and toes were frozen. The snow continued to fall, and the wind blew the unbearable cold right through his parka. Jack knew that the slope beneath the *bottleneck* was less steep than the couloir he'd just come down and decided to untie the ungainly knot that held him to the fixed rope so he could search for Logan. Rob Page said that she was at the bottom of the bottleneck, so *where the hell was she?*

Holding onto the rope as a guide, Jack moved tentatively down in the dark, having to stop every few meters to clean out the snow that blew through the crack in his goggles. Then he stepped on something that no longer felt like ice under his boot. He heard a weak squeal beneath him. He dropped to his knees and felt the snow-covered form of Logan. She'd made a sound, so he knew she was alive. Quickly he brushed the several inches of snow off her helmet and goggles and from her balaclava. He realized she'd been climbing without supplemental oxygen – a terrible, desperate mistake, he knew, after being on gas for the last three weeks – a guaranteed path to acute altitude sickness.

Jack stood up, reached under Logan's armpits and pulled her into a more upright sitting position. He dropped down onto her lap, straddling her legs with his knees and pushed her goggles up and pulled down her balaclava. "Logan! Logan!" he shouted. Then, again louder. "Logan, wake up!" He pulled out his water bottle and slapped her face lightly. He slapped her again, and again, more forcefully. "Logan! Wake up!" He slapped both sides of her face with his frozen hand.

He was about to slap her again when she moved her head and scrunched her face up into a scowl. "Okay, okay. Stop hitting me, Finn. What the fuck!"

Jack grinned and kissed her ice-cold lips. He brought the water bottle up to her mouth. "Take a drink Logan. Open your mouth." Logan took the water bottle into her mouth as Jack tipped the bottle up. "Slowly," he said. "Don't choke." He took the bottle away from her lips and searched for the pocket where his pills were. He searched for the larger Dexamethasones among the aspirins. He pushed the two Dex's into Logan's mouth and gave her the water again. "Swallow these," he ordered. "Make sure they go down." He had six aspirins and only a few ounces of water left. He pushed the pills into her mouth and gave her the rest of the water. "Drink it all," he instructed. It was a meager treatment for altitude sickness, but it was all he had. What Logan needed most urgently was to get lower very quickly.

"Okay," said Jack. "We've got to get going." The activity of descending the bottleneck and finding Logan had reenergized him with a release of adrenalin. He put her balaclava and goggles back in place and stood up, straddling Logan's legs. He reached under her armpits and pulled her to her feet, supported by the ice wall behind her. "Logan! Logan! Can you walk? Try to walk." Her body was still limp in his hands.

"Can't walk Jack," Logan breathed out softly. "Can't feel my feet. No Strength."

"Yes you can!" Jack shouted. He lifted her off the snow and shook her. "Logan, come on! Put some pressure on your feet. Wiggle your toes!" Logan draped her arms over Jack's shoulders but that was all.

"Can't Jack. Can't move."

She was dead weight on Jack's arms. He lowered her back to a sitting position on the snow. Jack knew the problem was that Logan's hemoglobin wasn't carrying enough oxygen and what there was, her body was sending to the vital organs – the brain and the heart – at the expense of her extremities. "Okay Logan, you're going to have to ride down."

Jack pulled Logan's coil of rope up over her head and played out about thirty feet of it onto the snow. He laboriously pulled his knife out, cut the rope and discarded the remainder of the coil. He sat on Logan's lap again and pulled her forward so he could search through her backpack. Jack found a headlamp, spare mittens, and an energy gel-pak. He tore open the gel-pak with his teeth and squeezed the contents into his mouth.

The Petzl lamp lit up the area around them like daylight. Jack tossed away Logan's backpack and stood over her. He reached down and pulled her up by her armpits and braced her against the ice wall while he threaded the rope through the two rings on her harness, ran both ends of the rope between her legs, and pulled the ends up behind her. He ran the ends of the rope over her shoulders, across her chest and under the opposite arm. The makeshift harness system was one more of the lessons he'd learned from Marcel Janot. Then, he was ready to load up, but there was one more job to do. He reached inside Logan's parka for the Walkie- talkie and pressed the green button. Morris O'Dell answered. "Morris, it's Finley," he yelled into the phone to be heard over the wind. "I've got Logan. I'm bringing her down. Gotta go." He clicked off and put the phone in his own inside pocket.

Turning around slowly, pressing his back into Logan's stomach, Jack pulled the ropes over his shoulders, crossed them again and tied them tightly to the carabiner on the belt of his harness.

"Finn, what are you doing?" Logan breathed weakly into his ear. "Just leave me here. We'll both die like this."

Jack pulled Logan's arms over his shoulders, squatted down painfully to pick up her ice axe, then stood up straight, lifting Logan two feet off the snow. He clipped one of Logan's slings to the fixed rope along with her descender. "Okay, here we go," Jack said, stepping off into the snow. "Go back to sleep for a while."

Morris O'Dell immediately buzzed Mathias at Camp 3 and gave him the news while Rob Page and Timmy Burns raced off to their tents to get suited up for one more climb. They stopped at the supply tent and grabbed several oxygen tanks, extra water bottles, some fuel canisters, and several coils of rope. They knew there was very little chance of them getting high enough in time to help, but they had to try.

Chapter 36

Glenda Craft sat at her expansive desk in her sun-filled corner office on the 47th floor of the Outdoor Sports Network building waiting for the satellite call from Marty Gallagher. To her right, through the floor-to-ceiling windows the East River shimmered in the morning sunlight. Behind her, ferry boats, tankers, tugs, and a massive cruise ship sent long, white wakes rippling through New York Harbor. It was a beautiful August morning – seventy-four degrees at 10:00am. Glenda thought about nine holes at Bedford Hills late in the afternoon.

On her desk were the notes from her staff about their next project – a caving expedition in Honduras. *Yes, someplace warm, with maybe even some decent restaurants!* She was done with mountains, and snow, and white upon white straining the irises of the cameras. She glanced at a paper on her desk and frowned, shaking her head. It was the synopsis of the ratings of the four weeks of the K2 project. It wasn't a complete disaster – the helicopter crash, Finley's rescue of the girl in the crevasse, and the video the women shot of the simultaneous summiting had some decent numbers for a few days in the U.S. and Europe, *but the rest of it was shit.* She should have known – she'd been warned. Mountain climbing wasn't a sport to be filmed. It wasn't even a sport. It was a slow-motion, time-lapse exercise in capturing the highlights of excruciating boredom. And the audio was worse than the video – grunting and gasping, sniffing and coughing, and voices muffled by hideous looking rubber masks.

Her bosses two floors above her were satisfied though. The ratings weren't great and the show was a financial loser due to the overhead, particularly the enormous satellite charges, but OSN had broken new ground, broadcasting real-time video from the Himalaya, further positioning the network as the leader in *live adventure programming.* And that was what it was all about. *A pity though, that they never got any video or an interview of the three women together...* her phone buzzed. Marty Gallagher was on the line.

"Marty, just sitting here thinking about how nice it would have been to get some video of the three girls after they came down."

"Yeah, well, not gonna happen. Sophie Janot's at a hospital in Islamabad having most of her toes taken off..."

"Ouch," said Glenda.

"Yeah, rough sport. The Korean girl's on a plane to Seoul, and Logan Healy is still on her way down."

"So let's get some video and an interview with her and Rudi when she gets down – we'll run an update – and that will be it. Then you can pack up the team and get out of there."

"They're hoping she'll make Camp 3 tonight and then get down here tomorrow afternoon. Most of the equipment will be on the Korean chopper day after tomorrow. The crew and I will be taking the OSN chopper."

"Well I'm glad she's all right. All the equipment sold off?"

"Yeah. We're taking the electronics and the cameras out to Skardu. Sold the trailer for five hundred bucks to the Pakistani guy who bought the generators."

"Oh the accountants will love that," said Glenda.

"Yeah, tough shit. It's junk now anyway. It's all junk, after a month in this place."

"Okay, good. You did a great job there Marty. Get home safely. Next week we've got some meetings scheduled on the Honduras project."

"Can't wait," Gallagher said, dryly. "See you in New York."

The snow had stopped falling and the sky was clear leaving a moonlit night of dropping temperature. Somewhere on the Abruzzi Spur, several hours below the Zermatt Camp 5, Jack Finley and Logan Healy lay in the snow where they'd fallen. Jack was on his right side to protect his ribcage, which was burning with pain. His left leg, totally unbendable at the knee, was braced against the slope to help keep them in place. He held tightly to the fixed rope, trying to breathe, trying to find another ounce of energy to enable him to get back to his feet. Logan, still lashed to his back, an arm over each of his shoulders, squirmed to pull her right leg out from under him. He rolled slightly to relieve the pressure on her leg. She burrowed her face into the space under Jack's neck to hide from the wind.

Jack turned off the headlamp to save what little battery power remained, and then they both lie still, resting they told themselves, although both knew that this was probably the spot where they were going die that night.

Jack had been carrying her for four hours, inching their way down the spur, most of it facing the mountain because of the steepness. He'd held tightly to the rope, releasing the descender carefully to avoid an uncontrolled slide and what would have been a catastrophic tumble. They went past Camp 5 because they knew there was nothing left there for them, and he needed to get Logan much lower on the mountain. He wasn't sure if they'd gone past Camp 4 or not, but it didn't matter, because he knew, once they stopped that would be it for the night and they weren't low enough.

But now, they lay in the snow with no protection from the icy wind and the ten-below zero temperature. Jack couldn't move his leg and knew he'd never be able to raise Logan up onto his back again. He could feel her nuzzling her face in under his neck, her mouth close to his ear. Her voice was weak. "Are we done Finn?" She coughed and squeezed him with her left arm. All she could manage was a gasping whisper. "Sorry Finn. Sorry I made you come here." She was sniffing back tears.

Jack turned his head to put his mouth closer to her. "Hey, still beats the hell out of selling insurance." He could feel Logan giggle. "You got to the top and that..." Jack stopped. Far down the mountain he saw something. A tiny pinprick of light. And then it was gone. He lifted his head off the snow to see more clearly.

"What is it Finn?"

Jack stared into the darkness for a few seconds. "Nothing. I guess it was nothing." Then, he saw it again. Clearly a light. It had the bluish tinge of a headlamp. "Yes, Logan, there's a light coming toward us, I think."

Jack switched on his own headlamp. He pulled it off from around his parka hood and held it up as high as he could reach with his left arm and moved it painfully from side to side, his ribcage screaming. Then he watched as the light from down the mountain moved slowly back and forth. "Yes, Logan, somebody's coming."

"Who? Who could it be? Everyone went down."

"Not everyone, I guess," said Jack. "Must be Mathias." He lowered the headlamp and breathed deeply. "Whoever it is, he's a long way away."

Jack started untangling himself from the ropes that held them together. It was an arduous task that left him breathless. He didn't want to take off his mittens to untie the rope from his harness, so finally he got out his knife and started cutting. When he was free, he rolled over to face Logan. He put his arm under her head and pulled her close to give her some warmth.

"We may get out of this yet," Jack said into her hood. "But you're going to need your legs. How do you feel?"

"I don't know." Logan coughed. "A little better. I think the pills helped. I think I can feel my toes. The air's better here."

Jack reached down with his right hand and started rubbing Logan's thighs. He squeezed and rubbed as hard as he could. "Try to bend your knees. Wiggle your feet and your toes."

"Yeah, I'm trying," Logan breathed out.

Jack turned and pushed himself up as far as he could to look down the mountain. He didn't see the light, but he knew that didn't mean anything. He went back to rubbing Logan's legs. "You're going to have to walk down from here."

"Yeah, I know," said Logan. "I will." She bent her knees slightly, then straightened her legs. Again, and again, each time bending her knees a little more.

She was tired, and Jack was tired from rubbing her thighs. They both went still. Jack put his right leg over Logan's legs to try to shield her from the wind and stop her shivering. Then they both fell asleep.

Jack woke with a start as Mathias dropped heavily to the snow, his knees straddling Logan's right leg. Jack started to sit up. Mathias was staring down at him trying to keep the headlamp beam away from his eyes.

"Jesus Jack, what happened to you?" The left side of Jack's face and his nose was completely black, and his beard and parka were covered with crusted, dried blood.

Jack patted Mathias on the shoulder with his mitten. "Had a bit of a tumble," he barely croaked out. "Good to see you Albie."

Mathias took off his backpack and put it in front of him to keep it from sliding down the mountain. "Okay, let's get her up." Jack could see that Mathias was totally exhausted and had lost a lot of weight.

Jack pushed and pulled at Logan as Mathias reached into his pack. "Logan, c'mon, wake up. We've got company." He shook her several times.

Logan finally opened her eyes and saw Mathias. With Jack's help, she sat up. "Oh Albie. What are you doing here?" She reached her arms out to him.

Mathias gave her an awkward hug with the backpack between them. "Hey princess. I took the chairlift up and skied down here." He reached forward and pulled down Logan's balaclava and pushed a black oxygen mask over her nose and mouth. He let Logan maneuver the straps around her head while he pulled from the knapsack a regulator and a long shiny oxygen bottle. "Here, try some of this. High-test Russian O's," he said, turning the regulator on to full-flow.

From inside his parka, Mathias pulled out two water bottles, pushing one toward Jack. "Here, save half for Logan."

Jack took a long swig from the bottle. "What is that?"

"Well, three hours ago it was hot chicken soup." Mathias reached into an outer pocket and brought out a pill box. "Take these," he said holding two Dexamethasones out to Jack. "And these," he said, shaking out a handful of aspirins.

Logan pulled loose the Velcro strap on the mask as Jack handed her the soup bottle.

"How do you feel?" asked Mathias.

"Better," said Logan. "I can breathe again." She took the pills from Mathias' hand and washed them down with the cold soup. "Hamilton, did Hamilton get down?"

"Yeah, he's down. He's fine." Mathias handed Jack the other bottle. "Water," he said. "Drink as much as you can. I have another."

"Sophie?" said Jack.

"Okay," said Mathias. "They flew her out to Skardu for her toes."

As Jack and Logan shared the water, Mathias looked around them at the tangle of ropes in the snow under them. He looked at Jack. "You carried her down here? All the way from the bottleneck?" He shook his head. "*Fucking incredible,*" he said, mostly to himself.

When Jack and Logan had finished the water, Mathias tucked the bottles into his backpack and took out a third bottle from inside his parka. He took a generous drink and offered the bottle to Jack and Logan. They each drank a little more. Mathias clipped the oxygen bottle onto Logan's harness. "Okay, we have to get moving. It's a long way to Camp 3."

Jack and Mathias got to their feet and pulled Logan up between them. They held her while she bounced on her legs for a while to get the circulation moving. She took a few steps and reached down for her ice axe. She was still clipped to the fixed rope. "Good," she said. "I'm ready." The oxygen and water had done the job. Mathias took out his Walkie-Talkie and had a brief conversation with Morris O'Dell, then they started down.

Jack went first, stumbling and sliding on his leg he couldn't straighten, hunched over with pain, dragging his axe on the steeper pitches. Mathias watched him with concern, but he knew Jack, and knew he would make it to Camp 3. He short-roped himself to Logan and they followed Jack. It had started snowing again.

The tent smelled like a wet dog. Sleeping bags used by dozens of climbers, on their way up and down over the last four weeks, covered every inch of the tent floor along with old food bags, and various pieces of spent clothing. A weak flame from the last fuel canister under the stove by the flap provided the only light in the tent. Jack had gotten half-in, half-out of a sleeping bag before he went out cold. Logan was covered over by a bag while Mathias pulled her boots off. He massaged her feet and examined her toes. "Don't look too bad," he lied, pushing her feet up under his shirt against his skin. But she was asleep. He found some old, abandoned socks in the rubble and pulled them over Logan's feet. They'd been used but were at least drier and warmer than her socks.

Mathias had to rummage through the food bags to find some freeze-dried chicken and rice, and a beef barley soup. He mixed them together in one pan and waited interminably for the water to get hot enough to make a meal. He found some energy bars and put them out on the tent floor in front of him. He knew it was important for them to eat something – as much as possible before they slept for the night. When the soup was ready, Mathias woke them both and made them eat. They only had one spoon, which they shared, passing it around with the pan of food. No one had an appetite and they'd soon had enough.

Logan pulled her legs into a sleeping bag and zipped it up to her face. Mathias put another bag on top of her. He turned to Jack, laying on a sleeping bag, almost asleep. Mathias switched on his headlamp and unzipped Jack's parka, then motioned to his fleece shirt. "Let me take a look," he instructed. Jack slowly pulled up his shirt with a grimace, revealing his stomach and chest. Mathias nearly gasped. *"Jesus Jack."* The entire left side of Jack's torso was black and the skin wrinkled and oozing pus in several places. The sharp end of a rib had pushed through the skin.

Mathias found the camp's small medical bag and spread the anti-bacterial ointment tenderly over Jack's ribcage and stomach. He used the entire tube. Mathias searched through the rubble of clothes and found a tee-shirt and laid it gingerly over Jack's ribs, tucking it in under his shirt as best he could. He pulled down Jack's shirt and zipped his jacket. Jack was asleep.

Mathias pulled a sleeping bag over Jack and noticed that his face was pale, and his eyes were sunken into their sockets. He turned off the headlamp and sat still, thinking about Jack, in this condition, carrying Logan down the mountain for four hours on his back. Mathias didn't try to stop the tears from welling up in his eyes and running down his face.

The last canister of fuel sputtered, and the flame went out under the half-melted pan of ice chips that Mathias had gathered before sleeping. He poured the melted water into a bottle next to a full bottle he'd already made. He wasn't going to bother with breakfast. No one would eat anything. Mathias unzipped the tent flap letting in the dull morning light and the cold air. As he put the stove outside the tent, Logan woke up.

"Need to get going," said Logan, in a hoarse whisper. She opened her sleeping bag, sat up and reached for her boots.

"Have some water first," said Mathias, handing her a bottle. "Sorry, no tea left."

Logan drank half the bottle and handed it back to Mathias. "Give this to Jack when he wakes up."

"Yeah, I will. How do you feel?" asked Mathias.

Logan was pulling on her balaclava and helmet. "Good," she said. "Better than I did last night." She edged toward the tent flap. "Need to get out and loosen up my legs before we start down." Logan pulled her gloves and mittens on. "Sorry Albie, I can't carry any of this shit down. Just leave it here."

"That's okay," he said. "Page and Timmy Burns are on their way up. They'll clean up."

"Yeah, that's good," Logan said, almost to herself. She glanced over at Jack, covered with a sleeping bag. "Don't let Jack sleep too long. We need to get off this mountain." She went out through the tent flap.

Logan found her ax and used it for support as she slowly walked around the tent several times, bending her knees, trying to get some circulation to her toes. She knew that her toes were worse than Mathias had let on, but she'd just have to ignore the pain now and climb down well on her own. She clipped onto the fixed rope and waited.

The wind was whipping the powdery snow into blinding clouds all around Logan as she waited next to the rope. *What was taking Mathias and Jack so long?* "Hey," she called up to the tent. "You guys coming?" But her weak voice was lost in the wind, so she waited, bouncing on her knees to try to keep warm. It was going to be a long, hard trek to reach base camp during daylight.

Another ten minutes passed before Mathias appeared at the tent door. He turned around slowly and zipped up the flap. Turning toward Logan, he just stood still for a few moments. He found his ax sticking out of the snow and walked slowly down to her.

"C'mon Albie," Logan yelled to him as he neared her. "I'm freezing my ass off here. Let's get going. Where's Jack?"

Mathias had his balaclava pulled down around his neck and his goggles up on his forehead when he reached Logan. She could see the tears running down his face onto his parka. Logan knew right away what had happened. She bent over and shrieked in pain. *"No, Albie! No!"* She reached out for him to support her.

Mathias hugged her tightly. "I'm sorry Logan," he said with a sob, "Jack won't be coming with us."

Logan buried her face into Mathias' chest and wailed with despair, the tears pooling inside her goggles. After a few minutes, her sobs subsided. "This was all my fault." She shook her head angrily. "I made Jack come here... all my fault."

"No Logan, it wasn't." said Mathias firmly. "It was nobody's fault. Jack knew what he was doing. He was doing what he loved."

"Yeah," she whispered. "Yeah, Jack loved the mountains." She separated herself from Mathias, looked up toward the tent for a few moments, then pulled her ax from the snow and started down the mountain.

Mathias watched her, letting her get far ahead of him, then took out the Walkie-Talkie from inside his jacket. He had a short conversation with Morris O'Dell, then started down after her.

It was late afternoon when Logan and Mathias finally reached the bottom. As they made their way up the glacier, a small group led by Rudi Joost, emerged from the basecamp to meet them. It was a subdued reunion. Joost hugged Logan for a long time, then they walked silently into base camp, to the medical tent where Eric Chen had a luke-warm frostbite treatment ready for Logan's feet. Morris O'Dell took Mathias' backpack and walked him silently to his tent.

There were no photographers or writers and Rudi Joost had uncharacteristically waved away Bruce Kinder and his camera crew. Marty Gallagher had a word with Kinder and sent him back to the OSN trailer to start packing up. The show was over.

That evening, Morris O'Dell hiked down the glacier to the Chinese basecamp and contracted, at a very generous figure, for four of the expedition's Sherpas to start up the Spur early the next morning to assist Rob Page and Timmy Burns in bringing down the body of Jack Finley.

Epilogue

July, eleven months later.

Chun Suek Yen checked out of the small hotel in the downtown bazaar section of Rawalpindi carrying only a small duffle bag slung over one shoulder. She liked to travel light, even on a twenty-two hour flight from Seoul. The streets, as always, were crowded at 8:00 in the morning with the usual crush of cars, lories, motorbikes and pedestrians.

It was already seventy degrees and the ever-present aroma of diesel fuel hung in the air, but Sukey decided to walk for a while before catching a cab to the airport. She had some time to kill before meeting up with Logan and Sophie for their flight to Skardu. Now, she was glad she'd turned down Logan's offer of a luxury suite at the Hotel Serena in Islamabad. Better to have some time to herself in Pindi, like the old days.

Sukey pulled a dark blue head scarf from her bag, dutifully covered her hair, and walked in the street, dodging the motorbikes, delivery vans, and the steady flow of pedestrians that never seemed to relent in the old capitol of Pakistan. She'd always enjoyed the tumult, cacophony and aromas of the streets of Pindi. They were a stark prelude to the silent world of the sterile mountains that followed. Even under the disapproving, quick eyes of the dark men, and the few women – always in twos or threes, in black burqas and loose flowing salwars – Sukey felt safe and free in the city.

Forced to the edge of the street by the traffic, something caught Sukey's eye. She gazed up at a small shop that looked very familiar and brought back nostalgic memories from years ago. In a window on one side of the doorway was a display of small tools, cleaning supplies, and other typical hardware store merchandise. The other window, the one that caught her eye, contained a dusty selection of mostly used climbing equipment... old boots, rusted crampons, dozens of well-used climbing axes, helmets, goggles, oxygen masks from a bygone era, assorted slings, a wooden bucket of pitons, and a pile of coiled ropes.

She smiled as she entered the store. *Yes,* she had been here before. She couldn't remember which expedition it might have been but she remembered buying a very useful pair of Marmot mittens for about half the price she would have paid in Seoul. The mittens were long gone, but at the time, an important purchase.

Squeezing her way through the meager racks of new parkas, vests and fleece jackets, Sukey made her way toward the rear of the store where the used goods were kept. She enjoyed running her fingers over the ancient hardware – the heavy wooden axes, rusted pitons and ancient crampons – and couldn't help imagining what historic expedition to K2, Broad Peak, the Gasherbrums, or maybe Nanga Parbat, the pieces might have come from.

A sales clerk appeared at the end of the aisle and eyed Sukey in silence. He nodded slightly then disappeared. Sukey wasn't sure if she was being ignored because she was a woman in a store, in a city, in a country where women were ignored as part of the culture, or if it was obvious, from the elegant, light-weight, cream-colored *Snow Leopard* warm-up suit, and the sparkling gold Rolex on her wrist that she wasn't really in the market for old climbing equipment.

The warm-up suit was part of the several hundred piece collection of high-end *Snow Leopard* fashions and outerwear that her new American agent had negotiated into the new five – million dollar revision of her personal services and endorsement contract with *Snow Leopard Industries.* She was surprised at how quickly her agent had been able to repair her relationship with *Snow Leopard.* International fame and celebrity had currency, her agent told her, even with Chairman Young Kim. Then came a multi-year, seven figure deal with Rolex which included a generous selection of luxurious watches. Her agent was ready to wrap up contracts with Apple and American Express, he'd told her, and they hadn't yet gotten back to Hyundai and Coke. Her ex-agent/ex-husband Mong had been shamed, but well taken care of.

The only other people in the store were three young men wearing shorts and t-shirts, who looked to be in their late twenties, leaning over a counter examining coils of rope. The men were all lean and sinewy with the weathered look of climbers. They were discussing the rope in a language that sounded like Polish to Sukey, but she wasn't sure. Behind the counter, a proprietor was pulling coils of rope from the shelves behind him and slapping them down on the counter. To overcome the language problem, he was writing prices on small slips of paper. Sukey watched the scene with a sense of deja vous. She had been there.

Sukey moved over to the counter next to one of the men. He turned and smiled at her. "Hello," he said, backing up slightly to let his comrades see the newcomer. They smiled at Sukey, welcoming her to their discussion.

Sukey said something in Korean, then laughed. "Sorry," she said. "*English?*"

The men grinned. "Oh, yes," said one, "always English. We are from Poland."

Sukey nodded. "Where will you be climbing? She asked. "On K2?"

The man next to her laughed. "Oh no, no. Not K2. Not yet. Maybe someday"

The man in the middle took over. "We will go to Gasherbrum. Gasherbrum one."

Sukey nodded. "Yes, very good. A very nice mountain." She moved within the circle of the men and looked over the selection of rope on the counter. "So you are buying rope?"

"Yes, just for our personal climbing ropes, but they are very expensive for us. We are thinking to buy used ropes."

Sukey reached over and picked up a coil of the used rope. She pulled a long strand out of the coil and ran her fingers over it as she examined it. She frowned and shook her head. "No good." She tossed it dismissively back onto the counter. The sales clerk glared at her. She rummaged through the selection of new rope on the counter, leaning in to examine the labels. "No, no," she said. "These are not what you want either." She looked up past the sales clerk, scanning the boxes of rope on the shelves behind him.

"You are a climber then?" said one of the Poles.

"Yes, I have done some climbing," said Sukey. Then she saw what she was looking for. She pointed to a box on a high shelf. The clerk pointed to a different box. "No, no. That one," she said, pointing to his right.

The clerk raised his eyebrows skeptically as he brought the box down to the counter. It had a *Sterling Evolution* label on it and was unopened.

Sukey turned toward the men. "It is important on the high mountains that you have *dynamic* rope, rope that will *stretch* under heavy weight on it."

One of the men chuckled. "Yes, yes, we know, but *way* too expensive."

The clerk sliced open the top of the box and took out a coil of green rope wrapped in plastic with a *Sterling* label on it. To put a quick end to the interruption by this Asian woman, he grabbed a slip of paper and wrote some numbers.

Sukey looked at it and shook her head. "Dollars."

The clerk frowned, turned the slip over and wrote "180 USD". The three climbers jaws dropped when they saw the price for a coil of rope. Sukey smiled. "It's a fair price," she said. "But we'll see." She took the pen from the clerk's hand and wrote on the paper: "$160 x 10. $1,600 for the box." The clerk smiled and nodded. Sukey placed her new American Express Black card on the counter.

The three young climbers protested her generosity but Sukey wouldn't have any of it. "Just climb safely," she told them. They thanked her profusely.

Sukey laughed. "Don't thank me," she said. "Thank Rolex." She looked at her glittering watch and started for the door. "Have to run. I'm late."

One of the men called to her before she got out of the shop. "Hey." Sukey stopped and looked back. "Have you ever climbed one of the 8,000ers?"

Sukey grinned broadly and nodded. "Yes. I've climbed them all."

As she left the store, behind her she heard an excited exchange in Polish, but made out the words *K2, Korea,* and a reasonable attempt at her name.

The elegant main dining room of the Hotel Serena was beginning to fill up for the elaborate breakfast buffet. White-jacketed waiters circulated among the linen-covered tables with coffee and tea. The round table set for four where Sophie Janot sat had a view of the entryway so she could look out for their guest, and for Logan Healy, although Sophie knew it was early in the day for Logan to make an appearance. She sipped the tea but her croissant was untouched.

Sophie was nervous about meeting the woman for the first time in person. They'd spoken on the phone three times; two months earlier to invite her on the trip, and then, a few weeks later to give her the travel and hotel arrangements, all prepaid by Mrs. Logan Healy Joost. The woman had objected to the complimentary round-trip, first-class Etihad ticket from Paris to Islamabad, and the luxury suite at the Serena. She would surely reimburse Logan for the cost, she said. Sophie had just laughed and told her to not even think about it.

The source of Sophie's anxiety was their first conversation, almost a year ago to the day. And now, she had to face Marie Chatelain for the first time since taking the phone in her daughter's hospital room in The Pakistan Institute of Medical Sciences, when they'd chatted casually about Sophie's famous father, skiing around Argentiere, and the weather in Cap Ferrat, before collaborating on Julia-Isabelle's death sentence with their cursory agreement that she should be sent back to Paris for medical treatment. It was a conversation Sophie could never get out of her head.

Marie Chatelain came into the restaurant and stood scanning the tables. Sophie waved to her and smiled broadly when she'd gotten her eye. Sophie had never seen Marie but she could instantly recognize a fashionable Parisian woman dressed for an activity she was unaccustomed to. The woman wore tight designer blue jeans, a flowing, comfortable beige blouse and what looked like brand new low-rise Zermatt trekking boots. On her head she wore a light-colored, floppy brimmed African safari hat. Sophie hoped that her own outfit – her customary long-sleeved green t-shirt, well-worn brown shorts, and newly-fitted orthopedic hiking boots – wouldn't make her guest feel conspicuous.

The women greeted each other with the customary European air kisses, hugged tightly, then both began to cry. It took nearly a minute for the tears to subside. Finally, they sat at the table, using the linen napkins to dry their tears.

441

"I'm sorry," said Sophie. Switching to French she repeated, "Je suis desolee." "I told myself I wouldn't do that when we met."

Marie Chatelain tried to smile, still dabbing her eyes. "Yes, I said the same thing." She laid the napkin on the table in front of her and attempted a smile. "Okay, no more tears. It was a tragic event for everyone. But, no more tears, okay?"

Sophie smiled. "Yes, I'll try."

"You met Julia on her trek in to the mountain, yes?"

"Yes. Jack introduced her to me when I was on my way out after Gasherbrum. Such a sweet, beautiful girl. She so much wanted me to autograph her magazine picture of Jack and I."

Marie smiled and nodded. "Oh yes, the *picture*, she treasured it. You were her idol. Julia had pictures of you all around her room."

Sophie teared up once again and reached for her napkin. Marie squeezed Sophie's hand.

"Thank you for being her friend and for visiting her in the hospital. That was wonderful."

Sophie shook her head and looked down into her lap. "I've always wondered... maybe, if I hadn't gone to the hospital..."

"No, no, Sophie, nothing would have changed. My husband and I were resolute on bringing her home. It was our mistake, entirely.

Sophie just nodded and smiled weakly. "And does your husband..."

"No," Marie interrupted, "we are divorced now." She added, very softly, "so, we have paid twice for our mistake."

Sophie turned away, toward the lobby to look for Logan. Marie caught a waiter's eye and asked for coffee. "So, now maybe on to some happier thoughts," said Marie, her eyes widening with enthusiasm. "What a superb accomplishment for you and Logan and um... the Korean girl."

"Chun Suek Yen," Sophie offered. "Sukey."

"Yes, Sukey. What an accomplishment for the three of you. To make it to the top of that mountain, and in such horrible weather!" She stopped to pour cream into her coffee. "I have read the book. I found it so fascinating!"

Sophie managed a polite smile. "Oh yes, the book." She thought about the *book*... *"The Last Mountain – The Untold Story of The Tragic Race To The Summit of K2"* by Samantha Ryan and Albie Mathias. They must have started working on it as soon as they left the mountain, probably on the plane out of Islamabad. Rumors began percolating in the press in early September about a seven figure advance. The world-wide mega-coverage of the event made a book written by *"two of the climbers who lived every minute of it"* a guaranteed international success before it was even written. The publisher's lawyers just laughed at the Zermatt NDAs. It was out for Christmas, published in six languages. Sophie saw a copy in the Serena's gift shop. There were rumors of more books; possibly by Morris O'Dell, and Rob Page.

"Did you find the book accurate?" asked Marie.

Sophie thought back to her reading of the book. Accurate enough, she thought, although, understandably, a little light on the details of her expedition and of Sukey's. "Yeah, it was fine," she finally replied, not wishing to get into a long discussion. Her main issue with the book was that maybe it was the cause of Mathias leaving his wife and two children in South Africa and moving to Colorado to live with Samantha Ryan. That seemed to Sophie like one more casualty of the climb.

Sophie looked out toward the lobby just in time to see a flurry of activity. Out of nowhere, it seemed, several photographers – the paparazzi of Islamabad – their cameras humming and flashing, formed up in front of two women walking toward the restaurant. A hotel security man moved to the front of the pack, ushering the photographers away from the women.

Sophie watched the show from her table with great amusement and amazement as her friend Logan Healy – even in hiking boots, khaki capris pants, a black t-shirt with a huge slashed Z logo across the front, and her blonde hair tied in a ponytail – looked like she'd just stepped out of a Vogue magazine ad. But it was Logan's companion that took Sophie completely by surprise. Anja Lindgren, the Swedish ski racer, with her trade-mark blue hair with green and yellow highlights, and a generous display of eyebrow, nose and lip jewelry, was as much a target of the photographers as Logan. The two women stopped near the entrance to the restaurant and had a quick chat and a kiss on the lips before Anja departed for the front of the hotel. A photographer pursued her.

Logan had a word with the hostess then strode confidently through the restaurant toward Sophie and Marie. Sophie couldn't help grinning as she watched Logan approaching them. She always had that effect on Sophie, as she had on most people. Logan was a show unto herself. They'd had a three-hour dinner together late the previous evening with no mention of Anja Lindgren. And now, photos of Logan and her friend were probably already on the internet.

Sophie pushed up from her seat awkwardly knocking her cane off the back of the chair. "Here's Logan," she said to Marie.

Logan picked up Sophie's cane from the floor, then hugged her warmly. "Hey Soph, how you doing kid?"

Sophie raised her eyebrows. "You brought a friend? Your pictures will be on Instagram this moment."

Logan laughed. "Not a problem. Rudi has become very understanding, now that we are married and he knows me better." She turned to their guest. "You must be Marie." They hugged. "I'm glad you came." She turned abruptly toward the buffet table. "I'm fucking starving. You guys should eat. Could be a long day."

Logan and Marie got back to the table before Sophie who lagged behind managing her cane and plate. "Oh, I'm sorry," Marie said to her. "I would have helped you. I didn't realize... how are your toes?"

Logan chuckled. "What toes?" She smiled at Sophie.

"Yes, I read in the book, about your frostbite," said Marie. "Was it very..."

Sophie smiled at her. "No. I manage very well. A bit of a challenge wearing heels though."

"I'm very sorry about your daughter," Logan said to Marie.

"Yes, thank you," said Marie. "Oh my goodness, I haven't thanked you for... for bringing Julia up out of that..."

"Yeah," said Logan. "I was wondering if you'd gotten that far in the book."

"That must have been so dangerous for you," said Marie.

"No. Not for me. Julia was lucky the best mountain climber in the world was following her up the glacier... or, she'd still be..." Her voice trailed off.

"Yes, that was so brave, but now I am hoping we could all put that behind us and move ahead..."

Sophie looked up from her plate and saw that it was now Logan's turn to press her napkin to her eyes with two hands. Logan sobbed silently, her shoulders trembling. This was so unlike Logan, Sophie knew, and realized that, like herself, a year hadn't been long enough. Finally, Logan dropped her napkin on her plate and looked at Marie Chatelain.

"What you didn't read in the book," Logan said softly, "was that Jack Finley gave up his life to try to save your daughter. He went all the way down into that crevasse, as far as he could, until he had no more rope. It was pitch black and freezing down there." Logan had to stop and take in a deep breath. "When Mathias and I got to them, I could see the end of Jack's rope. It was twenty feet above him. He'd untied himself from the rope to be able to get down to her, to hold her, so she wouldn't slide down any farther... so she wouldn't be alone. Jack knew he could never get back up that crevasse once he unclipped from the rope. But he got to Julia. He was holding her in his arms... like a baby."

Logan rubbed her eyes again with the napkin. "Then, a few days later, he carried me down the mountain on his back and saved *my* life." She tossed the napkin down on the table. She looked at Marie. "So, no, we can't quite put it behind us just yet. That's why we're here."

"At the Gilkey Memorial," said Sophie, "we'll leave a remembrance of Jack. He deserves that."

Marie nodded. "Oh yes, I've been looking forward to seeing the Memorial... and the glacier..."

"Okay," said Logan, reaching over and squeezing Marie's hand. "We need to head for the airport and meet up with Sukey."

Marie finished her cup of tea. "What time does our plane leave?"

Logan rubbed her eyes, then chuckled. "Whenever we get there."

A gleaming white Mercedes limousine left the Hotel Serena and drove south toward Rawalpindi. Logan and Sophie sat next to each other in the rear seats facing Marie Chatelain. The limousine had a full bar and several bottles of champagne, which the women ignored. They rode in silence for a long while until Sophie reached down into her travel bag and brought out another small suede bag with a draw-string closure. She reached inside the bag and brought out a six-inch diameter, half inch-thick disc. Sophie wiped away some lint and passed the disc to Logan.

"Poppi insisted on bronze," said Sophie. "So it would tarnish in the air and then hold up better to the elements."

Logan smiled as she ran her fingers over the raised image and the lettering on the disc. "It's beautiful Soph." She chuckled. "Jack would hate it."

Sophie laughed. "Yes, he would. He looks too handsome."

Logan handed the disc across to Marie. She had to take out her glasses to read the inscription beneath the image. *Jack Finley* and on the next line *Fayston, Vermont, United States*, and under it, *August 5, 2010.*

"I've only seen Jack's picture, in the book, with a beard," said Marie, handing the disc back to Sophie. "But I'm sure he would be pleased." Sophie tucked the disc back in its suede pouch and then into her bag.

At the Islamabad International Airport, the limousine turned off on a ramp to the *Domestic Charters* terminal and drove another two miles until it came to a gated security post. The driver showed the guard a pass, and the limousine was quickly waved through the gate onto the edge of the tarmac. A dozen private jets sat sparkling in the morning sun. Out on the tarmac a Cessna Citation XLS was pointed down the *private charters* runway. Its entry stairway was folded out and the plane's co-pilot stood at the bottom of the stairs, ready to receive their guests. Forty minutes earlier, the Citation pilot received a call from the limousine's driver, and now the twin turbo jet engines were warmed up, and the cabin steward was preparing lunch.

The limousine moved along the road at the edge of the tarmac and stopped in front of the Charter Terminal. When Logan and Sophie saw Sukey come running out of the terminal, they jumped out of the limousine to greet their friend. Logan ran ahead while Sophie limped behind on her cane. They'd both spoken with Sukey several times on the phone after the expedition, but this would be the first time they'd seen her since she had left them just below the summit of K2 to make her suicidal descent down the West Ridge to find Major Park.

Logan and Sukey were hugging tightly, both in tears, when Sophie reached them. Sophie pulled Sukey away from Logan and teared up herself. "Oh my God Sukey. When you left us that day, I was sure we'd never see you again."

Sukey laughed as she wiped away her tears. "Such confidence you had in me."

Logan pulled Sukey toward the long white car at the curb. "Come on, let's get in the air."

Settling into their seats on the Citation, Sophie introduced Sukey to Marie Chatelain, but the excitement and noise of the takeoff put an end to any further conversation. When the Citation had reached cruising altitude for the ninety minute flight to Skardu, Sukey reached across to Marie who was seated facing her, and held her hand. "I was heartbroken when I heard about Julia. I got to know her very well on our trek in to the mountain," said Sukey.

"Thank you," said Marie. "I'd forgotten that you were with her then."

"She was a wonderful girl." Sukey grinned broadly. "She and her friends put on such a show at the bonfire, singing that Lady Gaga song. I never laughed so hard."

"Oh Yes," Marie said, smiling, "Julia-Isabelle and Camille and Laure sang and danced all the time." She added wistfully, "The girls told me they were singing when Julia-Isabelle fell into that..."

"On the helicopter, we will try to find the spot on the glacier for you," said Logan.

"Will we find the crevasse where..."

"No," said Logan. "The crevasse will be gone because the glacier is always moving. But we'll get close to the place."

Marie nodded. "That will be nice. I brought one of Julia's favorite little stuffed animals to leave behind, a pink teddy bear."

Sukey wanted to change the subject. "And what about you Sophie? What have you been doing this past year?"

Sophie shrugged. "Oh, mostly hospital visits and learning to walk again. And, oh yes, the girls and I, we moved to Barcelona."

Sukey's eyebrows went up. "Barcelona." She smiled. "Carlos?"

"Yes," said Logan, "our Sophie has some exciting news for you."

Sophie seemed to light up at the thought. "Oui. Carlos and I are engaged."

Sukey reach across to Sophie to hug her. "That's wonderful Sophie. When will the wedding be?"

Sophie chuckled. "Oh, I don't know. Someday. But you will all be invited." The women laughed. "And you Sukey? Have you been to San Diego to see Mr. Hamilton?"

Sukey shook her head. She looked out the window. "No," she said softly. "I've been so busy." She turned back to Logan and Sophie. "Things have been going good for me in Korea. My new agent is wonderful." Sukey shrugged. "So maybe someday." She sat up with a start. "Oh, let me show you what I have," she said, reaching down into her bag next to her seat. She brought out a thin box and opened it to reveal a silver plate about eight inches across. She passed it around to the women. The plate was etched with a reasonable likeness of Major Park. Under his image, was the inscription: Major Park Jong-Su, 3rd Recon Battalion, ROK Army, 4 August 2010.

"It's very beautiful Sukey," said Sophie, passing the plate back to her.

"Yes. Dong Shin-Soo, our expedition leader, had it made. He asked me to bring it when he learned I was coming back. None of the other Korean climbers were coming to Pakistan this summer."

After a few moments of silence, Logan asked, "When you went home, did you go to..."

"Yes," said Sukey. I visited his wife and children. She was distraught over not being able to have a burial," she said softly.

Marie looked quizzically at Sukey. "But, why was there no..." Logan scowled sharply at Marie and shook her head quickly causing Marie to drop the question.

Sukey looked over at Logan. "And when you went back to Vermont, did you see Jack's wife"

Logan nodded. "Yeah, O'Dell and I flew Jack's body back to Burlington, and I met Jack's wife there. She wasn't very talkative. O'Dell and I left, then we went back a week later for the funeral. It was sad, with the kids there. Rudi came over from London, and Mathias and Samantha were there, and Rob Page and Tim Burns. And Eric Chen came over from Dartmouth, which was nice.

"Peggy didn't speak to any of us. And after the funeral, she came up to me and told me it was all my fault," Logan glanced at Sophie, "And yours too Soph... that *French woman*, she said."

Sophie smiled briefly at the epithet, then turned toward the window next to her. "She was right," Sophie said softly.

After a gap in the conversation Marie leaned forward. "And you Logan, I understand that you have been doing very well this past year. I see a picture of you and your husband in the magazines fairly often."

Logan shrugged. "Well, I *do* own this airplane."

The pilot's voice over the intercom speakers interrupted the conversation. "Five minutes to landing. Perfect weather. Sunny and sixty-two degrees in Skardu. Please buckle up."

The Citation taxied to a stop near the Skardu passenger terminal, and immediately a Land Rover pulled up next to the plane. Logan, Sophie, Sukey and Marie Chatelain squeezed into the two rear seats of the Land Rover. "Have to pop over to the terminal for a quick PR thing," said Logan. "Then, we'll drive out to the helicopter."

In front of the terminal, a small group of people were being arranged into a photo shoot behind a five foot *Zermatt Industries* banner held by two small local children. The arranging was being done by a woman wearing a burka and holding a camera. Behind the banner were several Balti porters wearing their ubiquitous Gilgit caps, and a man in a business suit.

The Land Rover pulled up to the group and Logan opened her door. "This will only take a minute. Quick picture," she said, exiting the car. The photographer greeted Logan effusively, as did the man in the business suit. The porters smiled and bowed to her as Logan took her position behind the banner. The photographer pointed out a spot next to the man in the suit, but Logan said something to her and moved between two of the porters with her arms around their shoulders. The porters beamed, Logan lit up her eyes and her smile like the world-class super model she had been only a few years before, and the photographer began snapping pictures. After shaking everyone's hand and a few words with the photographer, Logan was back in the Land Rover. They drove toward the helicopter section of the airport.

"What was that about?" asked Sukey.

Logan shrugged. "Not a big deal. We started a welfare fund for the Balti porters. Rudi and I gave them a million dollars to get it started."

"That's a nice thing you did," said Sophie. "Hard for them to make a living now with all the helicopters being modified to fly into the mountains."

"Yeah, the economics kill them. Won't be long before there aren't any porters working in Pakistan."

At the heliport, the Land Rover pulled up next to an old brown Pakistani Army helicopter. It had been modified by the addition of two rows of new, comfortable seats, but it was obvious it had seen at least a few years in the mountains and more than a few rescue missions. Two blue-uniformed pilots were walking around the helicopter making a final inspection.

"Sorry ladies," said Logan when they had exited the Land Rover. "I don't own this one. It's a rental."

The helicopter took off as soon as the women were buckled into their seats. Compared to the Citation, the noise was deafening as the helicopter roared away from the airport at treetop height. Rising quickly as it crossed over the Indus River, the helicopter left civilization behind and moved effortlessly across the dusty plain of the valley then over the rugged gorges and corridors of the foothills leading to the greatest concentration of high mountains anywhere in the world. Sukey leaned close to the window to look down on the journey that had taken her and Jack and Jay Hamilton more than a week to accomplish a year ago. Nothing looked familiar to her as the direct route of the helicopter was unconcerned with the campsites and walking trails used by nearly a hundred years of expeditions. Now, they would be over the Godwin-Austin Glacier in just two and a half hours, and then, back in time for dinner

The helicopter flew high and fast, enjoying the thick air at the beginning of the journey. But very soon the ground began to rise up to meet them and the pilots had to earn their pay as they carefully monitored the rotor speed and pitch in the thinning air as well as the volatile winds. Helicopters had alleviated much of the time, expense and effort required for high-altitude mountaineering, but they were still operating in one of the least hospitable landscapes on the planet. It would always be a challenge.

They flew for forty minutes over the huge Biafo Glacier at an altitude of a few hundred feet, fortunate that the mid-summer winds were gentle. The glacier was black and gray with little trace of snow, save for the shadowed enclaves at the base of the walls along the moraine on each side. It was apparent that the spring snows in the Karakorums had been sparse this year.

Flying low now, Sukey recognized the campsite at Paiju, their last encampment on the trek in, and knew they were over the Baltoro Glacier, and getting close. When they passed by the landmark Trango Towers on their left, Logan went forward and knelt between the pilots giving them instructions.

Twenty minutes later the helicopter turned slightly to the northeast and followed the Godwin-Austin Glacier. Soon, they were hovering over the K2 base camp area. A dozen colorful tents looked almost insignificant compared to the huge camp site of the Zermatt Expedition the year before. A fat, black Russian transport helicopter sat on the pad previously used by the ill-fated Zermatt CH-47. The mountain was concealed under a thick layer of low clouds.

"Not much to see up here," said Logan returning to her seat. The helicopter spun around and headed back down the glacier. The pilots flew lower now, searching for a landing spot near the Gilkey Memorial.

They landed on a sandy embankment on the moraine on the opposite side of the glacier from the Gilkey Memorial. It left the women with a hundred meters of rough terrain to cover to reach the Memorial, but it was the only suitable landing spot available.

It took the women thirty minutes to cross the boulder-strewn glacier to the base of the ridge where the memorial was located. Logan stood looking up to where the cairn was located, about fifty meters above them, on a ridge protected from rock slides and avalanches – Charles Houston and the rest of the 1953 American K2 team had selected Art Gilkey's memorial site well. Logan had scrambled easily up to the memorial several times before, but now she was looking at the rugged terrain and loose rocks as Marie Chatelain caught up to her and stood by her side. "Marie, I think you should stay down here," said Logan. "You're not used to this kind of thing. We won't be long."

Marie looked up toward the cairn and nodded. "Yes, I think that is best," she said, relieved.

Logan and Sukey made their way effortlessly up the grade, followed by Sophie on her cane. The original cairn was now surrounded by rock piles added on over the years to accommodate the many plates and plaques that now also memorialized the lost climbers of Broad Peak and the Gasherbrums. The three women slowly and silently edged their way around the memorial examining the plates and plaques, lightly touching those of climbers they had known or were most familiar with. The reverence of the site and the sheer number of climbers who had lost their lives on these mountains brought tears to their eyes.

Sophie knelt down at a spot near the main cairn that wasn't yet crowded with plaques and brought out Jack's bronze disc. "Here, I think, is a spot that Jack would like."

"Yes," said Logan. "He can look out and see the expeditions coming up the glacier."

"And check out the girls that are coming in," said Sophie, smiling at Logan,

"Perfect, I will put Major Park next to him," said Sukey, kneeling next to Sophie.

They drove thin anchors into the rocks and attached the discs with wire, securing them tightly to the rock.

As they finished, Marie Chatelain was standing next to them, trying to catch her breath. She was holding the tiny pink teddy bear. "Not so bad, getting up here," she said falling to her knees next to Sophie and Sukey.

"Well done," said Logan, squeezing in next to Marie. Logan ran her finger tips over Jack's plaque, and then Major Park's.

"I think," said Marie, "that Julia-Isabelle would prefer to be up her, with Jack, if it is allowed."

Logan looked at Marie and held out her hand toward the pink bear. Marie gave it to her. "Yes, I think that Jack would like that too." Logan tucked the little bear in tightly behind the wire securing the bronze disc to the rock.

Sophie put her arm around Marie. "Yes, Julia would like that," said Sophie. "She would like that very much."

The women came to their feet and stood still for a while, looking down at the plaques and the pink teddy bear, and said their private prayers and goodbyes to Jack and Major Park and Julia.

A light snow squall blew over them as they made their way back to the helicopter.

Acknowledgements

The Last Mountain is a work of fiction. The characters and the companies, *Zermatt Sports* and *Snow Leopard Industries*, are entirely the creation of the author and any resemblance to a real person or company is completely coincidental. Historical references to actual climbers, expeditions, and events, are presented as factually as possible.

This book would never have been written without the encouragement and support of my agent, Loretta Barrett, who read the first ten chapters of *The Last Mountain* before she passed away in 2014. Her enthusiasm for the story continued to provide me much needed encouragement throughout the long road to the completion of the book. I will miss her always.

The book would never have been completed or published without the tireless, selfless, and professional editing of my friend Roxanne Henke of Wishek, North Dakota. I doubt that Roxy, a much more accomplished writer and novelist than myself, realized what she was getting into when she volunteered to review the manuscript. Her guidance and friendship throughout the process was invaluable. Roxy improved the story immeasurably. Errors that remain are entirely my own.

I apologize to climbers of K2 and Cho Oyu for my simplification and distortion of the topography of the mountains. There was no other way. The account of the butterflies flying over the Northeast Ridge in Chapter 24, was shamelessly taken from Rick Ridgeway's *The Last Step*. It was too beautiful a scene to pass up.

When I first contemplated writing *The Last Mountain*, prior to 2010, there were twenty climbers who had successfully summited the fourteen 8,000-meter mountains. All were men. On April 17, 2010, Basque climber **Edurne Pasaban** summited Annapurna, followed a month later with a successful climb of Shishapangma, completing her quest to summit all fourteen of the 8,000-meter mountains. Pasaban is acknowledged to be

455

the first woman to accomplish the feat, although the record is mired in controversy over whether Korean climber **Oh Eun-sun** actually summited Kanchenjunga in 2009, and would have been the first to climb all fourteen after her successful summiting of Annapurna on April 27, 2010. In 2011, Austrian climber **Gerlinde Kaltenbrunner** summited K2 (her seventh attempt on the mountain) to become the second woman to conquer all fourteen, and the first woman to climb the mountains without the assistance of supplemental oxygen. In 2017, Italian climber **Nives Meroi** joined the club with her successful summit of Annapurna.

———————————

I am not a climber. I have never been to the Himalaya or the Karakorums. What I know about mountain climbing has come entirely from books and websites. Years ago I stumbled onto a reading hobby that has provided me with countless hours, months and years of engrossing, captivating and thoroughly entertaining arm-chair excursions into the great mountains of the world, side by side with the intrepid climbers and expedition leaders who created the history of this fascinating endeavor. The annals of mountain climbing are imbedded with the history of the last century – the great wars and border conflicts, and the hubris of the emerging countries as they competed for the fame and glory of conquering the tallest mountains.

For anyone interested in history, geography, exotic locales and the great feats of a truly rare breed of men and women, along with the gut-wrenching accounts of numerous tragedies, the literature of high-altitude mountaineering will provide years of engrossing reading. I recommend it highly. Following, is a very short list of some of the best.

• *Fallen Giants, A History of Himalayan Mountaineering from the Age of Empire to the Age of Extremes"* **Maurice Isserman** and **Stewart Weaver,** Yale University Press, 2008

- An indispensable read. A towering achievement. One of the best books I've ever read on any subject.

• *Into The Silence, The Great War, Mallory, and the Conquest of Everest* **Wade Davis,** Alfred A. Knopf, 2011

- Another must read. Includes an enthralling account of the Battle of the Somme (1916) and the decimation of a generation of the UK's top climbers leading to the elevation of the inexperienced Mallory and Irving as the lead climbers on the 1924 Everest Expedition.

• *Reinhold Messner, All Fourteen 8,000ers* **Reinhold Messner** The Mountaineers, Original German edition, BLV Verlagsgesellschaft mbH 1999

- The universally acclaimed greatest mountain climber in history. The first to climb all fourteen 8,000ers (without the aid of supplemental oxygen). Superb writing, history and photography.

• *K2, The Savage Mountain* **Charles S. Houston** and **Robert H. Bates,** Foreword by Jim Wickwire, The Lyons Press, 2009

- The classic account of the ill-fated 1953 American Expedition to K2, and the tragic loss of Art Gilkey. Mountaineering as it once was.

• *The Boys of Everest, Chris Bonington and the Tragedy of Climbing's Greatest Generation* **Clint Willis,** Carroll & Graf Publishers, 2006

- Indispensable story of legendary expedition leader Chris Bonington and his crew of dare-devil climbers in the 60's and 70's that made the UK a powerhouse of mountaineering.

• *The Boardman Tasker Omnibus* **Peter Boardman** and **Joe Tasker** *with a Foreword by Chris Bonington,* BatonWicks Publications, 1996

> - **Four books written by two of the UK's most accomplished and *free-spirited* climbers of the 70's.**

• *Brotherhood of the Rope, The Biography of Charles Houston* **Bernadette McDonald,** The Mountaineers Books, 2007

> - **America's mountaineering pioneer, leader of the 1938 and 1953 American expeditions to K2, Dr. Charles Houston was also a leading researcher into the effects of high-altitude climbing.**

• *Savage Summit, The Life And Death Of The First Women of K2* **Jennifer Jordan** Harper, 2005

> - **The heroic and heartbreaking story of the first five women to summit K2. A superb read that reduced me to tears more than once.**

• *The Last Step. The American Ascent of K2* **Rick Ridgeway** The Mountaineers Books, 1980

> - **A mountaineering classic. The gritty, unvarnished saga of the 1978 American K2 expedition.**

• *K2, Triumph and Tragedy* **Jim Curran** Houghton Mifflin Company, 1987

> - **Enthralling story of the tragic summer of 1986 on K2. Nine expeditions. Twenty – seven climbers reached the summit. Thirteen deaths – seven after reaching the summit.**

• Any book by **Ed Viesturs.** America's greatest high-altitude climber and still the only American to have climbed all fourteen of the 8,000ers (all, without the aid of supplemental oxygen). Viesturs books are filled with mountaineering history and superb photography. These are the books that got me started:

- *No Shortcuts To The Top – Climbing The World's 14 Highest Peaks* **Ed Viesturs with David Roberts** Broadway Books, 2006

- *The Will to Climb* **Ed Viesturs with David Roberts** Crown Publishers, 2011

- *Himalayan Quest* **Ed Viesturs with Peter Potterfield** National Geographic, 2003

GF
East Longmeadow, Massachusetts
June, 2021

CPSIA information can be obtained
at www.ICGtesting.com
Printed in the USA
BVHW031812181121
621979BV00012B/67

9 781647 198350